Emma Robinson

Dorothy Firebrace

Or, the Armourer's daughter of Birmingham. Vol. 2

Emma Robinson

Dorothy Firebrace
Or, the Armourer's daughter of Birmingham. Vol. 2

ISBN/EAN: 9783337251819

Printed in Europe, USA, Canada, Australia, Japan

Cover: Foto ©Andreas Hilbeck / pixelio.de

More available books at **www.hansebooks.com**

DOROTHY FIREBRACE

OR

THE ARMOURER'S DAUGHTER OF BIRMINGHAM

BY

THE AUTHOR OF 'WHITEFRIARS'

ETC.

IN THREE VOLUMES

VOL. II.

LONDON

RICHARD BENTLEY, NEW BURLINGTON STREET

1865

ARMOURER'S DAUGHTER.

— ✦ —

CHAPTER XXXV.

THE BLACK BOY AND WOOLPACK.

'How, master lawyer,' said Cromwell, attentively surveying Grimsorwe's glum visage, 'your looks also are
very secretly of our faction—all curds and whey! And
yet you have likely seen and heard how clearly the Lord
has owned the work in hand, how well we are rid of the
cavaliers this first brush, which is of infinite consequence
to further good success.'

'But I am glad of it, and of other good news I
bring. And you must needs confess you owe some part
of this to me, who assured you the King could send no
great ordnance against you, which would speedily open
a way through your chains and palisades,' replied Grimsorwe, striving to alter the expression of his countenance,
with but slight success.

'Nay, man, it was better as it was—all scowl and
gloom. It twists your nature out of all resemblance to
humanity to try and smile,' Cromwell observed, with

the grim humour in which he was not deficient. 'What ailed you, I say again, but now?'

'The woman who stood at gaze with you ere you left her at the road-head,' returned Grimsorwe, seemingly anxious to remove the impression that his heart was not truly with the cause he clandestinely served, '*she* passed me with an insolent flouting of contempt and misliking, and with her nose in the air as if a dung-cart were rumbling by her; whereby I plainly perceived Mistress Firebrace owes me some deadly spite for causing her to be detained at Aston; and as her fancy evidently runs altogether in the same strain with her paramour's, my brother, I marvel you——'

'Peace there, peace there, good bastard Richard! I will not suffer such a word to be used of the maiden without better or worser cause than any I have yet understood, saving your malice against your well-born brother and any of his favourers. Armourer Firebrace is a worthy stander-up, and as hearty in the cause as any man of substance can well expected to be, in one put to the edge of untried steel,' Cromwell sharply interrupted.

'I will prove my words at some fitter season, Master Cromwell. Yet I must needs repeat, I do marvel you suffer one who has shown herself an adverse and intelligencer of your enemies, to spy about in the streets at pleasure, and report, most likely, the liberty that is accorded me.'

'Well, I marvel yet more you should take it on so public an occasion, Master Grimsorwe,' returned Cromwell.

'I was anxious of the event. Had matters gone adverse with you of the town, I purposed to speed to

Deritend, and make my brotherly peace with Edward by guiding the cavaliers thither to his rescue,' returned Grimsorwe, with a smile of some darker internal consciousness than ridicule of the hypocrisy he declared.

But Cromwell's sagacity was not so easily thrown at fault. ' Was it so, Master Bastard?' he remarked; ' or to set the Anabaptists and the mob on your brother's destruction, as the cause of the ruin of their town? What for else have you these several times haunted in at the Black Chapel, out Bordesley way, and showed yourself so mightily edified with the ravings of the man with the hook?'

The Black Chapel was the designation of a miserable deserted barn, partially fallen into ruin, in the fields now covered with the haggard suburb of Bordesley, where the wildest fanatics of Birmingham assembled to discuss and expound the doctrines of their sect; and being a wooden erection, patched over at some time with coal-tar against the weather, its outward aspect well vindicated the epithet it had received, to the eye, while the opinions broached and propagated in the inclosure were supposed to merit it yet more in a moral sense.

Grimsorwe looked rather confused. ' I had a religious curiosity, mayhap, for the mind is much betossed on its first voyaging on the sea of faith ; and, besides, did half expect that one of my father's servants, who frequents that devil's synagogue, as they call it at Aston, would bring me some whispering thence,' he replied. ' But it is all of little consequence now, since the great enterprise I pointed out to you fails,' he continued, in a grievously disappointed tone. ' The King is surely safe at Nottingham, with his cavalry at Aston.'

'Why, man, man! what could I possibly do more than I have done? Have I not provided for the safety of the town until relief can come from the Earl of Essex; to whom I have sent a full account of what is intended, and an earnest entreaty that he would forward, at utmost haste, support to us in the success of the design, which I myself will undertake the instant the troopers, whom I hourly expect, of my own command arrive?' Cromwell replied, with angry vehemence.

'Well, then, sir, I am confident there are news for you from my Lord of Essex at the Black Boy; for even as I sallied forth, a gentleman, who announced himself bearer of despatches from *his Excellency*, had touched there on a spent horse. And who should *his Excellency* be but the earl who commands the Parliament's army in chief?'

'Aye, forsooth,' replied Captain Cromwell; and he seemed struck by the intelligence; for although it was not certain at that moment that the cavaliers would halt at Aston, and cease their useless rounding of the town, he declared his intention to return at once to his quarters, where the messenger was announced to be found.

Grimsorwe accompanied him, apparently aware that dissimulation of his intimacy with the Parliament chief was not likely to deceive the eyes for which it had been assumed. And it was this circumstance that produced an exclamation to be recorded from one of the parties in a small group of guests assembled at the Black Boy Inn, in the hostess's private parlour.

'What manner of doubt now, Mistress Mellons, of my well-witted god-child's true report? Here they come along, like Old Nick and his fiery shadow!' said a remarkably tall virago-visaged woman, who was sitting at a window whence she commanded a full view of the length of the outer street and back of St. Martin's Church.

' Troth, I have been all along suspecting as much ; for though I never lodged a prisoner before, I guessed there should be some restraint exercised towards them, Madam Cooper, and this was at none,' returned the landlady of the Black Boy to her distinguished inmate, who had become such since Tubal Bromycham had taken possession of the Moat House. ' But for the young maiden to venture on such a hazard as she proposes, to learn what is really astir between them, and even to so good an intent as the King's service and Master Holte's, methinks is a tempting of Providence. The Lord only knows what they may mean by the law military, which we all heard bawled by Accepted Clavers, at the market cross, this blessed daybreak.'

' The risk is altogether mine, good Mistress Mellons, and I am very willing to it ; for all you say assures me there is some devilish plot working against the young gentleman placed under my father's safe charge, whose blood will doubtless be required at our hand chiefly,' replied the sweet, musical-ringing, but resolute accents of Dorothy Firebrace. ' Give me my way, good friends, for once, and let us lose no time in locking me in the pantry cupboard of the captain's living chamber, where I can hear all that shall pass between him and Grim-sorwe and this newly-arrived Londoner, until you call him down to his dinner-mess. Not a long hazard, by the savoury scent of the roast from the kitchen.'

' Truly not,' said a personage, whose short, stout limbs, overweening paunch, and jolly rosy gills, trimmed

all round with white hair and beard, would have suited
well for a Falstaff; and he sniffed the air with visible
relish, as he added, ' Woe's my life, to think that it is
come to this with the high bailiff of Birmingham town,
that he must wait for broken victuals from a fanatic
dragooner's table to make his meal.'

' And scarce a full one then either, Master Cooper,'
sympathised Mistress Mellons. ' The man eats with a
live wolf in his stomach to go snacks; and their good
morning's work, with a wanion to it, will put them in
better appetite than ever. But what is to be helped
when the country-folks are so panick'd at the cavaliers?
There was scarce a basket of eggs or butter at the
market cross yesterday, and beeves and mutton were
as things unknown before the flood. Faithful Moggs
himself remarked on it as a judgment; there never
was so clean a shambles in Birmingham since the world
began. I saw it with my own eyes; not a gutter red
in it. Only I took the *judgment* my own way. But
the captain is provident, and had me store him in his
provender for weeks at once when the troubles began.'

' But he leaves the key of his store-room with you,
mistress, and will not suspect an eaves-dropper in anywise among his salt pork and loaf flour,' rejoined
Dorothy, with earnest beseechingness in her tones. ' I
shall incur little or no risk, and may do much good.'

' Truly, there are air-holes at which a body may
conveniently listen,' replied the landlady of the Black
Boy. ' And hé laughed merrily himself when he put
in the two pickled geese for Sundays; for, says he,
" I mind not *their* listening, and *they* mind not the
gallows!" which I could not understand at the time,
till I heard it cried that whoever fetched or carried any

tidings to the enemies out of the town, by the law martial, should dangle at a rope's end. How will you abide that risk, Mistress Dorothy?'

'That and any other! only we must lose no time; they are at hand!' exclaimed Dorothy, impatiently.

'Troth are they, fair mistress; but it goes against me, somehow, to risk it, though I am as true as another, I think, to the right cause,' humanely persisted Mistress Mellons. 'What say you, Madam Cooper? she is your god-child; would you have her run the risk?'

'By George and Dragon, would I; and run it myself a thousand times, stood I not too tall on my haunches, unless I could bend like a clasp-knife in the cupboard; and, besides, am rather hard of my hearing to strange voices,' returned Dame Cooper; adding, with a supremely contemptuous glance at her husband, 'Were John Cooper here a man in his soul as he is in his body, we were not to seek for one to incur a worser risk!'

'Who—I, good wife?' said the high bailiff, waking from a depth of reverie that might almost have been reckoned a slumber. 'What were you saying? Is it next Sunday? Your pardons, fair women; I was thinking of those same salt geese, and what a rare savoury dish they will make, over-baking a good batter pudding, a foot deep in the pan! But what talk you of me, wife, when you know as certainly as twice four I should fall asleep the moment they began buzzing and fuzzing their plots through the keyhole, and so betray all by my snoring? for well ye wot I do snore like a grampus when I am much aweary with clapperclaw.'

'Speak neither to him nor of him; had it not been for his dastardice I had held the Moat House until rescue, as sure as my name is, to my disgrace, Cooper!'

lamented the high bailiff's dispossessed lady. 'And to
think that a rascal smith should now pretend to be lord
of Birmingham! Odd's my life! and set up his apron,
bedaubed with colours, for a banner! Pardon, Dorothy,
darling; but I wot well you hold no more by any of
these traitors than myself. Let her have her way, good
Mistress Mellons; no great harm can fall of it to
Armourer Firebrace's daughter and Tubal Bromycham's
betrothed.'

Thus authoritatively counselled, earnestly importuned by Dorothy, and urged by a feeling of curiosity
on her own part—by no means the weakest of her
incentives—the landlady yielded assent ; and, selecting
one from a mighty bunch of keys at her girdle, invited
Mistress Firebrace to follow her up a flight of very
narrow stairs, which conducted to the upper floors of
the house.

Bailiff Cooper stared after the courageous girl in
amazement.

'I would not run her risk for all Birmingham and
Deritend to boot; and you her godmother, dame, and
counsel it!' was his commentary.

'You are good for nothing but to drink wort or old
ale, John Cooper ; but look that you talk not in your
cups to-night, or I will let the King's men know, when
they are masters again, what a faint heart you showed
throughout in his gracious service ; and mayhap then
the loss of your crown place will not be the worst that
shall betide you thereupon.'

Like other people in a passion, Dame Cooper did not
consider she was likely to do herself quite as much
mischief as the object of her indignation.

CHAPTER XXXVI.

MAJOR MONK.

MEANWHILE the fearless armourer's daughter unflinch-
ingly followed on Mistress Mellons's footsteps to a
small, very low-roofed upper chamber, furnished as
what we should now call a sitting-room. At one end
of this was a very narrow little bed-room, where Captain
Cromwell slept, and on a side of that a projection,
forming a jutting triangle with the wall, used as a cupboard, or wardrobe perhaps, at pleasure.

There were two holes like eyes at the upper part of
this door, to allow of some ventilation within. But the
scope of the interior was so very limited, and occupied
by provision stores, that slender as was the Deritend
maiden's form, she found some difficulty in ensconcing
herself in the recess. Such, however, was the purpose
in which she persevered, assisted by Mistress Mellons,
who thrust certain of the stores back, and contrived for
her a not very uncomfortable standing place, on the
whole, on the top of a firkin of flour.

This elevation would enable Dorothy to put her ear
to the air-holes; and finding she would persist in the
business, Mistress Mellons only further cautioned her
against the danger of oversetting anything, and exhorted
her, ' for her life, not to breathe,' and complied at last

with her desire to be shut and locked in the recess;
ably providing herself, also, with a measure of meal, to
account for her presence, if need were, in the upper
room, and muttering to herself that she could easily
manage to lose the key, if any suspicion arose, the
landlady of the Black Boy and Woolpack descended to
her bar at the very moment when Cromwell and Grimsorwe, making their way slowly through the eager
questioning throngs of the townspeople, re-entered the
inn.

It was doubtless a considerable hazard Dorothy now
incurred, and perhaps not quite in accordance with very
nice notions of above-board play in the game; but so
convinced was she of some deep, dark treachery at work
against the safety of her lover, that Dorothy could not
deem herself to blame in counteracting such by any
needful underhand movement on her own part. She
was convinced that everything was to be dreaded, from
observing the freedom of action enjoyed by the pretended prisoner, when he made his appearance at
Edgbaston Barrier; and the malice and fury flaming on
his countenance when, having had the impudence to
address her quite familiarly on their meeting, she turned
away from him in scorn, struck the conviction deeper
into her mind.

Unwilling to abide any further display of his audacity,
which might provoke personal reprisals, Dorothy then
determined to withdraw from the spot and return to
Deritend. But a thought occurred to her on the way
home, that Grimsorwe's absence allowed her a good
opportunity to go and see her friend Dame Cooper, at
the Black Boy; if possible, to put her up to some
watchfulness over the traitor's proceedings; and accord-

ingly she had made her way to the inn, and there not only diffused her own suspicions, but had them increased by other circumstances which had come to the cognisance of the expelled royalist bailiff's lady and her entertainer.

The chief of these was that a messenger had arrived from London, who demanded urgently to see Captain Cromwell, and not finding him there had left the house to look for him at once.

This person was apparently of the military profession, and probably of some rank, from his authoritative demeanour and gentlemanly attire, though he arrived in a plain travelling garb, and without attendance, in the town. His name was stated to be Monk. Dorothy was seized with dread, upon this intimation, that this stranger was the bearer of some decision on her lover's fate ; and she was determined, at every hazard, to ascertain what.

Neither had she long to wait in her concealment ere light seemed likely to be thrown on her perplexity. With a rapid beating of the heart she distinguished the sound of approaching voices, and in a few moments Cromwell evidently tramped into the apartment, in the heavy jack-boots he had assumed, with a full upper suit of armour, for the warlike action of the day ; and she knew that Grimsorwe continued his accompaniment, from hearing his voice at the same time. 'They of the house have misdirected the gentleman—purposely, to my thinking—to the defences Aston way ; but he will soon find out his mistake and return,' he was remarking. 'Know ye the man, sir?'

'Not I, indeed ; but he leaves word, I hear, that he is a major in the Earl of Essex's own body-guard, which is, I take it, of superior rank to mine; so, belike, the earl has taken it upon him to supersede me here, for, I misdoubt me, he is one of those lukewarm, half-hearted professors in the cause, which a great peer of large estate is likely to prove,' said Cromwell, evidently very peevishly.

'In that case, what shall you do, captain? Yield the fruits of your great courage and enterprise to another?' returned Grimsorwe, almost tauntingly in his accents.

Cromwell made no reply at first to the observation; but Dorothy had little doubt it produced some un-pleasing effect, for she heard the heavy boots crunch and crackle as the captain strode vexedly up and down the chamber.

'What shall I do? What *can* I do, Master Grim-sorwe?' he then answered gloomily enough; but, after another brief interval, resuming with singular fervour and exultation, 'Yet what boots to ask counsel of a fellow-worm of the earth? The Lord will open me a way, and guide me thereupon. He who took David from a-minding of silly sheep, to set him up as a leader of battle; yea, as a king and ruler over all Israel; the Lord's will be done, whatever it be. The mightiest of us all are but as chaff before a strong wind when the Willer willeth aught. And I do feel myself called upon, as by an inner voice, to kneel and ask of Him guidance over what is to follow. Truly, He hath been a gracious Lord to me this day, and removed all terror from my heart, which I looked to experience, of a surety, the first time I beheld the naked edge of the sword. Oft I have heard it said that the greatest and boldest of after-commanders have had their knees loosened with dread, in their first experiences of blood and death; though of a truth neither, through good precaution, hath befallen us to-day.'

And, greatly to the unseen auditor's vexation, as interrupting more profitable discourse between the parties, she became aware that the Parliament Captain had fallen on his knees, and was pouring forth a series of devotional ejaculations and entreaties for enlightenment direct from above. Nor did Grimsorwe himself venture to interrupt the paroxysm of prayer until Cromwell ceased of his own accord, and arose, apparently wiping his face, for he observed, ' This wrestling with the Lord in prayer is a hard though sweet exercise. Sooth, how the sweat pours from my skin, as an I were a reaper on a hot day! Much more of this will make me light enough for the saddle on my purposed midnight gallop to Nottingham.'

The expression struck alarmingly on Dorothy's hearing. Meanwhile, Grimsorwe's thoughts seemed to be running in another channel. ' They said below the messenger's name is Monk. Can it be the man of that name, a lieutenant-general in the King's army in Ireland, who was committed to the Tower just before I left London? From all I heard of him, he was of a sufficiently time-serving disposition to change his politics rather than remain in disgrace and durance. May it not well be he? '

Precisely as he spoke, Mistress Mellons entered, escorting a stranger; presumably, from his soldierly and commanding figure and manner, the officer from London.

He was, apparently, in the prime of his years; his countenance was handsomely featured and gentlemanly,

and stamped by an expression of great though quiet
reserve and gravity, not usually observable in men of
his age and profession. His demeanour was that of a
person accustomed to the good society of his time,
full of calm self-possession and nerve ; his language and
tones gentle and conciliatory, though not unmixed with
a certain inflexibility and composure of resolve in the
bland and affable accent that greatly puzzled the
hearer's judgment.

Dorothy could see little of this, even if she had hazarded putting her eye to the air-hole ; which she scarcely
did, lest some betraying gleam should light to detection.
But the first utterances of the stranger's voice gave
some notion of these other personal belongings. He
began to speak the moment Mistress Mellons had introduced him as ' Major Monk.' But, doubtless, as an
encouraging hint to the hidden witness, the landlady
interrupted by adding, ' Your honour's dinner wants
but another turn or two of the spit, so I do trust no
long delay needs be made to mar good meat!'

' So trust I also, good wife, for though my stomach
be ready enough for my meat (I thank my good morning's work for my appetite), cinders are hard of diges-
tion for an ostrich,' Cromwell replied, rather sharply.
' But as this gentleman I hope will partake with me, he
will hardly make his business, either, too tedious. From
London you say, sir ? '

' I have not said so, sir, but it is not the less true, and
from the Earl of Essex, his Excellency's head-quarters
in the city, sir,' replied the stranger officer, politely.

' Head-quarters in the Tower, did I hear you say ? '
returned Captain Cromwell.

Major Monk was evidently a little disconcerted. But

he answered quietly, 'You have heard, I see, of my in-
carceration therein, Master Cromwell ; but like other no
worse people I have espied the error of my ways, in the
time and solitude so afforded me, and have offered my
sword to the Parliament, which hath been graciously
pleased to accept it; whence it follows I am here with
this letter from the noble Earl of Essex's own hand, in
answer to one duly received and weighed from yourself.
But the subject, both ways, is of a secret nature, unless
this gentleman is as innermost as your own bosom in
the matter,' Monk concluded, with a visible expression of warning and wonder in his look.

'Far from it,' said Richard Grimsorwe, though with
inner reluctance, no doubt. 'I am the captain's prisoner merely ; most kindly entreated, it is true, and as
such withdraw myself.'

He suited the action to the word, while Cromwell
took the letter offered, and putting it in the hollow of
his left hand broke the large and pompous seal into a
hundred pieces with a stroke by the other. Major
Monk raised his eyebrows, but made no remark. Nor
did Cromwell make any apology for proceeding at once
to read the contents ; very slowly and deliberately, and
evidently more than once to himself.

During this perusal it would have been a singular
study for any person acquainted with the future desti-
nies of these two men—one the overthrower, and the
other the restorer, of the English Monarchy—to have
analysed their respective countenances. Singular but
vain ; for neither of them betrayed a glimpse of the
thoughts or emotions possessing them, under each
other's scrutiny ; of which each was vaguely conscious,
without any direct encounter with their eyes.

' Are you aware of the contents of this letter, Major Monk?' said Cromwell at last, deliberately refolding the missive, and asking the question in a very commonplace and ordinary tone.

'My instructions are simply to deliver it, Captain Cromwell,' was the cautious reply.

' Well, sir, you have executed your commission; but as for my part, I purpose to make it no secret to the entire nation anon of the strange balk contrived for me in a great enterprise, whereby a torrent of blood might be spared this people and kingdom. I would have you take notice that by this writing I am peremptorily ordered to abandon my plan to surprise the person of the King; leave this well-meaning but scarcely harnessed town at once, to whatever may befall it, in consequence of its brave adoption of my counsel; and draw, with all my raised forces in the three confederate counties of Beds, Cambridge, and Huntingdon, to the new rendez-vous of the Parliament army at Northampton.'

' Such are his Excellency's well-advised commands, I believe,' replied Major Monk, sedately. 'And I must add that, far from admiring the violence of your zeal in these affairs, Captain Cromwell, the Earl of Essex is sorely dismayed and horrified at the bare notion of so disloyal and insolent a design upon the sacred person of the King, which his Excellency's own fullest commission merely authorises him to set free from the hands of the Papists and malignants surrounding him, and place at liberty to hear honest counsels, delivered with all reverence, from his loving people and Parliament.'

' So 'tis worded in all the decrees and ordinances, sir,' replied Cromwell, with a laugh that clearly startled the cautious messenger. ' But deem you we shall be

arraigned for life and forfeiture of goods, in these silken
terms, should it fall to his Majesty's behest to require
the meaning of these acts of ours by judges and juries
of his appointment? It is a strange, it is a marvellous
thing how this delusion of words possesses men's minds!
Well, but, sir, have you done your mission now, or is
more to follow? Do you come to take military sway
and office among the good people here when I depart
to the rendezvous named, in obedience to my orders?'

'Of a surety, no; my Lord of Essex would never
think to set an officer of my service and standing at the
head of an undisciplined insurgent mob, though it has
not been thought fit to entrust me with so high command in the Parliament's service as I held in his
Majesty's,' returned the major, with evident disgust.

'Well, and in good truth, you are not the kind of
instrument to the work : you have served too regularly,
sir, I take it, for the business, which fits us poor half
civilians better. But how forwardly and trustfully
these worthy poor souls of Birmingham have put themselves under the ploughshare; or, rather, have suffered
me to place them! The King's cavalry already at Aston!
It yearns my bowels to think that I must leave them
to disasters I shall have been the main instrument to
bring upon them! Northampton! Why Northampton?
It is infinitely too remote for what should be the grand
purpose now, to fall upon the malignants, tooth and
nail, before they can gather to any strength round the
standard at Nottingham! Why Northampton, say I?'

He paused in the indignant query, seemingly for a
reply. But Major Monk only made the cold observation, 'In the camps where I was bred, no soldier
ever made questions of his general's will and decision,

whatever his subordination ; but above all, no officers, Captain Cromwell, of such subaltern degree as ours.'

'May only a major-general, or lieutenant-colonel, hold his commander a traitor or an ass, Major Monk ? If so, I did never so much long for preferment as at this moment !' returned Cromwell with startling suddenness and vehemence ; though he burst into a laugh the moment after, and added, ' But the Earl's Excellency naturally forgets not that he is a stream of the fountain of honour, which, if it be choked and dammed—what am I saying ? My dinner, sir, will smoke on the board anon, and I trust to see your ride has appetised you as well as our tramping to and fro in this town to-day hath ourselves, when you have had some space to dust yourself.'

The major now politely complimented Captain Cromwell on the skilful manner in which he had rendered an unwalled town impervious to a cavalry attack ; but with something of sarcasm and reflection in his tones that did not escape Cromwell.

'Nay, ours is but rough soldiery, sir ; yet it served the turn. You had the skilfullest of our trained military at Cadiz and at the Isle of Rhé with you, where I think I have heard you served ; but I know not that it fared so much better with you there !'

'In truth did it not,' returned the major, with evident vexation, ' but we were under ill captaincy—silk and velvet courtiers, who had never smelt powder, put to our rule !'

'Were you of *rank* to form any judgment in such matters *then* ?' returned Cromwell, demurely. ' I should say, by the reckoning of your present beard, you would but carry a pair of colours at the Isle of Rhé !'

'But I have served since in the Low Countries, and in Ireland during the horrid, hellish massacre there by the Papists,' returned Monk, rather betrayed from his wonted equanimity by the retort.

'In Ireland it was, then, no doubt, you acquired so profound a science in the salvation of the weaker numbers by the virtues of spade and pickaxe, that you speak so critically—which is to say scornfully—of our achievements here with the same?' returned Cromwell. And satisfied with the snubs he had thus administered to the self-sufficiency of the regular officer, he added cheerfully, 'But we own ourselves poor tyros in the sport, and hope to show to more advantage in an assault on roast beef and batter pudding mine hostess has nigh in readiness for us. And I can also recommend her ale and her strong waters. I say nothing of her wines, which, perhaps, better consort with gentlemanly liking.'

'I am beholden to you for the invitation, Captain Cromwell. We can be good trencher-fellows, if nothing else,' replied the major, rather sarcastically, both in words and tone. 'But I have not quite done my messaging: there is an order from the Committee of Safety in London regarding the disposal of the prisoners you announce yourself to have made and hold in this town.'

Dorothy's heart took a quick flutter at the words, and it was with difficulty she hindered the pant from being audible on the exterior of her place of concealment. It may be imagined if she listened with eagerness to what ensued.

'The prisoners!' exclaimed Cromwell, evidently taking the second paper with avidity. 'But I asked no instructions concerning them! I had intentions of my

own. What is said here? That I am to release
Richard Grimsorwe forthwith, and despatch Edward
Holte, under safe custody, to the Gatehouse Prison of
Westminster, to abide trial for high treason and other
his misdemeanours, in taking action against the high
ordinances of Parliament?'

'It is so determined, sir; the committee is bent on
making at once an early and terrible example, to deter
other gentlemen from such audacity,' replied Major
Monk, adding, with a suppressed sigh, 'They meant
the like against me, for my refusal to yield Nautwich
to the Parliament's summons, had I not made my peace
by submission.'

'That will never Edward Holte! And so they will
take the lad's comely head from his shoulders,' said
Cromwell. 'Hard measure that, and never meant by
me. Should it be? I did speak for the other, and
forward his letters to St. John and Master Pym; but
this is a bloody way to make bastards lawful inheritors!'

'I have obeyed my orders, it is for you to obey yours
now, Captain Cromwell,' said Monk, calmly. 'But I
know not why a simple gentleman's head should be so
rooted to the stem, when the noble Strafford's has
rolled on the block, and my Lord Archbishop Laud's is
so loose it needs but a waft of the axe to sever it!'

'Truly, truly, sir, yet it mislikes me enough. The
youth is a fair youth, and we have taken him at some
unhandsome advantages. But what other men do is
none of our doing. We wash our hands of the young
man's blood, when once we are quit of him from our
own restraint. Yet I could be sorry, too. But when
no choice is left us? What power have I, in either of

these matters, to withstand the decrees of my betters, were I so inclined? What power, I say?'

By a strange coincidence, even as Cromwell uttered the exclamation, in which indignation seemed to contend with some other restraining influence, a trampling sound became audible in the street below the inn, leading from the Bull Ring.

'Horsemen in Birmingham! what means this?' exclaimed the captain, evidently startled; and as clearly by the clatter of his boots, he rushed to the window.

What Dorothy Firebrace, helplessly imprisoned, would have given to have passed the deliberate and measured footstep of Major Monk, after the organiser of the defence of Birmingham!

She thrust her ear in strained anxiety to the hole in the store-cupboard; but the reverse of a relief was it to her agonised attention when she heard Cromwell exclaim, 'I was praying in my soul for an answer to my thought, and as the Lord liveth, they are here! My troop of God-fearing, man-despising horse are here, and plenty of armour ready for their casing and wielding! The God of Sabaoth—the Lord God of Armies be praised! Now can I speak with a straight back to any questioning!'

'What mean you, Captain Cromwell?' said Monk, stiffly enough now, indeed.

'Captain Cromwell! I tell you I feel nigh a major-general, or a lieutenant-colonel at the least, when I look at these stout fellows, I mean. Did I not tell you, erewhile, we should have beef and custard to our. dinner?'

'I do not understand you, sir,' said Major Monk, and it is very likely he did not.

'Captain, your troopers have arrived!' exclaimed an eagerly excited third voice at this moment, which Dorothy instantly recognised with a shudder.

'Are they so, Master Grimsorwe? In good time; but we are under sudden orders for Northampton, now,' said Cromwell, handing him the Earl of Essex's letter, and adding to Monk, 'I would have as many witnesses as I can that 'tis by no fault of mine this great opportunity is lost.'

'You are strangely communicative, captain,' said Monk, in a displeased tone, and Dorothy had little doubt he withdrew upon the word, from the tone in which the subsequent dialogue proceeded, without any intervention on his part.

CHAPTER XXXVII.

THE IRONSIDES.

'So then, at the very moment when success seems to ask but the plucking, you abandon the enterprise in obedience to this wavering Earl's commands?' said Grimsorwe, with disappointment and vexation in every accent.

'What can I else? You see how peremptory they are? how all aid is refused to this believing, zealous town, save information that Parliament commissioners will be sent down at convenient speed?' said Cromwell; and Grimsorwe burst into such a raging of disappointed expressions as fully revealed to Dorothy Firebrace the purposes he had cherished. But she was unprepared for what followed on the first cessation of this outburst, when Cromwell, receiving back his commander's letter, suddenly tore it into a thousand shreds!

'I will not keep this evidence,' he said. 'If I fail, it will but further sink me; if I succeed, who shall dare to question me on disobedience to such orders? My men have ten hours to rest and arm them till midnight; and at midnight we will commence our gallop to Nottingham.'

An undertoned but perfectly distinct hurrah burst from Richard Grimsorwe.

'Hush, hush!' said Cromwell, probably placing his hand on the imprudent lawyer's lips. 'You solemn prig below will hear us else; and I know not yet whether my men would obey me against superior command. But what is this you have been a-doing with St. John and Vane? They have sent for your brother to London, to have off his head!'

There was a slight pause, and then Grimsorwe laughed a laugh which made all the blood in Dorothy Firebrace's warm veins run cold.

'You see, then, captain,' he jocosely observed, 'you were wrong to impute to me a clumsy design to have him taken off by the Anabaptist rabble!'

That was all he said. Indeed, he had little opportunity to say more, for a tramp of numerous heavy feet on the old staircase outside announced the approach, probably, of the inferior leaders of Cromwell's troop of horse, anxious to greet their commander.

It plainly appeared so to the agitated armourer's daughter, whose brain whirled with excitement, but who discerned that the room filled with a multitude of persons, whom Cromwell appeared to welcome, man by man, with the most affectionate warmth and earnestness.

'What, Richard Pride, Richard Pride! is it you, good brother, whose sweet humility reverses your name? Hewson, my brave colourman, as fresh and lively as a bridegroom at the church, after your long ride! Harrison, my bedfellow, as prayerful, I trust, as when we last saw! Ha! Lambert, mine excellent lieutenant! what progress make you in book-learning for the wars? Master Hugh Peters, whom I would call reverend chaplain, but that the name is popishly abused; how fares it with ye all, dear friends?'

'The better for your asking, worthy captain; I do never hear your voice but I feel as if I had drunk wine —sweet, not heady wine,' replied Lieutenant Lambert, always obsequious and subservient, but secretly animated by an ambition that rendered him subsequently the bitterest, though most insidious, rival of his chief.

'I am well in body, dear captain; but my soul is sick with impatience to know what you purpose with us in this long cross ride. I know it is something of a most acceptable savour in the nostrils of the Lord; and we heard far and near as we came how you have stirred up this sweaty, hard-worked people to a real stench of godliness! But what is it, our Joab, what is it, that our speed must wear out our own and saddle-leathers too?' another voice enquired.

Cromwell seemed to make no direct answer to this question. It could not be called one certainly, what Dorothy heard him rejoin, 'Is that your Bible, Master Peters, you have slung at your haversack?'

'What should it be else, Brother Oliver? Lo, it is my bilbo of the good fight—the best of all fights! but I have told you I have no stomach for actual blows,' returned Master Peters.

'It was your namesake of old's fault, honest man! He could own Christ everywhere but at the cross; and yet Christ disowned him not for that trembling and weakness of the flesh, so good a Lord ours is! But what I wanted of you is to open the book, at a chance place, and see if you can light on any word of promise —any comforting or rebuke—in the enterprise I have on hand, but must not communicate to any until the hour of its execution.'

The chaplain readily complied, it appeared, with this demand : a strange superstition, but one in almost universal honour and vogue among those who professed the most to have cast off superstitions. For Dorothy heard a flutter of book-leaves, and then the harsh Puritanical recitation of the following very singularly apt quotation, certainly :—

'2 Samuel xvii. 1, 2 : "Moreover Ahitophel said unto Absalom, Let me now choose out twelve thousand men, and I will arise and pursue after David this night : and will come upon him while he is weary and weak handed, and will make him afraid : and all the people that are with him shall flee ; and I will smite the king only."'

' Says the Word that cannot lie even so ? ' exclaimed Cromwell, snatching the book evidently with vehement excitement.   ' Why then, what care I for the ordinances of man ?   So ye shall comfort your earthly Adam with the fruits and vintage of the earth, and clothe yourselves in the raiment which I have provided for you, while your horses rest a convenient season : and then I tell you all I will lead you forth on an enterprise whereto this oracle promises the blessedest success that ever was ! '

' Against the King's troopers, who are besieging you in this town, we hear ? ' enquired Peters, not by any means in the cheerfully exultant accents of a willing martyr.

' I am your commander ; you are to make no question, but follow me wheresoe'er I lead ! ' returned Cromwell. And the reproof was well received by the rest of the officers of the future indomitable ' Ironsides.'

' I am willing to follow you, captain, through the

flames of hell, to the restoration of the Throne of Jesus!' said the darkly-musing tones of Harrison.

' I will follow you, captain, as implicitly as one born blind must follow him who leads him by the hand,' said Lambert.

' You are the pillar of fire before us in the desert,' said another of the group, in fervid accents; ' lead on!'

' Well; but we are to dine first at least,' said Peters, smacking his thick lips. ' And by the scent that greeted us as we came in, should not have long to wait.'

' Go down to my landlady's great kitchen; you will find the board spread. But, hark you all, no talk before the pragmatic officer of the Earl of Essex you will likely find there. I will be with you at the shortest. Master Grimsorwe, I have a word with you.'

Grimsorwe had remained during this whole dialogue, it was evident; and Dorothy perceived he had intended to retire with the rest, had he not been detained thus alone with Cromwell.

' I had not time to tell you yet, Master Grimsorwe,' the captain now resumed, ' but the same order which transfers your brother Edward Holte a prisoner to London, directs your own immediate release. Here, therefore, is your passport out of Birmingham.'

In the pause of conversation that ensued, Dorothy then distinguished the scratching of a pen upon parchment.

Grimsorwe, it was pretty plain, received the document, but lodged a demurrer.

' I will thankfully use this, captain,' he said, ' to-morrow, when I have seen you sped on your journey, and my brother, as you call the unfeeling usurper of my birthrights, properly speeded on his way to London, under Major Monk's convoy, and that of a sufficient guard.'

' You thirst for your brother's blood then, man?' said Cromwell, in horrified and abhorrent accents.

' My *mother* was of nearer kin to me, and she was drowned in a filthy eel-pond, to make Edward Holte's a lawful wife!' was the malice-burning reply.

' Horrible, horrible!' ejaculated Cromwell. ' Howbeit, we are all but as instruments in the hands of the All-Overruler! Perhaps this young man's sacrifice is needed to cement the integrity of the good town to the cause. Howbeit, I will plead for him what I may with those in authority ; my cousin Hampden's honey voice shall be heard in his favour. Meanwhile, avoid my sight and presence from this time and henceforth, *fratricide*!'

As the dreadful word was pronounced, from which even Grimsorwe recoiled, so commonplace an interruption as the entrance of the landlady of the Black Boy, with a renewed summons to the Parliament Captain to dinner, occurred.

' My faith, worthy sir,' she exclaimed, ' the roast is on the board, and if you make not the better haste your men-officers will fall foul of it, and leave you as small a share as the last hound in the kennel ; they look so keen and famished at the viands! Good faith, your company needs rule! There's Major Monk already smiling and making his signs over the way at Blacksmith Clarges' rantipole wife, who shames the whole neighbourhood with her bold staring and audacity—more than her husband, who is the best singer in the town, can credit it!'

' He!—that grave and solemn gentleman?' said

Cromwell, laughingly. ' You must be mistaken, goodwife; but lead the way, mine hostess. I would lock
the door after me, to show whoever knocks the owner's
absent.'

It is probable the captain had Master Grimsorwe in
his intent as he spoke, for the latter sullenly remarked,
' I am going: forgive me if I show not so nice of my
manners, hostess, but betake myself at once to my
chamber, where you may send me such fragments as
the *hungry dogs* leave ! ' and so departed. For Cromwell assented, as it seemed, without reluctance to
Mistress Mellon's ready-witted saying, ' Nay, I will
follow with the key; I lack something from the stores.
Out on't, are they quarrelling below, by their clamour ? '

Thinking this no unlikely possibility, Cromwell nod-
ded, and strode out of the apartment.

Mistress Mellons then, indeed, turned the door-key
—but within—and flew to the closet. She opened it,
and Dorothy Firebrace fell forward senseless in her
arms !

CHAPTER XXXVIII.

A FUTURE DUCHESS SHOEING A HORSE.

LUCKILY there was plenty to occupy Cromwell's attention
during the very considerable interval that elapsed ere
Dorothy Firebrace was enabled to leave his dangerous
neighbourhood.

It was some time, indeed, before she recovered sufficiently to state the reasons of her being so overcome.
An almost desperate plan of counteraction had then to
be arranged between her and her sympathising Royalist
friends before Dorothy stole out of the back door of the
inn to return to Deritend.

In the first place, Cromwell, taking no further notice
for the time of his officers, turned into the street to
inspect his newly arrived troopers.

These were now drawn up in a well-dressed line—
scarcely a horse's head before another—in front of the
Black Boy, numbering probably about eight score riders.
For Cromwell had liberally interpreted the Parliament's
commission to him to raise a troop of horse—his popu-
larity in his county, and reputation as a gifted holder-
forth, as well as a courageous leader, giving him the
pick of its zeal and fanaticism.   Indeed, he was the first
to raise a body of men in the Parliament's service
endowed with the proper qualities to withstand the
dash and enthusiasm of the Royalist nobility and

gentry, at the head of their attached and hardy rural followers.

The 'Ironsides,' under which name, derived from their good Birmingham armour, Cromwell's regiment was destined speedily to be known and feared, were nearly all men of mature age, of grave and determined aspect, and of what was styled 'sober and God-fearing demeanour;' most of them, in truth, distinguished by a strong cast of gloom and austerity, supposed in those days to indicate depth and sincerity of religious conviction. All wore buff jerkins and high jack-boots, and were securely ensconced in what was called a *demi-pique* saddle, as if between the humps of a camel.

Cromwell was received with a deep solemn murmer, such as might greet the entrance of some reverend preacher into the pulpit, rather than by any more military sign of greeting to a commander. But it was plainly meant for an expression of satisfaction, and as such he accepted it; only, however, by raising his hat once as a general salute. But as he walked along the line he seemed to recognise each trooper individually, and by name, and to address to every one some friendly recognition.

'Ah, brother Moses Robson, with your beast as ever —clean and bright as new stacked barley, from your long ride! Francis Mallows, my good neighbour at Forelands, how left you the goodwife and the bairns at home? Fight-the-Good-Fight Wellesay, is it you, worthy man? and to what use hast thou put thy talent since we saw thee last? Thou wilt hear in this witnessing town that I have not buried mine in the earth! What! the good brothers Shadrach, Meshach, and Abednego! ye will find yourselves anon at the gate of the fiery furnace again! Save-all Daniels, we are coming fast upon the times when the dark sayings of God you are so moiled to interpret shall be interpreted by events and fulfilments clear as the sun! But I do joy to see how well treated your poor beasts are all, and what pains have been taken, as I desired, not to override them on the last stretch from Coventry. Well, there is yet some good rest in store for you awhile; but we must be in readiness for the saddle any hour of the day or night, the enemy being so nigh at hand as he is to this poorly-fenced town. But when once ye have donned the new steel coats I have had fashioned for you, ye will be as tough in the hide as any of the King's dragoons, and we will let them see anon that we know how to play the men as well as they. How, Philip Bendle, is it you? Are you not aweary, man, for the hour?'

'Yes, captain, even as a hart panteth for the brooks long I for the battle against the foes of Christ and His covenant! But I have changed my name since I saw your honoured face, and am now re-baptized unto God into Remember-Christ-died-for-you-on-his-enemies Bendle!' returned the trooper, with a dismal turn up of a pair of gleaming eyes, that seemed meant by nature for a very different expression.

'I am glad of it, good brother, very glad of it; I trust thy heart is re-baptized, as well as thine outward framework of man. Well, thou wilt find many good brethren of thine inclining on the steeps of salvation in this town. In especial one Sisyphus, a bellows-blower— I wot not what his other name may be—who is in possession of all the illumining over yonder, among the German truth-seekers. What though in his person he be as a broken and flawed pitcher? He smells in all his pieces of the good wine he held when he was whole and sound, ere the Amalekite dashed him against the wall.'

And with a word of this kind for almost every soldier he passed, Cromwell was some time ere he reached the last of his troopers.

The inspection evidently satisfied him. 'Soh! I know not but you are in marching order at this very moment, had you your arms well delivered. Yet, fair and softly goes far. Go now, all of you, across to yonder sheds, which you see now fronting on the market-place. They are shambles at ordinary times, but I have had them well cleaned out, and abundantly furnished of forage for the refreshment of your steeds. I see you are all, as I desired, provided with full wallets of provisions. But there is a kilderkin or two of ale ready to be tapped and rationed out to you, to moisten the salt beef and biscuit—and the town fountain for your horses. Do not overwater them, nevertheless. We may have to ride sooner than some expect. Let us be in this town, which has so freely placed herself in our hands, even as the shepherds in the midst of the flock, with the wolves prowling around. And we will have our staffs raised too. But we must put on the iron prods first; which shall be as soon as I have myself broken my fast this day with your officers; when look that ye be all in readiness to march peaceably down to a great smithery there is in the place, where I have all your new fighting gear in as good readiness to be fitted on as any Bucklersbury tailor's apparel.'

Again the solemn hum of approval passed along the ranks of the soldiery; and the officer who had been left in charge of the men, one Cornet Hacker—who

afterwards officiated, in the rank of colonel, at the
execution of Charles I.—received some further private
instruction from Cromwell, and gave a word of command which set the entire body in motion.

The manœuvre ordered—wheeling into line and
pacing to stables—was performed with a symmetry and
regularity that delighted the captain, who had devoted
infinite toil and study of his own to perfecting the discipline of his volunteers. He was then returning into
the inn when his attention was caught by the figure of
the tinker lad, Bunyan, who was standing on tiptoe,
gazing with intense interest at the military display—so
earnestly, in fact, that he seemed to forget he carried a
pot of glowing charcoal by an iron chain at his side;
suddenly now letting it fall, and giving a yell of pain as
he felt a burning touch of the implement on the flesh
of his naked legs.

Cromwell laughed. 'Let it be a warning to you, my
lad,' he said, 'lest by carelessness and remissness you
touch a greater fire than this! Do you take me, boy?
Do you understand the nature of an allegory?'

'It is an *a-leg-ory*, sir, since it hath burned mine;
but I know not why you should so scoff at me!' returned the boy, passionately. 'And I did think to ask
to become a trooper in your service; but I will go to
the cavaliers now rather, at Aston!'

'Simple child! Thou hast no gristle yet for the
hard work in store for these men of mine. But the
cavaliers, say you? A soul must not be lost for a careless word! Come to me anon, and I will explain that
I meant no jeer or jibe at you by my word "allegory."
Yet, stay now; thou art a wanderer in highways and
byways by thy calling, and of a shrewd capacity, me-

seems. Know you much of the country out away north-
wards from this, good lad? Let us say Leicester or
Ashby-de-la-Zouche.'

'Every step of it, even unto *Nottingham*, and beyond!' returned the lad, with a significance that made
Cromwell start.

He even seemed alarmed by the observation; and
after a pause of inner reflection said, ' Come in with me
at once; I will explain to thee my hard word. But if
thou hast any meaning in thine, keep it concealed, upon
thy life! Nor care I for the rest, what the fine gentle-
man-soldier from London may think of it. All men
are equal before Christ, and these are the days of His
manifestation, or the cause in which we contend is but
a rotten one. Thou shalt meal with me, and with him,
and all of us, begrimed and rag-clad as thou art; and he
who is too great for thy presence may remove his own.'

Cromwell returned with this strange invited guest
into the principal apartment of the Black Boy, where
he expected to find his officers and Major Monk.

They were there in reality, but not, apparently, on
very sociable terms. The officers were gathered in a
group, draining ample potations of ale, at one end of
the apartment, and Major Monk was sitting moodily
alone in a window-sill at the other end.

Cromwell, who was in hopes that the ' regular '
major must have seen and admired his troop's ma-
nœuvres, was rather annoyed to find he had selected a
window looking aslant into a dark back lane, without
apparently having had the curiosity to spy out at all
at the others opening on the main street leading to St.
Martin's.

It was, then, rather in sarcastic rebuke for this

inattention than as meaning what he said, that, on rejoining the grave and stately officer, Cromwell made the remark, 'How, Master Major, were you so taken up with ogling yonder slatternly young wench-wife shoeing the horse there, in Hog Lane, that you had no eyes for my picked yeoman riders?'

But now Major Monk himself, cold, polished, and impenetrable as marble as he usually was, blushed and started guiltily upon the word.

It is true, he replied: 'What wench-wife, captain? I see none. Nothing but a fresh-looking blacksmith boy, in a coally leather apron, grinning and hammering at a horse's heels, while his rascally, lazy, sot of a brother (is it?) sits drinking and roaring out all manner of senseless balladry on a cold anvil!' And he said this with such sedateness and settled composure of belief that Cromwell himself thought he was really mistaken, and laughed as if at the major's ignorance and lack of true observation.

'Why, you should level your spyglass at the object, Master Monk!' he returned. 'But, do you mean to tell me that, even without the affirmation of these petticoats under the grimy leathers—something of the shortest too, I grant!—you could not assure yourself that yonder full-flushed, rounded-cheeked, long, black, curly-polled, wicked, roving-eyed slut (I'll be sworn she knows we are looking at her, strike the iron rattlingly as she will!) with her teeth laughing like flakes of snow in her red, sooty lips—do you need me to tell you that yonder is Wild Moll, Blacksmith Clarges' wife, who doth the main work of the anvil, while he sings and drinks the Black Boy barrels here dry?'

'I do not need the information, sir; I concern my-

self nothing in the matter!' returned Major Monk, but
with an air of aristocratic disdain and disgust, and
turning away.

And yet, and yet! It is a sad story, but one that
forms the secret inmost wheel of the great event in
English history, styled the Restoration. For had not
this Wild Moll proved a false Venus to her Birmingham
Vulcan, and become in the course of time, and of her
husband's frenzied dissipation in his abandonment, wife
of General George Monk, yet continued scorned and
despised by the Puritans for her grave offence against
morality—who knows whether she would have taken
part with the congenially dissolute and gay Charles II.
in his exile, and have used the influence of her imperious temper and beauty over her husband to enlist his
powerful arm in the Stuart cause ?

Wild Moll was scarcely sixteen years of age at this
time, but the precocity of mechanic life, and her athletic
bringing up, had matured her person even so early, and
she might have been taken for a woman of three or four
and twenty in her Sunday clothes. In her usual working garments of black and greasy leather, wherein she
exercised almost all the offices of her husband's trade—
which his laziness and jovial drunkenness greatly dis-
inclined himself to pursue—a stranger might pardonably
have doubted her sex; unless, indeed, he had taken
into consideration the female coquetry and lively impudence visible under all the mirk that customarily
veiled Moll Clarges' ruddy complexion and saucy features, but could not the laughing provocation in her
brilliant eyes and smiles. Nor could the striking animal
beauty of her frame, visible in the free and vigorous
movements exacted by the manly tasks the young virago

seemed set upon, have eluded a soldier's eye so completely, one would think, as Major Monk would have
had it inferred.

The unfortunate though scarcely pitiable husband
himself—Blackbird Blacksmith, as he was called, from
his singing propensities—was a big, strapping fellow,
with a broad, rosy, drunken, merry face, decorated with
a profusion of shaggy black hair and beard; good-
natured enough in the main, but given to every species
of low dissipation and excess, known to ancient as well
as modern Birmingham. And his carelessness and
drunkenness doubtless contributed to make an unhappy
home, and facilitate the seducer's approaches.

But this is a story, luckily, out of the range of our
present narrative. It may turn away, with Major
Monk, from the contemplation of the vigorous beauty
and her tipsy blacksmith spouse, who sat swilling ale
and rollicking out some jingling chorus to the strokes
of his wife's hammer, and may follow Captain Cromwell
to the dinner table, which now began to smoke with
savoury viands.

A new subject of discussion, was, however, destined
yet to arise between the major and the captain. And
the former had certainly some reason to look surprised
when he found a tinker boy invited to join himself at
the repast. Nay, the very next seat to himself was
assigned to the shrinking and amazed lad, who evidently
little desired the honour.

'How is this?' said Monk, gazing at the dusky
apparition with anything but satisfaction. 'Do you
reckon tinkers among your cadets, Captain Cromwell?'

'This is only a visitor, but one of a many sweet soul-
experiences and awakenings; whereupon I think to

exchange some godly seasoning to our meat,' said
Cromwell sedately; but with a smile that was in truth
mocking and derisive enough, he added, ' You must
make up your mind not to sit altogether with gentlemen of born degree in heaven, major; and why not
also on earth ?'

' Not while there is another inn in the town where I
may fare for my money, Captain Cromwell, out of
the company of sweeps,' returned the major, indignantly; and slightly raising his hat to the Ironside
officers, he left the chamber.

' We are well rid of a tedious espial!' said Cromwell,
enjoying the success of his manœuvre, and the company
certainly seated themselves at much more freedom in
the absence, than had seemed likely in the presence, of
the aristocratic soldier.

Yet there was yet another slight interruption, besides
the lengthy grace which Hugh Peters now proceeded to
deliver before meat. Armourer Firebrace entered the
apartment with a perplexed and anxious look. ' Where
is my daughter, captain?' he demanded, without his
usual deference either of manner or tone. ' I left her
in your charge, and she has not returned to her home!'

Cromwell looked somewhat confused and amazed on
this query. ' She gave me the slip at Edgbaston
Barrier,' he replied, ' affrighted at the noise or the
looks of a grim fellow upstairs, who will persist to dog
at my heels. But she is safe enough—she will not
venture Aston way again!—perchance at the Moat
House, with her betrothed.'

Firebrace made some indignant though undertoned
observation, quite unaware—as indeed were all present
—that precisely at this moment Dorothy, perceiving

the coast clear into the back lane, had glided out of the
house; furnished, moreover, as some misdirection for
the eyes of the populace, with a cloak and married
woman's hood, belonging to Dame Cooper.

The armourer was then about to withdraw, when
Cromwell added, in no slightly imperious tone, 'But
look you, master armourer, delay not long at the Moat
House, and bring Tubal Bromycham home with you, as
fast as may be, to the Forge; for I am coming for the
armour you have fashioned there of mine, which is
fairly paid for, piece by piece; with the two hundred
brave fellows who are to wear it at my heels!'

CHAPTER XXXIX.

LOVE AND LOYALTY.

DOROTHY meanwhile sped home at all possible haste to Deritend.

Joy-bells were now pealing from the steeple of St. Martin's, and the entire aspect of things had passed from gloom and despondency to the exaggeration of triumph and exultation.

The whole population of the town appeared to have poured into the streets, exchanging all manner of cheerful gossip on the great events of the day.

Every one had some wonder to relate concerning the repulse of the cavaliers, and the distinguished part which himself or his neighbours had played in it. But, above all, everybody overflowed with praises of the courageous bearing of Tubal Bromycham and his fellows. And there were not wanting some to express an opinion that nothing but the Parliament officer's over-caution had prevented the townsmen, under his leadership, from sallying forth and effecting a complete victory. Indeed, this notion was carried so far that the arrival of Cromwell's troopers being now universally known, opinions were freely declared he had unhandsomely reserved the honours of the crowning defeat.

Dorothy Firebrace, no longer sympathising in any

degree with these feelings, lent no ear to their utterance.   Her experience in the morning had besides
awakened her to a sense of her disfavour with her
townspeople, and she knew not whether success would
add to or diminish the popular disgust.

Edward Holte, on his part, awaited her return with
extreme impatience, and, considering how much the
safety of the young creature, who had become to him
the dearest of womankind, as well as his own, were
involved in all that passed, it was no wonder.   Particularly as he had no means of acquiring the slightest
information on the momentous progress of events, shut
up as he was in a thickly-walled inclosure, at a part of
the town remote from the scene of action.

Unfortunately, too, on Firebrace's return, he had
overheard his anxious enquiries for his daughter, and
witnessed his abrupt departure to seek for her.

All this gave reasonable ground for renewed alarm;
and Dorothy's reappearance scarcely removed it.   Her
face was in reality too clear an index of the emotions
she was suffering to reassure him.   And when the
young lover clasped his fair beloved to his breast, and
besought her to reveal what occasioned her dismayed
and horrified looks, Dorothy wept some time on his
shoulder before she could reply.

But the interval of her father's absence was too precious to be wasted; and she forced herself to find words
to reveal to Edward Holte the repulse of the royalists,
and the dreadful information she had acquired, and by
what means.

It was doubtful which astounded Edward most—the
courage and devotion of the maiden in his service, the
depths of perfidy and treason made manifest in his un-

natural brother, the dangers that threatened himself, or
those assailing the person of the sovereign in whose
cause his loyal zeal was so earnestly engaged.

But from peculiar reasons this last idea speedily
worked itself uppermost in the mind of the young
cavalier; and he declared in tones of distraction, that
in comparison with the threatened sacrilege, his own
apparently assured doom scarcely deserved his attention.
It was by his father's fault, by his father's worse than
treasonable divulging, the noblest Prince of the earth
would perhaps soon be placed in the hands of a rabble
of black, designing traitors, who would not scruple, it
was possible, even to bathe their accursed hands in his
royal blood !

It was then that Dorothy exclaimed with a beautiful
blush, 'But if one could be found to venture all for the
rescue of his Majesty from so great and heinous a
danger, deem you not, dearest Edward, a generous
Prince would think he owed to his preserver even so
vast a recompense as our happiness in wedded love
together, say our harsh fathers what they will?'

'It cannot be doubted, my beloved Dorothy; but do
not think I will ever suffer you to hazard your dear
safety again for any hope of advantage to myself—no
not even for the preservation of my King!' the young
man replied. 'It would not matter much were I alone
concerned; my head is already plainly devoted to the
axe! And there is no risk I would not gladly incur
if——' he paused, with a full conviction of the hopelessness of any attempt he could make to escape from
the barricaded and well-guarded town.

'Listen to me, nevertheless, dear Master Holte,' resumed Dorothy, with fervour. 'Be in the first place

assured that were the danger such as I *could* take upon myself, and save your hazarding, I would never have communicated it to you, but have adventured on it at once. But it is not alone the King's captivity is threatened ; you also are to be sent to London—to the cruel, babe-murthering Tower—to the block! who can say? and without hopeful pause of any sort! Therefore your safety must be first provided for—must be fearfully hazarded to secure; and then the King's redemption will depend upon your loyal diligence and resolve! Are you willing to hazard much, dearest, for results like these?'

'I was thinking but now as you spoke, my Dorothy, of wrenching open the doors of this house, and making my way through all opposers, or perishing in the attempt, along the river behind your house into the open fields!'

'It would be an impossible enterprise; the river is staked below the bridge, and guarded by musketeers: you may almost see them pacing at their posts from the windows here,' Dorothy replied, very sadly; and her voice faltered as she resumed, 'But I have thought of a plan for your escape—with the assistance of some good and hearty loyalists, my friends, of the town—which, with God's blessing, can hardly fail of success.'

'What is it, my soul's adored? There is no risk, however desperate, I will not thankfully put to the venture; and whatever ill betide of it, bless you with my dying breath for giving me the chance to embrace!' returned the loyal cavalier.

Dorothy again visibly hesitated.

' 'Tis very sad,' she then exclaimed, evidently much embarrassed, 'that the treachery and wickedness of others must put us also on indirect means for extrication from the toils. This is of Mistress Mellons' device; but I see not what else can be done.'

' Keep me no longer in suspense, dearest, but declare your mind. There are few means, indeed, which such an end as the preservation of the anointed of the Lord cannot justify. For my own poor life, I put it not in the scale.'

' Yet, O my Edward! what are all the kings' lives of the earth to me compared in value ? But to proceed: I told you, did I not, of the dismissal given by Captain Cromwell to your traitorous brother, and of the passport which permits—nay, ordains him—to leave the town at the least possible delay ? '

' You did; and of the well-merited rebuke that accompanied it. True it is, men love the treason, but they hate the traitor ! '

' I suggested to Mistress Mellons that if we could but obtain possession of this passport——'

' How, dearest Dorothy ? ' interrupted Edward, in tones of great disappointment. ' What would it avail ? I have light, flowing hair; my traitor brother's is dark and soot-curled. We are much of a stature, it is true; but I am a soldier, and wear the laced garb of one. He is a lawyer, and wears the plain devil's robe of one. His person is now notedly known by these signs in the town. Of what use could his passport be to me, if even I had it ? '

So I told Mistress Mellons ; but she had an answer to all my objections. She hath a black wig, she says, left in her house by a player-man, a long time ago, of the King of Bohemia's strolling company, as they called themselves, who had not wherewithal on going to dis-

charge his meat, and so pawned it for the debt; which,
player-like, he hath never yet redeemed. But 'tis
ample; for the poor rogue played Holofernes the
tyrant in it, and when the mock head, severed by
Judith, was shown the gazers, the hair hung nigh the
length of her sword. So, if besides the passport we
can secure Grimsorwe's wolf-skin, what for but that,
favoured by the darkness and the general engagement
of men's minds in other matters, you may evade the
town?'

'There were some likelihood, perchance,' Edward
replied, not apparently much cheered by the prospect.
'But you might as well hope to steal a real wolf's skin
and tail from the creature's back unperceived, as this
robe and passport from Dickon's vigilance.'

'There lies our main difficulty, and the great hazard
that has therefore to be run,' replied Dorothy, with an
audible tremble in her bell-like accent, and blushing to
the deepest crimson of the rose as she added; 'for this
is what Mistress Mellons put it to me to do, to win the
means for your escape. She knows why I hate Grimsorwe so grievously, for I could not hide my agitation,
nor the cause, when I made from meeting him for
shelter to her house this morn; yet will have me
advised to let her declare to him that I have confessed
my aversion is but a feigned coyness, with a view to win
him to some declaration of honourable and honest
meaning in his suit. Having learned such particulars
at Aston to my betrothed's detriment, that I would do
anything to spite him—but find you, for your part, too
proud and cold! I can fairly enough, however, sure,
pretend to a bastard gentleman in the way of matrimony! And so Mistress Mellons would put it on

Grimsorwe, ere he leaves the town to-night, to visit me and offer his apologies for whatever so far may have been his misdoing towards me. Yea, this very night, she will let him understand, if he choose to accompany her as mediatrix, I shall expect them, in a friendly disposition, to hear what fair excuses he can offer, in the orchard behind our house!'

'You, Dorothy! meet that fellow in so solitary a place? But you mean me, doubtless, to be there and slay him first!' exclaimed Edward, fierce sparkles of jealous and vengeful feeling lighting up in his usually mild and beaming eyes.

'Not for the world! The man is still your brother, though the most detestable and treacherous of Cains; and you shall not shed one drop of your father's blood in his veins! Heaven forbid,' Dorothy answered, 'and therefore it is I have provided no horrible temptation of the kind shall be put in your way. You shall in no wise encounter with the wretch, Edward, be you right well assured!'

'And you will keep the rendezvous with him, then?' the lover returned, with an ireful doubt in his accents that was far from displeasing his hearer. But she put him as speedily as possible out of his alarm.

'Still less than yourself, dearest. Unless it be for a few instants necessary to carry on the stratagem, and for me to unpack my heart of all the scorn and hatred in it towards the villain. Know that I have sent a message to Tubal Bromycham, which I know well he will respond to, informing him that your life and my honour are in danger, and that only he can rescue both. When he comes I will confide to him so much as concerns the intention to send you for trial to London, and

Grimsorwe's visit; and will implore his aid in the project formed for your deliverance, and in taking a just vengeance on the plotter of all these inhuman intrigues. As my betrothed, Tubal hath a fair right to be offended at a private interview between me and Richard Grimsorwe, and he shall make a sudden appearance to disturb it. The traitor, alarmed, will produce his passport from Captain Cromwell, which Tubal will secure; and then, upon my complaint of all his insolencies, will order him to strip off his disgraced gown, and will fling him, in wrath, into the river behind our orchard. It is at a low ebb this dry weather, and can drown no man; but it will take Grimsorwe time enough to paddle out, and dry himself of the slush, and escape from the smiths' quarters, for you meanwhile to be far out of danger of recapture and the town, in his robe and likeness. How like you this plot, dear Edward? Dame Cooper, who in her youth saw Willie Shakespeare oft, and reads his plays with a truer relish, she doth confess, than her Bible, except Sundays, avers the Merry Wives themselves never devised a better to punish their fat luster in his carnal pursuit.'

Edward could not forbear smiling at the recollection of his favourite poet's mirthful inventions in the comedy alluded to; but the project seemed still not to please him much, by the objections he continued to raise.

'But Grimsorwe is no such fat, jovial Satyr of the woods; he is the worse devil of the towns!' Edward Holt resumed, 'He will become desperate, finding himself so scorned and outwitted. And ought I to suffer another man, even this new Lord of Birmingham, to run my risk?'

'The risk is little indeed. Tubal's strength were a

match for any three Grimsorwes! He will be armed: Grimsorwe, as a prisoner, weaponless. Certain of my father's smiths can be within call if their services are needed. If you refuse, Edward, I shall think you value a small punctilio of your own pride more than your King's safety—or my life, for that depends on yours!'

'Dearest creature! what can I have done to merit such goodness, such favour from Heaven! But is it certain that Tubal will so far stand my friend?'

'There is nothing he will not do to serve the *brother* of *Arabella Holte*. And the rather, I think, that the way of it in some sort returns upon Sir Thomas Holte indignities I have not hitherto mentioned, put upon Tubal at Aston.'

'For Grimsorwe, let him do his worst; there is nothing the traitor has not deserved of scorn and chastisement! But how is it to be thought the fellow dares venture near you, even on your gossip's encourage ment, after so much aversion as you have shown him?'

'Oh, he is infinitely conceited of himself, and has as low opinion of the fickleness and changefulness of women,' said Dorothy Firebrace. 'And see you not of what con- sequence it would be to him to win me over from your adherence, Edward? Truly, he hath importuned Mistress Mellons several times, she tells me, to make what he calls peace between us, and bring him to speech with me. When he met me by chance this morning at the barrier, he had the impudence to fall talking even so, and to profess himself so greatly enamoured of my beauty and *virtue*, forsooth, as to have made up his resolution to woo me as his honourable wife! and there- by seemed to think he must needs have outbidden my noble Edward! Anything whatsoever of falsehood he will do, and feign, to deprive you of friending and support, I doubt not. He will come, be assured, and Tubal will do as I desire him. Happen the worst, we can but fail, and throw ourselves directly on Tubal's benevolence!'

'That were to ruin him with his townsfolk—a thing not to be thought of,' said Edward, gloomily. 'We must try your dangerous device, Dorothy. But grant I have the disguise and the passport, how can I leave the house under your father's eye?'

'I have, therefore, named a late hour, at which he is certain to be weary and gone to bed. Or, at the worst, the disguise being brought you to your chamber, when you sally thence my father will conclude it is your brother departing from a brotherly farewell of you.'

'Suppose me then free out of Birmingham, what can I do afoot, when every moment will be precious, to hasten with the warning intelligence to Nottingham?'

'That also is provided for: Mistress Mellons will feign orders from the captain to her ostler to restore your horse to Master Grimsorwe, to return to Aston; and I have heard you praise it for its unrivalled wind and speed.'

'Ay, were I on fleet Dowsabelle's back, I would fear no overtaking. But the consequences to yourself, Dorothy! Know you not, abetting my flight may be held equal to an intelligence with the enemy; and has not martial law been proclaimed in the town?'

'Who can discover my accomplicing? And Cromwell and his men will be gone on their vain enterprise, and I will throw myself on Tubal's protection, who will remain master of the town, should any question be raised.'

'I must yield, Dorothy; but if danger threatens you, swear you will leave Birmingham at once, and throw yourself rather on the protection of one who will then constitute himself at once, at every hazard, your husband, openly, before all the world!' said the young lover, with passionate tenderness. 'But already we are plighted eternally one, and the Church can tie no band which is not already soldered round my heart by love and gratitude!'

It needs not to declare the renewed protestations of fidelity exchanged by the youthful pair, and their effusions of loving sorrow in the prospect of their approaching separation—in all which they were so earnestly engaged that Firebrace reentered in the dusk almost unobserved. Dorothy, in truth, having hardly time to disengage herself from her lover's fondly-clasping arms, and spring to a seat at some little distance, as the master armourer strode moodily in.

CHAPTER XL.

COUNTERMINING.

RAPIDLY and dexterously as the separation between the lovers was effected, it could scarcely have been altogether successfully so. Firebrace's glance expressed anger and suspicion almost equally as it fell on the youthful pair.

In truth, the natural bloom of Dorothy's complexion was singularly heightened, and could scarcely fail to excite observation. But perhaps the armourer was out of temper on other causes; he expressed himself to that effect, at all events.

'So, daughter!' he exclaimed, very sternly, 'where have you been these three good hours, since I found you not at your betrothed's new home, and it seems you took upon you to leave the masterful stranger's protection in which I placed and left you? Why did you so? Are all things topsy-turvy now, and do our very female houselings set our will at nought?'

Confused with these signs of anger and abrupt questioning, and anxious to turn her father's suspicions from Edward Holte, Dorothy answered, on her first impulse, rather imprudently :

'The captain betook himself nearer the assault at Edgbaston than I thought a woman needed adventure;

and was so altogether unheedful of me that the impudent fellow, his pretended prisoner, Richard Grimsorwe, overtook me, and was so insolent and forward in a kind of love-making he has undertaken towards me, and half the girls of Birmingham, that I fled from his affronts to my god-mother's refuge at the Black Boy; and there I found shelter all the time, till the just now of my return home.'

Firebrace's ill-humour increased. 'The man meddles in all things, in truth, and mars a great deal more than he makes,' he said. 'I know not why strangers should take upon them the rule of our town, and even of our houses, and goings in and out of them! He will tell us next, will Master Cromwell, how to bake our cakes, and at what hour to cover the fire for bed! Even but now he told me—but no matter what; we must obey, since he and his soldiers and his rabble have the whole town in their grasp.'

'You will soon find yourselves, I misdoubt me, in the condition of the horse who, to revenge himself on the stag, allowed the man to saddle and bit him, and mount with whip and spur!' Edward could not forbear saying.

The armourer looked at him very pettishly. 'Job lacked not his comforters neither. Master Holte, I thank you!' he said with bitterness. 'But methinks the poor dull beast that allowed himself to be revenged to his own enslavement, was not altogether of our Birmingham mettle. We shall kick and plunge rarely first! And, meanwhile, whom have we chiefly to blame, but you of Aston, for being driven on such ill-advised courses and alliance?'

Dorothy looked significantly at her lover; who suppressed the irritated retort that rose to his lips, and quivered for an instant on them.

'Nay, mine honoured host, I will bandy no further useless reproach with you. You are weary, doubtless, of your day's toil and trouble ; and I will betake myself at once to my chamber, that you may not be kept from your needful rest to watch my restlessness.'

So saying, Edward took a lamp which was usually set for him, and took a formal good night of the sire and daughter, and retired into the bedchamber he occupied in the Crown House. Not quite so guardedly, however, as he ought, in the farewell glance he exchanged with Dorothy as he closed the door, which, as previously mentioned, opened on the armourer's principal sitting chamber.

'What strange eyes the Holtes have! How they do gleam, like hot metal! Right glad am I that we are about to be quit of this fine young gentleman, our prisoner. And they say the country-side may hope for a sharp-edged deliverance from the race altogether, at the Parliament's hands in London,' Firebrace savagely remarked.

'I trust not! . . . It were a pity so good and old a name should vanish from our hearing,' said Dorothy, striving to soften the first vivacious energy of her expression, so contradictory to her angry sire's.

'You trust not? How concerns it you, minx?' rejoined the armourer, still more irascibly. 'Have we not a much better and older one—the name of our town itself—set up again, to fill the place of a score of haughty Holtes, and such like upstart novelties? And, well reminded, we must take the quicker care that the name of Birmingham fail not again in the land. This marriage between you and Tubal hath been long enough talked about now. He is established in his lordship, and as you grow so fast beyond my mastery, minion, I will place you in a husband's at the soonest. Why not at once—this very night? There is a good presbyter among these newly-arrived troopers, who will stand upon no ceremonies of church banns and proclamation, but will couple any two willing ones as man and wife for the asking. Tubal will be here anon on this business of arming the Cromwell fellows from our forges; I will speak to him about it, and he will spy as good reasons as I do doubtless in these troublesome times of war and soldiering to assure himself of his promised wife!'

Dorothy heard these words with the less alarm, aware as she was of Tubal Bromycham's real feelings on the subject. But she thought it best to attempt to pacify her father with some outward signs of submission. 'Nay, sir,' she said, 'leave it to me to bring all to pass more creditably to you than to turn suitor for a husband to your daughter. Tubal needs but a hint from me; a *command* from you would distaste him much, for, as you know, he never well brooked being set under control.'

Firebrace could not dispute the truth of this statement. He was, besides, soothed by the apparently ready compliance of his daughter. But he showed no intention of availing himself of Edward's retirement to seek rest also, though it was now quite the hour when his usual early habits consigned him to repose. Dorothy in vain suggested it to him as plainly as she dared, remarking upon his fatigued appearance, and how a white wine posset brought to him in bed would be

likeliest to give him refreshment and pleasant sleep after
the day's stir and tumult.

Firebrace at last peevishly told her that he must stay
up till their *Parliament Master* was served to his mind.
And probably observing how her looks fell, added that
he would not leave watching of the prisoner that night,
lest, hearing of what was in store for him, he should
attempt escape. 'To-morrow I shall deliver him to
those who will give me a proper discharge, and then I
will sleep a whole day to please you, Dorothy!' he
said, sarcastically; 'that is, unless the captain requires
us all to turn out on his heels against Aston!'

It was plain to Dorothy from these words that her father
supposed the newly arrived forces were to be directed
at once against the cavaliers at Aston. But she was
far from giving him any information to the contrary;
perceiving, moreover, that his suspicions were roused,
she no longer attempted to persuade him to remove
what she was well aware would be the great obstacle
and hindrance of his presence in her project to set
Edward Holte at liberty.

She turned the conversation in another direction;
and little pleased would Cromwell have been had he
been auditor of the skilful manner in which Mistress
Firebrace continued to feed the visible dissatisfaction
of the master armourer with the Parliament Captain's
latter proceedings.

It was clear that Firebrace was offended and annoyed
at the control exercised by this headlong stranger over
the government of the town; and, moreover, that he
felt himself and his fellows driven far beyond their
original intentions, into some vague and unknown but
stormily-working sea of change and revolution.

The conversation, nevertheless, speedily drooped between the preoccupied father and child, and both were
glad at the arrival of Tubal Bromycham, who now
made his appearance.

He brought with him the chief part of his young
men smiths, who proceeded to open out the forges and
prepare all things for the delivery of the armour and
weapons over which they had been so long engaged.

Tubal himself was in a strangely excited mood, and
clearly shared the armourer's error that an attack was
to be made on Aston.

' I am going with them,' he announced to Firebrace,
' to prevent their carrying the assault in too unneigh-
bourly a fashion. We of Birmingham do not want a
silence and a desolation at Aston ; but the uprooting of
the cavaliers there, and of yonder haughty, threatening
fellow who jeered so at us, and who they say is the
King's nephew. That is all well enough. And I trust
to show Sir Thomas Holte, and his family, I have as
much of the gentleman in me as I pretend to, by my
gentle return for their harsh treatment. Master Cromwell shall not hurt a hair of a Holte's head, or overturn
a stone of their dwelling-place ! '

Firebrace began to say something, to the effect that
it was fitter Tubal should attend to his own affairs,
regulate his own house, and drop other innuendoes,
which Dorothy very reasonably feared would lead to the
question of making her a bride out of hand. She therefore prevented her father's progress by asking Tubal to
give her his arm for a little airing in the orchard, feeling sick and faint at heart, as she said, with the day's
anxiety and fatigue, and wishful to discourse with him
on the future likelihoods of their affairs.

Firebrace understood this demand his own way, and Tubal his.

The former saw the pair go out together with evident satisfaction. The latter, the moment they had passed into the inclosed ground behind the Crown Forge, which was thickly planted with fruit trees, eagerly enquired what was the meaning of the message he had received from her by Mistress Mellons, of the Black Boy and Wool-pack, purporting, it appeared, that Edward Holte's life, and her honour, were in danger from the machina-tions of Richard Grimsorwe.

Dorothy declared to her betrothed, upon this, all that was necessary to induce him to act the part she desired in the rescue of her lover.

She told him of the plan to remove Edward for trial, and probable destruction, to London, at the instigation of his bastard brother ; of the insults offered to her by the latter; of the betrayal he had made of those Tubal had received in his wooing at Aston, and the pleasure he took in the detail : concluding by stating her belief that he hoped to cajole her, in the visit he would be induced to pay her that night, by false promises and love-making to join in the designs against Edward Holte.

At Edward's earnest desire she said nothing respecting the conspiracy to seize upon the person of the King. He feared the prospect would be tempting to all the Birmingham revolutionists. He was mistaken, but it seemed probable enough.

Sympathy for the brother of Arabella Holte—indig-nation against the unnatural half-brother—would have sufficed to make Tubal perfectly willing to afford the assistance in her projects requested by Dorothy.

But Tubal Bromycham's generous manly nature also suggested to him that he owed her every reparation in his power for seeming to trifle with her girlish affections, in offering her a heart so unchangeably fixed another's.

He agreed to all she required of him with the greatest alacrity; and it was arranged that she was to remain in the orchard until Grimsorwe arrived, when the proper moment for his interference was to be signified to him by Mistress Mellons, who was to seek him out in the forge.

It should be stated that the Crown House Orchard bordered the river Rea in a wide triangular space, considerably remote at some parts from the forge buildings, at others close upon them, in the elbow-like bend of its flow towards Deritend Bridge.

There was an approach to the orchard along a narrow path on the edge of the water, from the town; and, if induced to come at all, Grimsorwe was to make for the rendezvous by this access, which was least liable to observation, under Mistress Mellons' seemingly friendly guidance. A summer bower, formed of ivy and honey-suckle, the usual ornaments of an English garden at the time, was the appointed place of meeting; and it was conveniently near the low paling that separated the orchard from the river.

Our singular betrothed pair had scarcely time to complete their arrangement, when word was brought Tubal that Captain Cromwell had arrived with his troopers, and required his attendance. Accordingly he left Dorothy, and returned to the forge.

CHAPTER XLI.

THE BEGINNING OF THE END.

FIREBRACE was already there, engaged in delivering the
suits of massive armour, roped up in bundles of dozens,
to Cromwell, partly by the glare of the numerous
rekindled forge fires, but assisted also by a plentiful
supply of pitch torches which the captain had brought
with him.

Both Tubal and his betrothed's father were surprised
to find that the ceremony was not limited to the mere
delivery of the armour.   The troopers were directed to
equip themselves at once in their panoply, in divisions
of ten ; and as fast as they were fitted and strapped into
their strong casings by the smiths, they were marched
back to their quarters at the shambles.

Tubal speedily gathered from these signs that immediate action was purposed — action in which he was fully
determined to take his share, though chiefly with a view
to evince his still cherished tenderness for Arabella
Holte, and consequent wish to preserve her and hers
from injury.

He was anxious, however, at the same time, to fulfil
his agreement with Dorothy.   When the last squad of
the now fully accoutred Ironsides had left, he therefore
requested Captain Cromwell to give him a little time to

muster a picked body of the townsmen to accompany
him in the attack on Aston ; but, greatly to his surprise
and indignation, that leader demurely informed him
that he should not need his services.

'You are to remain on guard of the town, my good
lad,' he said, kindly enough, but imperatively enough
also, to Tubal Bromycham. And he continued in his
favourite Scriptural style, 'You can be of no assistance
to me on my present enterprise : but if the Syrians are
too strong for me, then ye shall help me ; as I trust I
have not been found backward in the behalf of this godly
city to-day as against the children of Ammon. But all
I require of you at present is to keep the gates, while
I go forward on the Lord's business this night. I tell
you again, you of Birmingham are to remain as the
female eagle in the nest, to guard the eyrie, while I
swoop downward on an errand of destruction and
salvation! I shall return—look to see it—with my talons
heavy with a mighty spoil. And then shall ye rejoice
with me, and all the land in peace and safety, every
man once more under his own vine and fig tree. Yea,
and throughout all the ages of time, your town shall
share with Oliver Cromwell the renown and heaven-
inspired salvation of the deed !'

Tubal was not at all satisfied with this cloudy
eloquence.

'I shall go with you to Aston, sir,' he said resolutely,
· or before you. The town desires no such plunder and
vengeance . as you seem to project against the place,
which is our chief ornament and palace in these parts.
Fight and expel the cavaliers if you will, but it is our
purpose here to protect the Holtes in their lives and
lawful possessions.'

He clung so obstinately to this statement and resolve, that Cromwell become greatly embarrassed and annoyed.

'What! the old leaven stirs again within you,' he said pointedly to Tubal, Firebrace being present. 'And for the sake of Holte's *fair, despising daughter* ye mind not what ye put to the hazard? Nay,' he continued, perhaps a little shocked at his own imprudence, observing Firebrace's surprised look, 'come with me both; and on your sacred pledge to secresy I will reveal what I truly have in hand.'

The two armourers accordingly, struck with the solemnity of the captain's manner, removed to some distance from the tired smiths and the forges at the back of the Crown premises, to a spot where Captain Cromwell, finding he could not otherwise secure the necessary aid and acquiescence, revealed to the two astonished Birmingham leaders his real intentions and plans.

It is little indeed to say that they were astonished: they were horrified and amazed to the last degree!

The impetuous genius of Cromwell, his audacity in action, and his purposes, had alike, at this period, far out-leaped the national movement and impulses.

At no period, indeed, of the whole tremendous struggle and tragedy did the feelings of the great mass of the nation—least of all of the middle and opulent classes, or of those that aspired to elevation on the established ideas of what *was* elevated—run to the overthrow of the royal dignity and power.

Firebrace, certainly a man of wealth and position as head of an influential trade, felt insulted at the total absence of recognition of the importance of these qualities under a feudal monarchy. But he desired their acceptance, not the overthrow of the power which it was believed could alone confer due honour and recognition to the claims of the new influences.

Tubal Bromycham, on his part, though a man born among the people—who had lived its hardest life—undergone its heaviest toils—had suffered its worst deprivations and insults—still knowing himself of the most anciently aristocratic blood of the land, thirsted only to resume the rights and distinctions of his highborn race. What wanted these men with effecting a seizure and delivery of the King of England, like some arrested malefactor, into the hands of the furious mobs and irreverend demagogues of London?

Tubal expressed himself at once with appropriate vehemence on the subject.

'Cross of God! lay hands on the most sacred person of the King himself! which to preserve my ancestor, William de Birmingham, suffered himself rather to be hacked to pieces at the Battle of Cressy, whereof the picture-book at the Moat House plainly tells! What treasonable sacrilege is this you talk, Master Cromwell?'

Besides sharing to the fullest this strong revulsion of loyal feeling, Armourer Firebrace was alarmed and irritated almost equally at the notion of the town being left with such dangerous assailants so nigh at hand.

'Mean you to say, Captain Cromwell,' he exclaimed, 'that you will go on this distant, treasonable, sacrilegious, most rash enterprise, and leave the cavaliers at Aston to harry us? Are you a madman, or are we all madmen that have trusted you?'

'I have shown you how you may keep your town against any imagination of danger in that direction; at least until I return with so mighty a hostage in my hands that it shall be as a ransom not only for you, but for the entire people of England! What would you more? The success of the enterprise depends altogether on its speed! Should the lightning, launched against some towering oak, play around the leaves and branches, or strike the sturdy trunk at once? All topples down with that—leaves, branches, acorns—all!'

'Rather I do suspect it is a cowardly desertion of us! And that having hurtled us on into a desperate jeopardy by your acts and exhortations, you are frightened away, with your spick and span new armour-men, by the mere sight of an equal enemy!' Firebrace furiously rejoined.

'You are an old man, Father Armourer,' Cromwell replied, sedately, but not without a momentary darkening of wrath; 'and fie on you, that snow-white hairs should cover so hot a brain! But the mere sight of the same cools me.'

'Then I trust *I* shall not be held too *young* for something braver than threats to an old man, captain!' said Tubal, also greatly exasperated. 'And I tell you, of my own part, that what you propose enters in no way into our notions here, and that we will not in anywise aid or abet you in the execution, but rather do what we can to thwart and prevent!'

'That can be little,' Cromwell replied. 'My troopers are armed—every man ready with a foot in the stirrup. I shall but ask a blessing on my enterprise with my valiant fellows to start upon it. As for you of Birmingham, how can ye help yourselves? Unless you would basely yield yourselves and all yours to the mercies of yonder haughty young German savage and his riders at Aston, ye must maintain the town manfully till my return with the King my prisoner; whereupon you may look to have the whole Parliament army engaged in your defence.'

'You shall never return into Birmingham with the King's sacred person disgraced and traitorously captiv'd!' returned Tubal, fiercely. 'I am Lord of Birmingham, and I tell you the true Lords of Birmingham have been and ever will be loyal to their Prince!'

'Lord of Birmingham, are you, and speak thus to him who hath made you so? By the Lord, then, you shall find that vipers' eggs hatch by the score to the brood!' Cromwell exclaimed, evidently now violently exasperated with the resistance to his will. 'Look to it, I say, my fine Blacksmith Lord! I will make half a dozen *lords* in Birmingham ere I depart, who will keep me a hole to creep in again when I return, be sure. "Sacred person of the King," quotha! Blacksmiths, stick to your anvils. Ye shall have all the swords, bucklers, pistols, breast-plates, back-plates, stirrup irons, and leathers—what not!—to make and fashion for the mighty men of war; but for the principles, and purposes, and means by which this war is to be fought out, leave them to men of study and understanding in such matters. What, man!' he concluded, turning suddenly upon Firebrace; 'you know not the meaning of your own sign! What should the crown and mason's level side by side portend, but that all men shall become equal again, and a great and glorious Republic, like that of the Seven United Provinces, make us all—and no one!—kings and masters in England!'

So saying, with a sternly imposing gesture, the Parliament leader turned away, and left the two chiefs of Birmingham rooted where they stood with surprise.

CHAPTER XLII.

THE ESCAPE.

A LONG pause and silence of astonishment ensued with the twain. But Tubal was even yet more amazed at the style in which Firebrace broke it.

'Worse times than ever at hand for all men, it is plain,' he muttered; 'and no man knows what may befall an hour before or after. Tubal, I would have my child placed in stronger protection than an infirm and wearied old man's; I would be free in mind, I mean, to encounter the adversities in store. Let us have this long-talked-of wedding at once—at once! not an hour's delay! Take your bride home with you to the Moat House this very night!'

Tubal was greatly taken aback; and no evasion occurring to him at the moment, he unintentionally increased the armourer's exasperation and suspicion to a high degree by his reply.

'Nay, sir,' he said; 'I will offer no restraint to Mistress Firebrace's free choice and will hitherto. And I must needs confess it has seemed to me of late to run strongly in another direction!'

'And speak you so calmly and indifferently of the same?' returned the armourer, violently roused and indignant, as much at the tone of the remark, as the remark itself, of his intended son-in-law. 'Ho! and what was that I heard Cromwell say regarding your zeal for Sir Thomas Holte's proud cate of a daughter?'

Tubal changed to a deadly pallor in his robust hues. Fortunately it was just then that Mistress Mellons made her appearance from the orchard, and advanced towards them, and Tubal took advantage of the circumstance to break off the conversation.

'I will abide in all things Mistress Dorothy's own wishes, father,' he said, hurriedly. 'I left her in the orchard—I will seek her there again. But here comes a stranger, a very gossiping woman, of the market-place. Pray you go in, and I will send your daughter to you; and what she decides shall be done without further wrangling.'

He retired abruptly as he spoke, and appeared to pass Mistress Mellons with the briefest interchange of courtesy between townsfolk and acquaintances. But the landlady of the Black Boy found time to whisper to him: 'Make haste; he is there—the villain is; but I would not the precious child were at the hazard of a five moments' alone with him! Quick! send me the other trappings to the great Bellows Forge. I have the tyrant's wig under my coats in readiness.'

Firebrace, out of temper with everything and everybody, and taciturn by disposition, was withdrawing himself from Mistress·Mellons' line of advances, dreading her gossiping propensities. But on reflection he wondered what the landlady of the Black Boy could want at his forge, and stopped to ask the question.

The good woman, however, had her answer ready: 'My lodger, the captain, has dropped his purse, as he supposes, somewhere in the smithies, and has sent me to look for it, good Master Armourer. And it needs no

cat's eyes for the task, with the fires so brightly alit that
I did hear some should say they thought the Crown
Forge itself was in a blaze. Most likely, in the great
Bellows Forge, he told me. But how fares it with your
fair daughter since her morning's fright, good sir?'

'Do not ask me; you women know each other's
secrets best,' returned Firebrace; and, afraid of further
palavering, he left the scene, and re-entered his house.

As he slowly remounted to the general sitting-chamber,
where he was determined to renew his vigilance on the
prisoner, something like a distant, stifled yell came to
the master armourer's hearing. It even seemed to come
from the direction of his orchard ! and he listened for a
moment with a deadly terror and anxiety at his heart.
Could Tubal Bromycham's outward composure have
concealed a secret exasperation against his betrothed?
And was it within the range of possibility that anger had
transported him to offer some violence to Dorothy, on
learning that her sentiments were changed towards him?

No; it was impossible—and yet !—

Struck with the deepest alarm, the armourer was
about to retrace his steps, when he perceived his
daughter herself passing rapidly out of the orchard gate
into the inclosures of the forges below.

She had a kind of bundle, he thought, under her arm;
but as all seemed well enough with her, and she made
towards the shed where Mistress Mellons was ensconced,
Firebrace considered there could be no occasion for his
interference, and resumed his original purpose.

The armourer seated himself with a gloomy and dis-
consolate feeling, nevertheless, in his ample fire-place,
keeping his eyes towards the door of his cavalier
prisoner's sleeping-room.

An ever-haunting, though vague suspicion, that all was not as he would have it between his daughter and this young man, continued to disturb the armourer.

Not alone Tubal's observation, much that he had himself observed, contributed to annoy him.

He felt no appetite, and declined old Mahala's well-meaning exhortations to take some food into his stomach, 'to lift up his poor heart,' as she said. 'Lackaday, and what ail'd at his worship to stare as wild as a baked herring in a dish? The young gentleman was fast asleep—had been as quiet as a mouse, these hours, in his chamber.'

Even with the zealous assistance afforded her, Dorothy Firebrace would thus have found some difficulty in carrying out her plans for her lover's escape, had not the old man's real exhaustion stood her friend also. The armourer had not seated himself very long in his chair ere he began to yield to the drowsy warmth and comfort of his hearth, after his day's fatigue; and, finally, he sunk into a slumber.

An uneasy and easily-disturbed one, however, since even so slight a tap as Dorothy Firebrace made at her lover's door, after crossing the chamber on breathless tip-toe, startled him. He resumed his senses, moreover, with a quickness that showed how slightly he had relinquished them; and having the presence of mind also to dissemble at once that he did so.

He saw the door open slightly ajar, and a hand put out, which pressed his daughter's, and then took from hers a closely-folded bundle, apparently of some dark stuff.

The door then closed again, and Dorothy, softly approaching her father, drew a chair, and seated herself directly between him and the line of view across the chamber.

It should be mentioned that the apartment was only lighted by the fire-glow, which, as it was still warm August weather, was only kept up for culinary purposes, and was at this time very low on the hearth. Consequently Dorothy had good hopes she was not observed; until, seating herself, her eye encountered the suspicion and anger gleaming in her sire's now opened orbs.

'What did you at the young man's chamber door?' the armourer enquired, fiercely. 'Are these maidenly manners, daughter Dorothy? or have you laid yourself out purposely to confirm your betrothed's suspicions? He hinted such to me but now; and if you have not consented at once to become his wife——'

'Dear father,' interrupted Dorothy, suppressing her agitation by a strong effort of self-control, and driven most unwillingly on the equivocation, 'I have—as soon as ever he is willing to become my husband. 'I promise you so, on my fair faith! But I know not how it should impeach my maidenly bearing to forward Master Holte a provision of clean linen Mistress Mellons hath brought him from his brother at the Black Boy, and other necessaries, for his journey to London; Master Grimsorwe himself having leave to return to Aston, and no further need of them.'

'Ay, so! I knew not they were so brotherly together; but I am glad of what you say concerning Tubal and your courtship, child. Methinks now I could eat a morsel,' said Firebrace, greatly soothed by those seeming good tidings, which were only true in sound. But how could it be helped?

This opening for delay was not in Dorothy's notions

at all. She was in hopes that her wearied sire would now at last have consented to go to repose, and leave the coast clear for Edward's retreat.

Still there was no remedy but patience and watching opportunities.

She therefore assisted Mahala to produce the contents of the pantry before the master armourer, protracting as long as she possibly could the lighting of the lamp necessary to guide him (however proverbially easy the operation) in the movements between plate and mouth. Firebrace had demanded light twice, and the second time with asperity and evidently reawakening suspicions, before the young girl unwillingly complied.

Still she had some reason to hope, in the disguise arranged, if only the presence in the house and departure of the supposititious Grimsorwe himself could be accounted for.

But difficulties seemed to multiply. One of the maid-servants, who had been staring down in the smithies —and perhaps enjoying same slight interval of court-ship with one of the young fellows there—came in to announce that 'a fine London gentleman wanted to speak with the master;' and on her footsteps followed Major Monk.

The major apologised for troubling the master armourer at his meal, with his accustomed bland polite-ness; and then producing a written paper, informed Firebrace that it was an order from Captain Cromwell for the delivery of the prisoner, Edward Holte, Esq., into his custody, and that of a couple of armed towns-men, assigned to his assistance, to convey the culprit to London.

'I was in no such hurry myself, and am concerned

to be thrust upon the business at such uncivil hours;
but Master Cromwell is a strangely peremptory and
changeable personage,' said the major, who certainly
looked a little puzzled. 'At first he did demur, methought, to any obedience at all to his Excellency the
Lord General's summons to a certain rendezvous I was
appointed to assign him and his troopers, south. And
now, nothing will serve him, but he will to horse and
ride away at midnight on the fulfilment! And so
hath sent for me, and rid himself by this writing of all
further care and responsibility at once regarding the
prisoner.'

'You shall be very welcome indeed to the custody,
howbeit, Major Monk, since that is your name; for my
eyes and heart are alike wearied out with the needful
vigilance,' said Firebrace, eagerly, and preparing to rise
at the very moment and summon the prisoner forth to
his fate.

Dorothy's wonderful courage and presence of mind
did not, however, desert her in the emergency.

'Give the *unhappy gentleman and his brother* a
little further time for their brotherly lamentations and
adieux,' she said, forcibly arresting the attention of both
her hearers on the words, and also speaking them as
loudly as she could, in hopes to reach Edward's hearing. 'I forgot to tell you, father,' she added, turning
to Firebrace, with an unquavering resolve in her accents
only the mighty passion that animated her could have
given, 'that a gentleman with black hair and in a
lawyer's robe—you must oft have seen now in the town,
and I to my sorrow this morning—but provided with a
sufficient passport, is in Master Holte's chamber, taking
his farewells there; whom, rather than hold much

speech with, I admitted, without troubling to wake you
for consent, so wearied as you were.'

There were formidable discrepancies in this statement,
if Firebrace had had time allowed him to consider them.
But he was besides thrown into a great passion by what
he heard.

'Pass a scoundrel through my chambers, before my
closed eyes, to my prisoner, whom you yourself accused
of great insolences not an hour agone!' he exclaimed.
'I am an old man, as I was told erewhile, but to chastise such an intruder will give me my youthful sinews
yet again.'

'Father! under your own roof—a man protected by
Captain Cromwell's pass—on lawful, and even com-
mendable business here now!' interposed Dorothy,
while her parent tugged with but indifferent success to
bring the handle of his sword round to his hand.
'Major Monk, I pray you interfere to keep the peace,
while I warn the worthless object of my father's wrath
to depart at once.'

Major Monk seemed willing to oblige in this respect,
and addressed some soothing observation to the irritated
elder, while Dorothy stepped across the chamber to the
prisoner's door.

The armourer himself, on reflection, was perhaps not
unwilling to be restrained; not to mention that his
weapon had become so entangled in his cloak that he
was ashamed at the efforts necessary to extricate it.
Dorothy had therefore the necessary time to execute
her own share in the manœuvre.

The door was now ajar, and she thrust it partly open,
exclaiming, with a well-assumed contemptuous and
angry accent, 'Come forth, Master ·Grimsorwe ; now,

as ever, you breed hate and contention wherever you
go; and you must put an end to your leavetaking, since
here is an honourable messenger of our masters in London, sent on a hangman's office to convey the unhappy
gentleman, your brother, thither at once.'

'Coming, sweet Mistress Firebrace; coming on the
word!' replied a voice which did not badly counterfeit
the oiled insidiousness of Grimsorwe's tones. 'Good
brother, so, farewell! I am sorry for you, but what must
be, will be.'

'Make haste in your own preparations, Master Holte;
but Major Monk will doubtless give you some half-
hour's space for them. For you, Master Grimsorwe, get
at once to your horse, which you will find well bestowed
at our courtyard gate, and get you with what speed you
may from the town. You leave an ill name behind you,
go when and where you will!'

'I am grieved to hear you say so, fair maid,' said
the person who now stepped boldly forward into the
little chamber, and who, in his lawyer's robes, with his
long black hair, broad-brimed slouched hat, and ink-
discoloured complexion, looked sufficiently like Richard
Grimsorwe to deceive any ordinary and casual observation.

Unhappily, however, Edward Holte, stimulated by a
natural longing to take a lover's farewell of his beloved,
and ignorant of the extremely offensive light in which
the armourer was likely to take any species of liberty
from a person of whose insults his daughter had already
complained, thought it sufficiently in the character he
had assumed to add, 'But I cannot leave you until I am
assured my peace is made at least with one fair townswoman of Birmingham, for whose sake I can despise

the anger of its men!' And he had the extreme indis-
cretion to fold her suddenly in his arms, and press a kiss
on her, sooth to say, now most unwilling lips.

In fact, Dorothy uttered a kind of shriek of depreca-
tion, but taken in a much stronger sense by her already
irritated sire. Firebrace in a manner tore his sword
from its tangles, and flung himself in headlong fury
and rage in the way of the escaping prisoner, with it
naked and raised gleaming in his hand.

'Defend your insolent life, bastard!' he yelled. ' I
am by descent a noble of France, and you are but a
half-blooded knave-born of England, and I will teach
you to dare to insult the blood of Audomar Fier-à-Bras
in his last descendant's child.'

Dorothy now indeed gave a cry of terror and grief,
and threw herself between the enraged old man and
her imprudent lover. Major Monk also advanced, but
seemed to hesitate what to do.

Edward did his best to retrieve the false step he had
taken.

' I crave your pardon, Master Firebrace—very humbly
I crave your pardon—and the fair maiden's. I must
needs have made too free with my landlady of the Black
Boy's heady ale to-day! Do not threat me, sir, for I
cannot stand upon my defence; I am still but a prisoner
on enlargement. Here is my passport, Major Monk; I
pray you stand by me and it, to see me safely out of the
house.'

In his agitation he resumed, however, but too plainly
his natural tones. Major Monk himself was struck by
the change; the armourer so confused and amazed, that
he involuntarily dropped the point of his angry weapon
to the floor.

This gave the former an opportunity to interpose. He took the passport, examined its brief contents, and returned it to Edward Holte. ' It is in due form,' he said, ' and recommends you to a free passage and assistance from all soldiers and others adhering to the Parliament. Proceed, sir; Master Armourer will make no further obstacle.'

But a series of ideas were striking like the rapid tinkle of a repeater in the armourer's brain. 'Stop!' he suddenly exclaimed, ' Stop, Major Monk! The passport concerns not this man! Who ever saw light amber hair growing under black? See yonder flowing love-lock! It is my—your prisoner, Edward Holte, escaping in disguise!'

' Indeed, but it seems strangely like!' said Major Monk, himself greatly struck with the phenomenon displayed. ' I'm sorry, sir, but you must await investigation.'

' That shall I not! Give me way! I am armed! I am desperate!' said Edward, and he now in reality produced a pair of pistols which Grimsorwe always carried in a secret pocket of his robe. ' Stand out of the way, Master Armourer,' he continued. ' Your grandsire's sword can do nothing against these loaded weapons. I mean you no harm. You are the father of Dorothy Firebrace. But I will be no longer stayed by any hindrance!'

' Your pardon again, sir,' said Major Monk; ' I have a competent guard at the door. It is not my way to thrust myself unprovided on enterprises. Come in, men, and level your carbines!'

The door of the chamber was, indeed, at once thrown open, and two tall young fellows, well armed, but whose garb rather resembled the livery of serving-men than that of townspeople, entered. And they were furnished with muskets, and Edward now, in truth, seemed confronted by overwhelming odds.

Dorothy herself, wild with dismay and grief, implored him to surrender. But on a sudden the young cavalier uttered a joyful exclamation—'What, my servants, Humphrey and Hodge, restored to me armed thus! Let no man stir from this chamber, good fellows, while your master's son escapes for his life! Farewell, dearest Dorothy!—fear nothing. My rescue must have been purposed by Master Cromwell himself, since he has chosen me such jailers!'

And with a sudden movement, passing the armourer and Monk—who found two muskets levelled at once at his breast—Edward rushed to the door of the chamber, and passed out.

Firebrace alone would have ventured pursuit, but as he turned with that purpose, Dorothy threw herself frantically into his arms, and exclaiming, 'Spare him, spare him; he is my plighted husband!' so embarrassed her father by her clinging that he could not stir without violence to her. And to crown the success of the manœuvre, old Mahala most kindly took the opportunity to overturn the lamp, hobble to the door, lock it, and hide the key in her vasty pockets.

Not but that she then set to work to make a feeble noise for assistance. But luckily the forges were now quite abandoned by the smiths, who had returned with their captain to his head-quarters at the Moat House; and as the windows of the chamber only opened on those premises, the armourer perceived it would be useless to summon aid in that direction. Major Monk, on his part, yielded quietly enough to the necessity of the situation, finding himself a prisoner, instead of a prisoner-maker, close under the muzzles of two hostile carbines.

'Master Firebrace, it is in vain,' he said, taking a seat; 'let us yield to the superior force put upon us; but your unhappy daughter and these men may have dearly to abide what they have done. Let us patiently await what rescue may be appointed us; and, anyhow, I shall remain in the town until I know the Parliament's pleasure in the matter!'

Major Monk was not sorry, perhaps, for a pretence to remain in Birmingham, in the neighbourhood of luckless Blacksmith Clarges' handsome young virago of a wife. But he himself possibly imagined at the moment that the duty he owed his new masters in this singular affair alone influenced him.

CHAPTER XLIII.

GREAT POLICY ON A SMALL SCALE.

CROMWELL, leaving Deritend in high dudgeon with what might be called the two loyal leaders of the revolution in Birmingham, returned to the Black Boy. On the way he resolved upon a course of action, which illustrated on a small scale his skilful balancing of men and parties in the tremendous national anarchy that followed the destruction of royalty in England.

He sent word to the escaped fanatic preacher, Wrath-of-God Whitchall, and to Sisyphus the bellows-blower, to join him in a thanksgiving he was desirous to offer at his quarters for the safety of the town, and to provide against further danger. Meanwhile, active arrangements were made for the secret midnight start he had in contemplation.

Sisyphus arrived the first from his outpost at the Parsonage, which he had occupied all the day with soldierly implictness to orders, though at the head of a band of zealots of the very lowest and most headstrong populace of the town. It was upon this former circumstance that Cromwell, who received him in his private chamber, complimented him dexterously, in the first instance.

' Indeed,' he said, kindly embracing the maimed and

desperate-looking figure before him, ' you and your
men are not held of any such honourable estimation in
the town, it seems; but to me you appeared models for
us all. Fie! how steadily did ye keep the house yonder,
as ye were bid, while the young man, Tubal, plunged
like an unbroken steed in harness, and would, if he had·
had his way, have ruined all by bursting out on the
cavaliers, which would but have let them in as easy as
riding a herd of oxen with the goad! But you remembered, no doubt, that scripture, " *He makes his people
willing in the day of his power.*"'

' I have been trained to the wars, captain; where for
so much as stepping out of the ranks unbid a man
should run the gauntlet of all his fellows, or come out,
as red as a lobster in his own blood, from the provost-
marshal's handling,' replied the Anabaptist, with a
gloomy glare forward into vacancy, but as if his mind
forcibly repictured to him some such scene of military
infliction.

' I'll warrant he has had a taste of discipline himself
of the kind,' thought Cromwell; but he continued aloud,
' Aye, aye, but we are more citizens here than soldiers.
But then again, I must say that if there be too little
discretion in some of our valour, there is too little valour
in some of our discretion. The elders of the town
showed themselves but faint-heartedly in the dispute
—Armourer Firebrace in especial. It almost seems to
me as if it would be an over-trust in the worthiness of
the cause to leave the disposal of things altogether in
the town—should any accident call me away awhile—
in either his or this pretended new Lord of Birmingham's
hands.'

He looked enquiringly at Sisyphus, who distinctly

ground his yellow wolf-like teeth, and repeated the expression in a tone of scornful mockery, ' Lord of Birmingham, forsooth !'

'Truly, I had forgotten,' Cromwell rejoined, with a smile, ' but you and yours do hold there should be an end of all kingship and lordship and knightship, and the like setting-up one above another of us poor earthly worms : is it not so ?'

' It was for holding and declaring that doctrine, in the camps of the father of the German Wild-Rider who has come against us, that I suffered—I mean, it was Bohemia himself who ordered me to be stripped naked, and lashed from end to end of the camp near Prague, for so exhorting the soldiers, after he had deserted us amidst the bitter ice and snow, and betaken himself to comfortable quarters with his wife, Elizabeth of England—who, however, mostly played the man better than he—while we were left to freeze and starve !' the Anabaptist returned, with a vindictive kindling in his usually ferociously still expression.

' Well, and it was enough to make you angry with such unthankful dignities, poor man !' Cromwell replied, very feelingly ; even tears started in his eyes. ' And yet it seemed you fought afterwards for that same unworthy prince and leader, even to the loss of some precious pieces of your outward framework of mortality. Was it not so ?'

' I was a soldier, hired for that,' replied the Anabaptist, raising his hook hand, and contemplating it with a look, for a moment, of intense sadness. ' But for this mishap I should have been a something more than a bellows-blower in the world ! I did always purpose it ; but who can resist his fate ? '

'How! you believe also in the inevitableness of things as they happen? — in a fixed and preordained destiny of man?' said Cromwell, now regarding the fanatic with a degree of interest in the question which seemed to express some fellow-feeling of his own on the subject.

'Could I change mine, it should be seen!' was the doubtful reply, but delivered with a passion and vehemence that startled the examiner.

'You are not content, then, with the condition in which it has pleased Providence to place you?' he said.

'CONTENT!' returned the Anabaptist, in the roar rather of a wild beast than of a man's accents on the word.

'How should I be CONTENT—to be styed in a filthy hole and corner of a dismal town—baked and choked in the summer heats—frozen in the winter chills—with an ugly hag for a wife, who has scarce preserved some fiendish mocking resemblance to the outward form of her beautiful sex — condemned to constant, endless, hopeless toil for the means to keep this mutilated carcass and pining soul together—with no portion in the savoury meats and drinks, the fine raiment, the sports, the revels, the triumphs of the hard taskmasters, whose wealth I, and such as I, create? You ask me if I am lower than *beast*, captain, when you ask me if I am *content*!'

'I meant no such rudeness, dear man; churn not your teeth at me,' replied Cromwell, rather unpleasantly struck with this fierce rejoinder. 'Alack, alack, the King and his advisers have much to answer for, in removing the old dams and landmarks, and setting the waters loose! Yet, who knows what God may purpose, even in our own days, in the resharing of Esau's

defrauded birthright? Even now, as I take it, you are
a man willing to earn better wages and accommodation
than any you now receive ; and I tell you, in the Parliament's name, that so long as you keep and hold the Parsonage with your fellows—which is a special inlet of the
town—I give to you and them exemption from every
other authority but my own, and pay equal to any by the
footmen in the Earl of Essex's army received. Do you
promise me to maintain the post, on these conditions,
against any, in or out of the town, who may offer to
take it from you, until my return ?'

'Ay, will he! against all the devils of hell blasting
fire from their nostrils!' returned the Anabaptist ; and
Cromwell himself scarcely liked the tone in which he
resumed, with a dark leer of intelligence in his savage
eyes : 'Give me but the time and opportunity, and I
will make myself master and ruler of the whole town,
so that you shall have no need to fear weak-hearted
counsels henceforth! Think you I love my master
Firebrace, who spurns my livelihood to me worse than
to a houseless cur ?—father though he be of the fairest
woman-girl in Birmingham — what say I ? — in the
world!'

'Go, go ; I purpose no such topsy-turvy mastery!'
returned Cromwell, with considerable disgust and anger
in his tones. 'And what ado has such a scum of man-
hood as thou art to remark that the maiden is so fair ?
Hast thou not a proper hag-wife, by thine own showing,
of thy own ? I do but ask and authorise you to keep
me this inlet of the town in readiness for my return,
which will be in a few hours ; and never dream, then,
that I and my soldiers will suffer any other mastery
where we are than our own !'

'You do only purpose an attack on Aston, then, captain,' the Anabaptist resumed, after a slight but seemingly ill-pleased pause, ' and would have your retreat assured ?'

' Why do you ask, now ?   This meddling and poking in higher concerns than your bidding will never do!' said Cromwell, very severely, and inwardly sorry, no doubt, that the necessity of his affairs compelled him to take up with such an alliance.

' Because—and I was coming to you with the news —a servant of the house there, who is under a spell to do obedience to a witch who favours the town for some cause, came whispering to me in the dark, that there are but some three-score wearied men and spent horses with the Palatine Prince there ; who may be easily fallen upon and put to the edge of the sword with such a force as is now unknown to them, at your command.   And so Master Grimsorwe himself bade me tell you.'

' Master Grimsorwe !' replied Cromwell, rather surprised ; 'I thought he meant not to depart till morning, and was in lodging overhead.   Are you assured the advice comes from him ?'

' It was dark night when I encountered him at the Bull Ring ; but I could not be mistaken in the man's black hair and skin, and lawyer's robe, and tongue-tied, careful lawyer's speech !'

' Was he returning on foot and alone, so late at night, to his father's house, with his hateful eyes unsatisfied of his brother's ruin ?' said Cromwell.

' Not on foot, sir ; on as cleanly-limbed charger as ever I espied ; and I have seen, to my sorrow, the finest of the wild Tartar breed,' replied the Anabaptist.

' Indeed ! why, where could he have hired it?   I

had laid strict orders that nothing four-footed, most of all, should leave the town!' said Cromwell, the energetic lines of his brows knotting into deep furrows. 'However, we will make no question now on these matters. I can, methinks, discern a reason why the traitor has changed his mind to return so suddenly — that he may feign his own danger in remaining, and pretend ignorance of our *assault designed*! Go now, good brother; you shall have your commission in writing. Here it is.'

The captain affected to let fall by accident, in these latter words, what he thought would mystify the Anabaptist on his present military intentions.

In reality he seemed so. 'I must go on first to the Black Chapel in the fields, that I may put my people aware of what is now toward. But Faithful Moggs meanwhile keeps my post,' he remarked, 'and you may depend on having your orders well observed, though I cannot read what you have written me here.'

Sisyphus retired, and Cromwell was left alone for some minutes.

He mused profoundly during the interval.

'But, no, no!' he said at the conclusion aloud, though but to himself. 'Turn not aside either to the right or to the left! Terrible judgments have ever befallen those who did not the Lord's will, even as He had willed it, and no otherwise. "*A lion met him by the way and rent him!*" No, no; or else it were a showy act to begin the doings of my troop with an overthrow of the King's nephew—attended, as he is, with but a third of our numbers, those wearied and disheartened, and never dreaming of so nigh a mischief!'

Shunning this temptation resolutely, and not as the

luckless prophet of old failed to shun his, Cromwell continued in thought until the fugitive apostle from Nottingham was announced.

This poor man entered with a wildly excited and eager countenance. It may be imagined that the tumult and confusion of the events that had occurred in the town since his arrival had not contributed to steady his disordered intellect.

'In good time,' said Cromwell, also embracing the maniac prophet as he had the fanatic leveller. 'But how comes it you are not properly cleansed and brightened of your apparel, worthy master? Is it not written, "He that overcometh, the same shall be clothed in white raiment?"'

'So it is written; but the godly poor man with whom I now sojourn, his clothes are rather of all the colours of the rainbow, being a dyer of his trade: and though he would have lent me of his raiment, is not that the Bow of the Promise? And who says that the time of the fulfilment is at hand?' replied Wrath-of-God.

'Thyself hast said it, and did speak the same most clearly, with thy mouth full—cram full—of a good gospel, when thou didst here arrive,' replied Cromwell. '"Behold I come quickly," didst thou proclaim, as with the voice of one crying, not in the desert, but on the mountain top, to all Israel and Judah. "Hold that fast which thy hast, that no man take from thee thy crown," I add. Dost apprehend me clearly, brother?'

'What, no! Thou speakest as if thou hadst heard the trumpet sound; but it cannot be that all the nations of the earth are about to utter the AMEN at last, as with one voice?' exclaimed the prophet, eyes and mouth alike gaping with expectation.

'Not quite so; but the way is to be prepared,' Cromwell answered. 'To speak as one of this world for awhile,' he went on to say, with a steadiness and coolness that seemed singularly to sober the imagination of his hearer, 'The minister of this town—a confirmed popisher, in all his practices, of the true Laudean breed —is to be turned out, as a wolf shepherd. I have appointed, in the Parliament's name, that a new one shall be chosen; yea, and as the custom ever was till the late archbishop's usurpation, by common suffrage of the people. Will you, who have come as an angel or messenger among them, undertake the charge, and also the establishment in this place of a small heaven, as it were, of the saints—the reign of Christ upon a little bit of the earth—suffering none other rule in Birmingham, but 'stablishing the Bible law in full power and dominion, and the way of holiness and righteousness in all things therein? I know that the major part of the people will no sooner hear you declare such sweet things of peace and holiness and all good rest, as you can—poor, blessed-hearted, over-worked souls!—than they will follow you, and abide by you; and your strength of charity and goodwill among men shall prevail, on the one hand, to keep down blood-thirsty and ill-designing creatures who are already a-brewing mischief among us; and on the other, shall hinder any return of carnal-minded rich men and others to the fleshpots of Egypt.'

Whitehall gazed with piercing earnestness at Cromwell as he spoke.

'Nay, he knows not—he knows not who and what I am: else would he stand and gaze thus unblenchingly, and would not rather fall down and worship?' the hapless lunatic murmured to himself. 'Nay, know I who or

what, myself, I am? There is a dark cloud in my
brain; is it the sun or the lightning that shall break
therefrom? Meanwhile speaks he not as one having an
assurance? I will do even as thou sayest, man of war!
And if the people do choose me for their pastor, is not
the voice of the people the voice of God? And truly
I will reign over them even as Samuel reigned in Israel,
by peace and godliness alone.'

Accordingly Whitehall assented on his part to this
division of impulse and power which Cromwell aimed at
producing in the town; and further agreed to remain
awhile to join in the prayers for a blessing on a certain
enterprise of the captain's, which he now declared his
intention of starting upon forthwith.

CHAPTER XLIV.

CUT-THROAT MEG.

MEANWHILE the dark-plotting bellows-blower, proceeding in the direction of Bordesley, seemed on a sudden
to alter his mind.

'I will go and warn her that she come not near me,
as she says she will, where I am ! What need I with
the hateful hag glaring at me there, now that so much
happier times are at hand for me, and all the joys of
life, so long withheld, but promised to the inheritors of
the kingdom on earth ?'

The Anabaptist turned, as he thus bethought himself,
into a very narrow lane, reeking with every species of
filth and abomination that could offend all the senses
alike, and which seemed, by a dull watery gleam at the
end, to open upon the River Rea.

It was a haunt of haggard profligacy and misery,
familiar as it seemed to his steps. His home was in a
house on the water at the lane-end, or rather a deplo-
rable wooden hovel, that admitted almost every species
of bad weather at its paneless windows and gaping
planks and rafters. It was built close on the edge of
the water, and might possibly at some period have been
decently tenanted, and used as a warehouse for goods
capable of transportation on a stream generally shallow,

though subject to violent floods. On one side was a
kind of open gallery, raised on piles that projected a
little into the waterway, with the remains of steps to
descend to it. But, like the rest of the building, these
were fallen into ruin and decay. In fact, from the river
it looked as if the whole hovel—walls, chimney, gallery,
and supports—was all aslant, and about to tumble into it.

The reputation of this abode was something on a par
with its external appearance.

It was dwelt in by a woman who called herself a
washerwoman, but who was believed to have very little,
if any, employment that way—a woman prematurely
old with debauchery and drunkenness in appearance, and
of a savagely ferocious and shrewish temper; who, after
a youth of the vileness that most disgraces her sex, was
currently reported in her maturer years to have become
the associate of thieves and profligates of the lowest
description, male and female, which the inferior corruption of that age could offer in a limited population
such as Birmingham counted in the seventeenth century.

There was not even wanting a report that deeds more
direful than robbery and pillage had occurred under this
baleful roof. A pedlar, whose body was found stripped
and covered with wounds on the river, and whose pack
had disappeared, was strongly rumoured to have come
by his ugly end beneath it.

But it was not for this reason that Cut-throat Meg,
as she was called, had acquired that horrid nickname.
The wretched creature had attempted her own destruction at some period of her desperate career, and the
haggled scar that deformed her throat, and which she
never took the trouble to conceal, remained to attest
the dismal fact.

Congeniality of poverty, and rejection by their fellow humanity, probably, rather than other feeling, had led to the union that existed between this woman and the maimed Anabaptist soldier. It was strange but certain that they were lawfully man and wife. And still stranger that the terrible, almost unsexed fury of passion and debauchery, was known to cherish a fondness and admiration for her bargain approaching in themselves sufficiently nigh to insanity to be scarcely at times distinguishable from it in the signs. In particular, if jealousy be a proof of love, never was a man more loved than the battered Mokanna of the Black Chapel of Bordesley; and possibly, when he grew in power and influence as a teacher of his pernicious tenets, and women, always forward in religious novelties, gathered around him, the feeling was not so unfounded as it is said sometimes to be. Yet what could it have been at this period but the very frenzy of the passion that preyed upon her vitals, which dictated the feeling of ill-will that certainly animated Cut-throat Meg against the fair daughter of her husband's principal employer? For it was she who by her snarls had attempted to direct the anger and fears of the populace, on the news of Prince Rupert's arrival, upon Dorothy Firebrace.

Sisyphus found no difficulty in entering the abode presided over by his fearful partner. There was no door to the lower portion of the house, which was nearly choked with the gravel and dried-up ooze of an old inundation. The stairs that mounted to the dilapidated chambers above hung almost loose, and broken away in wide gaps from their supports. He had only to push back a piece of coarse tarpaulin nailed over a doorway at the top of these, to find himself amidst his household gods.

Few signs of comfort appeared. The numerous broken panes of the narrow lattices were supplied with rags and clouts that could not quite exclude the gracious light of the now rising moon. In one corner there was a low truckle bed, covered with a mattress that revealed the straw it was stuffed with at various jags; with some bundles of black-looking coverlets, chiefly undressed sheep-skins. A few other miserable articles of household furniture completed the poverty-stricken aspect of things. A scanty fire, aglow in a sort of tripod on the hearth, had, however, a pot suspended over it that gave some promise of supper in preparation. And before this, huddled in a heap like a toad, sat a woman whose gaunt frame, grim looks, and wildly-gleaming eyes, might well have furnished a painter with a study for the infernal goddess, Hecate. The bellows-blower might be forgiven for not doting to any excess upon such a consort.

Cut-throat Meg seemed also considerably out of temper, and received him in no very winning style.

'What do you here, man?' she said, glaring haggardly at him. 'Did I not send you word I would bring you your supper to the Parsonage, and sleep for one night under a whole roof? I trow me, that is like to be the best of your day's wages at soldiering!'

'I come here because I would not have you come there: we want no women at an outpost, and *that* lies naked to the enemy on the fieldside. Where's my supper?' replied Sisyphus, in the tones of an ogre snubbing his ogress.

'Here's your supper; help yourself from the pot: you are old enough to care not to scald your lips with a mess of oat porridge and onions. But deem you I am going to stay alone by myself in this darksome rat-hole, while you tumble in the parson's down beds? What care I for the King's soldiers at Aston? I never heard before you were so troubled to keep me safe.'

'Nay; you and they would likely be good friends enough, soon enough,' returned Sisyphus, bitterly; 'and that is perhaps one reason why I will not have you so within hail-fellow-well-met of the jolly company! You shall tarry where you are, I say; at least until I know better where I shall myself remain for my last-ingness.'

'I can tell you pretty well, methinks, without asking the Witch of Aston!' returned the kind consort, pointing significantly downwards.

'No; the man who has been your husband on earth can never deserve to meet with you again below,' Sisyphus responded. 'And, for my part, I know not how I can have merited, other than by wedding thee, a fall so utterly from grace, which I know was once granted to me. I never murdered a pedlar!'

'And who says I did? Is it thou, liar and traitor?' the woman answered, with fury in her accents, but turning deadly pale in the complexion. 'And even were't so, is not the receiver as bad as the thief? and did not the very children screech to thee in the street on our wedding-day that I bought my husband with the pedlar's stocking-foot?'

'Be that as it may, the pedlar or the pedlar's ghost may keep your company to-night, for I will not suffer you away with me; even such ruffians as I have gathered about me would think scandal of your presence,' Sisyphus replied.

'And is this the queening and sitting on a throne you promised me when you courted me, wretched beggar and lousel as you returned among us from the wars?' said Cut-throat Meg. 'Fie on your lying, cheating tongue! nor am I the last or only one, I fear, it shall deceive. But you will not win the *armourer's fair daughter* by such witchery, old Devil's Claw! with the pick of all the handsome young fellows of town, and country too, offering themselves to her! and with her father's noble prisoner—for whose sake she puts herself in any jeopardy—an angel of light in the comparison of a demon with thee, broken handled glue-pot! And I'll take care, besides, that the people know enough of *her* goings on against them, some day, to tear her into calf's fritterlings!'

'Wilt thou hold peace, hag; or have all the hot gruel on thy grizzly head? Or, dost thou see, some say you killed the pedlar with this very chopping-knife: did he seem to like of it so well that you would have a relish of it in your turn?' Sisyphus replied, flaming with hatred and malice.

'But where are *thy* hands to do murder even on a woman? Will thy bellows-hook steady the cleaver for my skull?' Cut-throat Meg retorted jeeringly. 'Why, it were easier far for me to send thee tumbling over the water stairs after the pedlar, than for thou to do me the mischief that would likely content thy black heart's greed! What ails me, indeed, that I do not tear thy false, upbraiding, woman-cheating tongue from its roots, at least?'

'Silence, mad-woman! — hear your not that splash and struggling sound without in the gallery? Oh, can it truly be that the dead—that murdered men long buried, but unavenged, in their graves, can thus return to flout their murderers with dismal repetition of the deed ? Hark ! did ye drag him with that dripping splash of gore, to heave him over ? Good Heaven ! what means it else ? '

And the Anabaptist started up with an expression of intense superstitious terror in his aghast countenance, staring in the direction of the sounds he thus described, which were certainly audible on the exterior of the crazy pile towards the river.

But this excitement was as nothing compared with the horror of dread that took possession of every fibre of his guilty partner's frame. She shook and trembled, the powerful virago, in every limb of her gaunt frame: and clinging with abject fear to her husband's knees, 'Save me, oh, save me!' she yelled in a scarcely human outcry. 'Did'st not tell me thou had'st power given thee to pardon and absolve, as one endowed by Heaven with a special inward grace, that flowed out on whom thou willed'st to save ? I gave thee all the silver and the price of the goods that I could sell for the blood, to spend on thine own luxuries; and now keep the avenger off me!'

But Sisyphus's own consternation had culminated in the fact that a clout was suddenly removed from a shattered pane, and a ghastly visage, seemingly hung with black weedy mud, presented itself thereat.

'Mercy of mercies on me, liar and cheat that I am ! It is there, it is there, it is there ! But I never harmed thee, poor slain fellow-creature! I never killed but in fair fight ! It was before my time ! This is the murderess, and take her with you where you will ! '

'Sisyphus! Brother Sisyphus! is it indeed you?' said a most doleful voice now at the opening.

'Master Richard Grimsorwe! Am I dreaming, or mad?'

'No, no; it is I myself—none other—most vilely cozened, maltreated, stripped of my habiliments, thrown into this foul sewer rather than river, whence I have with such difficulty and slipperiness dragged myself, that I seem like a severed worm writhing to find its parts again!' groaned the voice. 'In the name of Heaven, let me in, good friend, and cleanse me of this mud and filth, that I may make my escape with what speed is possible from this accursed town!'

'It is a living man's voice; it is not Jacob Futvoye's!' exclaimed Cut-throat Meg, reviving in an instant from her fit of conscience and dread. 'Let us let him in; perhaps he may make it worth our while, unless he be choused of all. And even then, if he be of the town—and you seem to know him, Sisyphus—he hath been belike at no good, and must pay us to keep counsel!'

'Know him? ay, in truth. But how *here*, and how *there*, at the same moment? Come in, Master Grimsorwe, I pray you, come in; there is no way but by the lattice! And is it, indeed, you yourself, whom I met but half an hour ago in your fine black lawyer's robe, with your hair hanging like a mane to your girdle, on a steed that seemed to dance the air like the bonny bluebell?'

Speaking thus, the bellows-blower thrust the crazy casement so violently back on its rusty hinges that it fell half off, but allowed a space at which the person addressed scrambled headlong in. Then, regaining his feet, presented such a streaming mass of mud, weeds, rotten sticks and straws, and other river-filth, clinging round the likeness of a man, that Cut-throat Meg herself, albeit not given to the laughing mood, burst into a discordant clatter of the kind.

Not so Richard Grimsorwe. No sooner had he heard the words uttered by Sisyphus than he exclaimed, 'Oh, then, I see the whole treason now! By that malignant girl's contrivance Edward Holte has escaped the town, disguised in my garb! All is lost for me at Aston—and my only redemption lies in the success of the Parliament captain's plan! But what if they have discovered *that* too, and Edward hastens to reveal it? Miserable wretch that I am! the brutal giant that cast me into the river at the forge has so wrenched my limbs that I cannot stand, much less rush, as I ought, to set Cromwell in pursuit. What shall I do? I may seem to you, Sisyphus, to rave; but if Holte has gone to Aston there may yet be time to pass his intelligence and secure the King! Hasten with my words to the captain, good fellow! hasten, and the reward I promised you—for another service—shall be doubled. Hasten! I have not breath to explain, for my very soul is gorged with mud and slime, and my heart choked with them—and I can gasp no more!'

Indeed Grimsorwe seemed all but suffocated, and the convulsive action of disgust that heaved his whole bedraggled frame attested the efforts of nature to be rid of, it is probable, divers very unpalatable and unwillingly swallowed substances.

But Sisyphus waited not the result. He perceived too plainly himself the whole breathless imminence of the case.

'Attend to the misused, worthy gentleman, wife,' he
exclaimed; 'do him what service you can.   But life and
death hang on my speed now back to Captain Cromwell's
quarters! Fare you well, sir, for a space! Meg, *put the
chopper by,* and get your guest to bed!'

CHAPTER XLV.

THE comparison of notes among his enemies has certified the success of Edward Holte's plan of escape; so far, at least, as the then centre of Birmingham, at the Bull Ring. Thence let us now follow his flight.

Hazardous as he left the position of affairs in the Crown House, Edward had, however, too much good sense to attract attention by using any wild speed in his departure from Deritend. He found the horse on which Grimsorwe had arrived at the street gate, mounted it deliberately, gave the man the like niggardly fee that Grimsorwe would have given, and rode deliberately off. He could not help thinking, at the same time, that the steed recognised its proper master, from the thrill that visited its frame, the pleased snort it gave, and the lively action it exhibited at once.

Edward restrained this, however, as he passed up Digbeth; and he was proceeding at a very quiet pace across the dark inclosure before St. Martin's Church, when he encountered with Sisyphus, on his way to Cromwell's quarters.

Up to this period Edward had internally resolved to proceed at once to Aston Hall, which lay not much out of his direct route north, with intelligence of the

danger impending. Something, he thought, might be
effected by the cavalry posted there in delaying the
calamitous project formed to surprise the person of the
King. But what he now learned convinced him that
direct action, and at the utmost speed of horse and
man, could alone be useful in the conjuncture.

Believing he spoke to Richard Grimsorwe, Sisyphus
informed Edward Holte of the utterly exhausted condition of Prince Rupert's party of horse. All the impetus
of the fiery leader himself, and entreaties of Sir Thomas
Holte, could not get the wearied troopers to renew the
attempt to enter Birmingham that night. The other
officers themselves remonstrated with his Highness.
Yielding to necessity, therefore, he had quartered them
around Aston Hall, where, for the most part, they were
now buried in sleep, and heavy with the strong ales
liberally provided for their use by the baronet.

This intelligence could not be doubted, the Anabaptist said, since it was brought to him by so faithful
though secret a friend of the *good cause* as Adam
Blackjack, and by the order and instruction of Maud
Grimsorwe!

Edward learned with alarm and horror the treachery
and betrayal rife even in his father's household. But he
saw that nothing could be hoped from open resistance.
He had little fear, or rather the reverse emotion, that
Cromwell would be turned from his grand object by any
aside bait. He knew not well how otherwise to sustain
his brother's personation, and get rid of the bellows-
blower. The safety of the King was, besides, now the
all-in-all business. Happen what might to Prince Rupert
and his company—to his own family even—the devoted
cavalier conceived it proper to provide for that against

all risks. He therefore desired Sisyphus to hasten at once with his news to Captain Cromwell, and point out to him how easily the destruction of this detached corps might be effected in an unexpected onslaught.

Sisyphus proceeded on his way, and Edward Holte on his; the former no doubt more convinced than ever of his ally's superiority to every feeling of kinship and natural duty in his eagerness to advance himself in his brother's place.

Edward had yet to pass through some danger of detection when he reached the exit of the town towards Aston, at the Butts. But luckily the moon had not yet risen, and the men on guard there were very weary with their day's anxiety and vigilance. William Moorcroft imagined he perfectly recognised Master Grimsorwe, carelessly examined his pass by the light of a lantern, bade his late treater a civil good night, and God speed, and a portion of the barriers was cleared away to allow him to pass out.

Losing then no diligence, Edward rapidly skirted the long wall of Aston Park until it came to a sharp angle, where the inclosure turned off to the left. Directly fronting this lay Sutton Chace, the road through which formed a cross with the proper one for him to pursue, which lay to the right, into Leicestershire.

Edward Holte was well acquainted with the country he had to traverse, being, like most persons of his age and class, a keen hunter, and accustomed to follow the hounds great distances over it. He had no hesitation, therefore, about the way he should take, when he reached this point. Nevertheless, he reined up his horse suddenly as he came in sight of the spot, with an emotion of the greatest astonishment and wonder.

Nay, perhaps—so universally diffused and rooted were the superstitions of the time—with no slight sensation of fear.

Not without a cause! Precisely in the centre of the cross-road, beyond which on all sides extended a dreary, heath-like open country, he beheld a great fire kindled. Over this was suspended an iron pot, or caldron, from three iron bars united in a triangular support. This pot, from its bubbling, contained some thick liquid, and as it was red hot externally, the astonished spectator could not but conclude it contained some metal in a state of fusion.

And yet he was at full liberty to form the notion that some more horrible ingredients mingled in the contents. A very old man, almost idiotic with age, whom he recognised as the gravedigger of Aston churchyard, stood with a mouldy basket in his hand, in which there seemed bones and soil and some horrid rags that looked like the stained swathings of a corpse! And from it a most witch-like female figure—nay, the too well-known figure of the Witch of Aston herself—was busy ladling stuff into the caldron. And as if all this had been little, and could leave much doubt of the dismal certainties of the scene, all around, in the glow of the fire, sat some four or five horrible-looking old women, the terrors of their several districts, but mostly so infirm, rheumatic, and stricken with all the ailments of age and poverty, that it was a wonder, truly, how they had reached the place of the witch-meeting. Nothing but dotage, mingled with malice, curiosity, a vague belief in the dreadful powers ascribed to them by the folly and superstition of the age, and the influence of their grizzly chieftainess over them, could have given them the necessary energy—unless, perhaps, it was the temptation of the ardent spirit that, in all probability, circulated in certain transparent and singularly beautiful amber goblets emong them, and renewed for awhile the glow and life of youth in their time-drained veins.

Edward Holte was learned in the learning of his times, of polished manners and superior intellect. But he belonged to his times, and doubted not that he had come upon a *sabbath*, or assemblage of witches in the devil's name. The appearance of the group, the business in which they seemed engaged, the midnight hour—such it now was—the unlucky and ill-omened place of meeting—all conspired to force the notion upon him.

Unlucky and ill-omened to the Holte race certainly as well as to others which might be considered to have received injuries by their agency on this spot.

There it was that the ancestor of Tubal Bromycham had been so basely trepanned by the robbers, who afterwards pretended he had committed a felony with them on the person of a Holte. There it was that the miserable daughter of Maud Grimsorwe, and mother of Richard, had been interred, with all the horrors of the old laws against a suicide—a *felo de se*, as the phrase ran—with a stake through her breast on a cross-road!

Her grave was plainly to be seen at the junction of the cross-road from Aston to Sutton, inasmuch as her mother's cares had now for nearly thirty years kept the ground in good order, and mostly at the flower seasons bright with violet and primrose or wallflower and rose. The poor old wretch had even at one time a custom to buy a lamb in the spring and employ its tender teeth to crop the grass. But as the lamb was invariably stolen and butchered, in spite of the terrors of the witch, the frugal Richard had, of latter years, persuaded his grandmother not to indulge in so unrespected and costly a piece of sentiment.

Yet here it was that the woe-begone hag had collected her friends and cummers at this midnight hour, evidently to keep her company and assist in some direful rites that shunned the light of day and the observation of mankind; how could Edward Holte doubt of what diabolical nature when only a few years had elapsed since an Act of Parliament had been passed expressly forbidding the assemblage of witches on their unhallowed operations, and when persons exactly resembling in aspect and condition those before him were constantly undergoing the most dreadful tortures and capital punishment for the crime of sorcery, in all its forms and degrees?

So thunderstruck with amazement and dread he was, that the momentous nature of his own business passed for awhile from his recollection. And it is doubtful how long he would have remained transfixed and gazing, had not his steed, alarmed at the glare and smoke before it, uttered the usual cry of a startled animal of its kind.

In a moment a panic seemed to take nearly the entire assemblage. The gravedigger flung down his basket of dreadful relics; the old women who were squatting around jumped up and scudded off like frightened toads; and only Maud Grimsorwe seemed to have sufficient courage to remain. And she, turning her withered countenance round, with her back to the glowing gipsy fire, rather shrieked than said, 'The spell is of power— the spell is of power! My child has answered from her grave in this apparition, and her son shall be Lord of Aston Hall!'

Edward comprehended immediately, from recollection of an example with which a play of the great Warwickshire worthy had familiarised all England, that the dreadful old woman had been engaged in magical rites to ascertain the probabilities of her grandson's success in his criminal enterprises. The exclamation reminded him to continue his personation on an occasion when discovery would add so much to his risks. Even he fancied he spied some advantage in the circumstance.

He spurred his horse on ; which unwillingly, and with restive action, approached the blaze.

'I am no apparition, grandmother!' he said, in muffled accents, fearful of his ability to deceive ears so accustomed to the true tones of Grimsorwe's voice, and passing his horse beyond the hideous glare. 'But your prayers, if even they be to the Evil One, have proved of great influence in my behalf. The Parliament has received me among its adherents, and released me. But intelligence of my doings has been carried to Aston before me, and I am now flying from my father's anger and the cavaliers where best I may! Be sure, then, whoever overtakes me, misinform them of the way I have taken. I mean to make for Erdington ; but say I have fled over Sutton Chace !'

Even as he spoke a distant trampling of horses' hoofs came to his ears, as well as to those of the witch, who listened with apparent bewilderment.

'Ho, ho! Black Tom, Black Tom! art thou deceiving me?' she muttered. 'How shall my grandson be Lord of Aston, and flee thence for his life? And the cavaliers following him on the wind, whom I myself saw so lately all but dead asleep with weariness and drink?'

Edward had not, until now, noticed that the witch's

favourite companion, her starveling cat, formed a portion
of the company, and had not stirred from the comfortable
glow of the fire, in the general consternation, but remained purring and singing contentedly before it.

'Yes, yes, the cavaliers—a fresh party of them—you
will know them by their bright armour—but with Prince
Rupert still at their head,' Edward hurriedly rejoined.
'Hark! they come. He is the son of a crownless king.
Strive and detain him with some fine promise that he
shall be a king himself in good time; hear you! anything to delay and misdirect.'

The old woman brisking up at the prospect of mischief, Edward waved his hand in parting, and taking his,
proper right-hand road, bade her once again be sure and
say he had taken the left, and might be speedily overtaken. But swift indeed must have been the rider who
could have overtaken him, when upon that he jerked
the rein towards Erdington Woods.

CHAPTER XLVI.

A PURITAN 'MACBETH' AND 'BANQUO.'

THE sorceress herself, however, remained on the scene
of action, considerably puzzled.

'What can it all mean?' she muttered, tossing back
her white tattered locks in the wind. 'It was Sir
Thomas Holte himself, or Adam Blackjack lied, who
desired me to summon my witch-friends here—poor
dotard!—under assurance of his protection, and cast a
spell by which what is coming to pass in these strange
times should be known. He may well wish to learn,
wealthy and endangered as he is; and his dead children
attest my power to him from their graves! My curses
killed *them*, doubtless! Yet I never cursed young
Edward, and he is going, they say, to lay his goodly
head upon the block in London. My grandson must be
endowed with an equal power to harm with his ill wishes.
And yet he himself, it seems, is detected, and flying a
banished wretch from his father's indignation. I know
not if it will be of use now, if Sir Thomas comes to
warn him, as I purpose that his house and name will
never be built on any secure foundation, but shall pass
away like a dream, unless he acknowledges my daughter's
son for his true heir. No man, nor woman either, can
dispute he is the *elder*-born!'

The old woman's perplexity now changed its course.

'Strange, too,' she thought, 'flying at so breathless a speed from a company of worn-out men, who slept but shortly ago as if death had strewed the straw in the barns and outhouses they are lying in at Aston. So that, although some cursed me for a witch when I peeped in, not a horse-trooper of them all raised his tired arm to smite me. My troth! if all speeds well with Richard's contrivances in Birmingham, some of them will sleep the sounder to-night. No other male heir will remain when Edward's head is off, and so Sir Thomas must needs be reconciled to him. Yet was it Richard who passed just now, or some illusion of the Fòul One? Hath the Demon listened to me at last, after so often calling upon him in vain with my curses? Or is he putting a cheat upon me, as they say is chiefly the Old Deceiver's wont, when he seems to grant prayers made to him? The phantom showed most like my grandson Richard, it is true; the hair and tawny skin were his, but were the eyes and voice altogether so?'

Perplexed with growing suspicion, the witch still felt she could not be mistaken in the rapidly nearing thud of horses' galloping that came to her hearing.

This recalled her to the propriety of getting things in readiness for the new arrival; and she called to her dispersed companions to return.

'Nan Crookshank—Malkin of the Dyke—Winny Crossbone! Where are ye all? Come, my bats! come, my howlikins! come, my she-rats without tails! good friends, come! There is a jolly bake of offals from the Hall, for ye to share when the work's done, of the meal Adam Blackjack served whole to a Royal Prince this eve! What's your fear, sisters? We meet to-night by full permission, with the great man of Aston himself for a visitor.'

Some of the old women answered, but in distant screech-owl notes : 'Faggots and fire; Faggots and fire! Come away, Maud, mother! Come away! The devil himself cannot save us if once they get us into the flames!'

'Base-spirited hags! incapable of any good vengeance! Let them go—what care I?' muttered Maud Grimsorwe. 'Yet I gave them a bumper of *aqua vitæ* to put some courage in their marrowless old bones, and in the very cups from Sir Thomas's most careful stores, which Adam Blackjack would have me show to convince him I have the secret to walk his house invisibly, and steal! Would I had; neither silver nor gold should long deck his sideboard, unless my grandson were declared the true inheritor. But what is all this clatter now upon the wind? The pursuers come!'

Even as the wretched old creature uttered the words, two horsemen, in new and brightly polished suits of armour, appeared in sight, riding at the stretch of their powerfully-limbed chargers' speed. There was also a third in their company, almost abreast ; but he was a ragged lad, and rode bareback, with nothing but a halter in the mouth of a shaggy-looking pony to guide its advance.

These were Cromwell and Lambert, with their tinker guide, who, on the information of the bellows-blower, had started in pursuit of Edward Holte, and at a speed which it was evident had distanced the main body of newly equipped dragoons, though it was probable it was not far in the rear.

The spectacle that had alarmed Edward Holte was

somewhat diminished in effect by the absence of most of the other hags. But enough, it was plain, remained to challenge wonder and observation.

The furnace fire still threw its crimson glare. The unhallowed mixture still bubbled in the pot, and the moon having risen over the dreary heath which formed a considerable portion of Sutton Chace, illumined with a ghastly pallor the wild and weird figure of the Witch of Aston, as she stood seemingly awaiting the approach.

All this together produced a mingled exclamation of surprise and dismay on the part of the riders, and the three unanimously did as Edward had done—came to a sudden halt.

'What's this?' exclaimed Lambert. 'What strange woman have we here out on a desert place at midnight, who makes such signs of forbidding at us with her outstretched skinny arms?'

'It is a WITCH!' gasped the tinker boy, cowering as if to fall from his horse with dread.

'Indeed, but things look very like it; very like it, truly!' said Cromwell, also in singularly panic-stricken accents. 'I do remember me, in my unregenerate days, such a wild wretch as this they showed us for a witch at the Blackfriars' Theatre, that the playerman, William Shakespeare—who, they say, knew the secrets of both worlds—did devise and place before men's eyes.'

'Yonder, also, are the blasted heath and the aghast moon! Even in such a spot as this, truly, might he—being, as they say, a night poacher in woods and out-lands in his youth—have come upon creatures like this. And was he not of this Warwick county him-self?' returned Lambert.

'Let us go no further, sirs! The witch will put

some black cross upon us, turn us into dogs and fami-
liars, or ride us up and down the sky on broomsticks,
mayhap!' said Bunyan, quite in earnest, and terrified,
in the remark.

'The Lord being with us, what should we fear? Let
us tax her with her unlawful dealings, for there are
many statutes of most heavy charge, in the late King's
reign, against all manner of witchcraft and incantations,
upon which she seems now busy,' said Lambert, who
had been a lawyer before he took to soldiering.

'But let us be advised, brother, how we proceed,'
Cromwell replied, with strange tremulousness. 'I tell
you there was an ancestress of mine own, my Lady
Cromwell, wife to Sir Samuel Cromwell of Huntingdon,
who was done to death by charms and spells. But
you must needs have heard of the witches of Warbors,
some fifty years ago? Let us speak her fair and pass,
until such time as we have better leisure for judgment
and fulfilment of the law on this woman of Belial.
Come on, boy; why do you shrink and tremble thus
behind?

'It is my beast that will no further; his shoes are
clammed to the ground; I cannot move him by a step!'
returned the lad, who was holding his nag's head as
tight in the halter as if he had meant to strangle it.

'I believe thou liest,' said Cromwell, ' but we cannot
do without thee; loosen the rope, or look to have it
twisted as close round thine own neck. Come on, John
Lambert; we must clear this vermin out of the road,
or none of our following will dare to keep it!'

And putting evidently a strong force on his own
reluctance, the captain resumed his advance, clutching
the halter of the tinker guide's horse to make it keep

pace. The boy writhed and trembled, but could not help submitting unless he had slipped from his seat, which once or twice seemed likely enough.

Lambert himself, who had spoken most valiantly of the three at first, now held back, and was the last in the advance.

'What manner of woman are you, out on this lone spot at midnight—if woman you be?' said Cromwell, when they were nigh enough to be distinctly heard; but his voice quivered more than ever, strive to control the emotion as he might.

Maud Grimsorwe hesitated in her reply. She was aware of the penalties attached to the possession of the privileges of a witch; and tempted as the decrepit old wretch felt by the pride of diffusing fear, the consideration probably restained her.

'I am a poor old woman, sir,' she accordingly answered, after a pause, 'and time has so nigh done with me, neither do I take much note of time, if it be midnight, as you say. I am boiling a mash for some calving cows that feed out on the Chace, the male folks being very busy now with the soldiers at Aston Hall.'

'It is a strange-looking hodge-podge, howsoever, mistress,' said Lambert, peering into the caldron, and turning deadly pale. 'The mess seems to me more like unto boiling and bubbling blood than aught else; and if I am not much mistaken, that is a grinning human jawbone sharking at us from the hell-broth!'

'The colour is but the glare of the red flames, my master,' returned the old woman, scornfully; 'and what you espy as grinning teeth are acorns, to make the mash bitterly medicinal.'

'Peace, lieutenant,' resumed Cromwell; 'it is likely

enough what the old woman says. I was a cattle-
man myself once, and we gave our calving kine warm
mashes of the sort. But, now tell me, mother (we
must speak the devil fair sometimes, I tell thee, John!)
have you seen a man on horseback pass this way, in
a lawyer's robe? and if so, how went he?'

'In a lawyer's robe? Truly, yes,' the hag readily
replied; 'and yonder along the White Walk, over
Sutton Chace, he took his way, galloping as if he were
at race with the wind, and from the gallows!'

'Is yonder our turn outward to Nottingham, boy?'
said Cromwell to the tinker.

'The lad could hardly answer for the chattering of
his teeth; but he made shift to let it be known that
the one indicated was the reverse of the right turning,
until the witch's threatening glare fell upon him, when
he broke off inarticulate with fear.

'If it be not Nottingham way, our game shall not take
us off on a across scent,' Cromwell observed on this.
'Let him go his road as we will ours. Proceed in our
guidance, boy; we may take it the more leisurely,
that's all.'

'Do so, and a dry canker shall wither up thy bones,
boy, till they crack from thee like rotten twigs from a
bush!' the witch now exclaimed, thrown off her guard
by her own apprehensions for her supposed grandson's
safety, in fierce and menacing accents.

'Refuse, and I will hang thee up as firmly as the
greenest oak branch in thine own fancy rope rein,'
returned Cromwell, provoked out of his own fears with
this interference, which seemed also to confess the
attempted deception. 'And for you, foul witch, betake
yourself out of all Christian presence at once, or I will

overturn your mess, and try if you will not scald before
you burn.'

'Proud fool! you could not harm me; and I bid
you, in your turn, beware what you do! Ruin and
overthrow await you on this road if you pursue it; and
mere harmless village dogs shall go wolvish to devour
all of your company!'

'I will believe heaven rather than hell, which hath
promised me a good success,' returned Cromwell.
'Avoid the way then, beldam, or I will override your
shrivelled carcass to follow on't!'

'You speak greatly, master. But I tell you "There
is many a slip between the cup and the lip:" and though
Charles Stuart and all his family shall perish from the
land, and you shall sit on the throne of their desolation,
you shall be but the mockery and shadow of a KING,
and the gibbet shall swing your rotten bones at last!
But the blood is not yet shed which must flood you to
that height; and, though I wish you the devil's speed
in your work, 'tis but a poor beginning you make now,
to serve an old dotard's rage upon his son's life!'

'A king! Captain, you shall be a *king*, she says,'
Lambert repeated sneeringly. 'Prithee, then, good
woman—since fair words trade so well with you—what
fortune do you predict to me?'

'To be your *master's ape*! What more for such as
thou art?' the hag replied, with extreme bitterness.

'Thank you, that 'tis nothing worse. You might
have predicted a descent of kings from me, and so got
me my throat cut some night in a ditch, on my master's
coronation day; for look how he muses over your raving
lies,' said Lambert, mockingly; but he was plainly
much annoyed with the retort.

Cromwell, on his part, seemed offended with his lieutenant's allusion.

'Your head runs on a rantipole play, methinks, Lambert, and you see not how far this poor old woman's wits are astray, talking on as if we were thief-takers riding in a pursuit,' he observed. 'But at present, lieutenant, I charge you place so much credence on her words as to follow the escaped prisoner in the direction she gives; and if you overtake him, and he refuses to stay, kill him at once, without mercy! On my part, I will but wait till the troop comes up, to proceed on the main enterprise.'

'Methinks, sir, I should have some others with me also; the man is desperate, and escaped well armed,' returned Lambert, sulkily.

'How, do you dispute my orders, lieutenant?' resumed Cromwell, angrily and imperiously. 'Why, man, if I bade you attack a score, you should do it; and I send one armed man against but another now.'

'You are my officer, truly, sir,' Lambert replied, doggedly, 'and I must obey you. God be with you, captain, and do not listen to any temptings of the fiend from this weird woman's lips. Was Saul the wiser unto salvation of himself or his host, when he questioned her of Endor?'

He was then about to turn on the cross-road to the left over Sutton Chace, when a strange voice was heard from the angle of the wall over where this lurid scene took place. It exclaimed, in accents of fierce satisfaction, 'Ha, hag-witch! have I detected you at last at your sorceries? Look to broil at a stake for this, were you ten times Richard Grimsorwe's grandam!'

A strong-built man dragged himself up by the hands

to the top of the wall, as the words were uttered. But neither he nor another, who raised himself by the same means at the corresponding angle of the wall, expected the spectacle that presented itself.

The latter was yelling out, 'Now, witch, I cast off thy power and dominion for ever! So Sir Thomas has seen thee at thy witchcrafts, and——what armed men be these?'

The two first persons who arrived were Sir Thomas Holte and Adam Blackjack, who had fallen, apparently, upon a trick to seduce the Witch of Aston into a betrayal of her true qualities, and in a manner not to be mistaken; an effort to throw off the yoke that certainly partook of the disorder of the master-cook's mind, and very twilight sense of morality.

Maud Grimsorwe stared, in complete bewilderment, at the whole party.

'Is not this man the Prince Palatine, whom you allow to pursue your son Richard to destruction, Sir Thomas Holte?' she exclaimed.

'She is surely a madwoman, if these are real living men and soldiers. But how in nature can they be the Prince's troop, whom we left all fast asleep at Aston?' said Sir Thomas, almost equally astonished.

While he spoke, a redoubled and numerous trampling announced the approach of the main body of Cromwell's troopers.

In a few moments a long line, glittering in the new steel armour from Firebrace's forge, flashed past the astounded gaze of the baronet and his domestic. But just as they arrived, the witch threw something into the fire which exploded, and sent volumes of sulphureous smoke around, and for awhile darkened everything.

Very considerable confusion, amounting indeed to panic, seized upon the entire body of Cromwell's troopers upon this alarming reception.

In vain, shaking himself up from a kind of lethargy of brooding over what he had heard, the Parliament captain's voice rang out in loud and inspiriting words of rally and command. The horses, bestrid by those fear-struck riders, either became unmanageable, or followed the blind impulses of their riders' terror. When the smoke cleared away, the furnace was extinguished, the pot blown to atoms, the witch and the two detective observers over the wall had disappeared, and Cromwell found himself completely alone on the cross-road, with his troopers scattered in all directions, but chiefly over the open lands of Sutton Chace.

Much time was, of course, lost in the effort to re-assemble the soldiery; and when they collected in any number, it was at a considerable distance from the proper high road, near the ancient royal Manor-House of the district. Most of the paths and by-ways taken by the affrighted troopers converged on that.

But even when his corps was reassembled, Cromwell perceived very plainly that all hopes of a successful prosecution of his enterprise were at an end.

The superstition of the times and of his men was equal to their fanaticism, and somehow or other the report had become universal among the Ironsides that a witch had crossed their captain's path, and had denounced the enterprise on which they were going as certain to lead to the destruction of all concerned.

So far they had followed their leader implicitly, without knowing whither; but now a general, a panic-stricken murmuring at the prosecution of the design—

equally unknown as it continued—reached Cromwell's
cognisance ; and, with the true tact of a leader, he felt
it would be in vain to urge a project of so much hazard
and audacity upon men in such a state of reduced
morale.

Lambert, perhaps, who was all along offended at not
being trusted with the secret any more than the com-
monest trooper, took pains to spread reasons for dis-
trust and fear. What much he guessed of the real
object, rather stirred the secret envy and rivalry in his
bosom against his chief, than any zeal to second him
in an effort likely to lead to results so momentous, and
which would thrust Cromwell on such sudden eminence.

It could not have been Bunyan, the only other sharer
in the Witch of Aston's denunciation. The lad had
taken the earliest advantage of the confusion to effect
his escape completely from what he doubtless now
looked upon as an office under a fearful ban.

The circumstance that he had no longer a guide, and
was himself entirely ignorant of the country, had probably as great an influence as anything else in Cromwell's relinquishing the attempt on Nottingham. But
this failure also compelled him to take into consideration that he had no longer the chance of a brilliant
success to excuse an open and undeniable breach of
orders direct from his general.

Nay, in the strangely disordered and affrighted state
of his troopers' mind, he remembered with apprehension the nigh neighbourhood of the reckless Rupert and
his cavalry, whom intelligence must now have reached,
and whom a night's rest would put in condition for
action.

To return to Birmingham without engaging and de-

feating the cavaliers, would be to place himself in a
state of siege, in the midst of a town whose headstrong and divided counsels he felt he could not in such
a case control any longer. Or which might, on the
strength of his presence, rush upon some ruinous
demonstration of its own against the enemy.

On the other hand, his personal representations and
influence might be exerted to induce the Earl of Essex
and his officers to perceive the advantages of transfer-
ring the war to the neighbourhood of Birmingham. Its
condition would probably soon call for active measures
of relief, and the forward zeal it had exhibited in the
cause would compel the Parliament to forward his
representations in its favour. Perhaps the Earl might
even be induced by a true statement of the case to
advance the masses of his army upon the King at once;
or his own friends in Parliament might be brought to
urge the measure irresistibly on the public attention.

Upon these reflections—it could not surely be that
the witch's threats had any influence!—the sagacious
and usually calm-blooded leader came to the conclusion
that he would right his whole position in a single effort,
by announcing that he meant to proceed at once to
join the Earl of Essex, in obedience to his orders, at
Northampton.

He even gave it to be understood that such had all
along been his intention, and that he had left Birmingham so clandestinely only to prevent himself from being
annoyed by importunities to remain!

CHAPTER XLVII.

CHARLES THE FIRST.

IF Edward Holte had known these facts, he need not have made such headlong haste as he did on his journey to Nottingham. But he conceived himself anticipating what might well prove a fatal surprise for the King, and consequently his whole party. And the generous steed he bestrode seconding his impatience, horse and man arrived, all but exhausted, at the gates of Nottingham about noon on the day after his midnight flight.

Every stage of the journey more than ever convinced Edward of the certainty of the danger incurred, and the great likelihood that success would have crowned Cromwell's audacious attempt.

There was not a single garrison, or even outlying post of the King, south of Nottingham; and most of the intervening country was known to be strongly disposed to the cause of the Parliament.

So obstinately rooted, however, were the King's opinions of the inviolability and majesty of his person and office, that he even cherished a belief his subjects would never dare to meet him openly in the field. The supposed distance of any possible assailing force contributed to lull the vigilance of his scanty military attendance, and the news of Prince Rupert's victorious commencement of hostilities in Worcestershire, had recently arrived to swell the pride and confidence of the Royalists.

To complete the improvidence of the arrangements, the three or four hundred county militia who held the town for the King, and who were very slightly disciplined and ill-armed, were separated from the dilapidated old castle in which he resided by the rocky ravine surrounding it; and yet the approaches to the castle itself were no otherwise guarded: and the person of Charles I. was secured only by the swords of about sixty gentlemen, who had volunteered for the service, but whose high rank, and gay and careless habits, made them much fitter for courtiers than soldiers. Not to mention that they were perpetually quarrelling among themselves for position and favour with the King, and scarcely deigned to yield obedience to the captain he had placed over them, though allied to the royal blood.

Edward Holte distinctly perceived how easy it would have been for Cromwell to fall by surprise on the town, scatter the show of force collected in it, and thence have made his way into the castle. Inlet to that was easy; and the noble guard could have made but slight resistance in a fortress so ancient and ruinous that it was a fact none of the principal gates could be closed, and not even the precaution of a barricade had been raised in their stead.

Then again: strangely noticeable as was the whole exhausted and bespattered apparition of Edward on his arrival, in so troublous a time, it seemed to excite scarcely any attention. He was taken to be simply one of the numerous messengers who were arriving from various parts in the King's interest. He passed unchallenged through the town; and could hardly be said to be questioned even with a glance until he arrived in the principal court-yard of the ancient pile, built by an illegitimate son of William the Conqueror, and white and ghostly, even in the bright morning sun, with age.

In truth, messengers had ceased for some time to excite any very favourable interest at the Court of Charles, I. At this period they chiefly came with apologies for failures in promises, and craving for delay.

Since the erection of his standard, Charles had every reason to be disatisfied with the results that had followed. Even the nobility and gentry most devoted to his cause seemed taken by surprise.

Considerable portions of them had indeed no wish, by too early and overwhelming a triumph, to establish the King in the despotism his own inclinations were sufficiently known to point to, as the natural issue of a conflict. His fifteen years of absolute personal government and tyranny made his latter promises and assurances distrusted by the majority even of his own party; and disinterested men still hoped to the last that some means less arbitrary than the sword might be found to compose differences. The Royalists especially, believing they had the real power when they chose to exert it, were very backward in comparison with the adherents of the Parliament, which knew better what it was about, and was set on its purposes with inexorable clearness of resolution and design.

Things, indeed, looked so untoward, that on the very morning of Edward Holte's arrival in Nottingham, a council had been held, in which some of the King's most trusted and faithful advisers earnestly urged upon him the propriety—the necessity even—of renewing proposals of peace to the Parliament.

This advice was, however, so distasteful to the proud and self-willed monarch, that he had broken up the assemblage in a disdainful and angry manner; declaring that if deserted by all those who had promised him their fidelity and adherence, in the maintenance of his just rights as King of England, he would rather perish by the sword of the meanest rebel trooper than humiliate himself to sue for 'pardon and mercy' to the insolent *Parliament of Westminster!* •

So the King styled it, in distinction from the poor attempt at a rival one which he had lately assembled round himself at York.

In fact the principal councillors were leaving the presence of their irritated sovereign, who announced himself insulted by the base proposition made, at the moment Edward Holte rode into the castle-yard.

The King and his immediate attendants occupied the keep, or principal central pile of the building. Consequently, these grave personages—mostly with a rebuked and discontented look, and buzzing displeased remarks among themselves—were coming out to their respective lodgings in the fortress or the town. And it so happened that Edward's horse, being completely spent with the length and rapidity of its transit, stumbling over a loose stone, fell, after a slight stagger, so nigh the feet of one of the chief of these officials, that it was only by a hasty retreat he escaped a rather rude shock.

'Sain us! what manner of awkward rider is this, who

stables his steed on our toes?' exclaimed the personage thus assailed, but without asperity.

'Not only the council, but the councillor, shall be *overridden* to-day, it seems, Sir Edward,' remarked another near him, with a facetious and good-humoured expression, which differed from that of most of his associates.

'It is no great wonder; we see by his robe that he is only expected to ride a legal hobby to market. 'Tis a gentleman of your own profession, Master Chancellor,' said a third person.

At this time Sir Edward Hyde—the future Lord Chancellor Clarendon—was only Chancellor of the Exchequer to Charles I.; and one not overburdened with ways and means.

'Not so, sir; 'tis a diguise I have assumed to free myself from heavy thraldom and danger of my life, and to warn his Majesty of a most eminent approaching peril to his own, and the entire kingdom, so—I have scarcely breath—but for God's sake, let me see at once the gentleman who has the chief military command in his Majesty's quarters,' said Edward, and indeed in gasping pants for utterance.

'Danger to his Majesty's person! Have I not said so and warned so a thousand times? But how, sir, how?' said a deep, melancholy voice, from one who had not yet spoken, but whose noble person, fine though sorrowful features, and general air of neglect and carelessness in his otherwise rich garb, could not fail to command attention.

But Edward Holte was struck with the appearance of this nobleman—for he seemed of rank—for another reason.

'Lose no time to question me, dear Lord Falkland. You will conceive well I am no idle newsmonger, when I tell you that I am your old school and college-fellow, Edward Holte, come post hither with strange news out of Warwickshire. Nay, you know me not for this black wig. Now, what say you? Dear friend, no; let us leave embracings for aftertime. Fly to Sir Jacob Astley, and tell him suddenly to close the gates of the town, call every man to arms, and stand on the defence of the castle and of the King's person for life or death, against a large party of Parliament horse coming at full pace from Birmingham.'

'From Birmingham!' exclaimed several at once.

'Surely it cannot be. We have heard of no force on the Parliament's part nigher than Worcester; and that discouraged by a late defeat,' said Sir Edward Hyde.

'All will be lost, then, through incredulity. Lead me to the King himself, and I will speedily convince him. Meanwhile, no harm can be done by sounding the alert to the citizens and trainbands in the town,' returned the messenger, with a passionate excitement that supplied him with strength. 'Do you think I have ridden my good horse nigh to death for nothing?'

'In truth do not I, my dear schoolfellow. My lords and sirs, I can testify to you this is a gentleman incapable alike of falsehood or unfounded fear. Come with me, Edward; I will lead you myself at once to the King,' said the Lord Falkland.

'Good troth, then, I will see to the closing of the town on the word. Sir Jacob Astley is out hawking in the meadows below while we councillors were supposed to debate affairs,' said the good-humoured-looking personage who had before spoken.

'Do so, my lord Southampton; and let some groom attend this poor beast with a bucket of water,' said the humane Falkland. And offering his arm at the same time to Edward, he added kindly, 'Lean well on me, dear friend; I will be your guide to the presence of his Majesty.'

The help was very welcome and needful to Edward, who was stiff and faint with his long ride almost to an inability to move. He tottered, in fact, as if about to imitate his steed, for the first few steps. But luckily, a page passing with a ewer of water, Edward took a long drink from it, which greatly revived him, and then proceeded.

Lord Falkland kindly and prudently forbore to press the exhausted visitor for particulars of his intelligence; but he as considerately warned him that he should probably find the King in a very ungracious humour, and unwilling to be disturbed with any more disastrous news. 'Take your reception, whatever it may be, therefore, in good part, my dear friend, and answer his Majesty sharply and at once to the point. Indeed, your condition will suffer no otherwise. But here we are. Collect yourself for the effort; we are close upon the guard chamber; and what guard, you see, they keep!'

As he spoke, Falkland pushed open an unbarred door, black and worm-eaten with age, as if William Peverel himself had put it on the hinges; and then a curious and unexpected scene presented itself. A number of men, in a uniform gorgeous with velvet and gold lace, but with armour laid aside in full security, sat in groups at different tables in a long gallery, drinking, smoking, throwing dice, playing at cards, laughing, talking, rollicking, in the noisy confusion and uproar of a barrack-room; men nearly all of great quality and possessions, but who had even thus early adopted a tone of swaggering and debauchery as a distinguishing badge from the gravity and precision of their adversaries.

These guardsmen did not even notice the stranger's passage, though it is true the presence of Lord Falkland was a sufficient guarantee of his right to one.

A corridor thence conducted to a chamber in a circular tower at the end, and as there was no further let or hindrance, in a few moments Edward found himself introduced into the presence of the unfortunate sovereign, whose grandeur and fall present the most extraordinary and momentous catastrophe of history.

At the moment of Edward's entrance the King was seated in a deep recess of the round apartment in which they found him, writing by the full light which only in that part descended into its dark extent.

It looked like a haunted chamber of romance. The walls were hung with tapestry faded in all its figures to a ghostly indistinctness. The flooring creaked and crumbled as it was walked over, and was quite bare. The only good or even passable piece of furniture in the chamber was the desk at which the King was engaged, and which was a rich and elaborately finished piece of cabinet work, furnished with secret drawers, and curiously finished and ornamented in every detail. It is, in fact, the same preserved at Aston Hall, for the inspection of such of the curious as are allowed the privilege of a complete survey of the edifice and its contents.

At this the uxorious spouse of Henrietta Maria of France was engaged in composing a long and elaborate letter to his wife, accounting to her for the events of the day, and vaunting his own firmness and resolution in following up *her* ideas, in the rejection of peace on any terms but the full restoration of his abused power.

The numerous portraits of Charles I., executed by the greatest artists of his time, or of any time, have familiarised the world with his features and general expression ; but almost all of these were executed before his period of trouble and tribulation, when his court was reckoned among the most stately and magnificent of Europe, and he himself was served in it with little less than the awe and majesty due to a being clothed with most of the attributes of a divinity.

Even at this early stage of his reverse of fortune the naturally austere and melancholy countenance of the King had become more than ever the mirror of his unluckily compounded character. It was still handsome and princely noble in the general features. But in spite of the pride and reserve that marked every line, something of irresolution and infirmity of purpose flickered over the pale but easily excited complexion, and quivered in the corners of the unhappy and depressed, though well-cut and ruddy mouth. Nor could the cold and peremptory glance of the bright grey eyes, which in some lights became blue, disguise the anxiety and suspicion that lurked in their depths, and gave even their severest and haughtiest scrutiny a character of internal puzzle and weakness, which his craftier counsellors well understood, and worked to their own ends.

The long curling chestnut-brown hair of Charles I. was already prematurely grizzled ; and being subject in his youth to fits of stammering and hesitation, which he only remedied by speaking with great slowness and deliberation, this had now become an imposing and stately fashion with him, that gave all he said an air of being profoundly weighed and considered. But these circumstances made him seem older than he was; and the sombre richness of his apparel, which was chiefly of maroon or mulberry-coloured velvet, overspread on the shoulders with a collar of magnificent point lace, added to that effect.

To Edward Holte, however, this Prince was the incarnation of all that was great and august in human character and destiny; and if he saw him now shorn of some of his more glorious attributes, it was still the sun, though clouded by malignant vapours, which his worshipping gaze fell upon. Never knelt there a subject more loyal, heart and soul, than the heir of Aston Hall, when, the King turning sharply round on the noise of the entrance of his secretary with the unexpected visitor, Lord Falkland introduced him by name, and he sunk, utterly spent, on the floor, at the monarch's feet.

CHAPTER XLVIII.

THE COUNCIL OF WAR.

CHARLES himself appeared to have his natural sternness and arbitrary disposition, rather than his sympathies, roused by this display of emotion in a subject who presented himself so seemingly out of condition to render him the sort of assistance his affairs most required at the time.

'More excuses, is it, Falkland, instead of good weapons and stout men-at-arms to wield them?' the King said. 'If so, we are weary and desire to hear no more, come from what quarter soever they may. Consider your errand as done, sir, then, when you have named your senders, and trouble not to card us the usual wind of words of loyalty and devotion in our ears.'

'My liege, the young gentleman is well nigh spent with his haste to do you a most substantial service,' interposed Lord Falkland. 'And your Majesty will the readier believe so when I repeat he is the son of Sir Thomas Holte, of Warwickshire, who——'

'We need no further reminding, my Lord Falkland,' interrupted Charles, with a flush of anger and disdain. 'We remember very well Sir Thomas was of the forwardest to send us offers of assistance, as he has since shown himself of the backwardest to keep any pace in performance of the same. Not only has he not sent us a single man or horse of a pretended troop of cavalry he was raising in our service, but, as we hear, the town of Birmingham, which is as it were directly under hand-stroke from his fine new palace at Aston—an unwalled and every way unsoldiered and unprovided town—has burst into open sedition and declared for the Parliament, while he looks helplessly, or perhaps approvingly, on.'

'Not so, sire, oh, not so!' Edward Holte now exclaimed, with rekindled energy. 'My father has done all that lay in his power to fulfil his pledges to your Majesty: and no one knows so better than myself, his heir, who have barely escaped with my life from the fury of the misguided people there. But believe me, the townsmen of Birmingham are not in themselves so much to blame, as that they are in a manner driven on wild and desperate courses far beyond their inclinations by the wonderful zeal and industry in mischief of a noted Parliament man, who has lately taken to figuring among them in its name.'

'Why, so we have already heard, though not the traitor's quality or degree in treason. But what concerns it to know, when the least plotting villain of them all is a very giant caitiff of mutiny and insolence?' Charles replied; yet he continued in a milder way, 'Am I to understand, then, sir, you are the gentleman who was made prisoner on my behalf by those rebellious mechanics? and am I now to believe they have seen so speedily into the wickedness and danger of their sedition, and released you to be a suitor with me for pardon?'

Edward was obliged to reply that this was by no
means the case; that he had escaped with difficulty,
and with danger of his own life, to warn his Majesty of
a most flagitious and audacious project formed on his
sacred person itself by his.enemies.

'Charles looked at him now with visible alarm and
anxiety. ' Design on our person ! What, here in Nottingham ? Is the taint spread among our very servants
and followers then ? Stand up, man, and tell your
story, instead of gasping like a stranded fish on the floor
at our feet.'

Edward complied with this ungracious command with
a vivacity and spirit that perhaps rather startled the
King. 'What now, my Lord Falkland ? Do you say
you know the messenger ? ' he exclaimed.

'And can answer for his fidelity, sire, and perfect
trustworthiness, with my own life.'

' Well, then, say on, sir ; I would trust Judas on my
Lord Falkland's assurance, and am as attentive to you
as a man should be who is said to have a life-deep stake
in your utterances,' said Charles.

Edward Holte felt both chilled and repelled by the
kind of reception he experienced, but perhaps he derived
more courage from it than he might from a kinder one.
Accordingly he no longer hesitated, but revealed to the
King the project formed to surprise his person by a
party of cavalry secretly brought to Birmingham, and
flung upon Nottingham thence, and which in all probability he only anticipated by the briefest interval.

Charles seemed incredulous for some moments that
so audacious an act of treason and malice against his
royal person could really enter the head of his hardiest
opposer. But when he precipitately enquired who had

dared to project putting such an unimaginable villainy in execution, and learned, a very singular and powerful effect was produced upon him.

'*Cromwell!*—Captain Cromwell!—one of the Cromwells of Hinchinbroke, deem you? Heard you ever the man's Christian name, if such a ruffian can be said to have one? Was it Oliver—*Oliver* Cromwell?'

And the King's countenance changed as he pronounced the fated name, and a shadow seemed to pass over his spirit, as the ancient tradition affirms even the towering genius of Cæsar ever sunk rebuked in the presence of Brutus.

'Oliver, doubtless, sire, is the man's name who has stirred up the artisans of Birmingham, in ignorance rather than malice, against your Royal cause; for I am sure, at all events, the principal persons of the town have been made his instruments very unwillingly, and are showing evident signs how far beyond their own meaning and intents they are pushed by the man's desperation and the mutinous spirit of the rabble, always desirous of changes, and averse to lawful yokes and restraint.'

Charles gave a deep sigh as he listened; so deep that Lord Falkland looked at him with his own sorrowful countenance intensified in its characteristic expression.

'It is even so, then,' the King remarked, evidently as if in explanation, 'and *Oliver Cromwell* has grown to be the man of a most audacious and unrespective boy. I marvel not that if any man in England should be found to project so towering a treason, this should be the man. I do remember me, when I was Prince, being on a certain occasion of one of my late father, King James's, royal progresses, at this fellow's uncle's house

near Huntingdon; when, having the insolence to quarrel me at some remark I made on his clownish gait and
demeanour, on my offering to chastise him, the big
varlet struck at me, and hurt me much.   Yea, and that
same night, woke up the whole house with some mad-
brained vision of a giantess, that came to his bedside,
and offered him—as he openly stuttered to all who would
hear—a royal crown!   My father was not angry until
then, although I had complained with bitter tears of the
indignity put upon me; and still old Sir Oliver found
a way to soothe him through his favourite theories, with
assurances that the boy's family had been under ban of
a witch for more than half a century, which set them,
mostly against their wills, on all manner of mad defiances
and risks.'

'But these are times for madmen to flourish in, sire,'
Lord Falkland responded.

'Ay, so it seems, dear Lucius,' Charles replied, in
kinder and softened tones, 'and I do fear me now, more
than ever, they can only be cured as madmen are, by
letting of blood; by whips and straw, and dark chaining
to dungeon floors.   And, oh! but it contents me ill
that I must be the harsh phlebotomist and flagellating
keeper of my state.   What says our own Willie Shakespeare, whom we both love so well?

> 'The times are out of joint; oh, cursed spite,
> That ever I was born to set them right.'

'Such a man of forward action, truly, is more dangerous than the most silver-tongued talker of those
against us, sire,' Lord Falkland rejoined; 'and methinks your Highness owes much thanks to the zeal and
prudence of this young gentleman in warning you
betimes of his purposes.'

'Well, and I thank him; but I should owe a broad-landed lordship to him who had brought me the traitor's head,' Charles observed. 'Well, well, the time may come. *Patience, patience!* True, it is a word that is growing a little wearisome in my vocabulary; yet it is my great comfort and consolation against the injuries and insults of the times. God is patient also; yet ever and anon He clears the skies with thunder or the earth with deluges of fire or water. My turn may come.'

'But when it come, sire——'

'Tut, tut; I know thy chime now by heart, if ever I shall. "Pardon and peace; peace and pardon!" Is not this the everlasting ding-dong, my soft-souled Lucius, but not Junius or Brutus? Ha! you know not what it is to be a king, and feel the royal majesty of one so trodden upon in the dust as mine hath been! My purple robes trampled by such a swinish hue and cry as drove at my heels when I left London last! I must return thither on the wings of destruction, and sweep the way clear with a besom of fire, or never again shall I feel a king, or my base rebels understand that such I am.'

It was now Falkland's turn to sigh; and sigh, indeed, he did. But he dared not discuss the matter further with the King, whose towering pride, rather than motives of policy, made him thus set and inveterate in the hope of vengeance.

He only indirectly insinuated his opinion by observing, 'But at present, sire, the question is rather how *you* may avoid the vengeance of your enemies.'

'What mean you, sir? Of a surety, now, all of my subjects who are not engaged neck-deep on the contrary part, will rally to me when they shall hear of so unparalleled an atrocity devised against my person itself,' said Charles, as if astonishe the information had not struck his minister in this light.

Edward Holte eagerly took the opportunity to declare how much the audacity of the projected treason had disgusted the very chiefs of the revolt in Birmingham. The master armourer, and head of the smiths' guild, in particular; the young man. Tubal Bromycham, who was appointed its military leader, and who claimed to be the representative of its ancient and unjustly dispossessed lords; but, above all, he dwelt upon the fact that it was only by the matchless loyalty and devotion to his Majesty's service of the master armourer's daughter, Dorothy Firebrace, that he had himself been enabled to effect his escape, and bring the timely warning he hoped he did.

Charles looked greatly pleased at this statement. 'Nay, if the women take to us, their men will soon follow,' he remarked. 'I will make a note of this good wench's name in my tablet, and it shall purchase her and her kindred, if it may be, some exemption from the heavy destruction which must fall anon on the devoted town; for Birmingham is so, both in our thoughts and in our nephew's most inexorable resolve. Our latest posts from him brought word that he purposed a sudden onslaught on the town, and that he would give it up to fire and sword from end to end, as an example to all others in the like rebellious mood.'

'This inhumanity and impolicy have been tried and failed, sire; the town is well prepared and resolute in its defence,' said Edward, secretly moved to indignation with the bloodthirsty announcement. And on the surprised exclamation of the King and his secretary, he related the general facts of the repulse of Prince Rupert from Birmingham, which had come to his knowledge in his imprisonment.

Lord Falkland was specially and very ominously struck with the tidings.

'I like it less than ever, my liege,' he said, 'this Oliver Cromwell fellow seems to have the makings of a great captain in him; and the only way to mar his greatness ——'

'Yes, yes, I know what thou would't say. Still thy never-failing burden to all songs, "Peace, peace!" interrupted the King.

Edward eagerly put in his word upon this, in behalf of his neighbour town.

He assured Charles, with great warmth and eloquence, that he felt persuaded Birmingham might easily be brought back to its duty and true allegiance by mild treatment, and an assurance of pardon for what might hitherto be done amiss. Violent measures, he urged upon the King, would only throw both leaders and people resolutely on their defence, who were then by no means confirmed in disloyalty, and hesitating in their course. Were Cromwell but once cleared out of the town, he felt certain the sudden explosion his fiery genius had produced would leave no further effects. Perseverance in attack would, on the other hand, absolutely compel the Parliament to interfere in protection, and probably open the eyes of its commanders to the immense advantages of the general situation and country in the approaching struggle.

The amiable Falkland earnestly seconded this appeal.

Blood, he said, never cemented any work; it was so
slippery a fluid.

'Well, gentlemen,' the King said at last, rather pettishly at the contradiction, 'it will be time enough to
speak of mercy to any of my disloyal cities and people
when themselves deign to ask it of us.'

'True, sire,' said Edward Holte, feeling the disguised
bitterness of the remark, 'and the question is besides,
at this moment, rather of the safe disposal of your own
royal person.   That, methinks, can never be in a
crumbling ruin like this castle, even put on the alert as
your Majesty's defence now is.'

'Why not, Master Holt?' Charles hastily replied.
'The chief danger in the purposed attack lay in a possible surprise.   This (and I thank your zeal, and will
to my best of kingly power recompense) is doubtless
prevented.'

'The attack by Captain Cromwell and his cavalry,
possibly, sire,' Edward earnestly rejoined.   'But the
general design is of such likelihood and policy, that it
is reasonable to conclude the Parliament leaders will
take the hint, and pour their whole army round you
here from Coventry and Northampton, and I see not
what means of resistance attend your Majesty against
a formal siege by such a host as the Earl of Essex is
assembling fast.'

'The only refuge, sire, is evidently flight,' said Lord
Falkland, using an indiscreet word; a word which
roused all the pride and ireful disdain of the Stuart's
character.

'Flight, Lord Falkland!   And do you dare to advise
your Prince to so mean and cowardly a course as to fly
before his rebels?   Let them come.   Men will then

believe in my danger, and in the threatening ruin that
awaits all other chiefdom and preeminence in my person. I tell you, sirs, all England will rally round the
steeps of Nottingham, when it is known the King of
England is in hazard of life and royalty within its castle
walls.'

Lord Falkland, well acquainted with the obstinacy of
the King's character when he once announced a resolution, only ventured now to entreat that at least the
Council might be reassembled to hear the tidings, and
advise his Majesty upon them.

But Charles was not to be reasoned with in his present mood. ' No, Falkland, no !' he exclaimed ; ' I know
that it will only be to hear from them again base counsels of submission, and imploring peace at any cost from
my insolent Westminster masters. It is much fitter
that my soldiers should be called to counsel now with
sharpened swords !'

And moved by one of those sudden and violent impulses which he seldom supported in their consequences,
Charles strode to the door of the chamber, and opening
it, called out at the pitch of his voice, ' Ho ! gentlemen
of the guard, à moi, à moi ! (to me, to me).'

The response to this appeal was of a rather startling
character. The apartment in which the King had
hitherto given peaceful audience to the messenger of
warning suddenly became flooded by a throng of half-
drunken and excited men, who, pouring in with naked
swords in their hands, seemed inclined to make a victim
at once of the stranger. One of the foremost, at all
events, a man of powerful and rather handsome person,
though with a most debauched and ferocious expression
of countenance, advanced, staggering, but evidently with

overboiling zeal, on Edward Holte. 'Has the rascal
attempted some harm to your Majesty? Make mince-
meat of him, gentlemen!' this personage roared out,
flourishing his sword; and the King himself was obliged
to restrain his bloodthirsty violence.

'Retract that expression, Goring, and instantly, I
command you!' Charles said, well knowing what the
point of honour in such a case would require, even
under a drunken mistake, and seizing the ruffianly
upraised arm. 'This gentleman, on the contrary, has
put himself to great hazard to serve me. It is to communicate his intelligence I have summoned you. A
party of Roundhead horse, gentlemen, is riding hither-
ward to make your King their prisoner. May I trust
for my protection to your swords?'

'Against the whole world, sire, an't please your Majesty! Where are the villains?' yelled the before-
mentioned valiant personage, flourishing his sword now
wildly in the air.

'This is the man,' whispered Falkland to Edward,
'who lost us Portsmouth without a blow; having em-
bezzled the King's money for the defence so utterly,
that he had not wherewithal left to buy the garrison a
fortnight's salt.'

Edward smiled scornfully.

'The enemies are probably coming pretty fast into
the windmill swinging of your sword, now, Lord Goring,'
he remarked. 'But, before you destroy them utterly
off the face of the earth, I must ask of you truly to
withdraw your insulting word, or face one close at
hand.'

'I obey the King's orders in all things, sire,' the brag-
gadocio replied, in humbled accents; and Edward, by a

contemptuous nod, accepted the apology as sufficient, just as a personage, in the fantastic costume of court fool, who had scudded in with the rest, quietly added, ' Except in keeping of his towns, good coz!'

There was a general peal of laughter, which seemed not to be restrained by the King's evident displeasure.

' But where are these enemies, sire? Gentlemen, let us throw open the gates, and spare them what trouble we can in their approach,' said a splendidly-arrayed young cavalier of those noble guardsmen.

' You are but sixty, my Lord Denbigh, and probably thrice your number to the attack,' rebuked Lord Falkland.

, ' No matter; we will not count them; and the more they are, shall but the better show the King that men can fight even with what you style *golden swords*, Lord Falkland,' returned the impetuous youth.

The secretary had possibly made some such allusion to the supposed restraining influences of great wealth on valour with relation to the noble guard, who were nearly all of them of extensive possessions, as well as of the highest rank.

' Do not wrangle, gentlemen. Rest satisfied with this, that I shall place the life of your King in your hands, and will not stir from this place for any number of assailants likely to be brought against it,' said Charles; and the announcement was received with an uproar of triumph and joy.

Only the captain of the troop, Lord Bernard Stuart, did not seem so well content; and enquired if they were to take his Majesty's commands direct, or from the Major-General, Sir Jacob Astley, who was expected in every moment from a hawking-party in the fields.

Lord Falkland took the opportunity to renew his entreaty that the Council might be reassembled round his Majesty. But Charles interrupted him with passionate exasperation.

'No, my Lord,' he exclaimed, 'these are the only proper councillors now for an English king! The die is cast: this last immeasurable insult and treason has overflowed the measure of my so far exhaustless endurance. War, nothing but war, henceforth. If I made peace on such terms as the Parliament might accede to me, in my supposed present desperate circumstances, gentlemen,' he continued to the guardsmen, 'I may, indeed, remain the shadow of a king; I may be waited on bareheaded; I may have my hand kissed; the title of Majesty may be continued to me; and the King's authority, signified by both Houses, may still be the style of their commands. I may have swords and maces carried before me, and please myself with the sight of a crown and sceptre, though even these twigs would not long flourish when the stock upon which they grew was dead. But as to true and real power, I should remain but the outside, but the picture, but the sign of a king. My towns are taken from me, my ships, my arms, my money; but there still remain to me a good cause, and the hearts of my loyal subjects, which, with God's blessing, will recover all the rest—among whom I truly hold this gentleman, Master Edward Holte, not among the least. And now, gentlemen, to your several duties, as I must to mine; and, my Lord Falkland, see that your friend be well lodged and attended in our own household here. And so, farewell.'

He waved his hand, and bowed with a kingly grace and stateliness to the assemblage, who bent in acknowledgment almost to the ground, and all present retired.

Lord Falkland resumed his hold of Edward's arm.

' There's but one hope now of aught reasonable,' he whispered to his friend as they left the presence. ' I will hasten and communicate all to Sir Edward Hyde, whose eloquence sometimes has influence over our master when no man else can more with him than the wind on a frozen sea. But, indeed, if the King continues in his obstinacy, all we can do is to make ready to die loyally by his side.'

CHAPTER XLIX.

GRIMSORWE'S GRAND COUNTER-MOVE.

AFTER the excitement of this scene, Edward felt a very natural return of his fatigue. In fact he almost fell asleep in the midst of an attempt at giving some further explanations to Lord Falkland, who, observing his condition, humanely left him to repose in his own chamber, with the assurance that if the enemy appeared he would immediately call him.

It was late in the evening before Edward awoke, much refreshed, and found Lord Falkland seated at his bedside.

This kind friend had also provided restoratives of a more substantial kind, of which Edward was now well enough inclined to partake ; particularly when he heard that the day had passed off without any alarm, and that the most diligent scouring of the adjoining country and forest had failed to discover an enemy.

He readily accounted for this by stating that his escape was known to Cromwell, who, finding his pursuit fail, would probably despair of success without the advantage of a surprise, and relinquish the enterprise.

Falkland looked grave, and, though evidently unwillingly, did not conceal from his friend that the unpleasant result had followed that a degree of incredulity was thrown on the whole information. The King, especially, had relapsed into one of his most rooted prejudices—that his subjects never would actually dare to raise their hands against their sovereign, when they should be called upon to face him in person. ' Such a divinity doth hedge a king,' he believed with his favourite poet.

One good result had, however, followed the restoration of this self-confidence. The King had listened more temperately to advice, and Sir Edward Hyde had prevailed upon him to consent to hold another council, to consider whether terms of peace should be proposed for the last time. But the virtuous and clear-souled Falkland acknowledged with a sigh that the minister had been obliged to suggest this as a mere trick to gain time. He and the rest of the council, however, wished Edward to attend their sitting, to endeavour once more to bring conviction of the danger of his situation to the King.

After this the conversation of the two friends became more general.

Falkland was well acquainted with Edward Holte's family affairs and position, and the harsh species of domestic tyranny under which he laboured. Conversation on this point was, however, necessarily constrained; only Edward learned with little satisfaction that the Lord Keeper Lyttelton, father of the young lady to whom he had been betrothed from his childhood, without any reference whatever to his own feelings or selection, was with the Court at Nottingham.

This nobleman was no favourite with Falkland or his friend; and, indeed, he shared the general fate of selfish time-servers, and was an object of contempt with both the parties between whom he strove to trim.

He was, however, a lawyer of great abilities and position ; but having been raised to his dignity (corresponding to that of Lord Chancellor at the present day) to assist in saving the Earl of Strafford on his impeachment, he had craftily shunned performance of the conditions in a way that rather conduced to the catastrophe of that ' bold, bad ' minister. After subsequently wavering and hesitating between the contending parties, the violent proceedings of the Parliament, and his instincts as a lawyer, frightened him from their cause, and he had recently escaped from London with the Great Seal in his possession to secure a welcome with the Court. He had hitherto, however, received but a very cold one, for Charles cherished a life-long repugnance to all who had been in any way instrumental to the destruction of the most skilful and courageous instrument of his arbitrary designs.

But why Edward Holte least liked this amphibious politician lay in the fact that he was likely to prove one of the main obstacles to the success of his love affair with the armourer's daughter.

This was an unknown circumstance in his friend's history to Falkland, until the warmth of his friend's expressions respecting the young girl in question excited his notice and curiosity. Edward Holte then, very desirous to secure an ally so near the king, and unaccustomed to keep secrets from his friend, avowed to him his passionate attachment, and wish and purpose to make his brave rescuer his wife.

Lord Falkland received this statement in a manner Edward had calculated upon, from his knowledge of his pure and honourable and right-minded character. He confessed that nothing could be more unjust than constraint on such a vital point, and highly approved of the intentions avowed by his friend, to observe every species of good faith and honourable dealing towards the woman of his choice. But, although he was himself above the ordinary prejudices of his age, Falkland was quite well aware of them.

'Marry an artisan's daughter, a mechanic citizen's heiress! prefer to the Lord Keeper's the daughter of a man who heads a sedition against the King! If we supposed even the impossibility of your father's consent, my dear Edward, the King would remain rooted to objections! There is no stronger prejudice in his mind, derived from his sky-flying Scottish ancestry, than utter disdain and repugnance to a mingling of gentle blood with what is called that of the commonalty. It is impossible!'

'But I have told you the Firebraces trace their descent—as clearly as the Stuarts themselves from their royal progenitors—from the prime nobility of France,' said Edward.

'Still, nothing can efface the stain of their mechanic occupation in the equally vulgar eyes of kings and populaces!' said Falkland, with a mournful smile, for all philosophy is mournful. 'But if anything can, dear Edward, it will be the memorable service which conjointly you and this brave Birmingham maiden have rendered to the King.'

This was all the consolation Edward derived in his affairs of the heart from his friend. But in those of the intellect a rich fruitage awaited him in the society and conversation of the accomplished Falkland. A tender-

hearted and great-souled man, the famous secretary of
Charles I. united the rarest distinctions of humanity.
His comprehensive genius took in all that was exalted,
refined, and august in the qualities of the mind;
his generous and feeling heart all that was kindly,
faithful, affectionate, and heroic, in impulse and emotion.   Happy, then, was he who died so young, before
he had time to experience to the fullest extent how
misplaced natures such as his ever, ever are in such a
world as ours!

Edward passed a much more restless night than
might have been anticipated from his fatigue.   But the
council was held early on the following day, and Lord
Falkland presented himself betimes to be his conductor
before it.

The raillery with which he was received in the guard
chamber, even more than his friend's report, opened
Edward's eyes to the fact that his tidings began to be
discredited.

The young Earl of Denbigh came yawning up to him,
and smilingly reproached him with making him lose
his night's sleep for nothing.   'Had it been in the
expectation of some pretty damsel or dame, now,' the
sprightly cavalier remarked, 'but, fie upon it, to stand
stark in steel on a rampart from sunset to rise, looking
out for a foe that never appears!'

Lord Goring, also, mindful of his late rebuke, made
his reflections with characteristic swagger and insolence.

'You must have been very heartily afraid for the
King's safety, sir, so far to outpost pursuit.   We hear
there are witches in Warwickshire; mayhap you rode
hither on a discarded broomstick?'

'Your remarks abound in *salt*; it would have been

for his Majesty's service had your stores for a siege, Lord Goring,' interposed Falkland, checking his friend's visibly irritated rejoinder.

Edward's reception by the King and his assembled councillors was equally cold, and apparently incredulous in tone.

The Lord Keeper himself, though destined, as was supposed, to so near an alliance, fought extremely shy of him at first, as of a person under a cloud—a circumstance Edward was not grieved at. But it is astonishing how nigh men of vulgar natures are to the inferior animals, and how closely they resemble them in most of their procedures; and is it not known how the four-foot sick or wounded are treated by the herd?

These grave personages fell to questioning Edward with great minuteness upon the facts of his information.

Very soon he could plainly perceive that it was considered the right courtly vein to be unable to believe in the possibility of such an atrocity designed against the royal person and majesty as had been declared. The Lord Keeper frequently expressed his trust and conviction that such a height of blasphemy had not been reached even by the worst of the traitors he had left behind him at London, Sir Edward Hyde crossquestioned him with all the dexterity of legal practice, as if he had been a lawyer employed to establish an opposite chain of conclusions.

Especially was Edward annoyed by being called upon to explain exactly how he came in possession of the information he had conveyed.

From a feeling which had certainly in no way been exhibited towards him by his base-born and base-

hearted brother, he had hitherto carefully refrained
from divulging the share he had taken in the whole
transaction. But the object of the councillors, and
particularly of the King himself, seemed now to be to
ascertain by what means the enemy had become
acquainted with his slender provision against attack,
and the general carelessness of the garrison of Nottingham.

It was pretty plain that Edward fenced in his replies
to these questions, and as he also declined to state by
what means he had obtained the disguise in which he
now appeared, and had fled from Birmingham, several
of the councillors began to evince unmistakable signs
of dissatisfaction. Charles himself, indeed, had more
than once made the observation that, so far as he was
aware, in all Warwickshire only Sir Thomas Holte had
been put in possession of these facts, by way of inducing
him to hasten his promised levy. But, luckily, when
Edward in turn was beginning to lose patience, urgent ❦
despatches were stated to arrive from Prince Rupert;
and the King at once ordered them to be brought to him
at the council-board.

The messenger was accordingly introduced with his
letters.

He was announced as Cornet Titus, of the Prince's
own regiment, and, on entrance, proved to be a young
man of very confident and lively manners, which
scarcely even the presence of the King restrained.

Charles was no admirer of this species of individual,
and the gravity and austerity of his own demeanour
visibly increased when the jaunty officer of dragoons,
presenting his documents on both knees, declared himself perfectly able to explain anything that might seem

to require more light, as he was employed by his Highness in their composition as secretary.

This Titus was, in truth, the same who afterwards,
having reached the rank of colonel, composed the
celebrated Royalist pamphlet, advocating the assassination of Cromwell, entitled 'Killing no Murder.'

King Charles read the letter at first to himself, the
councillors looking on in silence, and immovably, with
the exception of the Earl of Southampton, who quietly
took the opportunity to pick his teeth, aside, with a
straw he found on the floor at his feet.

When the King at last raised his eyes from his perusal
and looked at Edward Holte, it was with a very peculiar
expression of surprise and blame.

'Methinks a brother's merits in the affair need not
have been so carefully concealed,' he then said, in a very
displeased tone, 'and even to the hazard of your own
story's somewhat discrediting! My lords, my nephew
writes to me that he had but just returned to Aston
Hall from the observation and pursuit of a large party
of rebel horse, secretly assembled in Birmingham;
which suddenly quitting the town in our direction, ascertained that surprise was hopeless, from Master Holte's
escape, and turned off to join the Earl of Essex, at
Northampton. These partisans were first observed by
Sir Thomas Holte himself, and a faithful servant of
his house; but only explained by the arrival of a gentleman of the Holte family (though but by a left-hand
acknowledgment, it seems), who had also been made a
prisoner in Birmingham: where, discovering the whole
mystery of the iniquity devised against us, he revealed
it to his brother—this Master Holte of yours, my Lord
Falkland! And rather than that any delay in the

warning to us should ensue—knowing himself to be no
rider to compare with his well-bred brother (being but
of the legal profession, which rather affects coaches and
slow Flanders mares, my Lord Keeper!)—and having
his passport to leave the place, he most loyally and
generously changed clothes, and gave it, to forward the
necessary diligence.   Which flight of Master Holte
being then by him purposely declared and confessed,
when it could run no risk of being stayed, has happily
turned aside the whole stream of mischief.   But I say
again, Master Holte, you should not have been so eager
to engross the whole merit of the service to yourself
and I know not what traitor armourer's daughter of
Birmingham, who does not appear, from anything
written here, to have had any real share in the transaction.'

It must be imagined, not described, with what
emotion Edward Holte listened to this statement.

He saw at once into what a trap he had fallen by his
own generous forbearance.   Conviction appeared in the
countenances of all who heard.

The Lord Keeper himself clenched the fact by remarking, ' Ay, ay, there was never any great love lost
between Sir Thomas's lawful heir and his natural imp!'

Edward felt that all he could say in explanation
would now come too late : that the most conspicuous
portion of the whole merit had been seized to himself
by Grimsorwe's unparalleled daring and dexterity.

Moreover, when he did begin to speak in some declaration of the truth, the King imperiously interrupted
him.

' It matters not now, sir, we have other matters to
attend to,' Charles said.   ' The Prince mentions that

this officer will expound to us the great conveniences and uses of Birmingham and its vicinity for all warlike business, and his Highness's consequent desire that we will incontinently forward to him some pieces of artillery, and what infantry can be spared, to force an entry into the town, and reduce it to a good subjection.'

Cornet Titus began a very fluent and lengthened military exposition upon this ; but as the King listened to it with evident attention and interest, no one ventured to interrupt. And it appeared to carry conviction to the royal mind ; for at the first pause in the overflow Charles turned to Lord Falkland, and desired him to write at once to York to expedite the sending of two large *culverins* (so 18-pounder cannons were then styled) with a competent guard of infantry, to his Highness the Prince, at Aston Hall, in Warwickshire, to reduce the revolted town of Birmingham.

Edward, however, could no longer submit in silence to this.

'Your Majesty will but thereby,' he exclaimed, 'make irreconcilable enemies of a people who, by gentle means, may, I am sure, be easily reclaimed to your obedience !'   ·

'And you have *fair* intelligence in the town, sir, or you would not have taken so much pains to persuade us that the daughter of the principal leader in the sedition, this Master-Armourer Firebrace, is a secret loyalist and friend of our authority,' said Charles, with a sneer, though it was a form of rebuke he was mostly too proud to use to his inferiors.

The Lord Keeper, who was sitting mopingly with his hands muffled in his crimson robes, now looked up, stared, and frowned.

Edward coloured, and felt it inexpedient to hazard any further reply.

Lord Falkland, however, true to his ever-urged policy of conciliation, spoke up alone among the councillors on behalf of Edward's proposition. 'Let, at least, gentle means first be tried!' he earnestly entreated.

Sir Edward Hyde and the Earl of Southampton also joined in an opinion to this effect. Upon all which a subterfuge extremely agreeable to King Charles's genius seemed to occur to him.

'Why, sirs,' he said, 'make what diligence we may, some considerable interval must elapse before the guns can be carried from York, properly guarded, to where they are asked for. And so let Master Holte make all use of his secret agencies and influence in Birmingham, to bring the people back to their duty in the meantime. On that condition I do offer them full pardon and remission of their offences hitherto. But if he fails, the guns will not arrive amiss, methinks; and for our more immediate protection I will have the Prince recall his cavalry from the west, and throw it over the country between us and Aston Hall, where, as he writes, he purposes for a time to fix the head-quarters of his command. And now, in what concerns the article of this message, you would have me send to London yet again, sirs,' the King went on to say, as if entirely dismissing the former subjects. 'I do yield, in so far as I think it may tend to daze the Parliament with hopes of my submission, and put some slacking on their efforts till I can think myself safer, and see myself more partisan than I am at present in my quarters here. But let it be well known to all ye who call yourselves my friends,' he continued, glancing at Edward, ' that there is nothing really meant by this towards a peace; which can never be till the sword has shown who has to dictate the terms. I hope to see you as a soldier next, Master Holte; and meanwhile inform your father's *other* *son* that I will find some means also to repay him his faithfulness and hazard in our service ere long.'

With these words it was evident the King dismissed Edward from his presence; and, in fact, all but the Councillors of State seemed to feel their own dispensed with, and retired.

CHAPTER L.

EDWARD'S RETURN TO ASTON HALL.

DISGUSTED to the last degree with what had occurred to him in this memorable interview, Edward speedily shook off the company Cornet Titus seemed willing to confer upon him, and made for the solitude he hoped to find in Falkland's apartment. Nor was he at all turned from this object or flattered by the cornet's polite observation—'I should have known you at the bottom of a coalpit, sir, from your resemblance to your beautiful sister at Aston Hall; who, I can assure you, the Prince Palatine himself declares the handsomest young lady he has set eyes upon in England as yet!'

Edward scarcely responded to the compliment, or perhaps noticed it; but if he did at all it rather added to the vexation he experienced at finding himself so wonderfully defeated and circumvented in all his most reasonable expectations by the infernal craft and artifice of his detestable and detested relative.

A kind of agony of powerless indignation and astonishment came over Edward's whole mind and heart when once he found himself alone, and free to pursue the windings of uncomfortable thought and apprehension which now appeared to his reflections.

The traitor who had usurped so unaccountably the

superior merit in the foiling of his own wicked stra-
tagems, of what more in the way of treachery and
contrivance was he not capable ?

Never before had Edward Holte dreaded his brother.
He had long suspected his hidden rancour against himself personally ; had despised his mean and calculating
nature, and wondered at the baseness of artifice and adu-
lation he exhibited in endeavouring to advance himself,
as the lion's cub might wonder at the underground
operations of a mole, whose progress is marked by the
dirt it heaves. Now he regarded him with a mixture of
fear in his horror and contempt, which the same noble
animal might entertain for the insidious snake.

Then what would Dorothy Firebrace think of the
great failure in all their plans, caused by his own senseless forbearance ?

If the wicked sometimes feel remorse for their ill
deeds, it is never probably so acute as that white species
of the same passion, when a good and generous nature
finds its displays of those qualities turned against
itself.

Punishment seems a natural recompense for guilt,
and is accepted as such by evil-doers, mostly with a
kind of consolation in the assurance that they are
reaping as they have sown. But to be afflicted for our
very virtues, to sow good wheat grains and only hemlock
to spring, seems unnatural and portentous even to those
who have had the longest experience of life and the
ways of men.

This feeling, that he had done wrong in sparing the
villain whom he felt he should have maimed for mischief by revealing his noxious qualities, tormented
Edward long. In vain he recalled to mind Dorothy's

exhortations to him not to forget that the wretch was
his brother.   The terror—we can call it by no other
name—inspired by moral depravity so matched by
cunning and audacity, deepened every moment in his
breast when he considered who, even more than himself, had provoked the hatred and vengeance of so
relentless a foe.

In the consternation of this idea his fancy presented
him a most alarming array of possible dangers awaiting
the object of his youthful but devoted love.   It seemed
to Edward Holte as if his own presence and unslum-
bering watchfulness could scarcely suffice to guard off
the perils menacing his betrothed from his unnatural
brother's resentment and craft.   Moreover, he remembered the circumstances under which he had left her in
Birmingham ; and, powerful as her friends were there,
who could say what might be the consequences in the
topsy-turvy state of things in the town ?   True, Cromwell, whose vengeance might have been dreaded, was
said to have withdrawn himself; but other and perhaps
worse dangers might be apprehended from the excited
passions of the populace, which there were so many evil
agencies to set in action.

Edward determined to lose not a moment in returning
to face his unnatural enemy at Aston Hall, and take
upon himself thence the necessary guardianship of his
soul's beloved.

Lord Falkland found him in this resolution, which,
indeed, he did not oppose.   He plainly intimated, in
fact, that the great service he had performed was by no
means properly appreciated by the King.   His Majesty
openly expressed an opinion that there was a singular
want of straightforwardness and whole-heartedness in

Master Holte's proceedings. He remarked suspiciously on the evident good-will and intelligence that existed between the heir of Aston and the revolted town; and Lord Falkland himself confessed he could not quite understand some points in his friend's conduct and explanations as regarded his brother.

Edward, upon this, burst into a full declaration, to this true and faithful friend, of the real circumstances of the case; but although Falkland personally was convinced and satisfied, however much amazed with the revelation, greatly to Edward's chagrin, he declared he thought it no longer feasible to bring the King to a true comprehension of the state of the affair.

'All this will seem to his Majesty mere after-thought and contrivance. I say it in sadness and in shame, but the King is so accustomed to tortuous inventions and subterfuge to remedy his own mistakes and faults, that he would likely believe much worse of you than now, should you attempt to force a knowledge of the truth upon him,' Lord Falkland observed. 'He will deem that, to secure the rewards and honour due to your courageous interposition, you are no longer content with an unhandsome suppression of your brother's share in the adventure, but aim at his removal from your path by unfounded calumnies and imputations of treason. But such a villain will be sure, in the long run, to reveal himself unmistakably. Meanwhile, were I you, dearest friend, I would indeed lose no time in returning to endeavour to disabuse your father of his confidence in this traitor, and protect your friends from his further ill designs; and if by any possibility you can, as you persuade yourself, recall Birmingham to the King's allegiance, it is impossible to do his cause and your own a greater service. Look, I have taken care to urge the point so earnestly upon the King, that I have procured you a full and gracious pardon for all of the town who submit to the King's mercy, ere force is applied. It lacks nothing but the great seal of England to it, which my Lord Keeper promises to bring from his lodgings hither and apply : and his Majesty promises, moreover, to give you a letter in his own hand to the Prince Palatine, commanding him to abstain from all attack on Birmingham, or infliction of punishment in life or goods, so long as you can give assurance or hope of the townsmen's return to their allegiance. But his Majesty himself will see you, and give you your instructions, or ere you depart.'

Edward expressed his earnest wish that no delay that could be spared him should be made, and Lord Falkland promised he would expedite the business as speedily as possible. He would take a proper time, he added, to put what respected Grimsorwe in its true light before the King, when other circumstances would probably have occurred to strengthen such evidence as could now be adduced.

In the midst of this conversation the Lord Keeper entered, with a small crimson velvet box in his hand, surmounted by a crown ; considerably to the increase of Edward's annoyance, who for private reasons of his own was not much desirous of the company.

He apologised to the Lord Keeper for the trouble he was giving him ; but the latter replied emphatically that he would rather trust the heart out of his breast, in another man's keeping, than the great seal of England out of his own.

'And if you only knew, good son, the trouble and

danger I have incurred to escape with it out of the clutches of the Parliament men in London, you would know what to think of the matter. And I do expect daily to hear they have declared me a traitor for my loyalty; but better so, at a distance, than clapped up in a dungeon of the Tower with my Lord of Canterbury, or some other faithful servant of the King's,' the Lord Keeper feelingly remarked; and he entered into a long narrative of the circumstances of his flight from London, and the infinite difficulties and dangers attending the enterprise.

'My house was watched night and day on the secret, by Master Pym's orders, and well I knew it was so, good cousin,' he went on to say; 'and, good Lord! imagine what my condition grew to be at last as they brought me treason after treason to stamp and certify with the magic in this little box. But the matter of raising the militia against the King did quite break me down in my compliances; it was such open and manifest treason. Yet was I forced to put the seal to this also, and the Earl of Essex's commission, merely to shut their eyes to my true intentions. Yet had it not been for Sergeant Maynard's assistance, I should never have known how to compass it; but he dressed up a figure in my wig and robes, that sat for a day hearing causes in Westminster Hall, while I took boat at the stairs, garbed like some mean citizen, and so on board a Newcastle collier, that conveyed me safe and sound, but with incredible anguishes of mind and dismays of pursuit, with the precious thing in my possession, to the garrison, and noble marquis of that place, holding it for the King.'

It thence appeared that the Lord Keeper, not having

been lately in Warwickshire, had a thousand questions
to ask of Edward Holte concerning the state of things
there; particularly how all was at Hagley, his family
seat, where his wife and daughter now resided.

Edward was a good deal embarrassed with these
questions, having been, in truth, very remiss in his
attentions to his betrothed bride for a considerable
time before even he made the acquaintance of Dorothy
Firebrace—facts which the Lord Keeper himself speedily
discerned, and Edward, perhaps, took no great trouble
to conceal. But his lordship was too politic to make
any direct observation on the circumstance; only when
he affixed the seal to the pardon offered to Birmingham
he expressed a civil hope that he should soon see his
friend Sir Thomas Holte again, and make use of the
first restoration of tranquillity to complete the happy
union arranged between the families.

'Amen' certainly stuck in Edward's throat to this:
but fortunately Lord Falkland, who had been for some
time absent, now re-entered the room.

This zealous friend brought good news for Edward.
The King had consented to expedite him his letter, and
permit him to kiss hands on his departure, immediately
after he had dined. 'And his Majesty makes no long
meals now,' said Falkland, 'and there is no need of a
great flourish of trumpets to signify the changes of the
courses; for indeed, until the plate came to hand from
Oxford, never was poor prince so moneyless for his
occasions as ours, who but awhile ago thought little of
expending a couple of thousand pounds on a single
night's masque, or other stage divertisement at court.'

Edward, with a blush, declared that at all events
his father had money at command, which he would

doubtless be proud to contribute to his Majesty's necessities; and a page summoning them at this moment to
what was emphatically styled 'the presence,' he was
very glad to leave my Lord Keeper's scrutiny and follow
thither.

He found the King in rather a better humour than he
had left him in the morning—one that might be called
severely gracious—and surrounded by nearly all the
principal persons of his little court.

It was plain Charles thought to make what has been
styled in modern times 'political capital' out of Cromwell's foiled audacity. Thanking Edward coldly for his
display of zeal, he expressed a hope that his father, and
other loyal gentlemen of the county, would now perceive
the necessity of immediately fulfilling the promises they
had made to him.

Edward respectfully renewed his statement that
nothing but arms were wanting for his father's tenantry
to form an excellent troop of horse; to which Charles
drily replied that if he succeeded, as he announced he
hoped, in bringing back the revolted town of Birmingham to its allegiance, the best possible sign of submission would be for the smiths of that place to furnish
the arms they were so well able. 'And you give us to
understand,' the King added, with an austere smile,
'that Venus is willing to use her influence with her
husband, Vulcan, in the sooty town, to forward your
designs in our favour.'

'No such goddess, sire,' returned Edward, indignantly
colouring, observing the titter and buzz that ran round
among the assembled courtiers, 'but rather the chastest
and noblest of them all, witty Minerva, mistress of all
the arts! The loyal daughter of the master-armourer

of Birmingham, sire, is a young girl of spotless honour
and repute ; and he who but smiles otherwise, saving
your sole Majesty, must answer to me for the gibe with
his sword.'

' Let us not further risk to provoke this ireful young
gentleman,' said Charles, hastily, and glancing re-
bukingly round his circle. ' Go, and speed with these
blacksmiths and their goddess daughters in any manner
you deem best—only *speed*.   Here is a letter to the
Prince our nephew, on whose delivery there shall be
peace awhile between his swordsmen and Birmingham,
if they also will have it so.   Promise what else you will
beside ; the keeping will be with us.   Tell the Prince I
will send further verbal explanations by Cornet Titus.
And now a good farewell to you ; and when you next
kneel to us, we trust it shall be to ask some suitable
recompense for yet greater service than, we would all
men note, we hold to have received already at your
hands.'

Edward thankfully received the document, knelt and
kissed the King's hand, and retired ; but, greatly to his
concern, Lord Falkland, who followed him out, advised
him to lose no time in returning to Aston, on a notion
he seemed to have taken that some double policy was
at work. ' It is the King's way but too much,' he said,
sadly ; 'and these verbal explanations to be sent by
Cornet Titus may very possibly be of a kind to thwart
the whole meaning of the written word.   To horse at
once, my dear Edward ; and, besides, I see you are too
honest and plain-spoken for a court as yet.   Would to
God that I had ever known so also of myself !   But it
is too late now ; and if this unhappy king is to be saved

at all it can only now be by honest counsels, which least of all he heeds, but which ever shall be mine.'

This suggestion was scarcely needed to hasten Edward's departure ; but he determined not to delay another hour in Nottingham, and begging Falkland to make his excuses in the hurry of his business to the Lord Keeper, the two friends embraced and parted.

CHAPTER LI.

THE VALLEY OF THE SHADOW OF DEATH.

EDWARD HOLTE's horse had not yet recovered sufficiently its express gallop of fifty miles from Birmingham to allow him to return at a similarly rapid pace. He was obliged to rest at night at Leicester on the way; but he met with no other obstacle, nor anything indeed to call for particular remark, until he arrived, about an hour before noonday, in Aston Park. He was then making the best of his way on his jaded beast to the mansion, when he came upon an unexpected movement.

He was about the middle of the great avenue, reflecting deeply on the best means to forward the objects he had in view, when he perceived a confused crowd of people suddenly swarming into it at the extremity.

For the most part these were on foot; and Edward, who was of course familiar with his father's servants and neighbours, easily discerned that the throng was chiefly made up of the former, and a number of the villagers of Aston.

Men, women, and children were intermingled; many of them with reaping hooks in their hands. as if suddenly called from harvest labours in the field by some unusual cause of excitement. He recognised Robert Falconer in particular, and the gravedigger of

Aston, who united to that office the seemingly very dissimilar one of a fiddler. Almost idiotic with age as he was, moreover, he seemed to preserve a good mechanical skill on his instrument, and was now scrubbing away at a lively sort of jig, or march, which evidently contributed very much to the cheerful movement of the company.

They came on at a rattling pace—talking, laughing, shouting—sometimes running indeed, to keep along with what was clearly a central figure in the movement, and which being on horseback made the exertion occasionally necessary. And besides, the poor animal, alarmed with the hubbub around it—perhaps struck or goaded on the sly behind, or hit by some malicious stone from a distance—frequently plunged, or kicked out, or darted headlong forward—varieties that greatly pleased the rabble, who raised the most uproarious shouts and laughter, and urged each other on to repeat the diverting exhibition; the chief part of the fun, it must be remembered, consisting in the fact that there was a human creature fastened on the horse by cords, through his naked feet, beneath its belly, but a human creature stigmatised by wearing a lofty paper foolscap, with the words 'traitor and spy' daubed in the largest red ochre letters on his bare back and breast, like a branded sheep.

If any doubt of the specific meaning of what was occurring could remain, the countenance, bloodless with terror, the shrieks and lamentable cries of the victim, and a thick rope round his neck, made things pretty plain.

One end of this rope was held by a pedestrian, of a tall, gaunt, rigid figure, dressed in a black leather suit, with a singularly large pair of scissors stuck in his girdle, and a sword of unusual and portentous length slung over his left shoulder. It was too long to be carried in the usual way at the belt. This was a man of a foreign appearance, with a long beard, but hair cut almost close to a strongly-developed, hard-boned, narrow, almost pointed cranium; a man of a physiognomy unalterably sedate and unmoved, who seemed to take the whole affair with the greatest imaginable nonchalance, holding his head stiff and upright, without regarding either to the right or left, and evidently equally insensible to the outcries of the victim and the disorderly movement of the village rout.

What was rather singular about this group was the fact that a personage who seemed an officer of rank, by his ornamented armour and waving plume, rode on the other side, also holding a rope, much thicker and stronger, and which was passed round the neck of the horse.

This rider appeared to be greatly enjoying the whole affair, encouraging the mob in their demonstrations by gestures, words, and applausive bursts of laughter, and frequently making his own mount execute various fantastic gambades and caracoles that added to the excitement and restlessness of the victim. He was a man of gigantic figure, and with a big, coarse, flat face, not deficient, nevertheless, in humour and vivacity of expression.

Edward was surprised and alarmed at what he saw. But it was not until he was close upon the whole party, which he pressed forward to meet, that he recognised in the horror-stricken wretch tied on the horse, the tinker-boy whom he had seen so busy aiding in pulling down

the old cross in Birmingham market-place on the
unlucky day of his own late visit there.

Doubtless the poor lad was now undergoing in his
proper person the horrors and tribulation he at a later
period depicted in his Pilgrim's passage through the
Valley of the Shadow of Death. A more dreadful
aspect of despair and frantic fear Edward had never
beheld. It awakened immediate compassion in his
breast, though it seemed only to excite derision and
amusement in all but the impassive military executioner
besides. Such Edward now supposed the tall man,
with the huge sword and scissors, in the black leather
garb, to be.

As a foreigner, and one well accustomed to such
scenes by his position in the camps of the ruthless
leaders of the continental warfare of the times, this
man's insensibility was perhaps natural enough. But
Edward could scarcely account for the ferocious enjoyment in the other accompanier's manner, until he heard
him speak. His accent then betokened him to be one
of a class of assistants in the bloody work known to be
at hand, whom Charles had most unadvisedly permitted
to join his standards—a leader perhaps in the then
recent horrible insurrection and massacres in Ireland,
when the Celtic portion of the population and their
chiefs had risen and nearly extirpated the English
name from the island; but doubtless, by his title and
foreign uniform of black and yellow, one of those
exiled soldiers of fortune of the Irish nation who had
previously earned distinction in foreign warfare. He
was called Count O'Taafe, and was Prince Rupert's
favourite companion, being in truth as jolly and light-
hearted a professional murderer (a mercenary soldier is

nothing else) as ever carved his bread with his sword.
A most gallant and devoted admirer of the fair sex
also, though he had rather a rough way of showing
it at times when he played a part in the storming of
a town, or was quartered at discretion in an enemy's
country.

'In the King's name, what is all this a-doing here?'
said Edward, confronting the uproarious group in a
manner that brought the whole to a halt, as he directly
crossed the advance of the intended sacrifice.

He was immediately recognised by the village people,
most of whom took off their caps and hats, exclaiming,
'His honour, Master Edward!' while the culprit
uttered a series of hysterical shrieks and exclamations
that he was innocent, and that they were going to
murder him, and implored mercy in such heart-rending
accents that Count O'Taafe put his hand over his mouth,
yelling, 'It isn't hanging you we are, sure, but a sow
and a whole farrow of squeakers we are ringing in the
nose. Will ye never cease the bothering noise of you,
now, until we can hear ourselves speak, and know what
we are about? Monsieur, I salute you,' he continued,
raising his hat in a courtly and polished manner to
Edward; 'but as you are a civilian, whatever your name
or rank hereabouts, you must be aware you have nothing
to do with an execution of the provost-marshal's justice
on a traitor and spy against the King.'

'I am none, I am none! I knew not where I was
going when I galloped upon the barn where the soldiers
slept! I was flying for my life from a witch!' shrieked
the affrighted lad.

'Well, my dear, you have run into the right sort of
hands to take care of it. I promise ye, ye'll have very

little further trouble with your life now,' replied the
facetious count.

'We are going, sir,' he continued, explanatorily to
Edward, ' to make an example of this young fellow, for
the amusement and entertainment of his fellow-traitors
behind their barricades, in Birmingham town hereby,
by hanging him, and his rebel hack of a horse too,
under him, on the tallest gibbet we can find wood for
near the place.'

'To hang the lad—and his horse! What strange
madness of cruelty is this?' exclaimed Edward.

The count had not failed to observe that his challenger
was a person of position and authority.   Probably,
indeed, he recognised him, as Cornet Titus had, by his
resemblance to his sister.   He continued, therefore, to
answer with an appearance of deference : ' Such are
the Prince's orders, sir ; they are known to be equally
traitors, man and beast, for the one was bestriding the
other as guides to the unspeakable rebels who lately
purposed to surprise his Majesty's own most sacred
person at Nottingham.   Sir Thomas Holte himself
witnessed the fact, who saw him playing the link-boy at
their head.'

' Oh, the Lord preserve me! the Lord preserve me!
What shall I do?   The Parliament men threatened to
hang me unless I did so ; but I meant to guide them
all awry, and leave them in some marsh or desert place,'
shrieked the affrighted lad.

' Heed him not, sir; he set them right when an old
woman would have misdirected them, of whom they
made question.   He has deserved the death ; the Prince
hath condemned him to it at the drumhead, after
hearing all he couldn't utter in his defence, for the

speech left him with fear. Only the trifle remains now of seeing the sentence carried out.'

Bunyan again renewed his cries of despair and supplication so vociferously that Edward could hardly make his own voice heard.

'Your pardon, sir,' he then observed to the officer, 'but I bear the King's express commands that no man shall be injured in life or limb, for any of these recent occurrences, unless by his direct commands.'

'Well but, anyhow, you don't call this spalpeen of a lad a *man?*' returned O'Taafe, with a great laugh at his own wit. 'And besides, the Prince's commission from his Majesty will bear him out in any manner of way whatever towards the suppression of this most horrible and unnatural rebellion. Robbery, murder, rape, fire-raising, all comes within our scope, and we mean to exercise our privileges, I can tell you, and like true soldiers and subjects of the King.'

'There is no commission can override this,' said Edward, producing the precious document, endorsed Charles R.

O'Taafe glanced at it rather surprised, but said carelessly, 'Oh, we gentlemen of Ireland have learned to go more by his Majesty's *maning* than his words. His Highness, I am sure, will not allow of any interference. Provost-Marshal Storcks, on!'

'Do you then refuse obedience to the King's express commands?' enquired Edward, with indignant astonishment. 'Where is the Prince? he will soon convince you better of your duty.'

'The Prince is close at hand, at the head-quarters of his troops, parading them before the Hall,' replied O'Taafe, looking rather embarrassed. Then, as if he

suddenly espied a way out of his perplexity, he continued, 'But come this way, sir; I will soon show you
that it is your duty to spare the Prince any trouble in
the matter.'

'Don't let them kill me, sir; oh, don't let them kill
me, and I will die for you most willingly myself!'
shrieked Bunyan, wringing his hands.

'That's their treason to the very marrow. They will
do the same thing to please themselves; but nothing to
do the King a service!' said O'Taafe, good-humouredly;
while Edward, much against his will, walked his horse
aside with him to ascertain what was meant. The
ghastly, yearning expression of the tinker-boy's countenance painfully irked after him in the movement.

'Well, sir?' he said, when they—the count and
himself—had reached the shadow of some lofty syca-
mores, at a distance from the crowd.

'This is the case then, Monsieur,' said the count,
evidently convinced that he had only to explain things
to remove the obstacle. 'Nobody of course cares a snap
of a pistol about this boy's haltering; but now the
Parliament soldiers have gone from the town we are in
hopes the Birmingham men will be so provoked to see
a comrade swinging—nay, and his horse at his heels for
·a makeweight—they will make a sally, and so open a
way for our cavalry to enter. The Prince and his
troopers intend to be in ambuscade behind the woods
here until we can see some signs of such a good result,
when they will pour on to the assault; and everybody
says it is a town of a rich citizenship, and with plenty
of pretty girls in, besides, to reward the soldier for his
trouble in cutting throats.'

'For this reason, most of all, I will suffer no further

steps in so bloodthirsty and mischievous a plan,' exclaimed Edward, scarcely able to refrain from some
more distinct mark of indignation. 'These country
people will support their master's son; and the Prince
himself, when he shall know the truth, will doubtless
lend a ready obedience to the King's commands. Robin
Falconer, turn that nag's head there, and follow me
home to Aston Hall with the prisoner.'

Robin, whose kindly nature had not hitherto gone
very heartily with the work, stepped cheerfully forward
and plucked the rope from the hands of the German
provost-marshal. The latter stared and looked at
O'Taafe, who muttered something to himself. But on
reflection, perceiving the preponderance of force was at
present with his opponent, he observed, 'Let us know
the Prince's own will in the matter, then,' and added
some words in a hoarse guttural to the official, which he
seemed to understand also in the sense of not offering
any resistance. Robin had meanwhile turned the tinker's horse, and in a few moments the whole procession
was retracing its steps to Aston Hall.

When this emerged from the green shadows of the
long avenue before Aston Hall, Edward riding behind,
to see that no trick was played, he perceived rather a
showy spectacle.

A solid squadron of horse, glittering in armour, was
drawn up in the great gravelled court-yard before the
mansion, with its principal officers assembled, but dis-
mounted, at the porch. Two personages, whom Edward
recognised as his father and mother in their stateliest
costumes, stood there in conversation with some of these;
while considerably at a distance, as if engaged in in-
specting the elaborate iron-work of the gate leading

into the gardens on the right, were his sister and a tall, powerful, rough-looking figure of a young man in armour, with a shaggy sort of a pelisse on his shoulders that looked like a bear-skin. This personage was leaning on his sheathed sword, occasionally using it to point out some feature in the design of the iron-work that appeared to strike him. But it occurred to Edward, painfully and at once, that his gaze was chiefly fixed upon the beautiful girl beside him, and with an intensity of admiration which had in it a good deal more of the trooper's boldness and licence than of the prince and gentleman's respect. And yet this he felt instinctively must be the Prince Palatine himself; and, without delaying to approach the house, he turned thitherward, and the whole *cortége* with him.

Rupert's falcon-glance was instantly caught by the arrival; but he was plainly greatly surprised and confounded by what he beheld.

'God's life, what's this? They cannot have passed the young cockatrice yet? no, they are bringing him back! What can be the meaning of it all? What stranger is this heading the rabble? Do not disturb yourself, mademoiselle, I will soon learn,' he said, in his rough impatient way, stepping from the young lady's side.

But she followed. 'It is my brother, Edward Holte, may it please your Highness,' she said, blushing deeply, with some strange secret consciousness, quite uncaused by anything apparent.

'Your brother! But nobody's brother under God's living sun has any right to interfere between my orders and their execution—the King alone. Well, gentlemen, what means all this we see?' the Prince enquired, in haughty and imperious tones, and stepping to meet Edward with so long and sudden a stride that the latter came against him with a degree of shock, as he alighted, out of respect, before he answered.

Edward apologised; but the Prince sternly interrupted him.

'A woman could not have struck lighter, sir; you are no rock at your breast; you have not bulged me!' he said. 'But again, Count O'Taafe, why have you and these people come back with my errand unperformed?'

'I have interposed, sir, by the King's Majesty's warrantry, who has empowered me to grant every species of pardon and oblivion regarding these late transactions, unless the people of Birmingham persist in their sedition,' replied Edward, with the gentle firmness which was a part of his character, but less to be overcome than the noisiest opposition of others.

Rupert stared grimly at him. 'The King is always meddling and marring in this strange way. But I do marvel to hear you have so interposed, if, as I take it, you are the gentleman—son of my most worthy host here—who have been the happy agent to do his Majesty a great service, with the loyal and devoted aid of Master Richard Grimsorwe!' said the Prince. Nevertheless, he continued in an angry, almost an insulting tone:

'But I have been warned of your weaker leanings and inclinings in the town; and give me leave to tell you, Master Holte, my commission authorises me to receive no commands or instructions but directly from the King in person. So I shall make bold to proceed with his rebels in my own way, till I hear from him by his own lips or hand to the contrary.'

'This letter is every word and line, sir, from his

Majesty's own pen,' replied Edward, producing a document which he handed over to the Prince.

He read it with visible impatience and disdain, occasionally uttering a species of wild impatient snort, and tossing his head disdainfully, like an unbroken steed that first feels the snaffle.

' It is most strange, but true; but if my uncle means to thwart the best-intentioned actions for his service thus, all is vain,' he exclaimed, and gnawed his nether lip for a moment's pause.

' You have a power granted you, it is true, Master Holte,' he then continued; ' yet I do hope that you are not under so strong a delusion and enticement in that traitorous town as hath been reported to me, that you will not rather aid me to bring it to just punishment and submission, than go about to use the restraints unwittingly put by his Majesty on his officers in your rescript here: the opportunity may not easily return.'

' I know not what has been represented to your Highness of my motives or inducements,' replied Edward, coldly; ' but I purpose to exercise the powers confided to me, under the great seal of England itself, to endeavour to conclude some happy peace and reconciliation with my father's neighbours here of Birmingham. And to begin, I do most peremptorily call upon your Highness and your officers to refrain from all further molestation of this poor lad, who, partly to my own knowledge, was an impressed and unwilling agent in Captain Cromwell's late design.'

' I was, I was, dear sirs,' gasped Bunyan, crying and sobbing bitterly.

' The boy's life is nothing to me, except for the service twisting his neck might have proved. Do with him what

you will; I must await the explanations promised me
from Nottingham. Mademoiselle, let us resume our
inspection of the garden gate. 'Twas a rare artist, rather
than smith, who has so devised it as we see,' said Rupert,
disdainfully turning away.

Rough and imperious soldier as he was, he had still
something of a German's taste and sensibility in art. At
a later period he was said to cultivate that of engraving,
and even to be the inventor of mezzotint, from observing
the effects produced in light and shade by a soldier
scraping the rust off his musket-barrel in parts.

'Release the boy,' said Edward; and Robin Falconer,
drawing his hunting-knife, made short work with the
thongs at Bunyan's feet.

'Come then, now,' said Count O'Taafe, during this
operation, 'we won't have our morning's work altogether
for nothing; and the next best thing we can do to hanging this young sniveller in his Majesty's service, will be
to make a dragoon of him. He sits a horse as if he was
born on the back. My good boy, will you put on breast
and back-plates, and fight the King's enemies instead of
mending their old kettles?'

'Only release me, sir; I will do anything and everything your honours are pleased to command,' exclaimed
the bewildered tinker lad.

'It's a bargain then, though I have not one of the
King's shillings by me at the moment for earnest.
Give him Randal Forster's suit, who had his neck
broken, slipping from the ditches before the town the
other day, and swear him in, Provost Storcks,' said
O'Taafe.

Thus it happened that John Bunyan shared for a
season in the violence and profanities which speedily

became rife in the camps of Charles I., and laid up good portion of that life-long enduring sense of remorse and guilt which appears in every line of his lowly but immortal work, but was possibly rather due to the delicacy of his awakened conscience and feelings afterwards than to any real occasion for so much spiritual anguish and doubt.

Edward himself thought this the best possible conclusion of the affair; and without heeding the somewhat offensive and derisive manner of the Prince, he raised his hat as he retired with his sister, and quietly watched the operation of loosening the unlucky tinker boy.

When this was effected, Bunyan made an attempt to rush to him, and throw himself at his benefactor's feet in thanks. But the poor lad's limbs were so paralysed with his long and cruel shackling that he fell after staggering a little to the ground, to the great amusement of O'Taafe, and some of the other officers, who had now gathered near.

Edward Holte, on the contrary, humanely assisted him to rise, and as he did so suddenly discerned a too well-known figure hanging over the balustrade of the central tower of Aston Hall, and gazing earnestly towards the spectacle, as if endeavouring to discern its meaning.

The sight reminded Edward, and bidding the boy be of good cheer, and dispose of himself as he thought proper, he rid him of his effusions of gratitude, and hastened forward to greet Sir Thomas and Lady Holte.

Almost at the same moment [the Prince rejoined Arabella Holte, and her brother would have been little gratified if he could have heard his words on doing so.

'It is your brother, mademoiselle, and therefore I
allow him his way! I shall soon have other instructions, I nothing doubt, from his Majesty, and
meanwhile what does one rascal life matter the more
or the less—or anything in such society as I now
enjoy?'

CHAPTER LII.

THE BROTHERS.

EDWARD made no further delay in approaching his
parents, who he now found discerned him; and was
speedily locked in his mother's arms. Sir Thomas himself made way to allow the meeting between the mother
and her child. And Rupert's officers, who were mostly
aware of the circumstances of the case, decently turned
their heads away, or strolled off from the scene of overpowering emotion that ensued between the poor broken-
spirited lady and her restored only son.

'Oh, my child! my dearest Edward! to see you again
after you have escaped from those barbarous rebels!'
exclaimed Lady Holte. 'What I have suffered in
terror and apprehension for your sake! my travail
when I bore you, my Edward, was less!'

'Dear mother, I was never in so much danger as you
suppose from our neighbours of Birmingham! Many
of them rather remembered how neighbourly we had
always been with them until these unhappy times,' said
Edward.

'The *fair ones* especially! Dear brother—dear
Master Holte, I should say—most welcome home! I
trust the King is content with all our zeals in his service; but, out and alas! what have you done with my

182		THE ARMOURER'S DAUGHTER.

pleading robes? A poor bachelor of laws like me
cannot replace them,' exclaimed a hateful voice at this
moment, and Richard Grimsorwe emerged from the
porch of Aston Hall, and threw his arms—yes, actually
through his arms—round the unwilling, flesh-creeping
frame of Edward Holte—in fond, fraternal greeting
home!

Edward, abhorring what had enveloped such a traitor,
had exchanged Grimsorwe's lawyer robe for a very plain
cloak in Leicester. This was the cause of his impudent
query and exclamation, which, however, was not ill-
contrived to break the impetus of the reply he might
expect.

But it was neither a place nor a time to enter dis-
cussions of a nature so involved and personal as Edward
Holte felt those must be between his brother and himself. Rupert's officers were now again gathered around,
and the Prince himself was seen advancing with Arabella towards the porch, at the young lady's own suggestion, who herself perhaps began to discover too
trooper-like a warmth and zeal in the Prince's pro-
fessions of admiration.

'I will explain what I have done with your dress
by-and-by, Richard,' said Edward, releasing himself
nevertheless urgently enough from the embrace; 'at
present I am very weary with nigh three days on horseback, circumventing the basest imaginable plans of
traitors and deceivers. Let me, if it please you, enter
my father's house again, and rest awhile.'

'Of all loves, yea—pray you, sir, make none of your
promised clearance of misapprehensions between Master
Holte and myself at present. Leave it, indeed, all to
me, who best knows on what his doubts may arise.

Brother, I will attend you in your chamber immediately,' said Richard, eagerly preventing his father's evident intention of saying something, of a reconciling nature probably, but which would more certainly have brought about the public explosion he was anxious to avert.

'Come, then; I shall be prepared for your suitable reception, Master Grimsorwe,' Edward replied, with every species of contempt and wrath in his accompanying glance. But he also felt how desirable and necessary it was to shun a quarrel with his traitor brother under so general an observation as now attended them.

Sir Thomas, for a man of his violent and imperious temper, had a singular habit of submission to Grimsorwe's wishes. He desisted, therefore, from any further interference between his sons, though pretty well aware of some exasperated state of feeling between them.

Not that he in the least suspected the atrocious plots and treasons of Grimsorwe in Birmingham. The latter had given another and most artful gloss to the alienation he knew must become apparent on his brother's return, and for which the scene Sir Thomas had witnessed, on Dorothy Firebrace's visit to Aston Hall, might alone have prepared him. But this new depth of treachery need not for the present be elucidated.

In other respects Edward had very fair occasion to ask some respite from society and conversation, on his return from his fatiguing excursion. He therefore requested to be excused from his father's now uttered desire that he would lose no time to dress, to attend the Prince's Highness at dinner. It was become the custom, it appeared, to serve a meal of the description in state every day at Aston Hall, where Prince Rupert had established his head-quarters; at its wealthy owner's earnest entreaty, certainly.

Sir Thomas, however, somewhat eagerly assented to the arrangement, while Edward remarked that his mother looked saddened and disappointed. But this was too much her usual state to set him on drawing any specially uncomfortable inferences; and the important business he had in view to transact was not, he deemed, to be postponed to minor considerations.

In his secret anxiety to the effect hinted, Edward was even well satisfied to allow the interview Richard Grimsorwe stated it was his purpose to seek with him. Whatever else came of it, it was possible he should glean some inklings of what might have occurred in Birmingham since his departure. And if even the ties of relationship, and force of circumstances, prohibited his taking a just vengeance on his traitorous kinsman, Edward had yet a kind of pleasure in the prospect of letting him know how fully he was aware of his treachery and plots, and how hopeless it must be henceforth to hoodwink him to their workings.

He retired, therefore, to his usual chamber in the mansion, and there awaited the result.

The heir of Aston Hall, of course, occupied one of the best apartments in it. He had a suite on the first floor of the north wing of the house, the bed-chamber in which is now known as the State Room, from its being of latter times dedicated to the use of guests of distinction. Sir Thomas had declared his intention to dedicate this entire portion of the building to the use of a separate household for his son, as soon as his projected grand marriage with the Lord Keeper's daughter took place. But until the arrival of Prince Rupert, the only other person of consequence inhabiting this wing was Mr. Lane, the family chaplain. Count O'Taafe and some of the other officers were now quartered in it. But Lady Holte had taken care that her son's apartment remained inviolate.

Resuming possession, and refreshing himself from his dusty journey, Edward had nevertheless almost forgotten the expected visitation. When Grimsorwe arrived he was plunged in reflections how best to open the negotiations for a peaceful arrangement with the town of Birmingham.

Grimsorwe made his appearance, following a domestic who brought Edward a cover from his mother's diningtable. And to do him justice, steel-nerved and audacious as he was by nature, he looked pale, and clearly entered on the business he felt he must go through with very reluctantly. Nevertheless he had made up his mind what to do with characteristic boldness and decision.

While the servant was in the apartment he poured out a series of voluble congratulations and assurances of his unbounded joy to see his dear brother safely once more at home; taking care to make no pause for a reply that might reveal the real state of the affair. But the moment the man retired, he brought himself up at full check, and observed, with a bitter laugh, 'It is no longer necessary to keep up the farce; loosen the torrent, brother Edward, which I see in your face is ready to burst upon me, and let us come as speedily afterwards to the best settlement circumstances now permit between us.'

'You call me brother, and truly; Cain was the first

brother!' Edward now replied; but he went on not at
all with the invective and violence Grimsorwe probably
expected. Contempt almost destroyed resentment in
his breast.

' Well, then, continue my brother, in that early sense
of the word; only understand that from this time forth
I am well aware that I have a *brother* who is contriving
by every means of forgery and false witnesses to oust
me from my birthright, and bring disgrace and annul-
ment on the lawful marriage of my mother with the
father whose true inheritor I am—a brother who, in my
late misfortune, left no stone unturned to procure my
assassination or destruction at the hand of unjust power
—a brother who, by fraud and the most audacious deceit
and pretence, has robbed me, and another dearer to me
than myself, of the proper rewards of our loyalty and
devotion to our sovereign—a brother who, I doubt not,
will continue in his villainous attempts, until I, too,
forget the base mingling of our bloods, and crush him
with my heel in the dust—like the serpent that he is!'

Grimsorwe looked a little astonished. He did not
possibly know how much was known, but he answered
with grim composure :

' If you are aware of all this, Edward Holte,' he said,
' still, on my part, I am assured you have no means of
proof of your allegations, and I defy your utmost hatred
and malice to produce any.'

' Dorothy Firebrace can witness—' began Edward ;
then reflecting on the danger of bringing her name into
the discussion, he suddenly paused. But Grimsorwe
had heard.

' Is it even so ?' he said, with peculiar bitterness. ' I
mean, is it this meddlesome girl who has pretended to

you all this strange catalogue of wrongs? But who
will believe her besides yourself? Will our father, fire-
sputtering Sir Thomas, who believes her to be your
mistress and paramour—lay not your hand upon your
sword; I have purposely brought none—and knows her
to be angered against me on some foolish trifle of
womanish complaint, which she has exaggerated into a
mountain of grievances to show off the brighter rainbow with true love and fidelity to you? Will the King,
who knows her whole kindred and alliance for a pesti-
lent nest of traitors and treason? And will it even be
to her safety with her own mutinous townspeople, that
she should declare to the world how she has played the
eaves-dropper on their councils for your sake, and exposed them to the imminent hazards and disasters that
now threaten them, forsooth, in detecting me?'

Edward was, at all events, greatly struck with this
latter view of the case; but he endeavoured to answer
as unshakingly as he could. 'I shall soon put the Birmingham people out of all dread for themselves, Richard
Grimsorwe,' he retorted. 'I bear the King's assurance
of pardon and peace, if they are willing for it; and then
how say you?'

It was not a discreet revelation. Grimsorwe's livid
complexion deepened in its deadly hues.

'And then how say I?' he repeated. 'No, Edward
Holte; I answer, how now! now that the suspicions and
anger of the Birmingham rabble are thoroughly roused
against your grimy Venus — now that they are well
assured she has taken part in your escape, yet know not
that was the sole means which thwarted a plan that
would have concluded the war at a stroke—I answer,
and I tell you, either you shall solemnly promise me

never to reveal ought concerning me or my objects you
may think you have learned by the agency of that artful
girl, or, driven to despair, I will pass over openly to the
Parliament, and reveal to it and the angry townspeople
of ￼Dorothy Firebrace all she has done to betray and
injure them.'

Edward was, no doubt, greatly startled at the prospect
of the calamity denounced.

He knew the tangible proofs that existed of Dorothy's
aid to himself, and the penalties she had incurred under
the martial law proclaimed in Birmingham on the day
of his flight. All the goodwill and energy of her friends,
he felt, could not protect against the rigour of the Parliament, if it was directed so formidably against her. No
man knew to what extent that body might carry its
terrorism or vengeance after the mighty examples that
had been made, and which caused even the Queen of
Charles I. to tremble for her own safety in his palaces
and castles.

But his consternation was much increased when Grimsorwe, perceiving the effect produced, informed him that
before he left the town, Sisyphus the bellows-blower
had raised a great tumult among the lower classes of
the people of Birmingham who had thronged to Firebrace's house, declaring they would have vengeance on
the false townswoman that had deprived them of their
hostage against the vengeance of the cavaliers at Aston
Hall; a tumult which he stated had been with difficulty
baffled in its objects by Tubal Bromycham, who, at the
head of his young men, had violently dispersed the
mob. But Major Monk still remained in the town, and
had written an account of all he knew of the occurrences to London. If proofs were then forthcoming of

Dorothy's full complicity, what might not be expected in the way of vengeance and satisfaction to the exasperated people on the Parliament's part? And Grimsorwe's evidence would supply all that could be required in that direction.

For the second time, of late, Edward Holte found himself totally overmatched and discomfited by the skilful combinations and remorseless use of means by his antagonistic brother.

His apprehensions for the generous Dorothy's safety were, in fact, too great to allow him to reason very maturely on the subject. Restrained also as he was from vengeance of a personal nature on the treacherous villain, little was to be gained by holding out as if he projected it; above all, it was necessary to gain time and opportunity for his plans of reconciliation between the town and its offended Prince.

Accordingly, when Chaplain Lane, secretly sent on the errand by Lady Holte, presented himself shortly afterwards, as if to congratulate his favourite pupil and friend on his return—in reality to preserve the peace, if there was need—he found the two brothers quietly, though sternly, concluding upon the articles of their compact.

No writing was of course employed. Nor did Edward in the least confide for observance of the conditions on Grimsorwe's part, in anything but his belief that it would seem in his interest to observe them.

Edward was to make no further complaints to his father, or declare more fully what he conceived to be the designs entertained by Richard Grimsorwe, and the means he was believed to have adopted to put them in execution. Grimsorwe was to keep concealed all that he supposed himself to know, or in his rancorous heart really knew, of Dorothy Firebrace's acts to achieve her lover's escape, and the King's deliverance from the great danger that had menaced him.

Chaplain Lane was a man of the greatest simplicity of character and tenderness of heart; too guileless himself to suspect almost the possibility of such a serpentine nature as that of the bastard son of his patron; too full of the milk of human kindness to doubt the easy forgiveness and reconciliation of two persons allied by blood, whose bitter reasons of animosity he was not aware of; he readily, therefore, mistook the calm and settled tone he observed between the young men on his arrival, as rendering his interposition unnecessary, and scarcely understood why Edward pressed him to remain, until Richard Grimsorwe, rising, took an apparently friendly though rather ceremonious leave.

No sooner, however, had he passed out of the ' State Room,' ere Richard muttered to himself, grinding his sharp white teeth—

' Easy fool! to dream that Richard Grimsorwe is the slave to sit down contented in failure and defeat, and leave the man and the woman—nay, the woman and the man—he most detests on the face of the earth to triumph over him !'

CHAPTER LIII.

A DRINKING BOUT TWO CENTURIES AGO.

ON the whole, Edward was not displeased to be rid at this moment of the necessity of carrying out the quarrel with his treacherous brother into all its harassing consequences, and interruption of his more important business. He felt there was no time to be lost either in his affairs of love or policy.

The discomfort, and perhaps danger, of his beloved Dorothy's position were pressing considerations. The King's changeableness of purpose, and unhappy habits of double dealing, rendered it very advisable to proceed at once to engagements which he could not decently annul or counteract, formed on the basis of his royal word.

After much reflection Edward decided on his course of action, and on the proper agencies to be employed; greatly annoyed, but perhaps hastened in his resolves, by some circumstances which added to his convictions that Aston Hall was not likely to remain very comfortable quarters for himself in the objects he had in view.

The mild spirit and timidity of old Mr. Lane clothed his statements in the most inoffensive words. But Edward could readily gather that the Prince, who was likely to prove his strongest opponent, was established in full sway and supremacy in the house; treated more, indeed, as if he had been a god than a man, and gratified in every whim and wish. Nay, the poor chaplain faintly hinted, with a slight pinky flush on his pale lean cheeks, too conspicuously so as regarded the beautiful daughter of the house, for whom Rupert openly professed an outrageous dragoon-like kind of admiration, which he took rather extraordinary means to display.

For example, he had possessed himself—how the chaplain knew not—of a breast-knot of scarlet and black ribbons worn by Miss Holte, and carried it now conspicuously stuck in his hat, in sign that he had dedicated himself as, what was then styled, one of the young lady's *servants*, or, as we should say in these times, suitors ; though perhaps that word expresses too much, as it did not follow that the ' servant' aspired to the honour of his mistress's hand in marriage. It was merely a vestige of ancient chivalric custom, when a knight would assign the service of his puissant arm and obedience for a time to some princess or forlorn damsel in need of aid ; most probably from the oppressions of a giant or enchanter.

Edward liked not much of this, knowing, especially, as he did, his sister's character; the vanity and coquetry which actuated her in her notions on such subjects. He was aware of her extreme beauty and unbounded powers of fascination ; but he was also much better aware than his father—having been in Germany, accompanying Lord Falkland on a secret mission connected with this very family—of the insuperable obstacles to any likelihood of a desirable termination of such an affair, in the pride of royal birth and position of the Prince Palatine of the Rhine.

It mattered little that, with the other personages of his family, Rupert was a landless exile and fugitive from his native country. It was well known that the descendants of the unfortunate Elector Frederic, who had lost their wealthy and beautiful inheritance in the attempt to grasp a crown, cherished always the hope and purpose to retrieve everything by the sword.

Nothing was certainly to be hoped from the justice or mercy of the house of Austria, or of the Duke of Bavaria, to whom the exasperated Emperors of Germany had transferred the dominion. But even in offering his sword to his uncle in the English commotions, it was believed that stipulations in favour of an attempt to wrest the Palatine back for its original owners were enforced upon Charles. And the King, on his own part, was sufficiently bound by the ties of blood and former treaties to be willing to hazard much on the behalf of his sister's family, in the event of his own triumph in England.

All this made Edward greatly regret the circumstance of Prince Rupert's being so intimately domiciled at Aston Hall.

The only remedy would seem to be to endeavour to withdraw his sister herself from the perilous neighbourhood. And strangely infatuated, by his own pride and ambition, as he knew his father to be, Edward thought it impossible he could remain blind to the considerations he felt it would be his duty to urge upon him.

And these feelings of irritation were not soothed by the discovery he made, in the course of the evening, of the kind of near neighbours he had himself acquired.

Towards midnight Edward Holte was startled by a sudden laughing uproar and confusion on the oak staircase, by which the north wing of Aston Hall is ascended; and found, on listening, that Count O'Taafe was being escorted by a party of riotous officers, only not quite so drunk as himself, to the apartment assigned him in that division of the house now called the Chinese Room, from the frightful oriental paper with which its walls are disfigured.

Among the voices—evidently perfectly indifferent to any neighbour's rest being preserved, or ignorant they were breaking it—Edward distinguished that of Prince Rupert, hectoring and peremptory, even in what was as clearly his own personal vinous elation. But still more vexed, and even alarmed, was he to recognise the impudent vivacious accents of Cornet Titus; since it showed with what rapidity he had been despatched after himself from Nottingham.

The revel was, in fact, very possibly in celebration of this officer's return to his corps.

Prince Rupert's dragoons were always glad of an occasion of the sort, or any other pretext, even when they feasted at their own expense, which would not now be the case. But it was likely enough the cornet brought acceptable tidings to military men, who must have felt themselves rather disgracefully foiled in their recent movement.

But what annoyed Edward the most was to hear, by his father's voice amidst the tipsy tumult, that he was clearly as far gone as any other there; or even worse, for he heard him bawling orders to some servants below to bring up a six-gallon cask of cider ' to drink off what they had drunk,' as he was pleased to express himself to his wild companions.

Not but that Edward was well aware his father was

a stout comrade at his cups; as was then generally the case, even among persons of the highest rank and gentility. King James I. had introduced the custom from his own hard-drinking land, and all the stately decorum and sobriety of his successor had failed to do more than check the passion somewhat among the new generation. But even that degree of good was likely to be neutralised by the habits of camps and warfare, on which the nobility and commons of England were henceforth for a long period to be cast.

Discomfort of mind would have prevented Edward from sleeping now, but the noise of the revel alone sufficed; and it was kept up for a very considerable interval, through most of the variations of a drunken debauch of the kind.

It seemed to Edward as if his father's house was turned into a riotous barrack, under his father's own leadership and prompting.

Songs were sung, evidently of a camp and bacchanal description, since they were received with shouts of laughter, and ever and anon roared to in chorus by the whole company to a clattering of swords and spurs.

Healths were as clearly given and as enthusiastically welcomed, but one in particular was received with thundering acclamations, and a curious noise that resembled the clash of a number of men-at-arms bringing their weapons and knees to hard ground to repel a charge of cavalry. And, to Edward Holte's extreme vexation, loudest above the deafening yell of military applause he distinguished his sister's name in the fierce accent of the Prince Palatine, and flourished with a German 'Hoch, hoch, ad cœlum!' ('Hurrah, hurrah, to the skies!')

To crown all, this wild glorification suddenly passed into another, but by no means unusual variation, in the display of the effects of too much liquor on men of such make. Edward almost immediately after distinguished a burst of voices, in very changed accents of fury—of expostulation—of enquiry—and then an universal confusion and uproar.

Some sudden quarrel and outbreak had clearly taken place; in which the heir of Aston would have interested himself very little had he not known that his father was one of the party, and remembered how choleric and passionate he was upon the least provocation. And, moreover, he discerned his father's in the rageful, though nearly inarticulate, tones that first reached his ears after the burst. Those of Cornet Titus next, shrieking almost with defiance and insult, as well as he could find utterance for drunkenness and rage. And lastly, the loud tempestuous thundering of the Prince, apparently endeavouring to enforce peace and order by dint of out-furying every other effort at exasperated expression. By this time Edward, throwing on his chamber-robe, and snatching up his sword, had made his way to his own door. And he arrived just in time to distinguish somebody hurled headlong out of the apartment opposite, and sent at a whirl, with very slight opportunity of resting his feet, down the oak staircase. The person, indeed, went past him with the heavy whirr of some missle discharged from a cannon.

Edward had no light to see who or what this object might be; but, alarmed with the notion that it might possibly be his father, he hastened as fast as he could tread down the stairs after it; and, to his unbounded alarm and consternation, found he set his foot, at the bottom of the whole flight, on the body of a man, lying there insensible, possibly in a degree with drink, but also not improbably stunned by his descent into unconsciousness.

At all events he made no answer to Edward's repeated demands to know who he was; and terrified and excited by indignation almost equally, the young man flew up the stairs again to knock at O'Taafe' door, and require a light and an explanation.

To his astonishment, however, not being personally much accustomed to such scenes, the previous joyous uproar had been already resumed. And to such an extent, that all the clamour he made for admittance either passed unheard, or only provoked peals of laughter from the revellers.

Such were at least very audible after each more violent renewal of his attempts to make himself heard. And it was impossible to enter the room without help from within, as the door could be secured by a massive iron bar, which Edward found was placed in the staples.

Edward finally abandoned the attempt on distinguishing his father's voice, who was clearly safe and sound within, since he was yelling a part in some uproarious song; at all events, joining in the wild military clashing of the time, for the song was in French—a language in which Sir Thomas Holte prided himself on having always found it impossible to acquire a single word.

Count O'Taafe, apparently revived from a more torpid state of inebriation by the recent concussion, trolled the leading part in rich, jolly, unctuous tones, though interrupted by occasional hiccoughs. It was a lay, however, of a kind which would scarcely bear Englishing, to a modern audience.

Edward did not await the whole bacchanal ditty out, but retired from his useless application when once he had ascertained his father's safety.

From motives of humanity, very undeserved if he had been aware of the full facts of the case, he then returned to see if he could render any assistance to the expelled member of the riotous jollification. But on reaching the foot of the oak staircase the fallen carcass was no longer to be found there; and grope about and feel with feet and hands as he might, and demand to know what had become of the victim as he did, all was in vain. No traces of him remained.

Satisfied on this score also that the expellee could not have been so much injured as he had feared, since he was enabled to take himself from the field of disastrous experience, Edward now again retired to his own apartment.

In reality he felt it would be much the best for him to make no appearance in a drunken revel, whose members seemed so ready to take offence, and exhibit violence. He determined even, unless he found his duty as a son, or some point of honour in that punctilious age engaged, to take as little further notice as he could of an occurrence which he could not think would prove in any case to redound to his parent's credit.

It would be necessary, however, for him, he knew, to ascertain, as quietly as he could, the occasion and circumstances of the quarrel.

It was plain the sense of the company was against the person who had been expelled with so much violence. But if Sir Thomas had resented some affront, real or imaginary, in his customary furious and headlong style, there was reason to apprehend a serious imbroglio. In

such a case his age might be held to excuse him from
granting the kind of satisfaction most likely to be demanded. But his son must step forward in his place ;
and Edward's real affection for his father, as well as his
own high spirit, suggested to him that he ought to take
the earliest opportunity to place himself, if necessary,
between him and his antagonist. But this conviction
added of course greatly to his anxieties and perplexities ;
and with all the reason he knew he had to confide in
his skill at his weapons, the idea that he might probably
be called upon to put himself in jeopardy of being
disabled from his pressing personal affairs, annoyed him
extremely, and effectually banished sleep from his pillow
nearly all the night.

Sometime afterwards he had, however, the satisfaction
to hear Count O"Taafe's apartment cleared, as he supposed, of all his visitors, who descended the oak staircase in a quieter style than they had arrived, their
heavier liquors having mostly fumed off, and the tart
cider in reality assisting in the sobering.

Perhaps, also, some of them had become alive to im-
pressions of a painful and disastrous character from the
events of the evening. Rupert himself spoke now in a
low and rather dulled undertone, and Edward distinctly
heard him—as if just for the first time made aware of
the fact—tell his companions to make no noise, lest they
should disturb young Master Holte, who slept, he was
told, in the chamber nigh at hand.

CHAPTER LIV.

FATHER AND SON.

WILLING to have his uneasiness either confirmed or removed at the earliest possible opportunity, Edward accordingly only awaited the dawn ere he dressed and presented himself at Count O'Taafe's apartments for an explanation.

Contrary to the fact of the night before, he found the entrance unbarred; and desirous to excite no superfluous attention to his proceedings, he pushed the door open at once, and entered.

Greatly surprised, however, was Edward Holte—surprised and more shocked and alarmed—when the first object he discerned proved to be Sir Thomas Holte himself, lying fast asleep in an arm-chair.

The early morning sun was beaming in through the latticed panes of the window full on the baronet's drowsy visage; and Edward Holte, who had scarcely ever before dared to make his father an object of direct scrutiny, now gazed with a singular mixture of emotions at the figure before him.

He perceived with pain that, relaxed in slumber from their habitually haughty and domineering expression, his father's features betrayed very manifest tokens of a mind but ill at ease.

Unhappy remembrances seemed to cluster on all the sunken lines of his lips, and to give them almost a character of anguish. The marks furrowed on his brows by an habitual frown were distinct enough; but the frown itself had vanished, and a gloomy, puzzled— one might almost say, dismayed and conscience-tortured aspect—had succeeded, which was even yet more uncomfortable to his son's observation.

With this exception Edward Holte's filial feelings were much gratified by noticing how little the progress of time had told upon his father's vigorous organisation. His black hair was rather grizzled, it is true, in the long clusters, but the noble though stern features kept all their lines unimpaired; the bare muscular throat was as firm and unpuckered in the flesh as a young man's of half his years in these degenerate days. His whole figure displayed power and vigour of nerve and muscle in all its yielding of repose, which obviously needed only to be startled to exhibit the most strenuous activity. To be sure Sir Thomas Holte was little more than sixty years of age at the time; and neither by himself, nor most of his contemporaries, was he considered at all an old man. At this age an Englishman of the old make began to reckon himself rather past his youth; that was all.

Edward remarked with less satisfaction other circumstances of the scene.

A massive table in the centre of the apartment was covered with the remains of the previous night's debauch. Numerous pewter cans, out of which cider was mostly drunk; an empty cask, stove in at the top, in which some flies were buzzing; a plentiful allowance of smashed tobacco pipes—attested the character of the revel. Edward besides observed a dint in the wall, about the height of a man, much bespattered and streamy with the yellow liquor ; below which lay a bulged pot, which accounted for the whole appearance. A missile of this kind had probably parted from some irritated hand on the previous night, and occasioned the row.

As for the proper tenant of the apartment, whom he came to seek, Edward's attention was speedily directed his way by a loud snoring. And he perceived the count at some distance, cast in his full regimentals—boots, sash, breastplate, and sword—on a bed contrived in an alcove, which in modern times has been removed ; or else a less miserable resting-place than a bare mahogany table might have been found, not long ago, for the body of the unhappy rope-dancer whom the misdirected taste of a populace, and unnatural greed, consigned to a dreadful death. The traces of blood are indeed not easily obliterated, since even that dark wood still retains a horrible outline of the massacred form deposited on it.

Edward's object was now to arouse Count O'Taafe, without disturbing his father. A difficult operation, as he soon found it : for he was obliged to use some degree of violence, even to shake the count out of his drunken torpor. And when he did succeed in the effort, the leader, accustomed to war's alarms, started bolt upright from the couch to his feet with a hideous clatter, and yelling '*Aux armes, camarades!*' with a noise that awakened his lighter fellow-slumberer at once, clapped a horse-pistol to Edward's head before he could dream of such an encounter. Nay, perhaps, in the first tumult of a soldier's ideas on such an occasion, might have discharged it, had not Edward stayed his hand by exclaim-

ing, 'My God, count! I am Edward Holte: what mean
you by this violence?'

'Ventrebleu! I was dreaming I was again at the
sack of Magdeburg, when the father of those two poor
girls sprang at my throat to throttle me, though we all
thought we had given him enough for himself in the
head!' exclaimed O'Taafe, with rather a ghastly and
bewildered stare. 'I am glad it is not the old madman again, however, for it was sickening work putting
him out of his misery! Who, say you, you are? A
gentleman on behalf of Cornet Titus, to our good,
though something choleric friend and host, Sir Thomas
Holte?'

This was light enough. 'No, sir,' replied Edward,
sedately, 'I am Sir Thomas Holte's son, and I am come
only to ask of you the causes for which it behoves me,
as my father's representative, to demand satisfaction of
so much younger a man.'

O'Taafe stared, and looked puzzled for a moment;
but he was about to reply, probably with an explanation, when Sir Thomas peremptorily interrupted.
And certainly in other respects he had started awake
with a full restoration of his wonted despotism and
control in his looks. But yet there was something
closely resembling a blush of shame in all the fiery
anger of the colour that mounted to his visage as he
spoke.

'Never answer a word on the subject, Count O'Taafe,'
he said. 'I shall hold you for no friend or well-wisher
to your host and entertainer, if you do. The quarrel is
altogether mine; and, as I informed the fellow himself,
when the Prince flung him out of the room, he would
find me here ready to answer in aught he may have to

allege against me in the matter. Edward, I command
you, ask no further questions in it. What I did was
rightly done; but I will suffer no man but myself to
abide the consequences of an act which as father of—I
mean, I repaid an insult with an insult; and if the
jackanapes, whose skull I laid open with a cider pot,
needs any further satisfaction, my arm is as unwithered,
and my courage as good, as any malapert boy's in the
kingdom, to do me right to the fullest extent.'

'Malapert boy, my dearest father?'

'Your father speaks not of you, sir, but of Cornet
Titus, who is indeed the impudentest young saucebox
rogue—I could slit his tongue myself, for a demi-stiver;
it is always making mischief—yelping on a false scent,
and spoiling the run for the whole pack, d—— him!
But the Prince himself, I think, will hardly suffer any
interference but his own in the affair. It was he who
assisted the cornet to make such a nimble exit out of
Sir Thomas's way, that I fancy he never lifted his feet
but once from the top of the staircase to the bottom.
Yet he seemed well and lively enough after the exercise,
too, for he came back for admission in a few minutes;
but we only laughed at him while he made hammers of
his knuckles on the good oak door.'

Edward hastily explained that it was himself who had
so applied, being alarmed with the noise and tumult,
stating also that he had left the body of a man stretched
at the foot of the stairs seemingly insensible.

'Oh then, *ma foi*! he may be lying there still, for I
do not remember any of us looked after him again, and
his Highness gave him as handsome a fling as a stone
from a wall in an escalade,' observed the count. 'Come,
Sir Thomas,' he added, with a wink, 'let us go and see

whether our young gentleman is still taking his ease at
the bottom of the stairs or no.'

'I will enquire meanwhile elsewhere,' said Edward,
who very well knew the man was not to be found where
it was proposed to seek him, and who now determined
to anticipate his father's researches with the cornet ; and
unmindful of the laws of precedence, he had stepped
before his father and his father's guest, when the door
suddenly opened, and the person in question himself
appeared.

Not alone either, for Prince Rupert was beside him.

Edward faced the intruder, and by no means with
any reflection in his own of the impudent smilingness
of recognition in Cornet Titus's visage, otherwise
slashed with a wound like a sabre-cut and considerably
bruised.

'I sought you, sir,' he exclaimed, fiercely. 'I hear
you have insulted my father,' and demand satisfaction.'

' Well, then, I'm here to beg your father's pardon, if
need be, on both knees, Master Holte, on my Prince's
command. And I am besides at present rather *hors de
combat*, with a couple of sword-thrusts in the arm and
hand, which his Highness did me the honour to inflict
this morning, in full satisfaction for the affront he put
upon me last night in escorting me headlong out of the
company, which I deserved for my rude behaviour,'
said the submissive loyalist, pointing emphatically to a
ripped sleeve and bandaged arm, which Edward only
noticed then.

' Your business is altogether with Sir Thomas, cornet;
lose no time on the way,' said Rupert, with a frowning
glance at the obstruction ; and Titus immediately took
the hint, in his own way, however.

Approaching the angry and disdainful-looking baronet, he said, very loudly and distinctly, ' I have to beg your worshipful forgiveness, Sir Thomas Holte, for my indiscreet allusion to the honourable young lady, your daughter, in relation to his Highness's well-phrased and most honourably meant toast.   He is not Achilles ; you are not Priam ; and Miss Arabella Holte is not your youngest daughter, Polyxena; and therefore I had no occasion to wish a better termination to the tale than for his Highness to lose his life from a birdbolt in the heel, by archer Paris shot.   Do you grant your pardon, sir, or must I kneel for it too ? '

' Kneel to God, to ask Him to make you less of an impertinent jackanapes than you are !   But trouble me no more with your senseless buffoonery, man, which is yet as full of mischief as a barrel of working yeast. Put a bung in your mouth henceforth, and let us have done with the whole foolery ! ' said Sir Thomas, in great confusion and exasperation, evidently at the revelation of the cause of quarrel before his son.   Then, turning with an air of laboured indifference to the Prince, he said, ' But your Highness has in this hardly used me well ; the minion's punishment should have been mine office.   Howbeit the hide is curried now, and there is nothing more to be said on the subject. Does your Highness's mind hold constant about our faring abroad to-day with the hawks ? '

' Most certainly, Sir Thomas; but we must all make it our study that nothing of our last night's foolish contention in our cups comes to Miss Holte's hearing; and she promised to let me be her palfreyman in the sport to-day,' the Prince replied, waving his hand to Cornet Titus, who made a deep bow and withdrew.

Sir Thomas also seemed anxious to finish with the scene.

'I will go and see Robin Falconer on the business, then, at once, and let us soon all meet at a jolly hunting breakfast : 'tis a fair morn for the hawks' flight. Thanks for your night's hospitality, Count O'Taafe, and your goodwill for the morning, though it has not been needful to put it to the proof. Come, Edward,' he concluded, observing the young man seemed to intend remaining, and yet with a pretty visible reluctance on his own part to taking him in his company; 'the Prince and his lieutenant doubtless have business together. Let *us* hence, so.'

Not seeing what better could be done, Edward complied; and he and his father accompanied each other in a dead sort of silence out of the chamber.

As they did so a figure hastily disappeared round the first balustrade ; hastily, but easily recognisable for that of Richard Grimsorwe.

Neither Sir Thomas nor his son, however, made any remark on the circumstance, both of them being occupied in their minds with a very different subject. But still the baronet had no wish to enter even upon this ; and he adopted a judicious, though usually rather feminine policy, by entering, as quickly as possible, on an angry discussion on the one which was by no means uppermost in his mind.

'You keep me company, Edward,' he said, 'and it is not amiss. I have not had any private talk with you since your return ; but what is it I hear of your strange interposition in behalf of those rebellious scullions of Birmingham, and prevention of the Prince's justice and vengeance on them, as the malignant seditioners and

muck-heap of treasons they are, and have proved themselves?'

To this speech Edward returned a temperate but firm
reply. 'I wish to bring back an important town to his
Majesty's allegiance; not by severities to cast in its
portion irrevocably with our enemies,' he said.

'Marry, fine talk, son Edward! But, plainly English'd, the story runs thus : You have a fair mistress in
the town, for whose sake you will put aside all high
considerations of policy, and hold back the sword from
the necks of incorrigible traitors, whereby you will
preserve a nest of hornets near us, when we might
smoke it out now at a word for ever.'

'A mistress, sir !' exclaimed Edward, with indignation.
'I recognise my vile brother's suggestion in that word,
whose dastardly violence towards a woman, and inducing you to break my safe-conduct, brought all the
recent danger and trouble upon me. Mistress! If
you speak, as I doubt not, of Mistress Dorothy Firebrace, clearly understand, sir, that in any ill sense she
is none to me ; that by her descent she is as good or a
better gentlewoman than I can pretend to be a gentleman, and in all personal worth and virtue infinitely
my superior. Nor should I dare to entertain a thought
concerning her unless in all honour, and with a view to
offer her my hand with my heart in marriage.'

It was a desperate venture. So Edward instantly
after felt it to be, and would fain have recalled his word.
But words are winged, and once from the perch cannot
be whistled back.

'In *marriage*! Marriage ? Did you say *marriage*?'
the senior roared out. 'Pray you, carry me with you,
Master Holte. Marriage! Marriage with a blacksmith's

daughter—an old mechanical traitor's brat of a pretty face! If I did not think you were jesting—to use the word— But we will put the matter out of doubt shortly now. You can no longer feign the impropriety of wooing a young lady to a husband's arms, whose father is absent and in mortal peril and jeopardy. My Lord Keeper is safe now, and his invaluable bauble, with the King. So my Lady Lyttelton came yesterday, with her good daughter, Mistress Penelope, to assure us. And as my soul lives, if ever you mean to inherit after me at Aston Hall, you shall wed the bride I have chosen you at the nearest conveniency!'

Edward perceived the necessity of withdrawal from so astounding a glimpse at his real feelings and purposes.

He had needed little convincing on the subject, but the utter hopelessness of obtaining his father's consent to such an alliance struck him more than ever. And with such an ambitious and insidious enemy in ambush to seize every imaginable advantage against him! He did his best to retrieve the slippery step he had made.

'Well, sir,' he said, 'I have not yet, that I wot of, openly demurred to your pleasure. But it would ill become us to deal in weddings and rejoicings at such a momentous and untoward conjuncture in our King's affairs, and when we have as yet done nothing in fulfilment of our pledges to him; with which his Majesty himself did feelingly upbraid me when I saw him of late at Nottingham.'

'He chose an ill time for his reproaches, then, Edward,' said Sir Thomas, rather soothed by the appearance of submission, 'just when your brother and yourself had hazarded your lives in his service.'

'My brother!' Edward exclaimed, but he recollected
at the moment the terms of his truce with Grimsorwe,
and did not follow on with the proper explanation of
his surprised and irritated accent on the word.

Sir Thomas remarked it sufficiently, however, to observe, 'Pish! what rancour is this about a foolish wench;
as if there were only one in the world! I trow me,
Edward, you will live to see the day when you will deem
yourself as much obliged to the rival who shall ease you
of your spoil as you now snarl and grind your teeth over
it to an otherwise conclusion. Yet, as the King says,
and as you say, we ought to fulfil our promises to him.
But how may that be, if we have no arms; and how
may we have arms except by lashing the Birmingham
men like mutinous galley-slaves to their forges?'

'It shall be part of the conditions of peace I purpose
to make that they shall supply both parties indifferently;
there are smiths of both minds in the town; and, besides,
they are all traders, and will not mislike an open market,' Edward replied; and, it must be confessed, Birmingham has generally preferred to be neutral in this
way.

'And is this noble blacksmith, forsooth, of Birmingham
to be confirmed in his lordship and claimed inheritances,
whereof part includes, as I have heard, the very land on
which I have built so brave a palace that the Prince
himself nothing disparages it in comparison with his
own native electoral castle on the Rhine, which is one
of the glories of Germany for magnificence and lustrous
ornament?' Sir Thomas enquired, with scornful bitterness.

It should be mentioned that Edward and his sire were
now crossing the terrace, between the Hall and the Fal-

coner's Lodge and other domestic offices of the building,
which yet afforded a very stately and imposing view of
a portion of Aston Hall. Sir Thomas looked round as
he spoke, and took a long and deep inhalation, as if his
fine stonework were also like some rich flower impreg-
nated with sweet odours to the breath.

He cherished, indeed, a kind of passion of admiration
and love for his noble masterpiece of art and expense.
But Edward himself was glad of the pause; it was, in
truth, rather a puzzling suggestion, that made.

'It would really appear, sir,' he at last timidly insinuated, 'that the unfortunate young man in question
has received some great wrong, ancestrally speaking;
but it will be for tribunals of the King's justice, most
probably at some quieter time, to right him, if it may
be. But meanwhile, I dare well assure you, Tubal
Bromycham will never seek or wish to trouble you in
your possession of this land. But for the Prince's Highness to compare it with the Castle of Heidelberg, it must
be in a most unbecoming mock. For the castle, when
it stood, was a fitting residence for a mighty king, but
is now little more than roofless wall and frontage, which
all the hatred of the most savage of conquerors and
ravagers— the merciless Tilly—could not hurl down its
mountain crags, with an army of plunderers' aid.'

Sir Thomas reddened. 'It is you who mock and
thwart me in everything, rather,' he said, angrily. 'I
know not that the Prince spoke of his castle as it is now,
or as it has been. All the world knows of the misfor-
tunes of his glorious family; you tell us no news there,
Edward. So then you promise me some manner of
mercy and forbearance from the Blacksmith Lord of
Birmingham, do you, whose title I propose to usurp, in

212 THE ARMOURER'S DAUGHTER.

due course of events, as well as his lands, and whose feet
have figured in my stocks as those of an impudent rogue
and vagabond? But some price will surely be demanded
from me for so much goodness; and so, instead of marrying my daughter to a descendant of the Emperor
Charlemagne, I must, I suppose, gratefully accept for
a son-in-law a Walsall collier.'

Edward was now thoroughly stricken with alarm.

'Good God! my dearest father, what is this you say?'
he exclaimed. 'I do trust you have no such perilous
frenzy in your mind, for it is nothing more nor less, and
puts to the hazard my sister's happiness, and all our
honours, most preposterously.'

'Oh, to be sure, I am a foolish old dotard, in my
second childhood—as weak in judgment as sinews, am I
not? Prithee, when was I put in tutelage? Is there
my Lord Keeper's seal to my superseding as well as your
pardon for the traitors of Birmingham?' Sir Thomas
answered, drawing up his towering figure to its haughtiest
strength and majesty, and surveying—almost contemptuously, and with visible suspicion and anger—his finer-
limbed and visaged son. 'You are the only wiseacre out
of Gotham among us, I presume, Master Holte? and I,
and even your scholarly brother Dick, must only go a
moon-raking where you show us the fine cheese in the
waters.'

'My brother again! And does he advise? Oh, my
dearest father, we are all made the playthings of a mon-
ster of treason and duplicity, that are to beat each other
to pieces jerked on his wires! I say it is downright
madness to suppose that the King's nephew can ever be
anything to my sister but a peril and a dishonour in the
association of their names. For God's own sake, then,

listen to me now! You know you have allowed me long
as your Deputy Ranger at Sutton Manor-House. This
haughty foreigner and I can never agree together, nor
shall I be able, even under our own roof, long to keep
at peace with his cut-throat ruffianage. Let me retire,
therefore, to Sutton, and assemble there and quietly put
in harness and preparation for the war—if war there
must be—the young yeomen of your tenantry, who are
to form my troop of horse. But more than all—oh, a
thousand times more—let me take my sister away with
me to Sutton, to keep house for me. The place may
easily be made tenantable and comfortable enough; and
she will be safe from any unhappy coupling of her name
with that of this royal soldier of fortune, who has evidently taken her into his besmirching homage and
admiration.'

'Hear to all this whipping of waters! what's to come
of it, trow, but froth? It must be indeed that I have
been deprived for incompetency, and put in ward of this
wise young gentleman, my younger son—at all events,
in the counting of years. Hark you, Master Holte,' Sir
Thomas now replied, with extraordinary vehemence;
'silly old goodman as I am, I do yet think I discern my
daughter's fair repute would run much greater danger
of scandal, should I find it necessary to make proclamation to the world the way you propose, and declare that
I find it impossible to trust her under my own roof in
the company of a high-born gentleman and prince! Fie
on you, for the mean, dishonest thought, which shows
well what manner of consorting you have yourself of late
enjoyed! But, for the rest, I am well content that you
should carry on your truckling peacemaking with the
Birmingham mobsters under any other roof than mine.

And methinks I could as little as ever guarantee your safe-conduct to the crop-eared knaves among his High-ness's brave followers. Go then to Sutton, and begin there your game at soldiering in his Majesty's service; but for a housekeeper, if one is so needful for you, invite thither your fair-faced Puritan Rosamund, the armourer's daughter. Take my word for it, there is no better cure for a runaway horse than giving him the spur till he tires; and a surfeit of sweet cake brings a man soon to see and acknowledge that plain bread is the staff of life. To Sutton Manor-House, I say then, with your fine mistress at once: and you will be the sooner ready to betake yourself to a plain but well-endowed wife.'

So saying, Sir Thomas strode indignantly forward, raising a silver whistle at his girdle, which he blew long and shrilly as he neared the Falconer's Lodge, while his son remained silent and sorrowful on the edge of the grass-plat behind.

215

CHAPTER LV.

THE HAWKING-PARTY.

CONCERNED as he was at his father's dangerous infatuation, Edward could not at the moment devise any other means of counteraction than those he had thus tried and failed in. But he thought some hope might remain in his sister's own womanly sense and spirit, which he resolved to make an attempt to rouse before he took his departure. And he had now fully made up his mind to retire to Sutton, feeling that his remaining at Aston Hall was powerless to prevent mischief, while it exposed him to embarrassing supervision and thwarting.

Moreover, he speedily found Sir Thomas was either really offended with his interference, or held him to his arrangement to be rid on his own part of what he probably looked upon as an inconvenient and crosswork meddling.

Edward was, of course, but little in the mood for an excursion of the kind. But partly to promote his own objects, and partly conceiving it his duty, as one of the representatives of the house, he presented himself at the grand *régal* which preceded the hunting-party now in progress.

Breakfast it was called; and a breakfast it was, in

the style of our hearty ancestors, who, as yet, dreamed
not of such wishy-washy foundations as tea and coffee,
but began their feeding for the day with as substantial
a meal of meat and strong brewages as the best of us
can now hope to dispose of for dinner.

The repast alluded to was served in the Great Hall—
almost, one might say, in the open air, the doors and
windows on all sides being thrown widely open.

It was a gay and bustling scene. The Prince was to
be attended on the excursion by nearly all his officers,
saving only those required to remain in charge of the
dragoons. About a score of cavaliers were therefore
thronging in the chambers, divested of their heavier
panoply, but still in their showy uniform, with white
plumes waving to their girdles from their dashingly
slouched broad-brimmed hats; with flowing locks, and
curled moustache, and pointed beard, well oiled; high
boots and gilded spurs, the rowels being as large as
sunflowers; and graceful, short-riding cloaks, thrown
carelessly over the shoulders, and fastened by an hussar-
like lacing of tassel and silver cord.

Among these fine personages Sir Thomas Holte and
his daughter were still conspicuous from the costly
materials of their hunting garb, which in both was of
light green velvet, profusely passemented, as it was
called, with gold brocade, in the young lady's case, and
further relieved by a cap of cloth-of-gold, and a brilliant scarlet feather. But Arabella Holte was yet
greatly more distinguished by her beauty; and her
brother's own saddening eye could not avoid appre-
ciating the heightened dazzle and glow of his splendid
sister's charms, under circumstances so exciting and
gratifying to her vanity and inordinate spirit of coquetry.

Very few women then living in England could in reality have contended with the daughter of the founder of Aston Hall for the prize of beauty. But no other lady was present save her mother, whose weak and faded outlines scarcely at all arrested notice ; and the vivacity and grace of the court-bred younger lady contributed to produce her extraordinary loveliness with the most varied lustrous effects, and to render her, even more than by the natural gallantry of a military society, the centre of universal homage and admiration.

Had that been all, it would not so much have annoyed Edward Holte, who was very well accustomed to see his sister an object of gallant devotion on the part of persons of his sex. But he perceived at once that a most particular and special dedication of his attentions was made to her by Prince Rupert, who seemed to have neither eyes, ears, nor understanding for any other person or thing.

The conversation was evidently chiefly between these two, and as clearly of a sprightly and interesting nature, since it even melted the saturnine reserve and hauteur of Rupert's usual manner, and lighted his harsh features, bending delightedly over his companion, as if by reflection from her laughing charms. And although Miss Holte had a remarkably fine falcon, hooded and chained by silver jesses on her wrist, to which frequent playful and fondling reference seemed made by the pair, it was plain to the merest novice that the bird was only a pretext and cover for the close and animated dialogue in which they indulged. Yet Sir Thomas appeared to take no notice, playing the courteous host in every other direction, with all manner of hospitable entreaties and recommendations of his

viands; little needed, for the most part, by his military
guests.   And this after so recent and demonstrative a
discussion, witnessed by so many of the Prince's officers
in person, and probably universally reported.

'My father has gazed himself into a madman, at his
fine house!' thought Edward. 'Yet if even his ambitious hopes could attain fruition, would my sister's
lot be a happy one as the wife of a haughty insulting
princeling foreigner like this, whose every look and
glance betray the harshest pride and despotism of character? I trow me not, since Arabella is at heart
herself as self-willed and disdainful of control and
supremacy as he! And then, poor Tubal Bromycham!
my mainstay and anchorage with him and the town
would be gone indeed.'

The company in the hall nearly all stood to their
refection, as was usual at an occasion of the kind, when
out-of-doors sport was in forwardness.   But huge
masses of corned beef, and brawn, and fried venison,
and mutton collops, disappeared under their exertions,
at the long boards set with the hunting fare. As for
the strong ale in the numerous hooped flagons, which
two or three were expected to share—and the claret
perpetually pouring from a massive silver centre-piece,
representing a rock and waterfall, from which the guests
helped themselves at discretion, in quaintly wrought
goblets and beakers of the same metal—it was who
should do the amplest justice to the liberality of Aston
Hall.

Meanwhile the wassail inside was not ill-matched
with the lively stir and movement in the courtyard and
terraces before the mansion.

Sir Thomas had determined to display his wealth

and magnificence to the utmost ; and all his choicest
horses and hounds, well groomed and caparisoned, or
straining in the leashes held by handsomely liveried
pages and other retainers for hawking or hunting,
crowded the inclosure; men shouting, horses neighing,
dogs barking, and the hawks flapping their wings and
jingling their bells, in a bright confusion of colouring
and sound, well canopied by a glorious azure sky, and
the glow of a cloudless autumn sun.

Into this cheerful company Edward Holte made his
way, without feeling himself much enlivened by the
association.

Nor did he receive many marks of welcome. A
brightening glance of recognition from his fond unhappy mother—a friendly squeeze of the hand from
Chaplain Lane—were for some time the only signs that
anyone observed his arrival. But while detained by
the passing of a singular triumph of Adam Blackjack's
skill in the shape of a besieged castle of gilt marchpane
or gingerbread, thronged with figures and waving with
little flags, on so large a scale that it was rolled in on a
wheelbarrow—Edward became aware of a pair of eyes
fixed upon him from a distance.

The eyes were those of Richard Grimsorwe ; who sat
in a recess of a window of the great inner chamber of
the hall, known as the saloon. Completely alone, too ;
in the congenial shadow of the branches of a stately
cedar that grew on the outside terrace.

He withdrew his gaze almost instantaneously, ap-
pearing to be deeply engaged in the perusal of a volume
in his hand. But in that brief interval Edward had
discerned a real fiendish and malignant expression of
mockery and enjoyment in them, that convinced him

his unnatural enemy appreciated the anxiety and trouble
with which he surveyed the scene before him.

Edward's action was quickened by the species of
echoing he found to his own fears in Grimsorwe's satisfaction; and under pretence of paying his respects to
the Prince, he gladly interrupted his public and yet
apart confabulation with Arabella. Nor would he allow
himself to be repulsed by Rupert's cold and formal
acknowledgment of the civility, and evident wish that
nothing further should ensue. He remained where he
was, and his presence exercised an immediate and
striking check on both the parties. The Prince turned
haughtily away, and Miss Holte bridled, bit her lip,
and seemed to seek some occasion to remove.

His annoyance much increased, Edward was about to
speak to his sister and ask her for a few moments'
private speech. But precisely then Sir Thomas joined
the group, and pronounced the unkindly resolute words,
'My son, sir, has come to bid your Highness and his
sister farewell. He proposes to fix the head-quarters
of his troop of horse, for which his Majesty has honoured
him with a commission, at a nigh royal manor-house we
have in these parts—that they may be less in the way
of your cavaliers. And besides, in truth, negotiators
from Birmingham—and he persists in negotiation—
would have but a sorry time of it among my tenantry!'

The Prince coldly made the remark that he trusted
his own presence at Aston Hall might not be found to
inconvenience its proper inmates; and a trumpet sounding at this moment for the hawking-party to form, he
offered his hand to Miss Holte, and walked off with her
at an unusually rapid rate through the company, which
of course all made way,

Edward followed them with his eyes for some moments, and saw the Prince himself, as the manner
then was, kneel to allow Arabella to mount the horse
by springing from his knee. And he then most distinctly perceived that as he placed the young lady's
foot in the stirrup, he stooped and kissed it!

What effect so extravagant a mark of homage from
so haughty and exalted a personage would have on a
vain, coquettish young woman like his sister, it was not
hard to conjecture. And while the rest of the company
trooped out after the pair, Edward turned with such an
expression on his face to his mother— who did not go
with it—that she almost cowered beneath his glance,
and said, 'I cannot help it, indeed, my dearest boy; I
can help nothing that happens in this house! But of
a truth, either your father will plunge us all into misery
and disgrace, or he will make his daughter a princess
by a marriage with the blood royal of the land!'

It was in vain that Edward, highly provoked at the
intimation, implored his mother to make some use of
her reasoning faculties, and remonstrate with his father
on the perilous course he was pursuing.

Lady Holte was a thoroughly spirit-broken woman
now, and at no period of her career had ever coped with
much courage or resolution against her husband's headstrong despotism. And when she found that Edward
himself had dared to make remonstrances on the subject
(which, by-the-by, neither of them again more plainly
alluded to), which had failed, she declared that any
attempt on her own part would only provoke Sir Thomas
to a still rasher following up of his own ideas. All that
Edward could obtain from the nerveless lady was an
assurance that she would watch most zealously over her

child; and if the Prince continued his attentions, engage him to some open declaration of his meaning, either by her own or her daughter's agency.

Meanwhile Edward's personal affairs and anxieties pressed heavily upon him, and he was obliged to adjourn for a while the consideration of his sister's perils in the efforts necessary to interfere with advantage in favour of the object of his own attachment.

CHAPTER LVI.

THE BLACKSMITH LORD OF BIRMINGHAM.

EDWARD HOLTE thus unexpectedly found himself sentenced to a species of exile from his father's house, and very few facilities remained in other respects at his disposal to effect the objects he had in view.

A messenger into the town must in the first instance be found, who would faithfully perform his mission, and could not be supposed to incur much risk in it.

These conditions he thought answered in the person of the Rev. Mr. Lane, whose mild and benevolent character secured him universal respect, and who was very well known in Birmingham.

The only difficulty was to overcome the extreme natural timidity of his character. But Mr. Lane had a great affection for Edward personally, and he agreed to everything required, when he found that unless he undertook the office, the young gentleman would again place himself, with no security but the good faith of some individuals in whom he declared he could confide, in the hands of the leaders of the Birmingham sedition.

Accordingly, shortly after the hawking-party set forth, Mr. Lane mounted a slow-paced ambling nag, and took his way to the town, the bearer of two letters, one directed to the Master Armourer Firebrace, and the

other to Tubal Bromycham. A servant in the Holte
livery was sent before with a white flag, and Edward
accompanied the gentle priest to the exit of the park,
giving him his instructions in detail.

Not knowing what might now be the state of Birmingham, or what fate might await his communications,
Edward was determined to proceed in them without
presuming upon any kind of goodwill or understanding
with himself on the part of the two leaders. In both
the epistles he merely asked for a safe-conduct, and
assemblage of the Town Council, that he might lay
before it the King's most gracious proposals to receive
Birmingham back into his allegiance and protection.
But Mr. Lane's private instructions were ample how to
influence the two chiefs of the town, in case of any
doubt or hesitation on their part.

Edward himself was to follow, at a suitable interval,
to the barriers, there to ascertain results. And in his
indignant feeling at his father's uncivil and peremptory
proceedings, he determined not to return to Aston, but
gave orders at once for a removal of his own more immediate personal appurtenances and servants to Sutton
Manor-House.

When these arrangements were effected, and he had
bidden his mother farewell, promising to see her as
frequently as possible, and earnestly renewing his cautions, Edward mounted his horse, and followed his
missionary of peace to the town with his credentials.

But he encountered quite a different sort of a personage some time before he reached the spot where he
had appointed to meet Mr. Lane, which was nigh the
Butts Barrier, as it had grown to be called, where
Grimsorwe had been stopped in his coach. A figure

presented itself in his way, in the ordinary leather garb
of a blacksmith, in whose herculean though stunted
proportions Edward Holte immediately recognised the
person of Tubal Bromycham.

A change had nevertheless come over the whole aspect
of the Blacksmith Lord of Birmingham, as Sir Thomas
Holte contemptuously styled him, which almost confused
his now friendly rival's recognition.

Tubal Bromycham's energetic and mind-stamped
features seemed to have acquired a new character of de-
veloped power and intellect, as if a sculptured lion had
become animate with all the vital instincts and supremacy which a lord of the forest in actual sinew and bone
could claim. This character of power had even attained
that highest evidence in man's moral organisation,
when it becomes, as it were, humorous and playful,
from a sense of the futility of the resistances opposed.
Edward Holte was struck with the bright and hopeful
expression of Tubal's countenance, which exalted the
rugged lineaments into an effect that, if not exactly
what is called handsome, was something more engaging
and noble than mere beauty of lines and colouring
could ever produce. And yet—he knew not well why—
this, as it were, sun-bursting of the brave soul through
its clouds, in the grand artisan, troubled the friendly
gentleman. He coupled it with the scene he had
recently left, and saddened to think to what cause
Tubal probably owed his Promethean animation of hope
and energy.

The two young men saluted in the most friendly
manner, Master Holte alighting for the purpose, as to
an equal, which he was well enough inclined to admit
Tubal Bromycham to be. There was no occasion for

any explanations between the former supposed rivals
now. Both felt and knew that Dorothy had rendered
their present relations perfectly clear and satisfactory.

But very important explanations were to be exchanged
respecting the business of the present meeting.

It was in answer to Edward's anxious enquiry as to
what had become of his messenger, that Tubal com-
menced his statements.

'Truly, Master Holte,' he said laughingly, 'the din
and uproar are so great in the town, and the rabble
there growing so heady and tumultuous in its dealings,
that the poor gentleman, as it were, lost his senses with
fear. And though I assured him, and truly, mark you,
that no man dares harm him under the safeguard of the
Lord of Birmingham, did so implore me not to be forced
to run the gauntlet of the crowded streets back again,
that I thought it best to put him into cool and safe
keeping in St. Martin's Church, as I have others threatened by the mob, and come myself to meet and tell
you how things stand.'

'But sure you do not mean to say, Tubal Bromycham, that the common sort are in the mastery in
Birmingham?' Edward enquired, much alarmed at the
intimation.

'They are striving hard for it, at all events, and under
the leadership of a desperate and determined fellow,'
Tubal replied, still smiling. 'Captain Cromwell—who
has, it seems, left us to our own exertions for safety,
after so committing'us openly against the King—hath,
besides, contrived us a legacy of tumults and all manner
of refractory proceedings, by turning out our regular
parson, and giving to the entire people the election of
a new minister. And this is what the town is running

mad upon just now, who shall be appointed to the vacant office, its sway from the pulpit, and emoluments; we of the Council, and most other upper substantial men, favouring a certain approved good preacher and martyr for the truth, who has lately fled hither among us, called Whitehall, and the rabble violently driving at placing a ragamuffin tub-ranter of their own—the Anabaptist knave, Sisyphus the bellows-blower—in Dr. Dugdale's pulpit and cushion.'

' Sisyphus the bellows-blower ! The villain who assailed Mistress Firebrace for favouring my retreat, and who instigated a base attempt at assassinating myself when a prisoner in his custody !' Edward exclaimed, who was still by no means aware of all the disobligations he owed the man.

' The same; and who, in my opinion, projects even worse and wider fulfilments of evil in his rotten and rancorous soul, to judge by the strange blasphemous overtures and promises he makes in his speeches, tow in the rabble over to bestow on him their votes,' replied Tubal. ' Yea, for he will have it that there are no longer to be poor and rich, kings, gentlefolks, and commons; but all men are to be equal, and to have all things in common. Beshrew my heart ! if the rancid rogue means not our women too ! for that the reign of the saints has come to pass; and he gives it out he knows by a vision and revelation he has received, that they have only to go in and take possession; to inherit the earth and the fulness thereof for a thousand years of happiness and joy— under, no doubt, his blessed sway !'

' Your women ! when the dastardly cripple has even endeavoured to hound the populace on to the destruction of his master's daughter!' exclaimed Edward, flushing deeply with indignation.

'And that is, indeed, still one of his main cries,' Tubal replied. 'He and his immediate gang are as clamorous as a field of cawing crows that Dorothy Firebrace shall be surrendered to the people (as they call themselves), and tried with all solemnity by them for treason against the good town. I have beaten their heads about pretty sharply already on this, without beating the idea out of them; and they grow the noisier because a Parliament man—one Major Monk—who is among us, declares, on the other hand, that she ought to be sent to London for calm judgment, and proper either acquittal or punishment. The howling curs are not to be contented without the rending of her in their own fangs!'

'But truly, Master Bromycham—if you be, as you say, true Lord of Birmingham—you will not suffer such atrocious mastery as this is likely to prove to exalt itself over your authority in the town?' exclaimed Edward.

'It shall be seen! But why give you me not the name of Lord, then?' Tubal replied, the light quickening in his blue Saxon eyes like the sparkles of a spear, and his strong hands knitting as if they grasped one. 'Howbeit, it matters not; men will give the name where they find the thing,' he continued, with a stern smile. 'And believe me, Master Holte, I am very specially glad you have come to witness—and report—how I bear myself in the rank and duties I derive from a thousand years of ancestry, and have resumed. They shall soon know in Birmingham who is lord thereof! But I cannot, as perchance you would have me,' he added, after a slight pause, 'interfere to prevent the

people of their free election, which they enjoy of as old
right and privilege as any under which I myself claim
and challenge the unlawful exercise of power that
deprived me of my inheritance.'

'Is it not certain, then,' said Edward, much disappointed, 'that, the rabble being so much more numerous, the election will fall upon Sisyphus, whose means
of mischief will thus be infinitely enlarged to the destruction of all law and decency in the town, and certain
rejection of the gracious pardon and terms I bring from
the King? For if once the mob are permitted so far
to gain the upper hand, who will dare to do or say anything likely to be unacceptable to them and their
leaders in their scandalous designs?'

'What are these terms?' said Tubal, suddenly as-
suming an air of dignity that greatly struck Edward.
'We will talk of the rest anon; but at present, I trow
me, there is no man fitter than the Captain and Lord of
Birmingham to receive and weigh the same.'

Edward briefly declared the advantageous conditions
which he considered he had obtained from the King.
An immediate cessation of hostilities on the part of the
near and dangerously-posted Royal troops, and a full
pardon to all concerned in the recent outbreak, on condition that on its part the town returned to its allegiance, and allowed its forges to be employed in the
service of all purchasers willing to give a fair price in
open market for the Birmingham manufactures.

'This were an undoing of Master Cromwell's work,
with a vengeance,' said Tubal, relaxing again into a
smile that seemed to indicate he saw nothing personally
objectionable in the notion. But a shadow darkened
over his visage as he continued, 'We must stipulate,

however, on our part, ere we throw our barriers down, that the King's ruffians be removed from so nigh a neighbourhood to us as Aston Hall. And, by all that is wonderful and strange! I do marvel that your father, Master Holte, should desire his mansion and — and family—to be given over to such rough occupancy and society as we all hear the Palatine's troopers exhibit in their demeanour at Aston Hall.'

Edward endeavoured to conceal the effect which these words had upon him, but was not sufficiently practised in disguise to prove so successful as he wished. Even the eagerness with which he clutched at the escape from his own fears, he thought he could discern in Tubal's demand, was rather betraying.

'I do trust you will insist on that condition—my father has his frenzies on some points—that the soldiers shall be retired. I myself have found them such uncivil company, that I have resolved to withdraw to Sutton Manor-House.

'You, Master Holte!' exclaimed Tubal, in spite, as it seemed, of a resolute effort to suppress his emotion, turning pale. 'You to withdraw from Aston Hall to Sutton Manor-House! There is, indeed, then, no time to be lost. But yet, no, no; with all her pride and her ambition, her unjust betrayal of my love, I am certain that she loved me once—must love me still! And when she hears that I have proved myself her equal in rank; that I have restored myself with mine own strong right arm to my rights, she will no longer disavow the love she once more than suffered me to believe she shared!'

'I cannot pretend to be ignorant that you allude to my father's daughter, Tubal Bromycham,' Edward now said, himself affected by the overpowering emotion which

evidently dictated this outburst; 'and I am grieved
indeed to be obliged to agree with you, that obstacles to
your generous passion multiply in my father's insane
spirit of pride and ambition, and, perchance, in Arabella
Holte's recklessness of coquetry, and pleasure in the
triumphs of her beauty and powers of fascination. Nay,
for I must candidly add, that though I know not on what
foundations you build, it seems to me scarcely possible
that she can ever have seriously meant to encourage
your devotion.'

'Ah, you know not, you know not; how can you
know?' the young man replied, with passionate warmth.
'But *I* know.   Oh, it is not in woman—in humanity—
so to feign!   What wanted she with the heart of a poor
artisan to trample on, that she should have taken so
much pains to win mine?   It was chiefly when I was
making her the virginals in my Lady Holte's withdraw-
ing-room, on which I know she still plays, for I have
often stolen up since to Aston Hall, and heard the music
bubbling from her bright fingers forth upon the night
from the notes.   And wherefore should she so often
keep my company, then, when she could not but see the
love and adoration in my eyes—and praise my skill till
I deemed myself some god of my grimy craft—and
smile at and encourage all the plain tokens of my
overmastering feelings, until, until that miserable hour
indeed——'

'When you declared your affection?   But did not
Arabella then most unkindly and repulsingly expel you
from her presence, and even carry her disdain and rejection so far as to reveal all to my father, and expose you
to the consequences of his well-known violence and
revenge?' said Edward, who felt an extreme repugnance,

on his own part, to work upon the noble-natured young
man's feelings further—as he so easily might—to his
own advantage.

'It is true,' replied Tubal, with a deep sigh, and a
dark shadow crossed his brows. 'But,' he continued,
with suddenly revived animation of hope and the loving
credulity of his nature, 'must I not forgive her when
I remember how beautiful she is—how proudly born
and reared—how skilfully in all womanly and ladylike
accomplishments—how worthy to be the wife of a
crowned emperor? Must it not have seemed to her an
insult—an audacity beyond compare—a madness worthy,
indeed, of whip and chains—for a mere artisan like me
(as such only she knew me then) to dare to throw myself
at the feet of one so exalted and so fair, and ask, as it
were, an angel of heaven to become the wife of a poor
smith of Birmingham? But soon, now, shall she, and
all men and womankind beside, know me for who I
am!'

'What purpose you to do?' said Edward, thinking it
uselessly honest to argue the matter further at this
moment.

'To let my good townspeople, in the first place, know
I am their lord, and by such a means as I hope will stir
Master Sisyphus and his fellows into open contention
with me for the mastery!' replied Tubal, beaming joy-
ously up again at the thought. 'But will you, on your
part, run some portion of the risk, Master Holte? For
I will let it be universally known in the town that you
are come to treat of peace between us and the King—
and we will make it openly—and measure strength with
all gainsayers! Nor is the risk so great as you may well
think, and Sisyphus and his followers will hope; for I

have lost no time to arm some score young fellows on whom I can depend, and who are ready to obey my orders for life or death; for the Lords of Birmingham hold the right of both!'

'It is no time to question of rights too nicely,' said Edward, much pleased at this revelation, 'and whatever the risk, I am willing to incur my share of it.'

'You can speak to our burgesses then, and declare the King's favourable will; and, if need be, perchance to the people. I have no skill in utterances by way of words, and you are scholar-bred, Master Holte,' Tubal replied; and Edward cordially assenting to the arrangement, nothing more seemed necessary by way of preliminary, and the young men resumed the road into the town.

CHAPTER LVIII.

EDWARD HOLTE'S MISSION.

HOWEVER well inclined to run any hazard in seconding
Tubal in his resistance to mob law, Edward Holte was
pleased to find his own eloquence not exclusively depended upon in the task.   On arriving at the barriers
they found a number of young men in readiness, who
obeyed Tubal's word of command, and formed themselves at once into an escort to accompany them to the
Guildhall.

These men were nearly all of the smiths' craft, which
at that time was by far the most powerful and well
organised of the trades of Birmingham.   And Tubal
proudly explained that, as lord of the town, all its inhabitants were bound to do military service to his
banner when called upon.   But the master armourer's
authority as chief of the smiths' guild, or company,
placed it specially at his devotion.

It is very possible, however, that Tubal Bromycham's
power was chiefly derived from the respect he was held
in as the best artificer of the town, and his general
courageous and popular character.

It is certain his now declared pretensions to a noble
descent and rank were very far from injuring him with
any part of the populace, saving the republican fanatics

of the Anabaptist persuasion, who were at the time in a
very low minority in the town. The smiths, indeed,
were extremely proud of having for a leader a young
man reared as an artisan at their forges, and in their
midst, but who also claimed to be legitimate lord of
their town.

This civic force was armed with pikes set in long
wooden shafts, and marched in attendance on its chief
and his friend with some appearance of military order
and discipline, Tubal laughingly explaining to his visitor
that hitherto he had only found occasion to set his men
on using the 'stick end' of their weapons. 'Come the
need,' he added, with peculiar significance, 'and we will
prod the rogues in the back with nine inches of as good
steel as ever made a more honourable hole in a soldier's
breast! But meanwhile, I have a rod in pickle for them
they little dream of.'

With a special purpose, as it appeared, of spreading
the news of the arrival in the town, Tubal directed the
march of this body in the first instance to the market-
place. The Guildhall, which was in New Street, on the
site of the present Free School, could easily have been
reached without passing through the then centre of
Birmingham at all.

Almost as soon as the incomers passed the Butts
Barrier, signs of popular movement and excitement
became evident.

The streets were thronged with an unusual number
of persons, chiefly of the lower order of the populace:
and of these it was to be remarked that by far the most
ill-clad and dangerous-looking carried various weapons,
and not altogether of the rough and rusty sort one
would have expected to find in the hands of the inferior

classes of a town, on occasion of so sudden and ill-
provided an outburst of warlike activity.   There were
to be seen muskets and pike-heads, set on long sticks,
like cattle-goads, which their owners carried with considerable swagger and determination.   Tubal remarked
upon these men to Edward that Captain Cromwell had
given them arms, during the late emergency, against
both his own and the master armourer's advice ; and
that having been posted to defend the entrance of the
town at the Parsonage, they had now the impudence to
pretend orders from him to retain the house for their
own and their leader's use, even before he was elected
to the office he now also pretended to.

'But,' emphatically repeated Tubal, 'we of the leadership of the town prefer the honest man Wrath-of-God
Whitehall.   For though he be a little cracked in his
roofing, still the cracks let in God's wholesome light,
and he speaks but of establishing Bible law to the fullest
among us ; of sweeping the hearth, and making the
house ready for the reception of the Master thereof, by
an universal cleansing and beautifying.   Not a pulling
down and defacing and mixing all things in confusion,
and stripping men of all that distinguishes each from
his fellows.   By the mass! (though that's a popish oath)
I almost think the Anabaptist villain would have us go
naked in the streets; and for aught I know, by-and-by, on
all fours !   And he hath had a filthy pond near the Black
Chapel, that a duck, which would gobble at a swine's
entrails, would not swatter in, consecrated—as he calls
it—with some devilish ceremonies, and invites who will
to come and wallow in it, and profess themselves thereby
his fautors and allies.   And there are not wanting a
strange many more than ever before to take the sum-

mons, because he goes about declaring that he is appointed to the godly work of bringing us all to a level, and rescuing all things to the common, as they were, he says, in Adam's time. Which truly might be when there was but one man and one woman on the earth, but must not and shall not be in Tubal Bromycham's; as the boldest and most headlong of the muddy rogues shall right speedily learn! For, howbeit, at present, there are not so many of them as to need any mighty suppressing, there is no knowing how they may gain ground, with such doctrines openly set forth and maintained.'

Besides the information thus received, Edward thought he could readily distinguish the members of this suspected and violent sect by their gloomy, fanatic visages, and challenging, scowling movements among the rest of the population. And few as they were in numbers, it seemed likely enough that the leaven of their pernicious principles might now become infused into larger masses, by the zeal and audacity of such a leader as the maimed but popular-tongued bellows-blower had of late exhibited himself.

So far, it was not easy to determine by what feeling the people hurrying along the streets were actuated; perhaps chiefly by curiosity, and some vague prospect of amusement, in sharing the commotion of an election by general suffrage.

The Presbyterian scheme of government in church affairs, which was then in the ascendency in the Long Parliament, would have made a regular doctrinal examination and acceptance unto the clerical office necessary, in conjunction with the choice of a congregation. But Cromwell, who had passed into the more advanced stage of religious revolt and enfranchisement styled

Independency, was glad of a pretext afforded by an old custom in Birmingham to declare that the place of the expelled High Church rector of the town should thus be filled. The custom related only to the minor incumbency of Deritend, but he widened its application to the whole town; and not, as we have seen, without some views of creating divisions and emulations in the place, which might increase the necessity and chances of his own arbitration.

But he had certainly not gone so far, in his wildest calculations, as to suppose that the Anabaptist bellows-blower—whom he himself looked upon as the refuse and scum of humanity—would dare to aspire to the vacant spiritual office and dignity.

On his part, Tubal Bromycham, with a natural instinct, supported the assertion of all popular rights, wherever they did not clash with what he conceived to be his own, as feudal chief of Birmingham. And he had, therefore, readily adopted the plan proposed, until he found what a dangerous candidature arose. Opposition then became necessary, and his energetic genius suggested it to him in the openest and most determined courses.

In the case of Deritend Chapel-of-ease the customary forms of a lay election were in use, in the exercise of this extraordinary, if not unique, privilege of the people of Birmingham to elect their spiritual guide.

The candidates were presented by a proposer and seconder to the people, and were then appointed to preach, upon successive Sundays, to all who chose to be auditors. After this preliminary, a day was named for the election. Friends and supporters eagerly canvassed for votes; opposition colours were displayed; harangues, squibs, and angry lampoons distributed; the taverns were thronged with bawling, contentious partisans; scuffles and altercations took place in all directions. Finally, the votes were taken in the usual way, first by a show of hands, and if a scrutiny was demanded, by a regular poll, sometimes lasting for days, even in Deritend, where only householders had the right to vote.

Tubal had thrown himself in the outset of this more general election into direct antagonism with Sisyphus and his supporters. He refused, and with the general concurrence of the upper classes of the town, to allow the church to be, as he considered it, profaned by the heathenish and unchristian doctrines avowed by the bellows-blower.

Sisyphus was duly proposed and seconded as a candidate before the townspeople, in front of the Church of St. Martin, with Whitehall; but he was refused the right he pretended to of holding forth in the building in his turn. And thus the express resolve of the Anabaptist and his partisans to enforce his claims to occupy the town pulpit and declare his principles, as a preliminary to the election, seemed likely to bring about a collision of the parties. For Tubal, continuing his explanations of the scene they were coming upon, informed Edward Holte that having locked up the church, and placed it under guard to prevent the intrusion, he was in hourly expectation of some violent attempt to take possession of it.

This was the stage of progress in the affair when Edward Holte found himself once more on the chief scene of action at the Bull Ring.

This considerable space was now nearly filled by a

confused multitude, evidently gathered together in ex
pectation of something remarkable coming to pass.
Windows and doorways were also occupied by the
owners of the surrounding dwellings, happy to enjoy
the spectacle without being forced to partake of the
bustle and buffetings. Women were there in unusual
numbers, as if they had some peculiar interest in what
was happening, though of a divided sort.

Clarges, the drunken blacksmith's wife, who was
amidst the crowd, standing with her arms a-kimbo, and
rolling her large, bright, impudent eyes in search of
some as yet unseen object, anxiously enquired of a neighbour, ' Is it true the bellows-blower will prove out of the
Scriptures we have all a right to be rid of our bad hus-
bands and wives, and betake us to others we like better?'
While Mistress Mellons, standing in a jolly blaze of her
autumnal charms at the door of her hostelry, with her
hands set on her hip bones, sneered to a gossip of her
own, ' Hear ye how the crippled beggar pretends to the
pick and choice among us all, in the Lord's name, with
never a plack to his purse, and scarce a hanging of rags
to his tanned hide!'

' He shall find he has reckoned without his hostess—
not meaning you, my fine madam—an' he do!' said a
gaunt third woman, who happened to overhear the
observation, in bitterly malign and railing accents. But
she was too well known as the jealous and half-savage
wife of Sisyphus the Anabaptist, to make it desirable to
enter into a wrangle with her on the subject.

Edward was further well satisfied to perceive that the
narrow churchyard before St. Martin's, raised almost to
a level on the inside with its walls by many centuries of
graves, was occupied by another division of Tubal's

smiths. Their leather aprons, bare arms, hammers, and
robust figures testified this, and seemed to promise very
indifferent success to an attack, unless of the most overwhelming numbers.

But in truth, when Edward looked around at the
thronging and haggard masses of the populace here
assembled, and remembered what likely materials want
and discontent offered to the reported inflammable
oratory of the Anabaptist, he scarcely, in his own
mind, applauded Tubal's energetic plan, especially when
he found that at all events Sisyphus intended to present
himself at the church for the purpose of formally demanding admission, at noon on that day, provided he
received encouragement in a certain 'seeking of the
Lord,' in which he and his most determined supporters
were at the time engaged at the Black Chapel in Bordesley.

In expectation thus of wonders at hand, the arrival of
Edward Holte and his accompaniers did not excite so
much notice as it otherwise well might.

Very few of the townspeople, it is true, recognised
the recent prisoner, who was little known in Birmingham during his college days, and had been kept out of
sight all the time of his captivity in Firebrace's house,
whence he had escaped in disguise. Everyone, indeed,
knew Tubal Bromycham, but, excepting in his relation
as the opposite leader to the expected assailant, his
advent could scarcely be looked upon as the signal for
any particular event, and it was events the people were
looking for.

But Tubal proceeded to work out his plans of bringing to the most direct and clashing issue, as it would
seem, the contest for the mastery in the town.

'Come, Master Holte,' he said, 'well bethought on.
We will begin by letting the townspeople know our intentions, and his Majesty's goodness fully, before we set
the grey-beards of the Council wagging over the news.
Let us get up on the churchyard side, and I will introduce you to these scarecrow lookers-on, and you shall
tell them all you have told me.   They are of the lower
sort of our commonalty; but such, I have always so far
seen, incline better to hear themselves spoken to by
scholarly gentlemen of your degree than ill-phrased
rascals of their own, like this Sisyphus.'

Edward, who was bred in sufficiently aristocratic
notions of the superiority bestowed by birth and position, made no hesitation to comply with his ally's
request.

Together, accordingly, they entered the inclosure before St. Martin's, which was strictly guarded against
general intrusion, and Tubal's voice of thunder speedily
demanded and obtained the universal attention of the
multitude.

He made no roundabouts of explanation.   'Hark ye,
my masters!' he exclaimed; 'lend your long ears
awhile to this worthy gentleman, Master Holte, of Aston
Hall, who newly comes to you from the King, with very
gracious proposals towards a peace with us, which,
methinks, as the Parliament has left us so unhandsomely to our own resources, we shall do well to lend
attention to.'

There was some considerable stir and movement
among the crowd at this intimation, and several of the
gloomy-visaged men alluded to as forming a portion of
it, without mingling, glided out of the assembly.

Edward Holte meanwhile—willing as much as in him

lay to support his ally's object—baring his handsome
head, addressed the assemblage in a very different style.
With a graceful air of deference, a sweetness and har-
mony of tones, a scholarly and elegant flow of language
that became the friend and fellow-student of the accomplished Falkland, he addressed the good townsfolk
of Birmingham, as he styled them, and declared the
occasion of his visit in the town.

An English mob, even of the most determined de-
mocracy of modern ideas, has a natural leaning to the
aristocratic. We are chiefly democrats because we want
to be aristocrats. Neither was it, as yet, the age of
democratic opinion, among the masses of the people,
so much in earthly as in heavenly things. Cromwell's
sudden impulse had but stirred the face of the waters—
not their depths—in Birmingham, as afterwards in the
entire nation. For the most part the assemblage
seemed to hear the announcement made with considerable satisfaction, though not without surprise ; and when
Edward had concluded his brief but exceeding appropriate and happily-phrased address, they said everywhere, ' It is Master Holte, of Aston Hall ; he says the
King wants to make peace with us. Let us make peace
with the King, provided he leaves us our rights and
liberties ! '

Edward, catching these latter murmurs, earnestly assured his hearers there was nothing his Majesty had not
promised to perform to give them every imaginable
comfort and security ; whereupon Tubal observed, ' Particularly the removal of the cavaliers from Aston,' which
was re-echoed in a great variety of accents, and seemed
to be accepted as a principle condition of the arrangement.

But Tubal was evidently desirous of some more direct
confirmation, for he now called out in his stentorian tones,
'Shout then, mates, for Peace, the King, and Master
Holte!' and the throng taking up the words, with the
rapid vibrations of popular impulse, sent them in a
rising and swelling wave of sound to its farthest skirts,
where it rippled over in the voices of the more timid
among the women and children, who had not ventured
deeply in.

At a moment so unfavourable to his purposes Sisyphus the bellows-blower entered upon the scene.

The Anabaptist presented himself in a somewhat
singular fashion.

He was scarcely garbed beyond the merest require-
ments of decency, and from his grizzly iron-grey locks
to his naked, ill-shaped feet, he streamed with water
and weeds, as if he had just been bathing in some
muddy stream. Of course his maimed figure presented
itself at its worst, and his virago spouse herself exclaimed, 'It must have been his witchcraft tongue!
his witchcraft tongue!' To complete this strange
apparition he carried a bucket of some black water,
equally weedy and foul, by his hook hand.

Sisyphus was accompanied by a considerable number
of the members of his haggard congregation, who, in
sign doubtless of brotherhood, walked arm-in-arm. The
eyes of these men were chiefly cast down, and nearly all
looked very pale ; but their brows were knit with sullen
determination, and their tramp was solid and one as that
of a herd of elephants. Their countenances were of the
most vulgar and animal type chiefly, and contrasted in
that respect with their leader's, whose fiercely fervid
aspect testified to the possession of mental power in

unison with his powerful and exasperate passions. But for these very reasons, perhaps, the general effect of the advance was the more sinister and menacing: a blind material force, under the control and direction of an evil spiritual agency, seemed there.

So at least it struck Edward Holte, observing the approach.

But what rendered the spectacle still more singular and questionable was that the five men abreast, immediately behind Sisyphus, all carried lighted torches, which smoked and flamed red and murky in the white dayshine all around.

The Anabaptist's favourite guard and henchman, Faithful Moggs, was in close attendance upon him as usual, his vividly-coloured hair looking as if it had recently been dipped in blood, and wielding his wonted weapon, a butcher's pole-axe. The gaping mouth and staring eyes of this bull-witted fellow did, nevertheless, not prevent the spectator from discerning an expression of fanatic trust and challenge in the zeal with which he kept his apostle's pace that promised no faint or half-hearted adherence to whatever obedience he might enjoin.

On the general assemblage the effect of this extraordinary arrival was doubtful and mixed.

At first there was a universal murmur of wonder and enquiry, followed by an explosion of derisive merriment. Then again, as the group came nearer to be scanned, curiosity evidently mingled largely in the popular feeling. So potent is the eye with the mind of man! The meaning of the show thereupon grew to be most eagerly canvassed before it came to a halt, which it did very soon after, on the place of the Bull

Ring. This gave an elevated stand for the Anabaptist, facing the churchyard, and his people then formed around him there, breaking into a harsh and untuned, but solemn psalm-singing, like the clamour of the waves on a sea-beach.

Edward Holte himself felt strangely impressed, while the populace became, as it were, hushed and awed to an expectant observation, insomuch that when the Anabaptist, having reached his elevation and set down his pail, suddenly turned round to them and exclaimed, ' I come from bathing in Jordan ; but not to preach peace, but the sword of the Lord and of Gideon ! Who talks of peace ? ' There was a moment of universal shrinking and silence, as if those who had so shouted found themselves rebuked and guilty of offence by one who had the power and the right to punish.

Tubal, however, broke the spell by answering from his neighbouring elevation, ' I did, and Master Holte, and all the good people of the town talked of peace, and do talk, bellows-blower ! And what have you got to say to the contrary ? Though, as for bathing in Jordan, you look more as if you had been dragged through a horse-pond, as would much better tally with your deserts.'

There was a general laugh at this retort, and a stir among the crowd, as if people were shaking off some oppression and drowsiness in the air. Tongues were unloosed, and ' What does the fellow mean by coming such a naked muck-heap before us ? ' freely enquired.

Until now it did not appear that Sisyphus, on his part, had taken any notice of the group in the churchyard.

He was perhaps too earnestly engaged in arranging his ideas for the oratorical occasion before him. But at the name of Holte he started; his eyes glared up with a truly savage and wild-beast expression; and Edward, encountering his glance, was struck with surprise at the blood-thirsty hate and fury in the flash of recognition. Of course he was entirely unsuspicious of the bellows-blower's secret motives for jealous indignation against the preferred lover of Dorothy Firebrace.

Nevertheless, Sisyphus possessed one of the prime qualities of the leader of an ambitious minority—command of temper, and patience not to dash himself against too powerful obstacles. He had been at a stern school for that, as appeared from the deep-wealed traces of the German provost-marshal's lash round his back and chest.

'Oh, is it but you, Master Tubal, my newly self-dubbed lord, and so another usurper in the true Lord's inheritance, who longeth for the occasion to beat and slay His messengers?' he replied, calmly enough. 'Yet I scarce expected, I must say, to hear you are turned traitor even to your own treason, to cry Peace where there is no peace, and never can be till Antichrist be wholly subdued. And who is Antichrist?'

We are not about to inflict on our readers a fanatic sermon of the seventeenth century, though it is necessary to declare with what intents and issues this most remarkable one of the Anabaptist of Birmingham, Sisyphus the bellows-blower, now teemed.

This man was, indeed, in most important respects, a Mormon blasphemer, two hundred years before the accursed sect of Joseph Smith planted itself upon the face of the earth—and flourishes apparently upon it in a whole province and city, like Sodom and Gomorrah before the rain of fire.

And now Antichrist, according to the levelling bellows-blower, was embodied in all the powers and dominations of the earth as then constituted—kings, lords, prelates, magistrates, and rulers of every sort and degree: who must be utterly overthrown, abolished, and driven forth of the land, so as to remove every species of rivalry and contention from before them, ere the dominion of Christ could be manifested and openly declared in His actual presence to mankind.

It is true, Sisyphus took not upon him to declare a new revelation. He had not the infernal audacity of the later false prophet; or else probably the beliefs of his time seemed to him sufficient for his purpose. But with almost equal presumption and lack of authority, he announced the fulfilment of all the old oracles of the will of God, and that the time of the promised inherit-ance of the Lamb of the Earth had come, and had been communicated to himself in a stupendous vision.

He averred that on that very morning, when he was engaged in wrestling with the Lord in prayer for the sake of the people of Birmingham, and enquiring what ought to be done for their redemption and security, in the continued absence of Captain Cromwell and the dangers that pressed upon them from Aston, he had sud-denly found himself lifted from the midst of his congre-gation in the Black Chapel and carried through the air thousands and thousands of leagues in the flash of a moment; that to his great terror and apprehension of total destruction, being no swimmer, he had found himself cast into a deep running water, bordered on either side with palm trees and rocks blazing white with heat, and knew that he was in the River Jordan, hurling along with the flow of the current to the fathomless gulfing of the

Dead Sea; that while thus proceeding, shrieking with terror and stretching his arms in all directions for help, he was suddenly caught in the garment by a Shining Man, who descended from the skies in a 'flame of sunbeams,' and stopped at last and brought to shore, though his clothes were nearly all torn off his back in the efforts necessary to effect his salvation.

According, then, to this profane wretch—for it did not at any time appear that Sisyphus was really mad—the Shining Man, in a long conference, informed him that he was the Christ who was crucified on Mount Calvary for the sins of the world, and who was now a-weary that for so many ages, the immense sacrifice had been made in vain ; and who was therefore coming in person to restore the entire earth to peace and holiness, and give the dominion thereof to the saints and faithful ones. So far, he and the stranger prophet, as he called him, Master Whitehall, were as one.

And the way—as Wrath-of-God, being partially inspired, declared—was to be made straight, the throne of the Lord exalted, His enemies put to the rout, Antichrist cast utterly in the dust. The King of Peace would then doubtless appear in all His glory, to reign a thousand years over the elect, who for that period would flourish without fear, without suffering or toil, or grief or death.

But whereas his rival candidate announced his intention merely to put the laws inscribed in the Mosaic dispensation into full execution, he, Sisyphus the bellows-blower, answered, ' Ere ye build, a clear place from the ruins must be spread before the Lord.'

Kings, nobles, prelates, and magistrates of every kind, being the visible form and outward limbs of Antichrist,

must therefore at once be deprived of their usurping
jurisdiction, and their powers thenceforth be exercised
altogether by the messengers and prophets of God.

Himself, Sisyphus went on to state, was appointed
such in the town of Birmingham, if he could find there
sufficient helpers and witnesses to the Lord to support
him in his efforts 'to make plain the way.' Yea, plain
even as the sandy desert before the heavy clod of the
camel on its way!

In this kingdom at hand there should be no more
poverty, no more sorrow, no more hatred, malice, and
uncharitableness; no striving of men against each other
in the rivalry of love or bitterness of hate; no lying,
cozening, cheating in the market-place; for all things
were to belong to all in common, without distinction or
distribution.

And here it was that the bellows-blower's instinctive
power to sway and direct the fanaticism of his times,
and the blind impulses of all ages among the multitude,
appeared in a most extraordinary manner.

To Birmingham—which had, as it were in a leaping
from slumber, shown the most zealous forwardness in
the work—was adjudged the high honour of making a
still more decisive advance in it. But still it remained
a marvel, Sisyphus modestly declared, how or why it
was that a poor and lowly man of the town, maimed of
his frame and unendowed with any good persuasive
power of any kind—though, he trusted, a resolved and
seasoned soldier of the Lord—was chosen out to declare
the great tidings to the good town, and also to carry out
the pleasure of the Lord, on the preliminary arrangements for His advent.

But with such a mission he declared himself graced,

by the special favour and selection of the Shining Man, in the town of Birmingham.

No wonder it is that, finding themselves in almost all ages oppressed and unhappy, the masses of the nations ever cherish a sense of unjust deprivation, and a longing for change, which compose the sure and exhaustless armoury of the demagogue. But, on the whole, the doctrine enunciated harmonised extremely well with the religious fancies and exaltation in mystical Biblical reveries of the time. To behold the completion of the great work of human redemption with their own eyes— the visible manifestation of the power and glory of God to mortal vision—what a prospect was here to those weary and worn with scanning the obscure assurances of bygone prophecy! Nor can it be denied that to be called upon in the name of peace and all righteousness to help yourself to your neighbour's goods and chattels of every kind could never be a very distasteful doctrine to a needy and toil-worn populace.

Like the modern Socialists and Mormons, the Birmingham prophet took good care not to reveal the corruption of debauchery and materialism which lurked in the depths of all his fine outward religionism and restoration of equality and fraternity among mankind. The suspected secret immorality of his life—the accusations of enemies—the instincts of sagacious minds— alone drew the inferences, which he was artful and skilful enough to veil from the ruder apprehensions of the multitude by a really extraordinarily eloquent and powerful generality of imaginative description, in which he figured the original paradise of man's innocence and delighted enjoyment of existence restored upon this earth.

.

•

CHAPTER LIX.

TUBAL'S GRAND ARGUMENT.

THE results appeared in a significant manner.

Aware of the power of outward symbols upon the popular feeling, the bellows-blower concluded his harangue by demanding if the people were satisfied to forward the cause of the Lord by giving him their votes and interest in the election of a religious ruler for the town? If so, they were to signify their consent to the passing away of all the old order of obstructions and usurpations to the glory of God, in a manner he should point out. Then, taking the largest of the five torches from one of the attendant Anabaptists, he presented it to the crowd, yelling, 'This is the usurpation of Charles Stuart, calling himself the King; are you willing it should be extinguished?' And numerous voices answering 'Yea, yea,' he tossed and flourished it frantically in the air, scattering sparks and drops of fire in every direction, and then plunged it into the pool of dirty water at his feet.

He did the like with a second torch, which he declared to represent a persecuting prelacy; with a third, which he styled an unbelieving, poor-man-trampling magistracy, amidst the triumphant yells and groans of Faithful Moggs; with a fourth, which he denounced as representing all the false college and book-learning and teaching, the law-giving and law-making of Kings and Parliament alike. And then he came to the last of his five blazing symbols, which he seized with an evident increase of exasperation and ill-feeling towards what it it symbolised in his thoughts.

'And this,' he yelled out, 'represents all that is to be hated, dreaded, and extirpated in all the rest—the proud Holtes of Aston Hall, who have brought the cavaliers into the country to harry and destroy us all, and who have already made corn so dear that the poor man can hardly buy him a loaf with a day's wage. I say, let us destroy the whole accursed, tyrannical brood, wherever we can find them, and lay the house of their cruelties and pride as level with the dust as the towers of Babylon of old.'

Strange to say, the very mob who but a few moments before had shouted for 'Peace, the King, and Master Holte,' now noisily clamoured vengeance and destruction on the whole, in their response to this appeal.

Tubal looked greatly vexed and nonplussed.

'We have done wrong to let those rogues fancy they have any right to a say in the town's affairs, the regulation whereof is altogether with the lord and substantial burgesses,' he said. 'But let them yelp their hearts out; if they attempt aught on you, I will make them con rather a hard lesson out of my hornbook. Let us go now to the Guildhall, and determine matters with the men of judgment and estate. Perhaps these barking dogs will go to biting, and I had as lief it came to the argument of blows now as at any other time.'

'They are more likely to attack us where we are,

nevertheless,' said Edward; 'or what is it they are
shouting now?'

A little attention speedily made this point clear.

Sisyphus had dexterously availed himself of the
emotion stirred in the populace.

'Why, yonder, then,' he roared, 'is the heir and
representative of the whole wicked and masterful race
of the Holtes, who has come among us, as it is said, to
seduce us into making a truce with the devil, and peace
with the hinderer of the Holy Ghost! Those who are
in earnest in what you have said, let them then follow
me over his insolent carcass into the church, where you
have promised to place me in the old dumb dog's
place we had erewhile; and whence I will declare to ye,
at a much clearer length, all the will and purposes of
the Lord; and thereby also shall we obtain possession
of the person of the traitress and espial of the enemy,
Dorothy Firebrace, who we all know is refuged in it,
with other enemies of God and the good town.'

'Good heaven! is this true, Tubal?' enquired
Edward, with much more alarm than any apprehensions
for his own safety could have aroused in him.

'It is,' replied Tubal. 'I knew no safer place, while
I was bound to be absent from Deritend and the Moat
House too, on this business; and so I have locked her
safely in the church, with her friends the Coopers, and
Mr. Lane. But she will be alarmed with this hurly-
burly, which she must needs in part overhear, though
not see. Take the keys, dear Master Holte, and go in
and comfort her, while I deal with this clamorous
rabblement.'

'Certes, no, while I can be of some help with my
sword by your side, Master Bromycham,' Edward re-

plied. 'Let us make ready for an onset, for I am sure they purpose it.'

'Let them come then,' said Tubal, with a grim smile, 'and taste the fiery breath of Bromycham's dragon. Ho, William Moorcroft and Philip Smalbroke! bring my cannon-piece out of the church!'

Tubal, as he spoke, handed a bunch of massive keys to one of his burly smiths, who, with a comrade, instantly made for the porch of St. Martin's; and almost as quickly as Edward could utter a remonstrance against opening the doors at all, to everybody's astonishment the doors opened, and a piece of artillery, of unusual size at that time, appeared in the entrance of the church, ready to be wheeled out.

'It is the first gun of the size ever cast in Birmingham, and perchance may be the last, for our trade lies not in such heavy war goods; but out of its mouth will I speak what shall satisfy all gainsayers its maker and wielder is master here, as elsewhere,' said Tubal, with an expression full of the triumphant haughtiness of successful genius. 'Loaded to the muzzle, and all,' he continued, uncovering a tow rope round a portion of the deadly instrument, and tramping with so strenuous a gesture on the sulphured end that it lit instantly into flame.

'Bring my dragon forward, mates,' he then said; 'let these good folks see well what they are about; and if they need a second blasting of his fiery breath, keep them well off the churchyard wall with your hammers and pikes while I reload. We shall see which will be weary first.'

But the portentous appearance instantly produced its usual effect upon an unmilitary multitude.

Even trained soldiers are with difficulty brought to face artillery directly, and no sooner had the excited throng in the Bull Ring, ready enough for a hand-to-hand conflict with the defenders of St. Martin's, espied the ponderous instrument of destruction emerge from its porch, than a salutary awe was stricken into the whole movement, and it was brought to a sudden pause.

In vain did Sisyphus, who, with all his faults, was a courageous soldier, endeavour to revive the ardour of his backers.

' It is but to make a brave onset, and take the culverin from them. It must needs be awkward and badly fashioned by a toy-smith like Tubal Bromycham. Had I but my arm and hand, I would soon let you see my meaning. Fie on ye, cowards! are ye turning tail already, before we know whether it will even go off or no?'

But the alarm had increased into panic in this brief interval, when Tubal, out-thundering every lesser sound, and holding the burning tow aloft with one hand, while with the other he pointed to the hour-hands on St. Martin's clock, shouted, ' Make the best of your next five minutes hence, my good friends, or you shall know to your costs whether Tubal Bromycham has spent all his leisure hours since these wars began for something or for much!'

This assemblage certainly was not disposed to doubt the skill in any species of manufacture in the stubborn metals of the prime artisan of the town. In spite of all Sisyphus's raving exhortations and entreaties, not a single person offered to continue the attack.

Even Faithful Moggs stared aghast at the preparation,

and muttering, ' Nay, master, for a man 'shall have his own head in a ditch a mile off ere he can lend the other's a crack,' would not stir a stump.

In short, ere the five given minutes were elapsed—or, indeed, half of them—the entire Bull Ring had become, in some strange and almost miraculous manner, deserted, and quit of all its noisy and threatening throngs.

Sisyphus himself, perceiving the danger he ran of being singled out as a sole mark for the indignation of his triumphant opposers, was reluctantly compelled at last to follow the general example.

But not completely solitary. His loving helpmate overtook him as he was turning into an obscure street out of the market-place, and ironically congratulated him on the events of the day.

' So you have saved what remains of you, Sissy, my dear,' she exclaimed. ' But you are not going to be King of Birmingham to-night; and the armourer's pretty daughter is safe in St. Martin's Church still.'

' Begone, hag !' exclaimed the infuriate prophet, turning angrily upon her. ' I repudiate and divorce you at once and for ever from my bed and board, and henceforth hold you no more a wife of mine than Lot his wife when she became even as a pillar of salt.'

' Aye, aye, Sissy, dear. But your law is not yet law in Birmingham. And who will help you to your meals and stockings if you cast me off? Will the armourer's beauteous daughter, whose lover has come so bravely on a visit to her now, and who doubtless means to carry her away with him ? '

' Ha, say you so ? I will rend him first piecemeal with this hook,' returned Sisyphus, whitening with rage.

Yet, perceiving the danger of further irritating his vicious consort, he said retractingly, ' But this is one of the maddest of your jealousies, Meg; and you would have acknowledged it so, if I could have made my way into the church. The traitress's head should have rolled upon a block, as comely as you deem it; and you should have shown it yourself as such, an' it had pleased you, to the people. The people! miserable dastards, to ˌfly before the gleaming of a piece of metal in the sun. What would they have done had they been with me at the storming of Heidelberg, whence I so right-fully deserted to the enemy, and led them up the rocks to the assault ? '

CHAPTER LX.

ST. MARTIN'S CHURCH.

MEANWHILE Edward Holte and Tubal exchanged a brief
congratulation on their bloodless victory.

'This is wonderful, but most exactly as it should be,
dear Tubal! The mob taught manners, anarchy effectually quelled, and yet no man hurt in his own person
or his friends to stir up a lasting animosity!' Edward
exclaimed, warmly shaking the hero of the occasion by
the hand.

'I am glad of it, too; I would be as mild a neatherd as the kind of cattle allows, in my rule; and
whatever the scholar's word you use, Master Holte, may
mean, I am satisfied I have shown who is to be master
in Birmingham awhile,' Tubal replied, adding, with a
smile, though with a slight quiver in his tones, 'You
may tell the story in as choice language as it likes you,
at Aston Hall; and let Sir Thomas moreover know that
he owes it to one whom he has little reason to count his
friend, that Aston Hall still stands whole and sound.
For had Captain Cromwell been aware of my possession
of this artillery, he would have taken it into his own
manage, and without doubt have tried what distance it
would carry from the Park to his walls. At least before
yonder Prince fellow and his dragoons arrived.'

s 2

'It is likely enough, and you turn out in all respects
very different from anything as yet apprehended in you,
either by friends or foes, Master Bromycham,' said
Edward. 'Neither, in the long run, do I deem the
commonalty will owe you any grudge for standing between them and the pernicious counsels of the wretch
who wants to establish himself as their leader. But be
certain so determined a fellow as this bellows-blower
will soon puff up a new flame of agitation; perhaps
against the peace we propose. I would have him expelled the town at once.'

'That is not so easy as crushing eggs, it fears me,'
replied Tubal, 'so to speak, for I know not fear in any
real conjunction with the handless rogue. But he has
established himself with a lot of his cut-purse renegades
at the Parsonage House, several of them not ill-armed,
and vows he will set it on fire and make the whole a
desolation rather than surrender the post to any but
the officer of the Parliament who he says gave it to his
holding. We must see about that some other day; but
meanwhile it will be as well to lose no diligence in
proceeding in your matter, Master Holte. Our town
councillors can assemble and give their opinions now
with no dread of a pelting, which some would allege
as a pretence to keep away, and I will send a summons
round among them to the Guildhall without further loss
of time. It is the bailiff's business, but at present I
have none. John Cooper would thankfully take office
under me, but his wife, who is his master, will not have
it so.'

'Meanwhile, then,' said Edward, eagerly, 'I may
devote a few moments to seeing Mistress Firebrace, and
assuring her of my unfailing love and fidelity. Said

you not she is in the church ? Though I did not espy
her there when the gates opened.'

'Have no fear,' said Tubal smiling, 'you will find
Dorothy safe within. Make use then of a short half
hour, which will suffice me to bring the master
armourer and other chief men to the meeting. But I
disguise not that Firebrace himself is possessed with
strange, and assuredly most undeserved, suspicions of
your intentions towards his fair daughter ; and is the
worse content, very likely, that he cannot hint me into
a jealously angry sharing of the same!'

Edward blushed with honest shame at the thought
that he could mean anything but perfect good faith and
honour towards his betrothed wife.

'My actions will always justify your confidence, never
the armourer's suspicions. Yet I blame him not for
his anxious care to fend off the possibility of evil from
his child,' he said. 'Farewell awhile now, Master
Bromycham, or rather Tubal, Lord of Birmingham, in
all reality ! I will strive not to exceed my leave, and
will be with you at the best speed I can make.'

Edward now proceeded into the old church, hearing
Tubal, as he did so, give general instructions to his men
as to the watch and guard of the precincts, and a proper
accompaniment of Master Holte to the intended assemblage of the chief citizens in New Street.

The mother church of Birmingham has little to
boast of in the way of architecture. But in point of
antiquity it rivals the oldest buildings in England, of
which aught but ruins remains.

It is said to have been founded upwards of a thousand years ago ; but the decay of so ancient a fabric
rendering repairs necessary, the vandalism of the

eighteenth century deprived St. Martin's of its great
claim on veneration in most external respects. The
crumbling stone walls were then encased in brickwork ;
the stained glass windows removed ; the flooring,
silently eloquent with records of the dead, repaved ;
and numerous time-defaced but interesting and solemn
memorials of the past, in the shape of monuments
and tablets, were cast, like the sweepings of a statuary's studio, to moulder in the vaults below the
church.

In 1642 St. Martin's still preserved the aspect of its
already great antiquity. The black, worm-eaten oak of
benches, pulpit, and altar-piece was an appropriate furniture to the time-grey walls, and the ghostly tenantry
of the statuary on the tombs, yellow and black with
extreme age.

These monuments were chiefly of the Birmingham
family, ancestors of Tubal, as were the principal parts of
the coats of arms emblazoned in the window panes,
which attested a long course of illustrious alliances and
intermarriages of the race.

The most ancient county names figured among
these: Astley, Someri, Seagrave, Peshall, Marmion,
Wyrley, Freville, Fitzwarren, Montalt, Beauchamp,
Latimer, Ferrers, and Townshend. The most ancient
monument in the church, with a single exception—
being the figure of a knight in complete armour, of the
thirteenth century—was of a Birmingham who had
figured in the wars of Edward I. And the exception was one so much worn and battered in the lapse
of ages as only to present the mutilated trunk of a
warrior in mail armour, lying under a canopy, with
armless hands crossed in devotion on the breast, and a

Latin inscription below, which had become illegible to any but antiquarian eyes.

Little of all this attracted Edward Holte's attention, whose eager glance sought a living lovely object of its own. But to his surprise, and perhaps alarm, he only perceived three persons present, all of whom he knew, and Dorothy Firebrace was not of the number.

These were the ex-Bailiff Cooper and his wife, and Mr. Lane.

The last was sitting on the pulpit stairs, propping his chin on his hands, and looking very pale and tremulous as if in apprehension of some great approaching disaster. And, indeed, his mud-bespattered clerical robe and general appearance denoted that he had already received rather unhandsome usage in his passage through the town on his embassy, doubtless from the Anabaptist mobsmen.

Bailiff Cooper had ' accepted the situation ' in a very different manner. He had taken possession of the clerk's seat beneath the pulpit, where he had fallen asleep, and was snoring lustily : while his consort stared, wakeful as an old but still eager and hungry hawk in its aërie, from the pulpit itself above.

Hearing footsteps in the church, Mr. Lane craned his neck forward with evident anxiety, and no sooner perceived Edward than he quite sprang to meet him.

And yet his first words expressed rather sorrow than welcome at the arrival : ' How grieved I am you have ventured into this trampling and goring watering-place of the bulls of Bashan, my dear Edward ! ' he exclaimed. ' I was only waiting for nightfall to effect my own escape, and implored the young man who has set himself up in the captaincy of the town—and who, I do confess, laid about him like a flailer in my behalf—to warn you not to come among such a lawless multitude.'

'All is well, dear sir, and the rabble dispersed with the mere show of armed suppression. But where is Dorothy; where is Mistress Firebrace, I mean, who I was told was refuged with you here?' said Edward.

The agitation and eagerness of the query evidently communicated a somewhat similar emotion to the weakly-nerved and sympathetic old clergyman. Or else some feeling of his own, quieted awhile by personal apprehensions, revived to trouble him. Mr. Lane trembled all over as he answered, 'Nay, my dear Edward, never ask me! What do you want, what can you want, what ought you to want with the poor girl?'

'What has become of her, Mr. Lane? You alarm me. Where is Dorothy Firebrace, I repeat?' Edward replied, with an increase rather than diminution of his excitement.

'Dorothy Firebrace! He calls her *Dorothy Firebrace* thus familiarly! My fears are confirmed. O Edward, Edward Holte! dearest youth! this, then, is the unhappy girl whom your brother Richard has declared to be the object of your unlawful attachment in Birmingham, and for whose sake you run such hazards in the unruly town!' groaned Mr. Lane. 'But, alas! need I any other information than her own tearful questioning on your welfare, and her strange probings to ascertain how matters stood between you and the lady you have been so long betrothed to at Hagley!'

'What is all this you say? I ask you only where she is?' exclaimed Edward, now almost wild with impatience and apprehension.

'And I answer you—It must not, and it ought not

to concern you, Master Holte! Consider who you are, and that Dorothy Firebrace never can be honourably yours; and pause ere you resolve to pursue the guidance of a cruel passion, which, feigning to love and cherish, can but bring destruction and disgrace and utter misery on its hapless object!' the good clergyman continued remonstrating. 'Consider, also, dear boy! it is no common victim you propose yourself: that Dorothy Firebrace is the daughter of one of the wealthiest townsmen of Birmingham, although he has unhappily allowed himself to be hustled into treason and rebellion by the crowding madness of the times! That, although exercising now a mechanical trade, her family descends from a nobler race than yours, as the most ancient monument in this church—yonder it is, the tomb of Audomar Ferre-Bras, Knight of the most Holy Order of the Temple, an exile by tyranny, but descended from an illustrious ancestry in France—her ancestor, attests! And that, to crown all, poor Dorothy is a girl as bravely-hearted as she is beautiful, who has saved your life, and who—who—who is the daughter of a woman whom I loved in my own youth! Vainly, indeed, since she preferred (and justly) a famous armourer of Birmingham to a poor chaplain and dependent on a proud master! yet for whose memory's sake do I, and shall I ever, live wifeless and childless to my grave!'

In the earnestness of the plea thus made, Mr. Lane actually clasped his hands, and crouched his limbs almost as if kneeling to Edward Holte.

The latter was moved by what he heard, but still more irritated.

'Good heavens, Mr. Lane!' he exclaimed, 'what has put it into your head that I design any harm to the

maiden? Have I as foul a reputation with regard to
women as the lying traitor who spreads his falsehoods
everywhere concerning his brother and a young girl, who
is as pure as snow newly fallen, and towards whom I
declare to you, by all that is holy, I mean nothing but
honour and—and—*gratitude*—if you will call it so!'

'In that case, Master Holte,' Dame Cooper now observed, with becoming solemnity, from her exalted seat,
'I take upon me to inform you, Mistress Dorothy has
gone up the belfry stairs, to spy from an opening there
is in the steeple how things are going on at the Bull
Ring. The moment she heard you were expected in
the town, and distinguished the noise and swaying of
the people outside awhile ago, she was no longer to be
restrained, though she had on one of her bettermore
kirtles, and it is as dusty and narrow as a chimney to
the roof.'

But ere this explanation was half concluded, Edward
was searching round for the means of access to the upper
regions alluded to; and spying a narrow door open in
the wall, he darted towards it, and found indeed a wind-
ing flight of stairs, almost as close and steep as a cork-
screw, comparatively speaking, but which he did not a
moment hesitate to ascend.

CHAPTER LXI.

THE CLANDESTINE MARRIAGE.

THE spiral passage terminated in a chamber in which
hung a peal of twelve bells, celebrated in the town for
their melodious cadences. And here Edward expected to
find his Dorothy. But her non-appearance, and an open
window in the front, satisfied him that in her eagerness
to obtain a view of the proceedings in the market-place,
she had ventured out on the shelving roof of the church.
Now as this was only protected at the time by a low
gutter without parapet at the edges, the notion greatly
alarmed him. And not without reason; for on looking
out he perceived Dorothy lying on the sloping tiles,
clutching fearfully at them, and seemingly afraid to
make any movement to extricate herself from her
dangerous and uncomfortable position! She had overlooked every personal consideration in her eagerness to
observe what fortuned to her lover, in the angrily excited scene below; but found it by no means so easy to
retrace her way, when the impulse of a more powerful
actuating motive than even self-preservation ceased to
exercise its influence on her mind.

Edward was exceedingly alarmed lest his sudden approach should startle her and produce some catastrophe.
And yet he perceived that assistance was required without

delay. He therefore said not a word, but jumped from the window, and placing himself astraddle on the arch of the roof, clutched his too rashly devoted betrothed in a strenuous grasp, almost before she was aware of any-one's approach.

'Fear not now, dearest! Draw yourself up; Edward Holte's strong hand is upon you.'

And Dorothy indeed feared no longer then. In a few moments she was safely beside her lover on the coping of the roof. In a few more moments safely supported by him into the belfry; and then, falling into his embrace, she swooned away.

'I saw you enter the church, dearest,' she mur-mured first, 'and only then felt on what a giddy shelv-ing I had placed myself, when I strove to return to welcome you. Alas, thus!'

Edward essayed the few remedies in his power, know-ing that it would be in vain to summon aid in their present elevation.

He had luckily a hunting-flask of wine in his pocket, and applying this to Dorothy's pale lips, and chafing her temples and hands, he had soon the satisfaction of seeing her revive. But, doubtless, had this nervous crisis overtaken her in her recent perilous position, great risk of a fatal catastrophe would have been in-curred.

We need not chronicle the first five minutes of the lovers' ecstasy, thus restored to each other. In fact, there would be little to be recorded save sighs, and tears, and kisses—numberless passionate pressings to each other's hearts—wild repetitions of each other's names, coupled with every imaginable endearing epithet; and then the whole fond delirium over again.

Dorothy was the first who recovered some degree of self-possession.

'It is enough, dearest,' she said. 'We cannot doubt each other's love; but, oh, if there were any witnesses, would not this meeting too much support the falsehoods of my enemies? Nay, what is harder still to be borne, the sad surmises of my poor father, in whose every word and look, since the night of our parting, I read suspicions that trouble my inmost soul. But what have you done for us at Nottingham with the King? Have we secured a royal patron there, at all events, to our persecuted love, at the cost of almost every other friendliness?'

Edward was a good deal embarrassed with this question. But it was necessary to confess and explain his failure, as it might well be considered, to the expectant maiden.

He did so as briefly as he could, and endeavouring to put the most favourable gloss on the King's demeanour towards himself on the occasion compatible with the inevitable truth.

Dorothy listened with an expression of intense disappointment.

'An unkingly King,' she murmured, 'that measures out his gratitude as a pedlar his tapes, by the ell-wand for a penny! Those who serve such princes do so of their own loyalty alone. And the traitor Grimsorwe to have so completely circumvented you! But who could be prepared for the glide and subtlety of the serpent in man's outward upright form? I blame you not, my Edward; it was a deceit past calculation. But the hopes you hold out in Charles's gratitude appear to me

little more than the fleeting promise of a rainbow on
the skirts of a tempest coming up fast on the wind.'

'You are indeed in great danger, dearest, in this town,
from much besides your father's silent disapproval,'
said Edward, mournfully. 'A portion of the mob
demand your fair head as that of an enemy to their
rebellious will and purposes. The Parliament's representative here, now Captain Cromwell is gone, requires
that you should be sent a prisoner before prejudiced and
merciless judges in London. Tubal Bromycham, who
has so courageously protected you hitherto, may not
always be on the alert, or have the means in readiness.
Who can tell what may be the progress of the war, or
which party may rise to complete ascendency in the
town? For all these reasons, dearest Dorothy, I implore you do not hesitate to comply with the earnest
entreaty I make you, and leave Birmingham at once for
some place of safety and quiet, where my love may constantly watch over your comfort and security.'

A blush, like a flame of fire, burst on Dorothy's
cheeks as she listened to these words, and seemed to
redden up even in her brilliantly excited eyes.

'What mean you by this proposal, Master Holte?'
she exclaimed, with sudden passionate vivacity; 'that I
should do all that in me lies to establish for truth your
dastardly brother's perjuries, and bring my father's grey
hairs with sorrow to the grave? Nay, to myself become
the thing I most abhor, a shamed and shameful daughter
of a name which, let me tell you, is emblazoned noble
on tombs more ancient than any Holtes in Aston or
Erdington. No; rather may the wild beast Sisyphus
rend me with his single talon, and fling me in shreds to
the cannibals of his faction to devour; or the Londoners

make a holiday to see my head roll on a scaffold on Tower Hill!'

Edward gazed with admiring despair at the beautiful, excited speaker, as she thus uttered a resolve so noble and true to her pure, and generous, and heroic nature, but which so evidently increased the dangers of the position.

He could perceive but one means of extrication, to which the passion which had taken possession of all the strongest energies of his being, also irresistably impelled.

'Not so, not so, my own Dorothy, my dearest all! Whatever ruin may come of it; whatever engine to my destruction it may put in the devilish Grimsorwe's grasp with my father; I ask you only to leave your father's house, and this raving town, as the known and declared *wife* of Edward Holte.'

Dorothy's indignant expression vanished on the utterance of the beautiful and sacred word which alone consecrates and exalts the destiny of woman on the earth. More; it changed entirely into one of the most adoring and ecstatic tenderness; and snatching Edward's hand in both hers to her bosom, tears burst in showers of diamonds on her lovely cheeks.

'Dearest, faithfullest, most generous of men and lovers,' she exclaimed, 'forgive the doubt, the selfishness, the fears, my demands must seem to imply. But if I lose thee, dear, most dear Edward, I lose the whole happiness of my existence; and what is existence without happiness? To eat, to drink, to sleep—who cares to live for these alone? And yonder kind and worthy, though too faintly-hearted chaplain of Aston Hall, who recognised me with tears as the child of a woman whom

he had himself loved in long by-gone years, warned me
of your betrothal to another—of your father's inflexible
will—and of how immediately he had determined on
the completion of the contract between you and the
Lady Penelope Lyttelton.'

'So he denounces, dearest; but I have always told
you it is hopeless to think to obtain my father's consent to our union.   In all probability he will be irritated
even to the extent of totally disinheriting me.   So he
has threatened me, if I dared dream of disobedience to
his will in this respect.   Grimsorwe, whose plots you
have yourself discovered are all laid to supersede me,
will be at hand to feed the flame.   But what matters
all this?   I shall have my sword still, and the woman
I adore, and so guerdoned will accept, smilingly, whatever the envy and malice of fate can do in all other
forms to mischief me!'

Dorothy looked yearningly in her lover's noble and
manly visage, instinct with the brightness of fidelity
and love and honour towards herself and her whole sex,
as it were, in the chivalrous candour of his devotion
to one.   And her tears fell faster yet as she resumed
utterance, in reply to that outburst of generous assurance.

'Dear life!' she sobbed, 'but can we not find some
means to baffle the hatred and malice of our enemies—
the cruel prejudices of these who yet love us well—
without giving ourselves up for immolation, bound
hand and foot?   A *private marriage*, my own Edward!
—a private marriage between us meets every objection
—removes every cause for dissatisfaction and fear—in
all respects save my poor father's headstrong wish to
have me wedded to Tubal, and so removed out of the

peril he so much and so causelessly dreads for his
child!'

'A private marriage! And you will accompany me
then to Sutton, where for awhile I am banished from
Aston to reside?' exclaimed Edward, with the eager
assent and hopefulness of youthful passion to such a
proposition.

Dorothy's splendid blush again reappeared, but of a
softer carnation, glowing all over her beauteous frame.

'But how were it then, dear Edward,' she said, gently
withdrawing from his clasping arms, 'with your wife's
fair fame in men's eyes, and my father's dreads? No
future declaration could ever clear my renown from
the blurts that would come upon it, or—if God should
so bless us—secure our children's true birth and legi-
timacy from cavil and sneer! My noblest Edward, no!
I would have you put all my doubts and fears to rest
by marrying me. But I would remain in my father's
house, unblamed by him and others, until—until circumstances might enable—might compel us—to divulge
our union. And meanwhile, dear husband of my soul
and heart, do not fear but that—but that—we shall
find place and occasion to meet and—and assure each
other of our everlasting love and constancy.'

There was a dove-like, billing intimation of tenderness and bliss in these latter words, which would have
overborne far stronger scruples of worldly interest and
prudence than ever found an abiding in the breast of
Edward Holte. But in truth, the scheme bore a great
appearance of reconciling the whole contradiction of
feelings and motives, that might have influenced
soberer calculators than two young lovers in such a
crisis of their passion's fate.

If Edward could not make himself altogether blind
to objections, he certainly uttered none.

'All shall be as you have said, my sweetest!' he
exclaimed, once more folding his bride-elect in his fond
embrace. ' Come the worst, then, you can flee to a
husband's protection at any time at Sutton Manor-House.
He will not shut the door upon you, depend, who would
open his very heart to receive you, if need were. Thus
shall we elude our fathers' suspicious and injustice, baffle
the bastard traitor's intrigues and malice of suggestion
in all shapes, and obtain time to improve what favour
our duties may have acquired with the King, by some
braver service of my sword in his cause. Nothing is
necessary but an inviolate secrecy, which I know your
love for me will well preserve. I have sworn to marry
you, and an oath in heaven should be kept as speedily
as possible on earth. Grimsorwe's calumnies will thus
but have worked to his own harming, and my perfect
happiness, whom he would so fain have consigned to
misery and ruin. Here is my hand in solemn plight,
Dorothy Firebrace. Accept it, and it is for ever
yours!'

'I do, dear love, I do! Take all I am in return, and
at the same time my promise to God of inviolable
secrecy until you yourself shall resolve and will to
blazon our marriage to the world,' said Dorothy, profoundly affected at the generous devotion of her young
lover. 'Neither to father, or family, or to friends—for
love, or fear, or foolish vanity—will I ever forget that
your ruin or prosperity hang on the faithful observance
of my word. No extremity of whatsoever kind shall
ever subdue me to the breach, though all the world
were clamorous round me to divulge, and every form

of grief and suffering circled me in with the true secrecy.'

'It needs no such oathing, my beloved girl! What more is needed now? Only a clergyman to receive our vows. We are in an inclosure dedicated to such hallowed purposes,' said Edward Holte.

'There is a clergyman provided also below, or was erewhile. The Reverend Mr. Lane will bestow the Church's benediction on us, Edward, if he is still under this roof.'

'The Reverend Mr. Lane, my Dorothy! You are ignorant, then, how timorous he is by nature; in what awe he stands of my father's displeasure,' sighed the purposed bridegroom, as if resigning any hope in the direction indicated.

'I am not ignorant of aught of this, dearest,' Dorothy replied. 'But I know also—for his emotion was too sincere and overpowering on recognising me, not to reveal the fact—that this good clergyman loved my mother in his youth. Mr. Lane, believe me, has all the kindness and pitifulness of a woman, with the weak fears of one. Leave it to me: I will prevail upon him, doubt not, to utter the words which will for ever rescue the child of the woman he loved from the fate he dreads for her. The witness we should need is also provided in the person of Dame Alice Cooper, who is a woman whose secrecy may be depended upon, if any woman's may. She most certainly dislikes Tubal Bromycham for displacing her husband, and will think you out-rival him by marrying me. And, besides, she is about to retire in disgust from Birmingham to her native town of Stratford-on-Avon.

'Be it so,' said Edward Holte. 'Let us descend into

T 2

the church ; we will not care for the snorer in the clerk's pulpit.'

We need not detail at length the consternation of Mr. Lane on the first divulging of the projected union to him—his first refusals to have anything to do in the matter—his affrighted representations of Sir Thomas Holte's certain wrath and chastisement of so great an act of disobedience on the part of his son, and abetting in the revolt on his own. Dorothy had calculated, with a true womanly instinct, on her means of overcoming this repugnance of fear, when emotions of such strength could be looked to, to influence on the contrary side. Above all, when she could appeal to the memory of that 'fond, foolish' past, if the reader will so consider it, which attached Mr. Lane, by a shadowy and mournful, but very loving species of paternity to herself; a memory suddenly revived, as it were, from the grave, in her strong and now matured resemblance to her departed mother, the gentle clergyman's love of youth.

Edward added his entreaties to his friend; his assurances that only more risk of discovery would be incurred by their being obliged to have recourse to another clergyman, as he was resolved nothing should hinder him from fulfilling his agreement with his betrothed.

Dame Cooper, who had been taken into the confidence, and who highly relished the whole romantic plan, which she declared (rather ominously) resembled to a nicety the stolen marriage of Romeo and Juliet, in her 'dear Willie Shakespeare's play,' joined her exhortations to Mr. Lane to fulfill his duty as a clergyman in making lawful the loves of two young creatures.

whom Nature herself had so evidently marked out as a pair.

The poor man yielded at last, though with infinite fear and trembling, vanquished by Dorothy's tears rather than any argument; but not until he had made all the parties to the act join in a solemn oath, upon the Bible, never to reveal the secret to any other human being but by one another's consent and allowance.

Mr. Lane hoped in this way to secure himself time for effecting a retreat from Sir Thomas Holte's resentment, should the discovery of his son's prodigious act of disobedience take place. He then finally consented to officiate in the rite, in his clerical capacity; and in a very, very brief period the words were said that cannot be unsaid, the vows were exchanged which only death could release, the whole solemn consecration of one man to one woman in marriage was gone through between the armourer's daughter and the heir of Aston Hall!

Dame Cooper's friendly zeal supplied the wedding ring from her own finger; and, if this alone were not unlucky enough, it was certainly no happy omen that, being too large, it dropped from the bride's finger as she knelt beside her newly-made husband to receive the final benediction. And the chink of the falling symbol on the stones, slight as it was, after the day's turmoil which he had overslept, like the last straw which breaks the camel's back, woke up ex-Bailiff Cooper in his snuggery. But before he could rub his eyes awake, and stare out astonishment, the rite was concluded; and the worthy could ever after acquiesce with a good conscience in his wife's assurances that he had not seen what he saw, but had awakened from a debauch of perry and ale, in which he had indulged to drown care, to *fancy* he beheld Mistress Firebrace and Edward Holte kneeling as bride and bridegroom, with clasped hands, before a white-haired, quivering priest at the altar's rails !

No argument, however, could ever persuade John Cooper that he did not perceive Edward Holte bestow a kiss on the fair forehead of Dorothy Firebrace as they arose. But he was left immediately after to his own conjectures, the whole group receding into the vestry of the church, where there was an ink-standish for the general purposes of the building; and where Mr. Lane, with a great increase of trepidation, so that he could hardly write, delivered to Dorothy a full attestation of her marriage, which was duly signed by all concerned.

Of course it was not ventured to make any formal entry in the parish books, though the keys of the chest which contained them hung up over the dispossessed rector's surplice plainly enough. But it furnished a remarkable piece of future evidence, that having no other paper on which to write, a strip of parchment was torn by Edward for the purpose from a very ancient and, of course, disused mass-book of the Catholic times, which Dr. Dugdale had, nevertheless, taken considerable pains to refurbish and cleanse from its dust of centuries, and had left conspicuously visible on a side table of the office.

Scarcely was this momentous business thus far concluded, when William Moorcroft, Tubal's most trusted subordinate, made his entrance into the vestry, with the announcement that Master Holte was waited for at the Guildhall.

Moorcroft was not a man of very rapid or acute observation, and probably he explained the scene before him to himself on some notion that the fugitives had taken refuge as remotely out of danger of observation as possible, and had there been found by their visitor. At all events he showed no signs of being struck by anything unusual in what he witnessed, and made no remark whatever in relation to it.

Edward, however, thought it best to comply at once with the summons; and only whispering some few words to Dorothy, which brightened her face with ‘ celestial rosy red, love's proper hue,’ he declared he would return as speedily as possible to *escort Mr. Lane out of the church and town*, and withdrew with his guide.

CHAPTER LXII.

OPPOSITES ALIKE.

THE Guildhall of Birmingham was a structure of very different appearance and proportions from the stately imitation of classical architecture dedicated to the uses of a town-house in the modern Athens of Industry. It was a very ancient Gothic building, chiefly of woodwork, with two projecting wings, and a central chamber of considerable extent under a low lantern-tower, where the rulers of the town—'the burgesses and worthy men thereof'—met to decide on most matters of internal government. In what specially concerned the lord and his claims and dues, an annual court was held at the Moat House, now occupied in that capacity by Tubal Bromycham.

To this ancient Guildhall Edward directed his steps, under escort, though the latter precaution seemed scarcely any longer necessary. Sisyphus and his adherents had in a manner drained themselves out of the streets, and were believed to have retired to hold one of their private conclaves in Bordesley. The rest of the population, either overawed by the recent display of determination and means of carrying out repression, or favourable to a return of peace and quiet, offered no

species of obstruction or insult to the progress of the
messenger of peace.

In the inclosure before the Guildhall, however, Edward was suddenly overtaken and detained by Tubal,
who came from the direction of Digbeth. He reached
at the cavalier's taller shoulder with his long arm, and
abruptly stopped him.

Turning, Edward saw that he was looking flushed and
disconcerted in a very unusual degree with him.

This was soon explained.

'What obstinate fools old men become!' Tubal passionately exclaimed to his fellow young man. 'Here
is Greybeard Firebrace knotted himself up against all
reason, and vowing to oppose every motion of peace in
the council unless I will promise immediately, and
without a day's further delay, to wed me to his daughter.
In self-defence, and not to grate unkindly on the old
man's pride, I have been obliged to tell him that it is
Dorothy who refuses any longer to accept me as her
husband, and to remind him that she has shown a most
evident preference for you. Upon which he has worked
himself into a ferment of discontent and upbraiding,
reproaching me that I was wilfully throwing his child
over to the licentious wooing of a stranger; that my
pride had risen, like a bubble in boiling lead, with my
foolish pretensions to lordship and mastery in the tur-
bulent town; and accused me that I am mad enough to
fancy myself a likely match for the proudest lady of her
station in the world, and who disdained me most—
Arabella Holte! He touched me there rather on the
raw—how he knows it I know not; and I answered him,
perchance, too sharply and peevishly, for thereupon he
grew angrier than ever, and declared that his daughter's

honour and safety were, at all events, sufficiently dear
to himself to make him resolve to persevere as much as
in him lies against any terms likely to restore the old
free resort and association between Aston Hall and the
town. And in this mood, and with these purposes, there
is much reason to fear he is coming to oppose our plans
with all the weight of his position and influence.'

Edward was exceedingly annoyed at this statement,
which seemed likely to act very injuriously to his political objects, and consequently his best private hopes.
It struck him, however, that some prospect of evasion
of the difficulty was offered in an idea that occurred to
him. He asked Tubal accordingly to bring him, if
possible, into an interview with the master armourer in
private, before the business on which he came was dis-
cussed. And although Tubal plainly expressed himself
of opinion that no good results could follow, in consequence of the armourer's exasperated state of feeling
towards him as a person who designed dishonourable
dealings with his only child, he persisted in the wish
until the younger chief of the town promised at all
events to exert his endeavours to effect the desired
meeting.

While they were yet speaking, passed by several grave
and dubiously-staring personages into the council-room,
and Firebrace himself then appeared, stalking gloomily
across the cobble-stoned yard before the Guildhall.

The grim austerity of the Puritan citizen's habitual
look and manner was certainly in nowise diminished by
recent events. And though Edward Holte respectfully
bared his head as he approached, and Tubal crossed his
way with a request for attention, it seemed likely enough
the master armourer intended to push on without notice.

He almost violently thrust the young smith aside, or else himself in the effort, and muttering ' I hold no private converse with the enemies of the town and Parliament!' was with difficulty brought to a stand by Edward Holte's directly facing him.

The firm though very respectful address of the young cavalier, and some apprehension, possibly, that a public wrangle might contribute to spread the scandals against his daughter, compelled Firebrace, much against his will, to a pause. When finding it could not be avoided, he assented to the earnest request made to him by Edward for a few moments' private hearing on a point of importance to be settled with the master armourer before the public proceedings took place.

He stepped aside, sternly bidding Master Holte follow him, into a small and darksome chamber in a species of watch-room at the entrance of the great hall, the solitary tenant of which was the figure of a giant, in Roman armour, cut in wood and garishly coloured, like the London Gog or Magog. This was supposed to represent St. Martin, the patron saint of Birmingham, and having fallen from an ancient niche over the entrance of the Guildhall, had been stowed aside as old lumber here.

By no means with any conciliation in his tones the master armourer then turned to Edward, and, with averted eyes, demanded his pleasure in delaying him from the town's business, whereupon he was come.

Edward had made up his mind what to do and say, to remove, as far as he should find it safe, the worst personal prejudices of the father of Dorothy Firebrace against him : at least, he fancied he was adopting the best means to this end. He replied, therefore, very gently to the armourer, by confessing that after recent

occurrences, unless properly explained, he had a right
to be suspicious of his own presence and purposes in
Birmingham.

'But,' Edward continued, with kindly warmth, 'your
misgivings are altogether unfounded, Master Firebrace;
and it is as an honourable suitor for your daughter's
hand in marriage that I presume now to ask you to
change your angry looks at me, and know me for a true
and honest friend, which I shall always prove. Your
daughter's heart is already mine, and her faith plighted
mine by links of love that bind firmer than adamant.
All that is necessary is that we should keep this happy
arrangement and alliance a secret from my father awhile,
as he is violently set on another match for me, and with
whom I have bitter enemies, who may use his wrath
against me in the disobedience to utter casting down
and ruin.'

While he thus spoke, Edward, who had expected that
all obstacles would melt like snow before this genial
sunshine, was dismayed to observe the deepening lower
on the master armourer's brows. Neither was the tempest long in bursting.

'What have I done, O Lord, that I am become as a
mockery and a derision among the Gentiles, and to my
own people likewise?' exclaimed old Firebrace, glaring
reproachfully rather than imploringly upward, and tossing back his long grizzly locks. 'Or am I some other
fulsome boy, licking up treacle poured forth to catch
flies? Or who do you think myself I am, my fair
master, that I should seek to thrust my daughter by
stealth into a family where I have no mind she should
wed, and who scorn and repudiate the alliance? I tell
you, were your father and his house of the royallest in

Europe, emperors and kings—know, Master Holte, I would not on such terms consent to let my daughter crawl up a throne! And do you come to me to offer that on certain conditions of present dishonour, suspicion, and mislike among all my townsfolk and friends I am to put my daughter in the way some day to find herself the bride of a disinherited beggar, of birth not half so well-blooded, truly, as mine own ; but far likelier, with all this fair show, the shamed and cast-off leman and mistress of a father-scorning profligate ? Go to, sir, trouble yourself to urge the matter no further; for I swear to you on the faith of my living soul, were you to present yourself to me as a son-in-law—fully consented by your haughty sire and all of his adherency—loaded with the favours of your King—with the lands and place of Aston to put in dower on your bride—I would answer as I do now, Woe worth the hour! Judge, then, if I will suffer an address which must be offered in a robber-like pacing of concealment, and under penalties but little short of his branding-iron and every other felon-forfeiture.'

The effect of this reply upon the newly-made husband of Dorothy Firebrace may be much easier imagined than described.

He perceived at once that not only were the chances of conciliation and indulgence towards their loves utterly hopeless on his own proud father's part, but on that of the equally, though in different style, haughty Puritan sire of his bride.

Every word was pronounced with the stern emphasis of the strokes of the hammer on metal, compelled into some irresistible form by the art so familiar to the master armourer.

Edward felt that further remonstrance would but increase suspicion and multiply difficulties. He therefore
resolved to attempt none; and, with certainly a pardon-
able hypocrisy, replied, 'I must then deem your consent
impossible to be obtained, and submit myself accordingly;' and he himself opened the door for Firebrace to
retire.

The master armourer would not, however, accept
this mark of deference.

'Age counts not against honour as yet in England,
Master Holte,' he said, stepping himself rigidly back.
'Take the way before me, which is the due of the heir
of Aston Hall; but you will not be followed by a seconder
of the proposal you come to entrap us withal from the
King!'

'As you will, Master Armourer,' returned Edward,
really now feeling himself wax angrily indignant at the
persevering repulse and hostility of the stern old man.
'But I trust I shall find some out-numbering of
reasonable men in your council, who will rather serve
the interests of the town and themselves than the
causeless animosities even of so chief a ruler in Birmingham as your office, I deny not, should make you,
were it more evenly balanced by judgment and temper,
to profitable issues for those ruled.'

And he took the precedence so scornfully urged upon
him with a very fairly provoked vehemence of gesture
and glance.

CHAPTER LXIII.

THE TOWN COUNCIL.

IRRITATED quite as much as discouraged by what had taken place between himself and his unconscious father-in-law, Edward proceeded into the Guildhall Council Chamber without deigning once again to look back.

It was a handsome apartment, particularly on account of its loftiness, the roof being open to the top of the lantern-tower. About a score of the principal burgesses, chiefs of the several trades, were present, for the most part looking considerably scared and puzzled, but wringing hands at every turn with Tubal Bromycham, and forming into little knots to hear what he said. And he seemed very busy saying something in his curt and straightforward way; probably explaining the object of the meeting.

Among these groups was specially noticeable a small, thin man, with a sharp and wizened, roguishly keen, indeed, and intelligent visage, and who seemed eagerly bent on acquiring all the information he could.

This personage was known to the general body of his townspeople as Johny-the-Rogue, his proper name being John Sainsfoy ; and he was a master-smith, who could turn his craft to as various uses as Firebrace himself, with the difference that he prided himself on

overreaching all who dealt with him, either in material
or manufacture, and in this discreditable manner had
acquired his by-name.

Johny-the-Rogue was notoriously reputed to cherish
a bitter ill-will against Firebrace and Tubal, whose
handiwork so far exceeded his own in other qualities as
well as honesty of metal and fidelity to contract in the
fashioning. His son, who resembled him as a weasel
does a fox, was said to have aspired to rival Tubal with
the master armourer's daughter; of course, with anything but good success. Rivals in trade the two forge-
owners had ever been. But all this did not prevent
Johny-the-Rogue from addressing Tubal in a very soft
and cringing manner, as he came on with his explanations, congratulating him greatly on his success in
putting down the mutinous movement of the populace
in the forenoon.

'These are troublous times, troublous times, Master
Bromycham; but you are the man born to sway them.
For my part, I should never have ventured out of my
smithy smoke to-day had I not heard with what a high
hand you swung the rabble back into their holes again
by their tails. Not a rat among them will squeak for a
month again. And so also there are good tidings of a
peace forward, are there, God be praised?'

Tubal knew that this man would be sure to back
terms of peace if they also promised profit, and he
endeavoured to respond to Johny-the-Rogue's ques-
tionings as conscientiously to the purpose as he could;
and he was thus engaged when Edward Holte entered
the room, followed, at some interval, by the slow and
brooding steps of the master armourer.

Tubal, probably tired of the unaccustomed part he

was playing, immediately took advantage of the arrival to break off his conference with the sly and insidious old man, and begin the business of the meeting.

'I am no speechifier,' he said, abruptly addressing the good company, but in those tones that always commanded the remotest attention, and made his whispering neighbour start. 'What I have to say, I mostly say it with my right hand and arm. But there is Master Edward Holte come to you, my masters, from the King, and he will tell you why himself.'

Edward took the hint; and animated now by so many additional motives to complete the task he had assigned himself, addressed the burgesses, as they were then styled—not town councillors—of Birmingham, in a still apter and more earnestly persuasive harangue than had previously proved so effective, for a time, with the general assemblage of the townspeople.

He began by giving the King much more credit than he deserved, for an anxious wish to prevent the seemingly now inevitable calamities of a civil war; at all events, to narrow to as definite and few issues as possible the decisions put to the unreasoning arbitration of the sword, and to confine, as far as possible, the theatre of misery and bloodshed.

The matters in dispute between the King and Parliament, according to the young Royalist orator, were now in reality reduced to this one—which of them should wield the executive power of the state, which for all the known times of England had been confided to the sovereign.

The King had granted every demand made upon him that could possibly tend to the security of the liberties and religion of his people. He had surrendered his

dearest friends, and the faithfullest servants of his will
in his former way of government, to the utmost fury and
vengeance of the factions opposed to it; to public and
national justice, if it so pleased them of Birmingham
to consider it, as no doubt many wise and honourable
men, and true subjects in their hearts, might hold it,
and did. The noble Strafford had poured forth his
loyal and generous blood—whose purple was richer than
the robe of the empire he perished, as it were, by his
own consent to preserve—on the scaffold. Laud, the
archbishop, was in a dungeon of the Tower, expiating
the severities and oppressions of a too harsh, however
well meant, zeal in the establishment of church influence
and domination, which he doubtless confounded in his
own pure and virtuous mind and purposes with religion
and the supreme sway and enhancement of morality.
But not contented with all or anything of this, the
Parliament insisted on sequestrating the whole kingly
authority and rightful prerogatives of the crown into
its own hands, and of thus establishing a worse than
Venetian oligarchical tyranny, with a more phantom
Doge still at its head, in the realm and constitution of
England, which of all time had been royal and free.

The question of the militia, of the direction and
control of the public sword, was that upon which alone
the King remained firmly and inexorably resolved never
to yield to the tyrannous spoliation attempted to be
made of his rights. And upon that it was, and which
was relied upon as the supreme effort to reduce himself
and his people to so miserable a slavery, that the Parliament had prompted and abetted the most furious
and insolent seditions and violences against his Majesty
and his royal family, and had finally driven him away

from the proper capital seat of his government and state.

London, in fact, the well-spoken Royalist proceeded to declare, was the real and main offender in the whole affair, and the sole reliable support and abetment of the Parliament in its unjust and traitorous designs. It was on London, therefore, alone that the King's indignation would most reasonably and properly be directed. His Majesty deprecated nothing more than the multiplication of obstacles in his way, and the necessity of inflicting chastisement on towns and cities in their hearts faithful to him, though in some instances either shamefully coerced or led astray from their duties, as Birmingham had of late become.

True representations had, however, been made to the King by some honest gentlemen, their friends, of the real state of affairs there; how the good town had been for awhile transported and driven out of its accustomed moderation in opinion, and attention to its own industrious pursuits, by the sudden outloosing of a tempest-blast of fanaticism, and the violent control of a military force. But now both had ceased of their tumultuous and unlawful influence, and though the surface of the popular wave was still something ruffled and tossed, it was only froth and foam that showed above the calming billows now. They were quit of the armed oppression lately exercised among them, and the proper authority of their lord and the worthy burgesses of Birmingham had been duly and most efficaciously restored. They were free then now—as they must all have heard, within so brief an interval—to exercise their own will and judgment truly in the affair, and decide whether they would return to the quiet and

peaceful exercise of their trades and occupations, which
promised to become more profitable than ever, under
his Majesty's full protection and pardon, or expose
themselves to all the inconveniences and ravages of war,
already close at their doors, in the hardly-restrained
exasperation of the King's cavalry at Aston, and certain
very speedily to present itself in overwhelming power
and vengeance, in the shape of a royal army marching
on London from the north and west, well provided, by
the Queen's diligence, with artillery and other means of
destruction, whereby their town might be laid level
with the dust at the least word of a bidding, whose
utterance it might no longer be possible to entreat
refraining.

What could Birmingham, whatever her spirit and
courage, an unwalled and unfortified town, do against
so formidable an advance, supposing her citizens so
madly set against their own interests and preservation
as to persist in the seditious movement effected by the
artifices and violence of an intriguing stranger? And
it was plain that Birmingham, having been led or drawn
into so dangerous a strait, had been deserted to her fate
by the Parliament, which had withdrawn its one scanty
troop of horse, and need not look to their distant
London army for assistance of any sort.

Supposing even that a most unlikely chance of
victory on the part of the London cockneys and
frenzied fanatics over well-born gentlemen accustomed
to arms, and their hardy tenantry, ensued, the royal
army would first have marched through their county,
and inflicted whatever justice or vengeance might be
decreed. And Edward Holte very truly assured the
meeting that there was a strong disposition among

many of the trusted councillors and favourite advisers of the King to inflict some memorable chastisement on a town which, destitute of the means of defence, had cast itself with such fury and violence into rebellion, and set so bad an example to others in the like predicament.

It was for them, therefore—the chief men and masters of the town of Birmingham—to resolve upon its fate, which the orator now committed, in the King's name, to their deliberation, on terms that, with their kind permission, he would proceed to disclose.

The reader is already aware of the nature of the conditions which the King affixed to a 'full and gracious pardon, and receiving back into his protection' of his good town of Birmingham, and which indeed were most indulgent and ample, had they been sincerely meant.

All that seemed required was that the town should professedly return to its allegiance, open itself to all lawful egress and regress, and engage to allow of the furnishing of the King's armies freely for their money, with the warlike implements and engines that formed an established portion of its manufacture.

In confirmation of all which Edward produced his credentials, and the conditional formula of pardon, duly signed and sealed, and requiring only acceptance on the part of the people of Birmingham.

This speech was listened to with great though, for the most part, silent attention, thus far; not, however, without an occasional murmur of assent and approbation. But men seemed more intent on watching the effect on their neighbours than in giving utterance to their own conclusions. Yet it was plain enough the general result was favourable, and particularly the last part of the stipulations seemed agreeable to the taste of Johny-the-Rogue.

'I was always for a fair and open trade with all customers myself,' he remarked, 'and no questions asked, but that the payment should not be in King James's clipped money, come by whose hands it might. Yet I am but the deacon of our craft, and the master armourer decided otherwise.'

'Still, of a surety, father, it something marvels me,' squeaked out the falsetto tones of the younger Sainsfoy, known as 'the Weasel,' 'how the town can return to its allegiance without receiving back into his authority the Crown Bailiff, Master Cooper, which methinks Master Bromycham here, who sets up for proper Lord of Birmingham, will by no means allow.'

'My interests shall not stand in the way of the town's, Wynkyn Sainsfoy,' replied Tubal, cheerfully. 'If Cooper will accept the office again, he may hold it under me by what authority he pleases, until the King shall be put in full and true possession of the rights of my case by Master Holte, when I shall as certainly expect justice from his royal hands as from any mob of upsetters in the world.

'Ay, ay! kings are greatly changed in our time from what they were in your great grandfather's, when he was (so unjustly, as you say) condemned to gibbeting and forfeiture as a highway robber.'

Tubal was about to make some angry reply to this sarcasm on the part of his despised rival, Wynkyn Sainsfoy, when he was cut short by the sharp and vindictive utterance of the master armourer, who suddenly exclaimed, 'Say'st so? How are kings changed? Only by adding worse perjuries and beguilings, they and their satellites, to their old violence and tyranny, which well this bedazed young man will learn to know.' And, to the great surprise and unfixing of the opinion of the meeting, whose members always expected to see the master armour and his intended son-in-law of one mind, he rose, and pronounced what in its way was a most singularly virulent and passionate but effective counterpoise to most of the arguments towards the restoration of peace, and acceptance of the conditions proposed from Nottingham, brought forward by Edward Holte.

Firebrace was very well known in his town for the Puritan tendency of his religious opinions, and the warmth and earnestness with which he had from the first supported the general movement of the Parliament and nation in that direction ; but no one suspected his political opinions had attained to so deep and violent a cast of republican repudiation and hatred for the established forms of government and authority which his present outburst betrayed. Nor had it hitherto appeared that he had been so convinced and zealous an agent in the late revolt as his now open profession of absolute and unswerving devotion to the cause of the Parliament implied.

Indeed his considerably broken and confused forms of expression declared no slight internal dislocation and disarrangement of ideas, and greatly added to the puzzle of the auditory, among whom he had the reputation of a concise and unwinning, but clear-minded speaker, on the few subjects of a mundane nature he deemed worthy his attention.

Above all, there was no mistaking the personal animus

and exasperation of the master armourer's tone; and not alone against the terms of peace themselves, but their offerer.

He adopted with the utmost virulence all the arguments in popular use against the possibility of placing any kind of confidence in the King's promises, and reluctant relinquishment of the tyrannical form of government he had maintained so long, until the necessities resulting from his maladministration compelled him to resort to a parliament for support.

Nothing, he maintained, but Charles's surrender of the power of the sword could furnish his unhappy people with any security against his grasping spirit of despotism, and visible reversion to most of the superstitions and observances of Popery to please a Popish wife.

The Londoners were most nobly and righteously engaged in this just cause, he declared, in support of the Parliament, and Birmingham had bravely and fittingly thrown in her weight on the side of the religion and freedom of the people of England. And were they now about to exhibit themselves as a pack of headlong children, following the suggestion of any leader for the moment, and then running wild with fear, and rushing into exactly the contrary extreme the next?

What had they to dread which they had not abundantly shown their ability to withstand? The cavaliers at Aston? But had they not already repulsed with shame and open discomfiture, aided only by a few chains and ditches, the worst these vaunting enemies could do or threat? And for this success they had been indebted to none but themselves, for the Parliament

officer had merely brought his men into the town for a
few hours, to don their armour, after the attack had
failed. And as for this wonderful army, which was to
come over Warwickshire in' a cloud of destruction and
overwhelm all opposition, where was it? Master Edward
Holte, he was certain, had not seen it at Nottingham.
And on such childish threats and bugbears were they to
take panic terror, and resolve to throw Birmingham
open to the dissolute and debauched soldiery and supporters of the King, who would immediately use their
opportunities to introduce every species of licence and
profanation into their as yet honest and God-fearing
town?

What mattered the heady stirring up of the poorer
sort of the place, which has been so much enlarged upon,
but was chiefly on the side of gospel truth and the
spreading of religion, in reality, compared with the
contamination and ruin which thus awaited them?
Everyone knew what manner of man was Sir Thomas
Holte, of Aston Hall; and what kind of better behaviour
should be expected from his allies and guests? What
safety would there be for the town from the most
solemn assurances, from such perjurers, if they once
relinquished its guard and close defence?

Therefore himself, the master armourer, declared he
never would consent to any kind of pretended peace
and making up of differences, which could not be, since
those he spoke of were as between darkness and light;
but would faithfully adhere to the declaration made by
the town in favour of the Parliament, with whatsoever
strength of friends and adherence might remain to him.
And as for the freedom of trade declared, it was verily
a liberty granted to serve either God or Baal, at men's

pleasure; and only the idolaters of Baal, in their secret souls, would demand or accept the privilege.

Johny-the-Rogue, who felt himself strongly glanced at in this latter remark, contented himself, nevertheless, with retorting, 'Ah, my sir, but you had secured all "God" first to yourself, with the Parliament Captain; and poor under-craftsmen, like me, cannot make our wine-presses overflow by looking over hedges into our neighbours' flourishing vineyards.' And the force of the observation was evidently appreciated by a considerable number in the assemblage.

The master armourer's opposition did, nevertheless, as clearly produce a great effect. It visibly much troubled Tubal, who muttered, 'Nay, if the town's councils be thus divided, we shall have nothing come of it all but ruin and misery!' But his eye at this moment falling upon Edward Holte's anxious and excited countenance, his ideas seemed to sustain an electric shock of change, and, with a sudden fierceness and masterfulness of look and manner and word, which diffused a new emotion through the audience, he exclaimed, 'I must let you too, then, my masters, know who is Lord of Birmingham; and how of old time and usages it was always the Lord of Birmingham that spoke for the town, and fought for it, and had the good ordering of it, and you burgessess had nothing to do in the matter except to obey, and carry out his will. So now, I say, I will accept the King's peace offered us, and I will see it enforced in all its points; conditioning only, Master Holte, that the soldiers of the King are ordered to leave quarterage at Aston, and approach us no nearer than as we shall give fair permission to them under my hand and seal.'

'Why, Tubal, can you write ? I thought not ; and it is not much the use of our craft,' said the audacious Wynkyn Sainsfoy, who was aware that, from the circumstances of his early rearing, Tubal Bromycham's education in scholarly respects had been extremely deficient, even in that unschooled age.

He looked rather alarmed, however, as to the effect of the taunt, and shrunk his spare little framework of mortality as far as might be out of reach. But somewhat to his surprise, Tubal answered quite pleasantly, 'Yes, Weasel, I *can* write now ; and I do purpose to make myself, at whatever toil of hand and brain, in all other respects what a gentleman of my degree by birth and descent should be.' And quietly turning to Edward Holte, he enquired if he consented, on the part of the King, to the conditions named.

'I think—I am sure—there can be no objection to so reasonable a demand,' Edward replied.

'When it is assured us, I will then open my town to all in-comers, and its trade shall be free again to all the world,' returned the Blacksmith Lord of Birmingham.

'And truly herein we have a fair specimen of the kind of government, or rather masterful and unlawful tyranny, we may ever expect from kings and their pretended representatives,' exclaimed Firebrace, fiercely. 'But since you take on you so, Tubal Bromycham, take also notice that from this moment I withdraw from you all leading and command over the smiths' guildsmen, which you only exercise by my leave and licence, and which I resume now in my proper hands.'

'It must not be, Father Firebrace,' returned Tubal, with a firm but regretful expression. 'All men who draw the breath of life in Birmingham are bound to do

suit and service in arms to the lord thereof whenever
called upon.　Deem you I have not made some use of
my learning to look into the old books in the Moat House,
and see what authority and right are truly mine?'

'It shall be seen, however, Master Bromycham,
whether the smiths of Birmingham will obey their old
chief and master, or a Walsall collier lad preferably,'
returned Firebrace, giving way to his indignant feelings.
'I will go and discharge my workpeople at once from
attendance on you and your cannon at St. Martin's
Church, and take my daughter home to my own safe
keeping and custody; for I am not one of those fools
whom experience cannot make wise: and will leave to
you solely and wholly the rewards of the confidence you
profess in the goodwill and honourable dealing of the
Holtes of Aston.'

So saying, the passionate old man withdrew in an
evident fury of disappointment and suspicion, leaving
Edward Holte apparently victor, but no triumphant
one, upon the field.

In other respects, the acquiescence in Tubal's decree
seemed general; particularly after Johny-the-Rogue had
observed, with his crafty smile, 'What our lord does is
none of our doing, then, it would appear; and for my
part, I am content both King and Parliament should
remember it.　But in the way of trade, Master Holte,
if you be still so minded as to weapon your troop in the
King's service in Birmingham, I think I can supply you
at as reasonable a cost as the Crown Forge doth the
Parliament, and am willing thereto.'

Edward courteously acceded to this offer, anxious
to conciliate a person who seemed of influence, and
to secure himself a good pretext for future visitation

in Birmingham. Perceiving, moreover, the doubtful balance of opinion and authority in the assemblage, he determined to take Tubal's declaration as a sufficient acceptance of the proposal he had made on the part of the town. He therefore dexterously thanked the good burgesses of Birmingham for their loyal and reasonable demeanour on the occasion, promised that he would immediately procure from Nottingham a confirmation of all that had been done, took a graceful farewell of the meeting, and retired.

CHAPTER LXIV.

SUTTON CHACE.

TUBAL followed his Royalist friend out of the Guildhall, and rejoined him in the street. Discussing what had occurred, the two young men then turned, by tacit consent, to retrace the way to St. Martin's Church.

Both agreed it was a great disaster, Armourer Firebrace having exhibited himself so openly hostile to all that was proposed.

' Many of the precision elders of the town will follow where he leads,' said Tubal. ' And it is true the most part of my young men look up to me chiefly as the representative of the head of their craft. Saw you not I dared not put it to the vote, but was forced to take it all upon me, like this poor King, with his refractory Parliaments? It is almost as well there are the Anabaptists, swearing vengeance against Dorothy, to keep the greybeards and Firebrace in awe, and compel them to look to me always for safety and defence. How say you, Master Holte?'

' It little likes me, howbeit, Dorothy should remain in a town so tossed with feuds and ready for mutiny,' replied the clandestine bridegroom. ' But when you can no longer rely on yourself and your friends for her protection, Tubal, I trust you will send due word to me at Sutton, where I shall soon have assembled a troop of horse at my devotion and yours, in that case.'

'Nay, Master Holte,' exclaimed Tubal, with warmth ; 'never dream that I purpose or will suffer any such treason to my town as to admit armed men, come whence they may, to the control. But nothing shall injure Dorothy while these arms of mine can heave a hammer, nor will the Anabaptists soon again try conclusions with me. You may depend, too, I *fear me*,' he continued, with a smile, 'on Master Firebrace's diligence in looking after his child, whom I doubt not he has already taken away home to his strong-barred house, from the church.'

Edward had little doubt of this fact either, though he struggled to hope on against hope.

'However it be, Tubal,' he said, after some final suggestion that they might yet find Dorothy in St. Martin's, 'I owe to you much gratitude, and trust yet to owe you more, for your furtherance of my honest love.'

'You know how to repay me, Master Holte,' said Tubal, with emotion.

'I will not fail,' Edward replied sadly and evasively of what he knew was meant, 'to send due word to his Majesty how faithfully you have bestirred yourself in his affairs here, and place before him in the same breath the unmerited wrongs of your ancestors, and your just claims on such rights and restitution as are yet in the power of the Crown to afford you in Birmingham.'

Tubal, however, seemed highly satisfied with the promise, for a reason Edward had overlooked, and knew not still what reliance could be placed on.

''Tis as I would have it, then, in all respects. For your glorious sister has only to know that Tubal the

blacksmith is a gentleman, and with some means as
one, to forgive his former presumption, and restore him
to the happiness else for ever lost!'

Edward suppressed the deep sigh that rose in his
breast; and yet this confident reiteration infused some
degree of hope into himself, not unmingled with
curiosity to ascertain whether there was any better
foundation than the delusive sorceries of passion for the
young man's belief.

What was apprehended was found to be the case at
the church.   Only the Coopers and Mr. Lane remained
there—Dorothy was gone—when Edward re-entered
St. Martin's, leaving Tubal, he knew not why at the
moment, behind, outside.

Dame Cooper readily explained. 'Within the shortest while after you were hence that we could expect to
hear of any mischance, enters me the master armourer,
looking so black and angrified that methought he had
discovered all, and was as ill-content his daughter
should become a gentlewoman as another would be to
have her wed below her degree.   But, by good mercy,
he knew nothing at all of the matter, only was very
peevish, and set on his daughter's leaving at a moment's word, as if there were fire and powder in his
'Come, minx, and look to keep close house awhile in
Deritend!' And when she asked but leave, all weep-
ingly and whimperingly, poor soul, for me to accompany her, he would not have it so by any means, but
croaks me out that henceforth he had taken his part,
and intended that all of his house should do the like,
and so would suffer no royalist spies of whatsoever
sort within his doors! And she was obliged to go
at once.'

Edward's intense disappointment showed plainly enough in his face.

'Alas, Dame Cooper,' he said, 'now will the stern old man bar me of all access to my gentle bride, and I am as one who has looked into paradise only to have the grating dashed in my face.'

'Nay, nay, good Master Holte, say not so, and with so lackadaisical a crossing of your arms on your poor breast. What! the art of twisting rope-ladders is not yet quite lost among mankind, and where there's a will there's a way—nay, there are half-a-dozen ways, to my knowledge, into the old Crown House. Ay, and there are dark nights enow to be hoped for yet in Birmingham, though it be the full harvest moon at present, to cloak a lover's secret steps. Nay, rather than so kindly a pair should be altogether disfurnished of a dovecote to bill in, I will, methinks, consent to remain awhile in this mad town, and make you welcome to some poor home I yet may call my own.'

Edward upon this eagerly explained to the wife of the ex-bailiff how, under present circumstances, she might conscientiously allow her husband to resume his duties and residence at the Moat House; and he was repeating what Tubal had said on the subject to the friendly woman, when the young smith rejoined him abruptly in the church.

Tubal's aspect had so remarkably gloomed over, in the brief interval of their separation, that Edward noticed it at once, and enquired the reason.

''Slife, sir, how came you not to miss the cannon-piece as I did when we first arrived? And find now that Firebrace gave orders to a party of the smiths to wheel it back to Deritend; and here is William Moorcroft come to tell me the armourer has secured his strong gates, and ordered the great furnace to be got in readiness to melt the cannon into a clump of iron again, lest, as he pretends, it should fall into the hands of your cavaliers.'

' Can you not rescue it ? The artillery is yours, not Firebrace's,' exclaimed Edward.

' And come to blows with a man whom for years I have looked upon as a father ?' said Tubal, and Edward felt it was useless to say any more on the subject.

Such was the state of disruption and confusion of policy and interests, private and public, in which Edward Holte was obliged to leave Birmingham after that day of contention and strife, which had yet included the marriage of two lovers so tenderly and truly devoted to each other.

One little satisfaction, however, he secured ere he went, Dame Cooper consenting to allow her husband to resume his office and residence at the Moat House, on the conditions previously assured by Tubal.

' She had no animosity against Master Bromycham himself,' she said, ' who was as good an artisan of his trade as need be, put by his craze to fancy himself a lord, and there was room enough and to spare for Noah and his ark in the Moat House ; and for any harm the blacksmith gentleman had done her and hers thus far, she was even'd with him, tit for tat, and might be more so yet !' And Edward, who knew the significance of his secret ally's phrases, and that no real injury was meant Tubal by himself, was well content to find he had secured a trysting-place, easy of access from outside Birmingham, as soon as the vigilance of his unconscious father-in-law should abate.

Tubal and he parted with mutual and sincerely felt expressions of friendship and good-will, Edward promising to keep him well informed as to the further results of the business they had just concluded.

The comparatively quiet of the streets no longer called for alarm on the part of Mr. Lane, as he and Edward Holte rode together out of the town. Not to mention that the poor clergyman's mind was now possessed with a new and engrossing subject for anxiety. Edward indeed was quite wearied with the ceaseless cautions to preserve the recent event a secret; if for no other reason, for the sake of his unfortunate friend and tutor, who had so madly consented to place his all at stake to pleasure him. And on this account he was glad when they reached the gates of Aston Park, where they separated; the culpable chaplain to return to the Hall, Edward to pursue his arranged plan of retiring to Sutton Manor-House.

But the former had yet another nerve-shaking duty imposed upon him; which was to convey to Prince Rupert, and all else whom it might concern, the statement that terms of peace had been arranged with Birmingham, which would be duly certified to his Highness as soon as they had obtained the royal approval.

This instruction given, Edward and the chaplain parted, and Master Holte took the way quite alone over Sutton Chace, to the ancient manor-house known by the name.

At this period the extensive district, still dearest to the holiday-making Birmingham artisan, from its wild but picturesque freedom from limits and inclosure, was considerably more varied in characteristics than at present. Its wastes of broom and bog were relieved by

deep masses of woodland, carefully pierced with paths
for the convenience of the deer, in which the district
abounded, as well as with various winged game.   The
Bowen Pool was almost entitled to take rank as a lake,
and the extensive marshes, from which its sedgy bed at
later periods could scarcely be distinguished, were
covered with a forest growth of immemorial antiquity.
William the Conqueror was said to have built the Royal
Manor-House situated in the deepest part of this sylvan
territory, and to have hunted in Sutton Chace six hundred years even before Edward Holte traversed it on
this occasion two centuries ago.

Indeed, so faithfully does popular tradition preserve
the feeling of bygone ages, it was a current superstition
all over the district at the time, that the stern Norman
Nimrod's apparition still haunted the scene of his early
delights in the flesh over Sutton Chace; not in any
pleasurable enjoyment, it is to be remarked, but as a
kind of purgatorial punishment for the wrongs and
cruelties he had been guilty of, in clearing the vast districts he dedicated to his favourite sports of their
nobler original inhabitants, to leave the solitudes necessary for deer and boar.   In truth, the story ran,
that whenever the apparition crossed the affrighted
vision of peasant or keeper, always in the form of a
gigantic knight mounted on a gigantic steed, horse and
rider both seemed to glow red-hot with internal fire!
And the impression was confirmed by the fact that
wherever encountered, the apparition seemed always
urging its way, through forest and brake and tangled
waste of every kind, towards the Pool; wherein it
usually concluded the spectacle by plunging with a
hissing noise, and the usual splutter of fire and water

encountering—doubtless down to its native hell, in the belief of the despoiled Saxon, who probably first beheld or fancied out so suitable a punishment for the oppressor.

This was not a pleasant association to accompany even a brave young cavalier in a moonlight ride over the three or four miles of desolate and shadowy way which Edward Holte must traverse to his new home. But luckily his mind was too anxiously and absorbingly employed on other thoughts, in which the deepest satisfaction was strongly intermingled with something of dismay and awe, when he reflected on the events of the day. He, Edward Holte—the husband of Dorothy Firebrace, the armourer's daughter of Birmingham—against his father's consent—unknown to him—plighted by him to another wealthy and high-born bride!

When Edward remembered his father's character—the adverse influences surrounding him — he was at times amazed at his own audacity; and nothing but the passionate attachment that glowed in his heart and every fibre of his youthful being for the fair woman he had made his own, gave him courage to sustain the reflection of the dangers and troubles so evidently attendant on the event.

Yet it cannot be denied Edward was startled rather vividly back to the recollection of the dreary legend of the Waste, as the part of Sutton chiefly haunted by the red-hot apparition was called, by suddenly catching the ring of the metal of a horse's hoof in the distance before him.

He was approaching the Manor-House, but the view forward was obstructed by a remarkable eminence in the ground, called ' Loaches Banks '—long the puzzle

of the antiquary, being surrounded evidently by arti-
ficial excavations, like a moat, but with no sign of ever
having been occupied by a building.

Some supposed the spot to have been the site of a
Roman camp; others of a Druidical temple; others,
again, declared for its having been an ancient place of
interment, whose peculiar sacredness had accumulated
the bodies of the dead into this mound. But no remains
whatever attested the validity of any of these supposi-
tions, unless the last may be considered as proven from
the generally credited report, that on All Souls' Night
the hillock flamed round with corpse-candles. The
traditions of Sutton Chace were, it must be confessed,
not of a very lively order, but such as were naturally
prompted by its characteristics of gloom and solitude,
at most seasons of the year save in the early green and
bloom of spring.

But if Edward Holte's fancy dwelt with a moment's
superstitious excitement on the recollection of the fiery
Phantom of the Waste, it could scarcely be considered
a relief when he recognised in the bright moonlight,
turning from behind the banks, the figure of his detested
brother, Richard Grimsorwe.

What did he there?

Edward believed Grimsorwe capable of every atrocity,
and almost suspected him of some design of crafty assassination. As a precaution, therefore, he drew a pistol
from his holsters, and by no means dissembled that he
held it ready when they encountered face to face.

Grimsorwe, however, burst into a discordant, ringing
laugh.

'What, brother Edward! do you take me for a high-
wayman?' he exclaimed. 'And I have been to Sutton,

by Sir Thomas's wish, making all manner of arrangements for your comfort there. For when our good
father came to think of it, he grew of your lady mother's
opinion, that more pains should be taken in arranging a
household for you, than you were likely to take for yourself. So I have been with a rare convoy of all manner
of household goods for your use, and instructions to the
keeper and his wife at the Manor-House, which will
save you trouble in every way.'

'I am beholden to my father, whom you also style
yours, Master Richard Grimsorwe,' replied Edward, yet
not much in tones agreeable to the intimation. 'But
believe me, after the complaints made to me by Gaspar
Feldon of your conduct with his wife, and my forbidding you the Manor-House while I shall be deputy-
ranger there, I am surprised that even your zeal in my
service should have induced you to venture within
range of Gaspar's quarter-staff again.'

'Nay, but I knew the good fellow was out on his
duties in the Chace, which often enough betides with a
keeper of Sutton,' returned Grimsorwe, still smilingly;
' and Esther Feldon and I may have our little signs and
signals from afar. Though I say not that it is so. It
is, indeed, all the foolish forester's staring at antlers
has put them in his head. And Sutton Manor-House
is not a place the son of my mother,' he continued,
with a suddenly changed and ferocious look in his eyes,
' whether you deny me a father or not, Master Holte,
would choose to make the scene of an unlawful amour!
Along this fair White Walk here, it must have been,
my mother made her escape from Adam Blackjack and
his persecutions, with her baby in her arms—to throw

herself for mercy at the feet of Sir Thomas Holte—and
find it only at the bottom of Aston Swan Pool!'

'However all this may be, I am not your injurer,
Richard Grimsorwe,' Edward Holte replied. 'Only of
this I am resolved—and I intended it all along— I will
not have spies of yours posted where I am ; and I intend
to find another housekeeper than Esther Feldon as
speedily as may be for Sutton Manor-House.'

'And that is precisely what my father will not suffer,
and forbids your removal of any person whom he has
retained in service at Sutton,' Grimsorwe answered ; adding, in a jeering tone, 'But what espial can so perfect
a young gentleman in all the virtues as the heir of
Aston Hall dread to see set upon his immaculate and
loyal doings of every kind and sort ?'

Edward reflected.

'It is true,' he then replied, as if satisfied by some
quiet reasoning to himself. 'Let your spy therefore
remain, and carry what intelligence between Sutton and
Aston she likes, provided she keeps a little on this side
perjury in the leasings and inventions you will put into
her mouth.   She will have little else awhile to come to
report, but the words of discipline for a troop of horse ;
and so, if it pleases you, let us meet as seldom as we
can henceforth, and as goodnight to you as your kindness
meant to me deserves !'

Edward touched his horse with the spur, and passed
Grimsorwe without relaxing his grasp on his weapon,
and was speedily out of sight of his enemy.

Richard gazed motionlessly after him for several
minutes.

'No!' he then ejaculated, 'never again shall I, by
any artifice or persuasion, induce this man to trust in

me. But not the less shall my vengeance follow perse-
veringly in his steps, until I can stand equalled with
him, if not in honour, in disgrace! Yes, on the very
scene of my hapless mother's shame and woful doom
will I retaliate like with like, as rigidly as the old law
exacted and denounced, " An eye for an eye; a tooth
for a tooth!" '

CHAPTER LXV.

SUTTON MANOR-HOUSE.

NOT greatly cheered on his own part by this interview,
as may well be imagined, Edward Holte meanwhile
pursued his way to Sutton Manor-House.

This ancient hunting-seat of Norman kings was, at
the period, in spite of its considerable elevation near the
hilly little town of Sutton Coldfield, almost completely
embosomed and lost to view in depths of coeval forest.

The enormous height of the ancient trees which surrounded the old Royal Lodge gave it, in addition to its
own tumble-down and ruinous aspect, a very gloomy
and shadowy effect, excepting under the strongest beam
of day. But, indeed, by far the greater portion of the
original château had either wholly fallen into decay,
or exhibited only what it had been in shattered and
scattered bulks of masonry, glaring white amidst tufted
mounds and hollows in the ground.

No inconsiderable portion of the timber and lighter
building materials had at various periods of neglect and
disuse been plundered and removed by unlicenced
spoliators or grantees of unthrifty sovereigns. What
remained was chiefly a low stone house, battlemented
on the top of the wall, which ran between the empty
and dismantled remains of two towers, and had originally

formed a square central mass, known still as the 'Donjon,' or Keep. But the greater portion of the back
premises having undergone the processes of dilapidation
described, the Holtes, on becoming hereditary rangers
of Sutton in the reign of Henry VI., had so far repaired
and rebuilt the inclosure that it presented a comfortable
lodgment for a hunting-party, even in considerable
numbers, and had often been so used by Henry VIII.;
while there was abundant room for the head-keeper and
his family (when he had one) on the ground-floor
chambers of the tower to the east, which was nothing
like so shattered and rent by time as the other remaining one.

It is true the chief of these apartments were almost
unfurnished, it being the custom of the kings of England, in the good old times, to remove their conveniences about with them to their different temporary
residences for amusement or business. And they were
exceedingly low in the ceilings; very gloomy and dark.
And although Sir Thomas Holte, in his younger days
being devoted to the chase, had fitted up a portion of
Sutton Manor-House for his own use, with no inconsiderable display of the taste for decoration and enjoyment he afterwards exhibited on a grander scale at
Aston Hall, few vestiges remained to Edward's day.

Report, indeed, would have it the baronet had made
these improvements and embellishments with a view to
contriving a secure and unmolested seclusion for the
unfortunate mistress whose tragical fate has been so often
alluded to in this narrative. But Sir Thomas never
resided at Sutton after his marriage, and consequently
the suite of chambers running the length of the ground-
floor building, of which Edward's hereditary taste for

field sports had early induced him to take possession, were in a sad state of mouldering and decay. But his attention being otherwise devoted, he had concerned himself only to restore some of the chambers to decent habitable order.

The entrance to the 'Donjon' was through the Keeper's Tower, as it was called, upon which numerous well-kept passages and clearings through the thick surrounding woodland conducted. Edward had, therefore, no difficulty in making his way to it, and the weary snorting of his steed might alone have announced his arrival, when he came to a halt; but a horn hung over the gateway for the purpose.

Edward expected the door to be opened by the keeper, Gaspar Feldon, but it was his wife who responded to his appeal. And then he remembered it was unlikely Richard Grimsorwe would have visited the house, except in the absence of the keeper—a man of a sturdy and determined character, of enormous size and strength, and with whom he knew himself to be an object of the bitterest suspicion and dislike, for reasons the most exasperating, even if not established on very clear and undeniable foundation.

Esther Feldon, the wife, was, however, by no means what one would have supposed a likely person to figure as an occasion for strife in the prosecution of a wicked intrigue of the kind. She was a tall, thin, Puritanical-looking woman, with a long melancholy countenance, whose characteristic expression was singularly whimpering and woe-begone, in consonance with the apathetic sadness and monotony of her habitual tones and language.

In truth, it was strange how reports could have arisen to the disadvantage of a personage seemingly of such starched and glum demeanour, and who, besides, had always enjoyed a reputation for unusual strictness and propriety of conduct, until Grimsorwe intruded himself —some time previously to the events we have related— upon his brother's society at the Manor-House.

To be sure, Esther Feldon was not altogether in good odour in the neighbouring little township, in consequence of being reported a frequenter of the conventicles of the Birmingham Anabaptists; but her personal appearance ought in other respects to have guaranteed her. Apart from her unpleasant and unhappy general expression, both her eyes were remarkable for an indirectness of vision—not exactly amounting to a squint, but giving the face a screwed-up and sinister cast. Her complexion, however, though pallid, was very clear, and her hair of a bright raven-black, though plastered as closely to the head, under her plain linen cap, as the paint which represents that adornment of the sex on a Dutch doll. And she was certainly a woman of a mind and education considerably above others of her class; which might be accounted for by the fact of her being the daughter of a parish clerk at Sutton, who in his day had so great a reputation for learning that he was currently reported to be able to give the Psalms out in Hebrew if he thought proper.

It was never very easy to guess at Esther Feldon's real sentiments from her words, or look, or manner. And Edward Holte could not at all divine whether his arrival displeased the woman or otherwise—was expected or not by her, from anything she said or looked. ' Master Holte,' she observed, without the slightest intonation of any sort, much as if she had been an automaton machine fashioned to sound the words.

Nevertheless, Edward had no reason to doubt Grimsorwe's statement that he had been beforehand in making arrangements for his comfort. He was in reality almost startled by the changes which in a few hours had been effected by the surprising zeal of his brother and his satellites.

Under their labours, an unsuspected richness of hanging and gilded ornament had reappeared on the walls and cornices from the dust of a quarter of a century. The principal living-rooms were carpeted; and some handsome pieces of furniture transported from Aston Hall gave the two principal apartments an air of comfort and even stateliness.

These opened one into the other, and consisted of a saloon, a bed-chamber, and a small cabinet stored with all the materials for hunting and fishing—there being some famous preserved sheets of water for the latter purpose within the extensive range of the Sutton territory. And from the windows of these apartments, pleasant though shadowy views into the neighbouring forest were caught, and from the farthest one a wide opening revealed an expanse of gorse-blooming heath and hillocky lowland and upland, terminating in the wild and picturesque elevations of the Beacon Barr.

Esther Feldon led the way, with a dim taper in her hand, through these improvements without making any remark, or seeming to think that any was called for. But Edward's surprise certainly took a strong shade of anger and vexation when he observed that some of the alterations seemed specially adapted for feminine use.

Above all, a toilette and press were arranged in the sleeping apartment of a showy and elaborate device, which he felt it was almost an insult to have fitted up for the accommodation of a solitary bachelor sportsman, who besides proposed to himself the training of a troop of newly-raised recruits.

'Body o' me ! did Richard Grimsorwe imagine his mother is coming back to her old habitation?' he exclaimed in a passion, much excited by the notion that it was pretended he purposed following in his sire's unhappy steps, in his habitation of Sutton Manor-House.

'I know not; what is done is done by order,' the apathetic Esther replied. 'But I would fain hope not, Master Holte ; though Adam Blackjack ever asserts he has traced young Maud's ghost hundreds of hundreds of times, in the white night-clothes she escaped in, over the waste from Sutton to the Swan Pool in Aston pleasure-grounds.'

'Adam Blackjack is a madman, and worse than a madman ; I will have my father admonished of his dealings with our worst enemies, and the frenzied calumnies he spreads !' Edward angrily responded. 'But who else then, prithee Mistress Feldon, is expected to take up her abode here of your sex?'

'I know not, sir; I made no questions—never do. I did what I was bid ; but, truly, I heard some talk that perchance your sister, Mistress Arabella.'

'I trust it shall be so; and in that case let the trumpery remain,' said Edward, endeavouring to soothe himself into the belief that such might possibly be the true explanation. But, at all events, he determined to foil the intention if, as he now began to expect, it was supposed he would make some outbreak on the subject which would call attention to it, and admit of any

variety of misinterpretation. Then declining the offer
of the keeper's wife to furnish him with some supper,
and only requesting her to desire her husband to attend
to his horse on his return, she glided gloomily out, and
he was left alone.

321

CHAPTER LXVI.

LOVE'S LABOURS.

THE first use Edward made of his retirement was to write a full account to Lord Falkland of the success of his negotiations with the town of Birmingham.

It must be excused to the lover-husband of Dorothy Firebrace if he presented by far the best side out of all the circumstances of this affair.

He almost totally suppressed the part taken in opposition by the master armourer, ascribing the degree of repugnance he had experienced to his proposals to the natural unwillingness of men to own themselves practically in the wrong, or to have been forced into actions against their own better judgment.

It was not easy to exaggerate the courage and goodwill exhibited by Tubal Bromycham in suppressing the revolutionary movement of the populace in Birmingham. But Edward certainly made the best of it, and took the opportunity to represent and urge the claims of the Blacksmith Lord on a restoration of his rank, and of the possessions of his family the Crown had it easily in its power to grant. His friendly zeal represented in shining lights the advantages of such an act of justice to the Crown itself, exhibiting as it would to all the world his Majesty's sincere desire to remedy all real abuses in

VOL. II.   Y

administration, since he even repaired the wrongs of his
predecessors.   It would secure an adherent of dauntless
courage and resolution, able almost alone to retain the
important place in question faithfully in his sovereign's
allegiance.

It may be thought Edward Holte took still more
special pains to declare the dangers encountered by
Dorothy Firebrace in her faithful adhesion to the royal
cause, and to dwell upon the heroic courage and resig-
nation with which she had endured the consequences
of the popular exasperation.   Edward was too good a
logician not to confine this ill-feeling to the lower classes
of the town, where in reality it chiefly prevailed.

On the other hand, he was enabled with truth to state
that a large proportion of the masters and upper workpeople of Birmingham desired nothing so much as to be
left to pursue their trades in peace.   Of course he concluded by stating that his Majesty's offers towards such
had been most thankfully received by the persons of
influence in the town ; and that they had agreed, on full
consideration, to accept the terms proposed, on one only
and very fair condition, which the safety of the town
certainly demanded : this was, we know, that before they
threw down their barriers and opened their forges to the
supply of the King's army his Majesty would be pleased
to direct the removal of the cavalry force from Aston
and any other near vicinity.   And this condition, Edward
went on to say, being so reasonable and just in itself,
and the best means to prevent further danger of concussion and outbreak, he had taken upon himself to
all but assure in his Majesty's name.

Edward urged the immediate confirmation of this
arrangement upon the friendly Secretary of State, with

all possible warmth and earnestness -natural enough under his circumstances ; and, to add every weight to his entreaty, announced that he had himself retired to Sutton Manor-House in order not to annoy the towns-people with the neighbourhood of his own troop of horse, which he was now proceeding to assemble, arm, and discipline with all imaginable diligence.

And to effect this object, Edward Holte most zealously bestirred himself at once, conscious of his increased burden of responsibility, and that every moment was of consequence in providing against the dangers certain to follow on a discovery of his secret engagements.

Only the most powerful protection and patronage could be of use in this way ; and Edward knew no better means to secure the King, than to show himself forward and eager in arms on his side. Moreover, the bustle and activity of the movement were likely to divert the suspicion and espionage which he had so much reason to consider fixed upon him.

The occupation also divested his mind from the tedious anxiety with which he expected news from his clandestine bride in Birmingham, by the aid of the friendly services engaged there in his behalf.

Sutton Woods and Manor-House accordingly—in a few hours, one might say—became the head-quarters of the Holte Dragoons, as Edward had determined to name his corps. And about six score hardy young yeomen, who had long been expecting the summons, joyfully joined the standard of their landlord's heir, for the most part as volunteers, well mounted on their own horses, and ready and willing, with a very little instruction, to form a dashing and enterprising corps in the service of their King.

In reality, it happened as Charles had expected on the conjuncture. The tidings, which he took every pains to spread, of the audacious design—hardly frustrated—on his person, aroused very greatly the zeal of his partisans, and awakened them to the conviction that the war was a real war, and must be met as such. · In every part of England the loyal nobility and gentry were seized with alarm and indignation, and preparations which might else have continued to languish took all the forms of movement and activity. But at the same time the undesired result followed, that the formidable man whom it was most the interest of Charles, if he had known it, to keep in the background, was suddenly brought forward into a notice and publicity that sped him faster on his path of preeminence than almost anything else could.

These military occupations, and softer and more engrossing cares of the heart, filled up Edward's time so absorbingly, that day after day passed without his noticing the superfluous lapse of time that intervened before he received any reply from Lord Falkland. Neither had Mr. Lane communicated with him from Aston Hall.

But matters continued apparently quieted in Birmingham, under the energetic handling of Tubal Bromycham; insomuch that the Anabaptists apparently withdrew the claims of their champion, and Whitehall being elected minister of the town, the bellows-blower retired of his own accord, without awaiting an ejectment, from the Parsonage. Even Firebrace's exasperation and suspicions appeared in some degree lulled, and somewhat more friendly relations were resumed between him and his long-intended son-in-law. Nay, on the latter proposing himself as an escort for Dorothy in taking some necessary air and exercise (for she began to look very ill in the confinement to which he at first subjected her), the armourer allowed her to leave his precincts in charge of her quondam betrothed. It was plain, in fact, that the old man's favourite hopes revived, ignorant as he was of Tubal's overmastering motives to lend aid in the progress of his supposed rival's happier fortune.

But even 'Master Shakespeare, of the Globe,' indeed, has said nothing truer than in his famous lines on the always thwarted and perplexed course of 'true love.' And Edward Holte was painfully disturbed in his enchanted dreams of successful love and military glory, almost as soon as he had raised the brimming nectar— of the former draught of paradise, at all events—to his lips.

A reply reached him from Lord Falkland, which, in parts favourable to his most earnest wishes, was wanting in some most important points, and visibly disastrous in others.

He was informed that the King approved of all he had done in effecting the peace, with the exception that his Majesty insisted on the town of Birmingham laying itself open at once to the quartering or passage of his troops, instead of so undutifully demanding that they should be removed elsewhere.

The principal reason in receiving the town so easily back again into pardon and grace, it was declared—after its seditious outbreak, with the means of punishment ready at hand—was its alleged great convenience for military use.

In the opinion of its value in that respect Prince

Rupert so entirely joined, that he had resolved as speedily as possible to fix his head-quarters in Birmingham; and, meanwhile, would not think for a moment of leaving Aston Hall, where he found himself very well situated for intelligence and communication with most of the other scattered gatherings of the King's forces. And would remain more needfully so, as his Majesty himself intended to retire on Shrewsbury, to place himself at the head of the now considerable army collected in the west, and from Wales and Ireland, in his behalf. And to Shrewsbury Edward Holte was ordered with all possible speed to hasten with the mounted levy he announced himself to have formed, his Majesty's forces in this direction being chiefly of infantry, and cavalry specially requisite and desirable for the guard of his royal person on his various extended movements among the loyal population of the west.

In addition to the exceeding distastefulness for a young bridegroom, in the first bloom and glow of triumphant love, to be called upon to leave his adored, Edward Holte could not but vaguely surmise something of sinister and plotted in all this arrangement.

It seemed strange that the only condition upon which Birmingham insisted, should be the only one denied. Strange and ungracious too, in the last degree, to add so much that was unsavoury and menacing in the demand that the town should be thrown open. Very strange that such importance should be attached to the attendance on the person of the King of a raw troop of volunteer horsemen, who had hardly yet received their arms, much less exercised them. Something pointed and confirmed in the summons to him and them to remove so far from the neighbourhood of a town

with which the young captain had evinced such kindly
sympathy.

But besides his own reflections, Edward Holte found
a few lines affixed to Falkland's official communication
which greatly added to their discomfort and suspicion.

The amiable secretary expressed himself in a cautious
. way, as was natural, considering the disturbed times and
the chances of interception. But he stated to Edward
Holte that he apprehended persons and opinions that
meant no good to the town, whose interests he desired
to serve, had gained a great ascendency with the King.

A certain Count O'Taafe, an Irish soldier of fortune,
who, under a great appearance of jollity and freedom of
demeanour, concealed singular talents for intrigue and
cajolery, had arrived at court from Prince Rupert.
Charles had lent a ready ear to his statements and
opinions on the subject of the town of Birmingham :
and he, Lord Falkland, had good reason to believe that
all that had been resolved upon in relation to that place,
was by the advice and insinuation of this Irishman.
The Council had scarcely been consulted on the matter,
the King insisting on the condition he named in the
most peremptory and determined manner, and refusing,
in fact, to hear any reasons to the contrary ; so possessed
was his mind with the artful suggestions made to him.

Not a single word was said about Tubal Bromycham !

Edward Holte knew enough of the character and
double-minded procedures of Charles I. to feel that the
information he received gave scope for the greatest
anxiety that some ill turn in the whole transaction was
to be dreaded. This uneasiness was, however, greatly
heightened in more than these respects by a communication he received shortly afterwards from Aston Hall.

Having been expected in vain for several days, Mr. Lane arrived at last at Sutton, with a face more than customarily full of ill omen and disaster.

Besides being so absorbingly engaged in personal affairs, Edward had refrained from sending to enquire the motives of this absence, from consideration for the panic alarm of the poor old man, and his dread of implication in any discovery of the recent transactions. And unwilling to subject himself to scrutiny, offended almost equally with his father's and brother's behaviour towards him, and having hardly a moment's time to spare, he had not himself made any visitation to Aston. He wished, besides, not to present himself before Prince Rupert, whose peremptory manner he so little relished, until the business with Birmingham was settled, and his Highness in fair course at least of removal thence.

Now this hope was over. The Prince seemed rather confirmed in residence at Aston ; and from all Edward learned from Mr. Lane, seemed more than ever to regard his quarters as fixed.

Far from removing them, the number of his troops was swelling constantly, so that Aston Park began to put on the appearance of an extensive cavalry encampment. Trumpets and kettle-drums resounded in all directions, night and day. Artillery was expected from York. And not only had the Prince treated Mr. Lane's announcement of the agreement arranged with contempt and disdain, but he openly declared his conviction that as soon as his royal uncle was placed in possession of the real facts of the case, he would disavow the absurd bargaining which had assured the worst rebels in England exemption from the due penalty of their misdeeds. Nor was it at all concealed that Count O'Taafe was despatched to court with earnest advice to this effect.

The kind old man had been alarmed from bringing this intelligence sooner, hoping to divert the suspicions he apprehended might have been excited by his attendance on his young patron into Birmingham. Yet, he confessed, he had been so closely questioned as to all that happened there, by Sir Thomas, and cross-questioned by his lawyer, that he frequently grew confused and alarmed, and scarcely knew what he had said.

But the most disquieting part of the intelligence remained to be communicated, and Mr. Lane proceeded upon it with evident marks of discomposure and anxiety. But he could not in his conscience, he declared, with tears gushing to his kind simple eyes, but state that from what he had observed, Prince Rupert was likely to crown his influence with Sir Thomas Holte by marrying his fair daughter. All who saw them together remarked what lovers they had become, and it was the general talk and expectation of the house and village at Aston, that the haughty young lady there would be fitly wedded at last to the nephew of a king.

It seemed not to have entered the loving-hearted clergyman's head to doubt but that matrimony must be the end of all this wooing and company-keeping he described between the royal dragoon and the beautiful daughter of his host.

Mr. Lane had spent the greater portion of his life in dependence on the wealthy baronet, an admiring spectator of the development of his grandeur and greatness. Even so exalted an alliance seemed, therefore, by no

means out of the possible culmination of these glories;
especially as the Prince was so poor and Sir Thomas so
rich, and the latter talked openly and very significantly
now of doubling, and even trebling, the fortune he had
originally intended for his daughter in case she married,
as he thought she could not fail, to his mind.

Mr. Lane was only concerned at the disastrous influence these demands upon Sir Thomas's purse, and
his increased pride in so illustrious an alliance, might
have in reconciling him to the one contracted in secret
by his son.

But Edward was assailed by a deeper and less personal apprehension. He was, besides, conscious that he
was scarcely fairly reciprocating Tubal Bromycham's
generous helpfulness in his own love affair. He determined, therefore, to ride over to Aston Hall at once,
and endeavour to obtain some decisive understanding in
the affair. Above all, if possible, to discover his sister's
real sentiments as regarded her devoted admirer in Birmingham, and to put her unmistakably on her guard
in the perilous hallucination in which she seemed to
consider herself safe and triumphant, dancing on the
verge of a precipice.

In deference to Mr. Lane's alarm, however, he deferred
the visit till the following day, that it might not seem
prompted by any report of his. And, moreover, while the
good clergyman was partaking of some refreshment with
him, Gaspar Feldon, who had been for a portion of the
contract with Johny-the-Rogue, and had his orders to
call on Dame Cooper at the Moat House, brought also
a billet, written in a tremulous hand, but which seemed
to the enamoured young husband like a sunbeam shaped
into letters.

'I have fair leave from the master you wot of to go
with our good friend, whom also you wot of, to the
Cherry Orchard this afternoon; yet, in good truth,
shall be at the *Moat House* on a dearer visitation, if I
may hope to encounter there with one to whom it shall
seem rather a palace of love, built so that at least the
windows may overlook Paradise!'

END OF THE SECOND VOLUME.

LONDON
PRINTED BY SPOTTISWOODE AND CO.
NEW-STREET SQUARE

www.ingramcontent.com/pod-product-compliance
Lightning Source LLC
Chambersburg PA
CBHW031337070726
47496CB00017B/1187